GALLOWS GOD

LOKI'S WOLVES

MELISSA SNARK

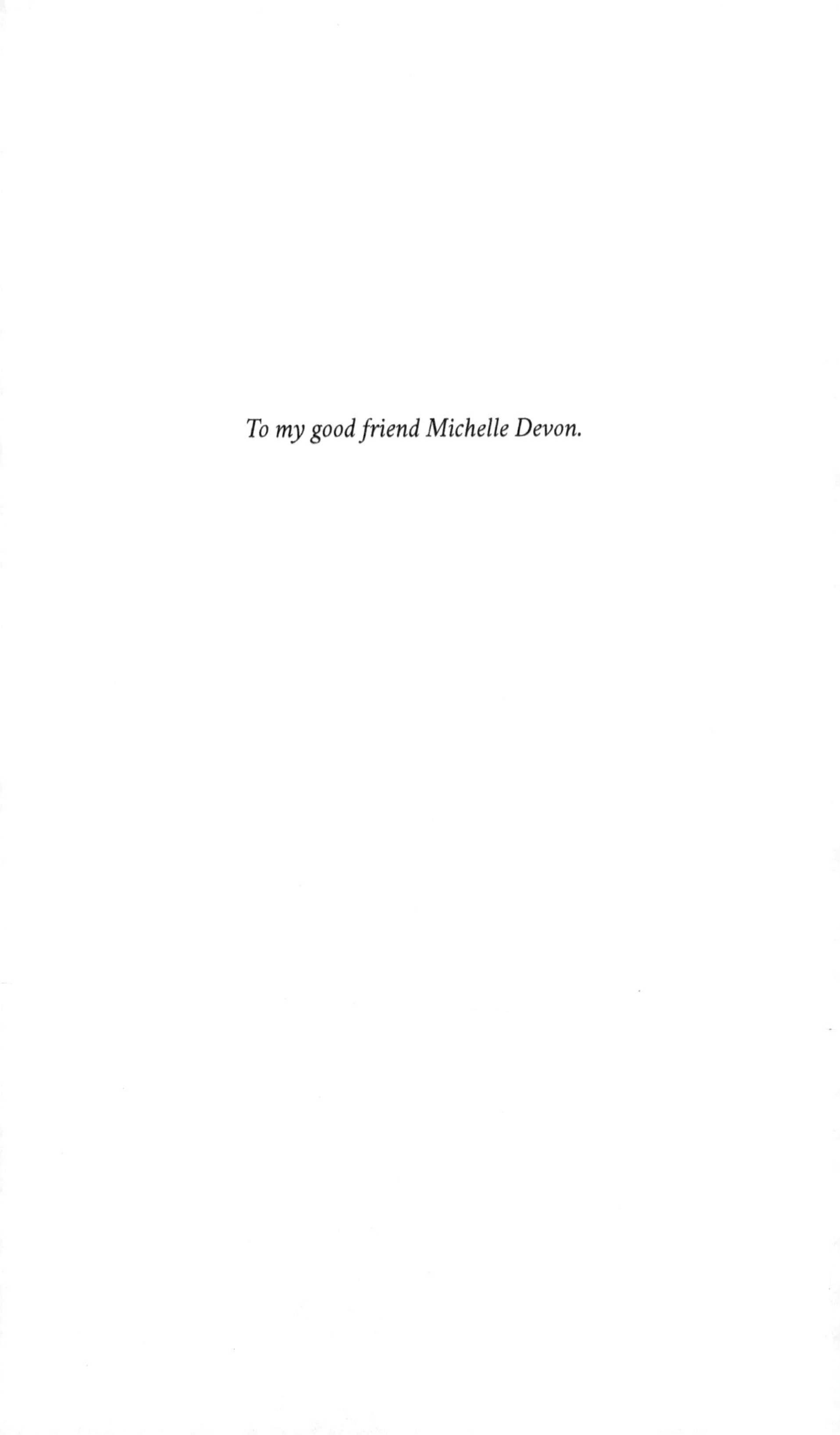

To my good friend Michelle Devon.

ACKNOWLEDGMENTS

A great deal more work goes into the production of any novel than the author toiling alone at their keyboard. My thanks go to Jennifer L. Carson for the invaluable advice she provided during the development of Wolf's Cross and the still-to-be released Blood Brothers. I wish to express my appreciation to the many people who provided feedback and support: Sheryl R. Hayes, Michelle Devon, Lynn Hunter, Rissa Watkins, Lisa Rayns, Pamela Altman Talley, Becky Oviatt, and Heather Hungate. Thank you also to editors, Marjorie AJ Cooke and Shay VanZwoll of EV Proofreading.

GALLOWS GOD

Universe: Loki's Wolves

Series: Ragnarök: Doom of the Gods

ISBN-13: 978-1-942193-19-7 (ebook)

ISBN-13: 978-1-942193-16-6 (paperback)

BOOK DESCRIPTION

A Norse trickster god with a bad rap becomes an accidental hero when he saves a boy from the curse of vengeful witches. He swears on his villainous heart, no more Mr. Nice Guy.

Mind your own business. Keep your head down. Shenanigans are for suckers.

Loki has learned his lesson and learned it well. He's the original desperado hiding out in the American frontier. Unfortunately for the god of lies, the Norse goddesses of fate are up to dirty tricks—targeting a six-year-old boy and his faithful dog for termination.

These witches made a fatal miscalculation by angering the world's savviest trickster. Loki rides to the rescue. But as they say, no good deed goes unpunished—centuries of staying off Odin's radar blown in a heartbeat.

Old enemies are reunited. While Odin and Loki square off for a showdown, bloody warfare erupts between various supernatural factions, including hunters, wolves, and Odin's worshippers.

Before Ragnarök ends the world, Loki must choose. Does he want to be a champion or a destroyer? He has a notion of protecting the nine worlds from total obliteration, but it means trusting the blood brother who betrayed him.

CHAPTER ONE

From his most ancient beginning, flight exemplified freedom within his heart and soul. As a hawk, Loki soared high above the suburban oasis carved from Arizona's austere desert. He drifted upon a rising column of warm air, wings angled to induce enough drag so he didn't outpace the child he followed. Far beneath him, the figure of the six-year-old was tiny, but enhanced avian senses permitted the Trickster to drink in every sight and sound.

The boy's fleet feet splashed upon the wet pavement, running beside a small twig boat while the swift-flowing gutter stream swept the tiny craft along. Michael Allen Fraiser had light brown hair and an olive-toned complexion as well as a lean, athletic build designed for speed. The child ran with joy; he ran with confidence. No hesitation in his stride or caution in his manner. His arms extended straight from his sides and his throat produced a steady hum, like the engine of a small plane. As if at any moment, he would find liftoff as the wind carried him high into the sky, far from worry and fear.

Weaving a delicate spell, Loki spied upon the boy's thoughts and caught a glimpse of pure imagination, a sweet dream of freedom almost powerful enough to be magic. Michael lacked the skill to focus his longings and shape reality, but the fantasy was nonetheless charming and oddly compelling.

Chasing his makeshift ship, Michael turned onto a curved pathway, following the trough that channeled runoff into a park. The sidewalk sloped down through wide patches of multi-colored gravel.

Floating over the expanse, Loki surveyed the landscape below. Favorable air currents created by the June storm faded and the updraft ceased, forcing him to bank and circle to maintain altitude. None of the scraggly trees offered a satisfactory perch. The scattered lamp posts were higher than the branches. Those manmade constructs were all situated along sidewalks and the paved playground, too far from the boy's route to provide a satisfactory vantage point.

When Michael darted off the pathway and sprinted across a rocky patch, Loki remained aloft to stay close. Near the bottom of the hill, the drainage ditch emptied into the pond created by water collecting in the lowest part of the park. Riding the tide, the twig boat sailed toward the center of the pond. The pool of water was completely opaque, dark even at the shallow edges where light should have penetrated.

The child's stride shortened. The soles of his sneakers skidded across the rocky surface, and then brought him to a halt upon the muddy bank. Indecision etched every line of his slender frame while he considered whether the toy's recovery was worth wet feet and ruined shoes.

Folding his wings, Loki entered a steep dive and plummeted toward the earth. Just before he crashed into the ground, his hawk form dissolved into a swirling column of smoke and coalesced into a boy. An unruly mop of black hair topped his head, and his skin was warm brown. He chose to appear eight years in age—young enough to seem unthreatening to a suspicious six-year-old, but old enough to exert some authority. Standing a few paces behind Michael, the Trickster pulled ribbons of magic from the air and wove them into garments to clothe his body. Nothing elaborate—just a T-shirt, board shorts, and Nikes.

The sun brightened as it crept from behind the clouds. He squinted to shield his eyes. A quick dip of his head produced a red baseball cap with a wide brim. Chin tucked to his chest, Loki watched while Michael kicked at clumps of bushes.

After a minute, Michael turned up a thin branch less than two feet in length. Holding the implement as an extension of his arm, he returned to the puddle's shore and probed the murky depths. Concentric rings spread across the water.

Dead center, fat air bubbles swelled to the surface.

The boat bobbed just beyond reach. A cry of frustration issued from the boy's throat, and he edged closer until the toe of his shoe dipped into the puddle. He balanced all his weight upon one leg and leaned outward. The tip of his tongue poked between a gap in his front teeth, and his straining form embodied a single determined thought—just a little farther.

Uneasiness roiled Loki's gut, coiling like a confined serpent. As an accomplished freebooter, he recognized a golden opportunity when one presented. This unwary child was low-hanging fruit, an easy shot at revenge. Loki didn't even have to get his hands dirty.

All he had to do was stand aside and watch while Fate murdered the boy.

Air hissed between clenched teeth. He didn't like this at all. Oh, how he loathed the monster he'd become. He'd done many perverse and malicious things in his time, but he also possessed a certain twisted code of honor. As a general principle, his more spiteful pranks trapped unwitting adults, not children.

The boy wasn't special or remarkable. Aside from a fertile imagination, he possessed no special abilities or magic. Not the son of a god or even a monster. Loki wondered what he was doing there, even though deep down he acknowledged the compelling curiosity driving him to investigate the child.

He had to know what it was about Michael that Jake considered so damn special. The child must possess a secret, a hidden quality significant enough to qualify him for adoption into the Barrett family.

The pond's surface rippled as the air bubbles grew larger and migrated closer to the oblivious child. When the boy wobbled on the verge of toppling into the water, Loki sucked in a sharp breath.

Impulsively, he barked, "Hey, kid! Don't fall in."

Emitting a startled yelp, the boy flailed his arms. Twisting on one leg, he spun and barely caught himself. The branch fell from his hand and landed in the water with a crisp splash.

Loki exhaled, long and slow. Tension bled from his coiled frame. He released the ball of magic clutched in his hand and was shocked to discover he'd prepared to go to the child's rescue. But why? He wasn't a hero or a do-gooder.

He wasn't even nice.

Wide-eyed, Michael stared. "W-w-who are you?"

"A friend." His gaze flicked to the bubbles and then to

Michael. Reaching behind his back, he conjured a small sailboat from one of his countless treasure stashes. The item appeared in his hand. "Did you lose a boat? I found this."

An elven toymaker had handcrafted the tiny sailboat, the product of hours of loving labor. The sleek hull was ornately decorated in gold overlay upon a field of dark green, and two elegant masts supported crisp white sails.

It gleamed like a jewel.

"Wow, it's beautiful." Michael's eyes widened with amazement and then blazed with yearning. Suspicion forgotten, he hurried toward Loki on eager feet, stumbling in his excitement. His arm extended, hand grabbing.

"It is yours, isn't it?" Loki asked.

Michael froze.

Fascinated, Loki observed the conflict between conscience and greed as it played out upon the boy's face. Small teeth sank into his jutted lower lip, and a tremor coursed through his body. His arm jerked and then fell.

Shaking his head, Michael said, "I lost a boat, but that's not mine."

Honesty. How curious.

Loki cocked his head. "But you want it. Why not lie and take it? I wouldn't know any different."

Michael's stance solidified. "I know, but stealing is wrong." Then a haunted look appeared in his eyes, and he shuddered. "Bad things happen to people who steal."

Loki's stomach gurgled, a belch sour with bile. He thrust his open hand toward the child. "Take it. I want you to have it."

"I don't know..." Michael stared at the ship, his gaze intent with longing. Such self-restraint was remarkable in a child his age.

"It's not stealing if I give it to you."

After a split-second of indecision, a smile blossomed on Michael's face. He reverently lifted the tiny ship from Loki's grasp.

"It's beautiful," he said in a breathy voice. "Thanks."

An adult would have questioned Loki's motivation or wondered where he'd acquired the exquisite toy. The boy simply accepted his reasoning at face value. He could be faulted for naivety if not dishonesty.

"You're welcome." Warmth replaced the nausea, a percolating cheerfulness that made him sneer. His interested gaze lingered on the boy. "It's not made of glass. You can put it in your pocket or a backpack."

Michael's wary eyes regarded him. "Okay. What's your name? I'm Michael. Are you from around here?"

"Ben." The lie rolled off his tongue without a second's consideration. He waved his hand vaguely toward the far side of the park. "I live over there."

"Do you want to be friends?" Michael asked.

Loki blinked. "Friends?"

The child nodded. "Yeah, you know. We could hang out."

"Friendsssss..." The word terminated in a sibilant hiss. He scowled while a storm of conflict raged within. He understood the basic principle of friendship. Loki and Odin had once been loyal companions. But once burned, twice shy. He'd refused to place his trust in another person ever again.

Loki regarded the boy with hardened suspicion, trying to discern his angle. "Why? You already have the boat."

Michael's brow knit. His gaze dropped to the sailboat and then lifted to consider Loki again. Sorrow skewed his face. Stepping forward, he thrust out his hand, offering the coveted toy. "I'd rather be friends."

"Really?" Loki glanced at the boat. "How odd."

The child frowned. "You're weird."

"So I've been told." Well, not in those exact words. Reaching out, he pressed the child's fingers closed around the ship. "Keep it. We can be friends."

Somehow, he would adapt. Life had thrown enough absurd and challenging puzzles his way. If necessary, he could fake friendship well enough to con a naive six-year-old. Hell, it might even be fun.

"We can?" A beaming smile transformed the boy's face. "Great! We're going to be best friends."

"Best friends," Loki agreed, marveling at the childlike simplicity. As an adult, acquiring a best friend had taken him centuries, not to mention huge risks. Vulnerability had exposed him to hurt. Trust placed his lot solidly in the hands of another.

Centuries invested in building up a single relationship only to have it vanish in the blink of an eye, lost to misunderstanding and distrust. Pride and ego set even the closest of comrades at each other's throats, and when the dust settled... sons died.

Sons paid the price of their father's sins.

"How old are you?" Michael asked. "I'm six, but I'll be seven August third."

"Eight," Loki tilted his head to gaze skyward. Too much time had passed since he'd last been a boy. He recalled childhood as a short, brutal experience that probably didn't have much relevance to a modern kid. His slang needed updating and he hadn't gotten into a video game since his total obsession with Mario Kart in the 90s. However, his repertoire was extensive, his shape shifter nature adaptable.

He'd figure it out.

"Wanna try out the boat?" Motoring with childish

exuberance, Michael turned toward the standing puddle which percolated with agitated froth.

Lashing out, Loki seized the boy's elbow. "Play with it at home. Stay away from black water."

Face rounded with fear, Michael spun toward him. "Why?"

"There are witches who lurk just beneath the surface, waiting to drag unwary children under."

Blanching, the boy shot the pond a terrified glance. He hastily backed away from the puddle. "You know about monsters?"

Satisfied he'd instilled a healthy sense of caution, Loki began, "I—"

"Hey, Michael!" The voice of a teenage male sliced through the air.

As soon as the child turned, Loki changed to a fly and buzzed high above him. Through multi-faceted eyes, he watched Michael glance over his shoulder. Upon finding his new friend gone, he frowned and turned in circles, looking for Ben.

The teenager shouted again. "C'mon. We're gonna be late for the game!"

"Coming!" Clutching the exquisite sailboat to his chest, Michael whirled and ran toward the two older boys approaching from the distant side of the park.

Once he was sure he was alone and unobserved, Loki adopted his new persona as Ben. Standing on the shore of the impenetrable pond, he cocked his head. His gaze pierced the darkness to what lay beneath—the frustrated fingers of Fate, angered at being denied her prize.

Feral viciousness edged his smile. "I do know monsters. Quite well."

CHAPTER TWO

A man's smoky voice carried on the strength of his tenor and captured Freya's imagination. It resonated, uttering indecipherable words, but there was no mistaking his throaty murmur. His was the voice of a lover and a poet, sensual but strong, pleasing in all ways to the feminine aesthetic.

The Norse goddess of love and war pivoted on the ball of her foot and changed her course. Her mission of moments before was forgotten, as fleeting as the random musings in the dreamer's mind upon awakening. A faraway smile curving her lips, as she followed the alluring sound, rather like a sailor chased a siren.

She drifted through the windy corridors of her hall, Sessrúmnir. Her adventure brought her to the enclosure which housed the giant cats that pulled her chariot. The magical felines were gifts from Thor, the god of thunder. They had the tufted ears and stocky body-type of a skogkatt, but were of an exceptional size and strength. The tiger-sized felines were: Tregul, named for his liquid amber fur, and Bygul, a glossy golden female.

Ah, what a shock to discover a burglar in her cattery! On stealthy feet, Freya sneaked closer to the curved archway of the catio. Just outside, she paused and tilted her head to eavesdrop upon the man within who fawned over her chariot cats. Near enough now to put a name to that seductive voice, a secretive smile curved her lips.

"Aren't you a handsome fellow?" The man crooned his praise.

"Mrrrow." Tregul's cat-voice rumbled in purr, deep and brassy.

His mate, Bygul, issued a jealous chirp of complaint.

"C'mere, sweetheart, mustn't ignore you. Mmm, aren't you the softest pussy? You'd make luxurious slippers..."

PHOENIX, *Arizona*

The bat's sharp crack carried to the farthest reaches of the ballpark.

The ball soared high and hung suspended at the pinnacle of the arc, bright white against clear blue. The rotating sphere began a slow descent toward the bleachers where the fans all sat with their necks craned skyward to follow its trajectory.

"I've got it! I've got it!" Glove hefted high, Michael danced atop the bench in the stands, limbs flying in constant motion, a determined bid to catch the foul fly ball.

"Get under it, Champ." Jake Barrett's arm mirrored his instructions to his adopted son, but he refrained from reaching out to guide the child's hand. The boy had to succeed or fail on his own; victory and defeat each taught a distinct and valuable lesson.

Michael adjusted his glove, and the ball thwacked leather. An immediate cheer arose from the fans of both teams for the boy who danced and whooped. Holding his glove aloft, his grinning face swung toward Jake.

"I caught it. Did you see?"

"I saw. Good catch, Son." Smiling, he patted the boy on the back.

"I caught it." Michael jumped down and collapsed to a seated position upon the bench. Grinning like mad, he gazed at his prize. "I caught it."

The afternoon sun cast long, angular shadows across the bleachers of the high school ballpark. Tugging the lid of his cap down to shade his eyes, Jake rested his hands on the tops of his thighs and leaned forward. The weathered plank creaked as his weight shifted. His intent gaze coolly surveyed the baseball diamond.

The game was in the top half of the ninth inning. The home team's players, the Red Devils, were on the field and the visitors, the Bulldogs, were at bat. The scoreboard read *Home 3* and *Guest 2.* A runner sat on first base with one out.

Jake's teenage sons were on the Red Devils. Gage played second base while his fraternal twin, Jonas Dean whom everyone called JD, manned the shortstop position. On the bench beside him, his adopted son, Michael Allen Fraiser, milled his legs with the furious, pent-up energy of any six-year-old. So far, the child had shown admirable restraint in occupying a seated position through the entire game.

"Can I try?" Michael begged as the visiting team's batter emerged from the dugout.

He feigned skepticism and cast the boy a sideways glance. "Do you think you're ready?"

"I'm ready!"

The Bulldog's batter made his selection and warmed up with a half dozen heavy swings before he walked out to home plate.

"Go ahead." Jake dipped his chin.

Michael exploded off the bench and landed with his arms flung into the air. Then he cupped his hands to his mouth and launched into sports-sing. "Hey! Batter, batter! Swing!"

Around them, heads turned and people grinned to hear the child's voice soar in the music of baseball—the all-important heckle. Jake patted the boy on the back, delivering wordless approval on a job well done.

Pitching for the Devils, Andre Hedford worked through a warm up on the mound. Even though he was sixteen and a junior, the lanky teenager was the tallest member of the team. Once the batter stepped into the batter's box, the pitcher lobbed a fastball dead center across the plate.

The batter swung and missed, and the umpire barked, "Strike!"

The guest team's fans groaned in protest.

Dancing in triumph, Michael added his voice to the shouts of celebration from the Devils' loyal supporters. While the pitcher prepped, the boy heckled again. "Pitch to 'em underhand!"

When the next pitch flew high and wide, the batter passed. The umpire called it, "Ball!"

Jake shot to his feet. "Flip over the plate and read the directions!"

"What? Are you blind? Get some glasses!" the boy piped up. He tilted his head, looking to Jake. Those wide eyes sought approval and reassurance.

"Good one, Son." He patted the boy's shoulder, earning a smile in return. Being the focus of such intense hero-worship humbled him. His own sons by blood were almost adults. At seventeen, the twins were the youngest of the Barrett brood. Both young men were independent and self-sufficient, whereas Michael was at the age where he still sought adult guidance and approval.

As father and son, he and Michael were in a tentative, transitional phase. The boy's mother had been murdered in December of the prior year by a monster who fed on guilt. Jake had slain the beast, but Michael still suffered from nightmares. He saw a counselor but couldn't discuss the true source of his trauma with a woman who didn't believe in the supernatural.

The decision to adopt was easier than Jake would've ever expected. Michael had no living relatives, and the modern foster care system wasn't equipped to handle the boy's needs, so the child would be raised by hunters who believed that things that went bump in the night were real. Many of the teenagers on the field had a parent or other relative who was a member of the Phoenix-based hunter organization which had its headquarters on Red Butte. The private high school provided additional security, year-round schooling, and special accommodations to facilitate the unique dangers and demands of the lifestyle.

Jake's knowing gaze swept the stands, noting the underlying signs of duress in the spectators. Many were suffering despite the trappings of an idyllic afternoon. On the aisle row, Marie Sanders, a middle-aged woman with puffy eyes and a red nose, clutched a fistful of tissues while she put on a brave show for her son, the Red Devils' center fielder. Her husband and the father of her children, Neil, was one of the fifteen men missing in action in Tucson. She didn't know it yet but she was a widow—Neil wouldn't be coming home.

Those deaths weighed on him—an onus. Jake hadn't announced the deaths yet. He'd only just found out a couple hours before himself. Maybe it made him an asshole, but he perceived no benefit to ruining the last ball game of the season. The spouses and families of those lost would know soon enough.

"I can't see!"

Michael's complaint forced Jake's attention back to the game. He looked down, noting how most of the audience was on their feet, obscuring the boy's view of the field.

"Hey! Sit down!" Michael bounced left and right, up and down, but his short leaps failed to propel him high enough to obtain an unobstructed view.

Leaning over, Jake hooked his hands beneath the child's armpits and boosted Michael onto his broad shoulders. The youngster barely weighed anything.

"Better?"

"Yeah, thanks."

The Devils' pitcher heaved another fastball, and the batter swung with all the finesse of a bull in a china shop but managed to connect. The bat cracked. The ball soared, flying sharply to the left of the shortstop. The batter dropped the bat and ran for first while the Bulldog player on first sprinted toward second base.

Cheering his sons on, Jake roared at the top of his lungs, and the crowd thundered along with him. Michael's high, enthusiastic voice filled his ear, encouraging JD and Gage to victory. A wave of visceral excitement swept through the fans, building toward a crescendo. They screamed for blood, a call to conflict that harkened to an earlier era. Not quite the same as combat, but the instincts to fight remained integral to human nature.

Following the ball's trajectory, JD fielded it across his body in a skillful catch, while Gage covered second base. The shortstop pitched the ball straight to his brother's glove in a seamless maneuver so smoothly coordinated the twins could have been two hands of the same body.

Continuing the play, Gage tagged the second base before the runner reached it. He performed a neat 180-degree pivot and launched the ball to the first baseman. A sudden hush fell over the stands, silence as reverent as a church service. The ball whacked the first baseman's glove at the exact moment the batter's foot struck the bag in a classic bang-bang play.

Tense anticipation reigned. For all the good-natured heckling and competitive catcalling, the fans were respectful at their core. Jake likened them to honorable warriors, both the players and parents of both teams. Among all modern sports, he loved the game for its nobility of spirit and strategic complexity.

"He's out," the umpire announced, throwing his thumb over his shoulder.

The home team had won.

A cheer erupted from the Devils' loyal fans as they celebrated their team's triumph. The outstanding double play was the jewel in the crown and the closeout to a spectacular winning season. Home and visitor fans alike delivered a standing ovation while the two teams lined up and shook hands.

"That was the best game ever." Michael's arms waved with so much enthusiasm, he whacked Jake on the back of the head. The second his feet touched ground, the child sprang into motion before his father let go.

"You're right. It was a great game." He released his hold on the boy, who shot forward. With a rueful shake of his head, he watched the child's swift passage down the stairs. Michael's small size allowed him to weave around obstacles and squeeze past the legs of slower moving adults.

"That boy is a tornado in a trailer park." The other man's deep voice came from two rows back and up. Henry Hedford, aptly nicknamed Skinner, stood and made his way toward the staircase bisecting the bleachers. The burly African-American man had a shaved head and many intricate tattoos visible upon every square inch of exposed skin. Despite being on the high side of fifty, he was as hard as nails and meaner than a wolverine.

"He's a handful, all right." Jake stepped onto the stairs.

Skinner shook his head. "Don't know what you were thinking. Taking on a boy that age without a wife..."

"It was the right thing to do," he replied in a flinty tone. Privately, he wondered the same sometimes, questioning whether he'd bitten off more than he could chew. His beloved wife, Sarah, had passed away over two years ago. Cancer had robbed him of her company, and he bitterly resented their unplanned separation. His professional calling as a hunter was dangerous but required long hours and frequent travel. He refused, however, to voice his doubts aloud. The adoption was a done deal. For better or worse, Michael was Jake's responsibility.

Jake's reputation as a renowned warrior and a man who commanded powerful magic preceded him far and wide. He had a number of monikers, some ruder than others, including Hunter King and Master of the Hunt. Within their organization's formal hierarchy, Skinner acted as his second-in-command and right-hand man. The two men had served together in the Marine Corps prior to forming their own private paramilitary organization, and they'd had each other's backs in countless confrontations. Jake trusted no one more.

Here, among civilians, they weren't hunters. Here, they were simply fathers watching over their sons. Side-by-side, they followed the stream of humanity pouring from the bleachers. Friends and family members mingled with the players, delivering congratulations and chatting. Their boys gravitated toward them, and soon Andre, JD, Gage, and Michael joined them in a loose circle near home plate.

"Dad, the team is going out for pizza," JD explained, employing teenager code which meant that (A) Parents weren't welcome, and (B) He needed money. He held out his hand in expectation. The firstborn of the fraternal twins, JD was quick-witted, competent, and clever. A natural protector. Like his father, the young man was tall and broad-shouldered with brown hair and eyes. He took after his mother as well, having inherited her grace and compelling charisma.

"Boy, you need a job. When I was your age..." Grumbling entirely for show, Jake fished his billfold from his back pocket.

"Geez, Pop. When you were our age, dinosaurs roamed the earth and there were no jobs," Gage chimed in. The teenager was a couple inches taller and slightly huskier than his twin. He had light brown hair with blond highlights he'd inherited from Sarah. The youngest of the four boys, he had always been a diplomat and negotiator, and was by far the most empathetic. The peacemaker, just as his mother had been. Patient and considerate.

JD snorted. "Actually, dinosaurs hadn't evolved yet."

"Man, you think your father is old? Mine knew dirt when it was still rocks," Andre tossed out, setting off another round of old-age jokes.

While the others got a good laugh, Jake separated four bills from the others and slapped them down on his son's palm. He caught JD's gaze. "Make sure you're home by ten. You still have school tomorrow."

"Sure thing," JD agreed with a cheeky grin.

"Can I come?" Michael asked in a wistful voice. He wore his hope on his face. The boy worshipped the twins and followed them everywhere despite the considerable age difference.

They all turned to gaze down upon the child. Jake inhaled, biding his time. A look loaded with meaning passed between the twins. JD's brow furrowed, and his head jerked back and forth. Gage pinned his brother with a shaming glare even as he mouthed, "Aww, c'mon."

"Pleeeaaaase..." Michael pleaded. The boy was a pitiful vision, rounded eyes and jutting lower lip. He raised clasped hands.

"Okay." Shrugging, JD gave in fast. He shoved the money into his pocket. Without saying goodbye, the pack of boys drifted away.

"You have him home by nine," Jake called after them.

Two fingers tagged JD's temple in a quick salute.

Gage leaned over to talk to Michael. "Listen, Champ. You've got to help us impress the girls. Can you do that?"

"Sure, same as last time?"

"Let's vary our strategy..."

"Hell." Skinner settled his hands on his hips. Grinning, he rolled his head from side to side. "Don't you miss being young."

"Humph." Jake sized his friend up but held his tongue. Instead, his gaze tracked the carefree youths as they gallivanted off to join their friends. In his heart, he acknowledged a bittersweet truth. Even if youth restored his body to robust vigor, age weighed heavily on his soul. He lacked the capacity to indulge in an untroubled existence.

They stood in silence for a while, waiting by mutual consent until the baseball diamond was empty. Some conversations required privacy.

"You got plans this evening?" Skinner asked eventually. "Winnie is making lasagna."

He chuckled. "I recognize that tone."

"What tone?"

"That my-wife-put-me-up-to-it whine."

His friend scoffed. "Bull *shite*."

Through narrowed eyes, Jake pinned Skinner with a knowing stare.

The other man caved like a soggy house of cards, throwing up his hands. "Alright, ya got me. She's invited over her younger sister."

"Denise?"

"No, Talia."

Heaving a sigh, Jake glanced skyward. "I'm a married man, Hal. You know that."

"Yeah, I get that, but Winnie doesn't get it. All she sees is that it's been over two years since Sarah passed away. She thinks you're lonely, and she thinks that little boy needs a mother."

"Well, she ain't wrong. Tell Winnie thank you, but I wasn't feeling social." The entire gist of the exchange disturbed him. While Skinner understood Jake was a god, Winnifred didn't know. Her husband had never told her and never could.

"I'll do that." Skinner dropped a curt nod.

"Good."

Conversation over. In the last two minutes, they'd engaged in more oversharing of their feelings than at any point since Sarah's death. They were hard men, and intimacy didn't suit them. With so many unspoken concerns, uneasy foreboding lingered in the air.

From the look on Skinner's face, the man had something on his mind. Jake waited until his friend got around to parsing it out. Still, he couldn't wait to get out of the sun. He was hot and thirsty, and stank like day-old roadkill.

"It's not right." Skinner fisted his hands.

Jake quirked his brow but the other man required no encouragement.

Skinner flung his arms wide. "Us sitting here—watching baseball and eating hot dogs. As if the whole damn world wasn't coming undone around us."

"Enjoy these moments of normalcy, Hank. They're precious." Soon, they too would be gone in the trouble and turmoil to come. These good memories would be what they clung to.

"Any further word from Tucson?" Skinner couched the question as a demand. He remained unable or unwilling to accept Jake's perspective. "The fires are still burning and refugees are still trickling out. If any of our people are still alive..."

"We're not going to hear from anyone else." Upon issuing the flat denial, Jake shook his head. "Consider anyone MIA in Tucson dead behind enemy lines."

"No fucking way." Skinner hollered the protest. The warrior ethos was deeply ingrained in his psyche. *No one left behind.* Anger energized his entire body, and he shifted to a fighter's stance.

"I activated the hunter's marks of every missing man and used my second sight to determine their fate." Jake offered the rebuttal in a flat, hard voice. His facade remained stoic. Not that he didn't care or feel. He did. His heart ached for each and every one of the people they had lost. Their deaths weighed upon his soul, and he was tired. Exhausted. And opening the door to his foresight, which he normally kept locked away, had plunged him straight into the grip of awful depression.

"They're dead? All of 'em?" Face set in a rock-hard mask, Skinner stared at him. His jaws clenched, teeth grinding like stones.

"All fifteen." Jake dipped his chin, sick in his heart. Fifteen plus the previous eight hundred and eighty-five men and women they'd managed to confirm were killed in action.

"That brings our losses to nine hundred." Skinner fumed, locked in place. Then his fury erupted. Bellowing like an injured beast, he threw up his hands and stomped in circles. He shouted profanity, foul and scathing, aimed at the undead and the Necromancer, their enemy. He cursed Loki and the Fates and threw out a final disparaging challenge to Odin.

Jake gave the man his space, and refrained from taking offense. Every last hunter in his organization—except one—had offered him a vow of personal fealty. As their general, he made tactical decisions and sent them into battle, and he also bore direct responsibility for every last man and woman who died in his service. As their god, Jake sent his Valkyries to gather the souls of those who fell and escort them to Valhalla.

Long ago, a Viking king had once stated it far more eloquently: *"We fight. We die. We go to Odin. This is glory."*

"Nine hundred," Skinner repeated once he'd calmed. He halted, breathing hard, clearly struggling to reconcile with their staggering casualties. "Nine hundred. We took a thousand of our best-trained and equipped soldiers to Tucson, and we lost nine-tenths of them. Only a hundred of us made it out."

"I can do the math," Jake said in sharp irritation. He'd done the math. Even with a thousand men, they'd been outnumbered by vampires. Overwhelming odds. Not just ten to one. More like a hundred to one.

Neither of them mentioned the uncounted innocent lives that had also been lost that night. Some things were beyond their control, and certain paths led straight to the pit of despair. If they descended into it, they'd never get out.

Over the last six months, the undead population in cities along the U.S.'s southern border had exploded out of control. Attacks were frequent and unpredictable. The number of civilian casualties had mounted until it defied the government's ability to suppress the truth. Rumors leaked to the general population, stories of magic and monsters, and civil restlessness grew with each passing day. Rebellion percolated and brooded, another giant of a problem, which defied even Jake's prowess as a problem solver.

"How is it that we're even still alive?" Skinner asked, grappling with disbelief. "I was there. We shouldn't have been able to escape. We were surrounded on all sides by motherfucking undead..."

Jake had died in Tucson—three times over the course of a single night. However, he kept his mouth shut since his death didn't count. No matter how awful or grievous the injury, he always got back up in the end. Whole and sound in body, if not mind.

"They drove us out. The Necromancer is playing with us. I don't doubt he's taking direct orders from Loki." Jake summoned his worn patience. He and Skinner had already had this exact conversation and a couple variants of it over the course of the past three days since their defeat in Tucson.

"What the fuck are we going to do, Jake? We can't win." Opening and closing his fists, Skinner looked to Jake for answers. An awful thing to witness, such a strong man reduced to beseeching.

As second-in-command, Skinner's crisis of faith fairly represented all hunters as a whole. The spirits of many in the ranks were flagging. As a result of the death and destruction of the last several months, his people suffered from severe battle fatigue. Even a fresh infusion of new recruits, courtesy of the U.S. military, hadn't alleviated the stress. They needed Jake to be strong, now more than ever.

"That's what Loki wants. To instill defeat in our hearts. He desires to reduce us to despair and agony. Seeing us suffer means more to him than simple death. So that's what we must deny him. I refuse to allow him to win." Jake infused his voice with unwavering resolve. Drawing on the magic that connected all hunters, he projected his determination to Skinner and on to his followers.

"Right. The bastard won't win." Skinner squared his shoulders, set with renewed conviction. "We're dug in. Our defenses at Red Butte are as ready as they're going to be without reinforcements. Sir..."

The other man's uncharacteristic hesitation set Jake on edge. He tilted his head back but the position produced pain from the knotted muscles in his neck and shoulders. "What?"

"Are we going to move our families?" Skinner blurted out the question. The man never hesitated to risk his own life, but his wife and son were another matter.

"Not yet." Jake's tone allowed no refusal or discussion. He suffered similar anxiety for the safety of his own sons, but evacuating their families did no good if there was no safe place to send them. He had a possible sanctuary in mind, but it wasn't time.

Not yet.

"What about Finn and his people?" Skinner asked of the White Mountains Tribe of wolf shifters, the potential allies they'd been courting since the short but bloody hunter-werewolf war had ended. In the natural course of things, wolves detested the undead with a fiery passion. The wolves were few in number, but powerful.

And as contrary as a woman convinced of her rightness.

Jake suppressed the impulse to swear. Fucking werewolves never stopped complicating his life. Instead, he said, "I'm still working on that."

Skinner grunted. "Better work faster."

"Yeah."

After he and Skinner parted ways, Jake drove home and parked in the driveway of his single-story suburban home. The house was quiet but not empty. As he entered through the garage, Michael's Rottweiler mix, Rascal, met him at the back door. The dog's tail wagged in greeting, but the animal gazed past Jake, seeking his master.

"It's just you and me tonight, mutt." He patted Rascal's head in passing. For all his complaining, Jake had a marked rapport with both dogs and wolves in particular. A poet might have called them kindred souls.

Rascal whined but followed him. Ultimately, the dog's empty stomach trumped the inconvenience of second-rate companionship. The canine accompanied him through the empty halls of the home he'd shared with his wife. Since Sarah's death over two years before, he hadn't changed a single thing. The interior remained intact, just as she'd left it.

Jake fed Rascal canned food and zapped leftover pasta in the microwave for himself. He passed the evening in the family room, lounging in his favorite armchair with *Good Omens* by Terry Pratchett. A heavy weight resting upon his knee drew him out of the story. He peered at the Rottweiler, and an involuntary smile cracked his hard face.

"Sorry, boy. You're stuck with this old man for a few more hours." Jake closed his book, and he stroked the dog's silky head.

With a mournful moan, Rascal stared at him with pleading eyes. In response to the attention, his tail produced a half-hearted thump but the dog clearly missed Michael. Having survived a traumatic ordeal together, the pair was inseparable. Initially, it had proven to be a challenge to convince the boy he had to leave the animal while he was at school.

Hours passed, and the ratchet of slamming doors and competing voices shouting over one another signaled the return of his sons. Barking, Rascal leapt to his feet and galloped from the room. A short time later the boys burst into the kitchen which was open to the family room. Rascal trotted on Michael's heels.

JD made a beeline for the pantry while Gage opened and hung on the door of the refrigerator, gazing into the cavernous depths. The teenagers appeared energetic in sharp contrast to Michael. The laggard six-year-old wandered into the room last, covering a yawn with his hand. All three sounded jovial as they argued music, naming bands Jake wasn't sure he'd ever heard of and probably didn't care to know. His tastes tended to old time rock and roll.

"Did you have a good time?" He noted the time—half past nine—but decided not to reprimand them. Instead, he closed his book, set it on the side table, and eased to his feet.

"Yeah, it was great." JD extracted an armful of various

boxes and bags from the pantry and dumped them onto the counter.

"Yep." Holding a gallon of milk, Gage dug out a package of tortillas.

"Didn't you go for pizza?" Jake entered the kitchen as the twins added even more food to the rapidly expanding pile. His critical gaze swept the collection. He sighed.

"Geez, Dad. That was three hours ago." JD swept past the hanging pot rack and snatched two frying pans.

"Make sure you clean up the kitchen afterward."

"Will do."

He directed his next words to Michael. "You ready for bed, Champ?"

"Yeah." The boy nodded, smothering another yawn.

"No story tonight. It's late."

Michael agreed without protest, a sign of how tired he was. In short order, the boy brushed his teeth and changed into pajamas while Jake let the dog out one last time. Then, he tucked his son in with Rascal stretched out across the foot of the bed.

"Are you ready to sleep with the lights off?" Jake asked before he left.

"No. Leave them on." Michael gripped the sheet covering him in clenched hands. "Please."

"Good night, kid."

"Good night."

The lights were a concession to the boy's nightmares, the same as the dog on the bed. With his older sons, he'd always forbidden pets on the furniture. Lately, though, he'd gotten downright soft as far as discipline went, and the twins never missed an opportunity to give him a hard time about it.

The child fell asleep immediately.

Leaving the table lamp on, Jake padded from the room

and closed the door behind him. He rejoined his older sons and passed another hour hanging out before they went to bed. He double-checked all the doors to be sure they were locked and checked in on Michael one last time.

The child slept safe and sound, and forlorn longing filled Jake's heart. If only he had it in his power to keep it that way.

CHAPTER THREE

SESSRÚMNIR, FREYA'S HALL IN FÓLKVANGR

Freya sprang forth and revealed herself with a flourish that set her gown to fluttering about her luscious feminine form. The intruder lifted his face and regarded her with an unblinking stare that was markedly similar to that of both cats.

Arik Koenig, former attorney-at-law and the general of Freya's army, sat on the raised lip of a planter bursting with ferns. In his late thirties, the man was fine in both fitness and form, though there was a touch of gray in his brown hair. He had a broad chest and shoulders, muscular arms and legs. His features had splendid symmetry, though a silver scar on his right cheek marred his perfection. The shape of his brow, nose, and lower face hinted at a distant Roman heritage. High cheekbones alluded to his Nordic blood.

"How dare you threaten my precious Bygul with slipperification!"

"Slipperification?" Arik arched a querulous eyebrow.

"I heard you say it with my own ears. Don't bother

denying it... Cad." Freya freed a playful smile, but then she schooled her expression to sternness. She glided with cultivated grace across the marble floor. She possessed absolute confidence in her irresistible charm. In all the nine worlds, no other woman was comelier than she. Her golden hair cascaded about her shoulders and then flared artfully about her cleavage. The sheer material of her gown left little —but enough—to the fertile male imagination. She was the embodiment of desire.

"I confirm nothing, I deny nothing." He shrugged in philosophical fashion while holding his arms immobile, fingers splayed. Bygul obliged his attention. The tigress banged her head against his palms with relentless persistence until he scratched behind her ears.

PHOENIX, *Arizona*

Absorbed in his book, Jake stayed up past one until fatigue eventually overwhelmed him. Even though he possessed staggering stamina, his human body required rest. *Sleep.* He despised the mortal weakness more than any other because it was when he was at his most vulnerable.

He possessed the curse of prophecy, an ability to perceive the awful future where everyone he knew and loved perished. While conscious, Jake kept his second sight closed up tight. Sleep weakened the barrier. When his consciousness was submersed, nightmares plagued him. Visions of what was yet to come.

In his dreams, the world burned—inevitable, inescapable doom.

Entering the attached master bathroom, he stripped and

showered, rinsing away a day's worth of sweat and stench, base products of human existence. He'd endured the indignities of aging without complaint. Salt and pepper dappled his once dark brown hair. The harsh desert sun tanned his skin to a color and consistency like weathered leather.

His mortal body bore evidence of every wound ever sustained and healed. Scars layered atop scars. Silver lines crisscrossing his body, forming elaborate fractal patterns. Three tattoos remained intact, protected from damage by virtue of their innate magic. One was the stylized dagger hunters wore on their bicep as a badge of brotherhood. The second were two words over his heart: *Absit omen.* It was a protective invocation, translated—*May what is said not come true.*

The final tattoo, a double-sided dagger with a straight blade, stood apart from the others. A larger version of the membership symbol, it ran the length of his forearm. The image had a raised textured surface, and the surrounding flesh puckered and burned as if molten metal had seared his skin. When drawn, the tattoo became a physical weapon, a knife with a molten blade. The dagger was *Stakhla*, whose name meant Standing Fast, an enchanted weapon that dated to antiquity even though the few surviving sagas made no mention of it.

Many more ancient stories had been lost than recorded.

Although in perfect health, sometimes his head ached or his stomach soured. He loathed admitting it, but his aging muscles took longer to limber up. His reflexes had slowed and his joints ached. Over the years, he'd grown accustomed to the inconveniences of a mortal existence.

When he emerged from the shower, the clock's digital display read 2:04. Rubbing his hair dry, he headed straight to the bed. The towel lay where it fell. He crashed to the mattress, surrendering to the greedy grasp of sleep as his head hit the pillow.

He plunged straight into the nightmares he dreaded—the gaping jaws of a monstrous wolf swallowing him whole. His sons fallen before sword and axe. Thor perished before the serpent's fangs. Sun and moon snatched from the sky. The world smothered in ice, and then consumed in fire. He endured until the moment he realized—

He wasn't alone in the dream.

Unease coiled about Jake's slumbering form, a sly serpent impinging upon his sleep, sliding neatly past the mystical wards that were supposed to protect him from intruders. Naked except for a sheet tangled about his hips, he lay prone upon the king-sized mattress.

He opened his eyes. Blinking, he looked around and registered the familiar profile of his bedroom. Nothing appeared out of place. No obvious threats lurked in the shadows. Restless, he rolled over and flipped the sheet off. He stretched his long limbs, steel-tough sinew flexing. His heart rate sped. Reflexively, he reached cross-body, fingers brushing the stylized dagger tattoo on his forearm. His fingertips followed the raised, rough edges of the blade that overlaid scorched scar tissue like a brand, one twist and it would become real in his hand.

"Hey, Jake. You awake?" Loki's sibilant voice rolled out of the darkness, perceptible as full on surround-sound.

An annoyed huff burst from his mouth and morphed into a moan. "Loki, what the fuck do you want now?"

"That thing we discussed..."

"We didn't discuss shit." Disgusted, Jake withdrew his hand from the tattoo. Judging from the Trickster's chatty tone, he wasn't looking for a fight. "We haven't talked in months."

Loki scoffed. "What's months between gods? Our dialogue began millennia ago and will continue until the very end."

"At last, a good reason to welcome the world's destruction." Jake sat up and glanced at the nightstand. The digital clock radio read 3:23 a.m. He'd never get back to sleep. No point in even trying, especially since the opportunity to thwart any attempt would delight the Trickster to no end.

"Hardy-har-har." Loki clucked his tongue.

Groaning, he ran his hands through his hair and dragged them over his face. His mood was the color of phlegm. Exhaustion hung over him to the point where moving was a chore. Taking the lazy route, he beckoned to Loki. "Come here so I can throttle you."

"Geez, what's with the foul mood, old man? Here, I've suspended hostilities, enabling you to spend these last several idyllic days with your family. Aren't I at least entitled to a nod of gratitude? Would thanks be out of order?"

"I lost nine hundred men in Tucson, and you want a nod of gratitude?" Patent disbelief infused his voice. He tried and failed to keep his astonishment and anger off his face. The smart move would've been to show nothing and deprive the Trickster of the satisfaction of a reaction, but the devastating loss in Tucson had robbed Jake of more than just his composure.

"It could've been an even thousand." Loki's tone sharpened with irritation before he drew an audible breath and continued calmly. "Look, I didn't challenge your army to a final showdown at the OK Corral. That was your idea. As soon as I found out what was happening, I called off my dogs, but most of your people were already dead. The best I could manage was to have them clear a path so the survivors could escape."

"*You* called off the vampires?" Jake asked with unvarnished skepticism, even though Loki's words had the ring of truth. He and the handful of his men who'd survived the vampire assault in Tucson had pulled off a miraculous escape. Experience informed him that things too good to be true must be lies. Ah, and what a coincidence. Here, he had the god of lies spinning stories for him. Yet wisdom contraindicated what common sense dictated to be a simple matter. Nothing involving Loki was ever entirely what it seemed; nothing should be accepted at face value.

"Who else?" Loki asked in a smug tone. Finally, the Trickster's voice had attained directionality and definition, no longer a disembodied manifestation. He'd either produced a tangible illusion or actually taken on physical form.

"That's a question." Jake reached across to the end table and turned on the bedside lamp, casting dim illumination throughout the room. His legs dropped over the side of the bed, so his bare feet touched the cold tile floor.

A youth on the cusp of manhood sprawled on a wicker chair at the far end of the room, close to the French doors which led onto the pool deck in the back yard. The Trickster's physical experience seldom mattered, but Jake studied his rival anyway, noting the other's elven appearance. A curtain of burgundy hair, some strands loose, others woven with copper filigree. A tarnished silver key dangled from a braid behind his ear. He wore forest green garments, brown boots, and looked like he'd wandered too far from a Renaissance fair.

Loki rubbed his chin. "I even ordered our troops to

withdraw so you could recover their souls. A few had already turned. Not much to be done for that."

"Why?" Jake asked, point blank. Not that he would believe the answer, but he wanted to hear it anyway.

A shadow crossed Loki's features. "Because things have gone too far. This whole thing..." He swept his hand in a wide circle meant to encompass some vague generality. "...began as a means of screwing with you. It's taken an ugly turn, and it's getting out of hand—"

"Why?"

"Thousands of mortals are dead. You *don't* think this is out of control?" Loki gaped at him with patent disbelief.

"No." Apparently, he needed to clarify the question. "Why did you pull back the troops in Tucson? Why not just finish it?"

"Oh." Loki crossed and uncrossed his legs. "I didn't order the attack in the first place. My minion—"

"The Necromancer?"

"The Necromancer initiated the attack without checking first. Not that I'm denying responsibility. I encourage my followers to be go-getters..."

"It's not like you to plead ignorance as a defense."

"I'm not defending what happened," Loki's jaw jutted at a stubborn angle. "Or apologizing."

"What the fuck are you doing?"

"Explaining. That's all." Loki huffed.

"Well, ain't that special." With a grunt, because he was old and grumpy, Jake pushed to his feet.

"Where are you going?" Loki shifted, so the wicker chair creaked.

"I need to take a piss." Jake padded across the room toward the master bathroom.

"Ah, doesn't it suck to be mortal?"

Sometimes it did, but Jake wasn't about to grant his nemesis the satisfaction of an admission. He stepped into the bathroom, not bothering to close the door. The unexpected midnight visit annoyed him more than surprised him. A few months ago, Jake had made the mistake of engaging the Trickster while at the hunter's primary facility, which was located on Red Butte in the mountainous desert north of Phoenix. Ever since, he'd expected to kick over some rock and have Loki come crawling out. The rascal craved attention like a troublesome child, but even more so, he delighted in provoking his rivals.

He returned, hoping but not expecting to find Loki gone, however, the obstinate Trickster still occupied his chair. Cranky from the lack of sleep, Jake walked to the bureau and pulled a pair of shorts from the top drawer.

"Couldn't this have waited until morning?"

Loki snickered. "It could've, but it wouldn't have been as much fun as waking you up. Nor as satisfying."

"Go ahead." He stepped into his boxers and pulled them up his muscular legs. The elastic of his waistband snapped against his abdomen. Obviously, the other god wasn't leaving.

The redheaded youth sat straighter. "Are you listening to what I'm trying to tell you?"

"Yes, I'm listening." Suspicion and paranoia defined his mindset, but as a fatalist Jake preferred to follow the path of least resistance. He understood Loki too well. The only way to be rid of the overgrown pest was to humor him until he got bored and wandered off. Besides, he might as well take advantage of the opportunity to learn what his rival was up to.

"Are you? This is important."

"Yes." If he could have breathed fire, an inferno would've consumed the wicker chair. "I'm listening."

Their gazes locked.

Loki paled with rage. He embodied seething, pent-up anger. A manipulative creature to his core, the Trickster wore many masks. He could fake any emotion from grief to joy, and Jake had seen countless performances in the eons they'd known one another.

The white-hot anger was real.

"Has it ever occurred to you that you ask too much?" Loki leveled an accusing finger. "You take too much for granted."

"Your brain is addled," Jake snapped. The accusation wasn't what he'd expected. Not in the least. Here, another Loki truism held—the Trickster always surprised. Even those with the longest and closest associations, friends and lovers with insight into that duplicitous heart, could seldom predict what the god of lies would do in any given set of circumstances.

"Those wretched Norns cursed us to this. They predicted we'd become enemies and so we have... I attack your forces. You retaliate. Thousands of mortals die and we redraw the maps." Loki struck his palm with his fist for emphasis. "Can't you see? We've played right into their hands?"

"Don't play the hapless victim with me. I know you too well." Disgusted, Jake turned away and got out a pair of faded denim jeans, a shirt, and socks. With swift efficiency, he dressed and then once again pinned Loki with his gaze. "The Norns didn't force you to murder my son."

Loki drew a sharp breath. His mouth turned down at the corners even as he forced his lips into a smirk. "No, they didn't. That makes it even worse." Disgust curdled his voice. "I've become predictable—playing the villainous role as I was cast."

"How galling for you."

"You've no idea." Loki's slump morphed into a crouch, reticent of an irritated cat. His eyes fixed on some far off point, the focus of his frown. His ring finger tapped out a rapid beat upon the armrest.

Gauging the Trickster's demeanor, Jake paced closer, moving with measured, unhurried steps. He couldn't tell whether the redhead's body was a real physical manifestation or an illusion. Magic always made his skin itch and Loki invariably set him off like a swarm of fire ants.

Nostrils flaring, Jake stopped before Loki. Braced to get down and dirty, he leaned over and rested both of his hands upon the armrest. When the Trickster looked up quickly, he was ready.

Surprise flickered in Loki's green eyes. Long centuries of experience clued Jake to the Trickster's true feelings. Everything about the *Jötun's* appearance and behavior were predictably fraudulent, but even the god of lies had tells.

"Why so pensive, Loki? Have you tricked yourself into a corner?"

Loki's frown deepened to a scowl. "How do you do that?"

"Do what?" Given the opportunity, Jake wasn't too big to pass on a self-satisfied smirk. "Read you?"

His narrow chin lifted and then flowed into an elongated snout. Wolf's eyes. Glistening canine teeth. Pointed ears migrated high on his skull and flattened. A snarl curled in his throat. "Accurately."

"Your hubris exceeds your cunning."

"Well, duh." Loki rolled his eyes.

"I see you. I see you for who you are. Not who you'd have others believe you to be." Jake ditched irreverence, imbuing his words with the full force of personality. Loki stopped laughing. The stared at one another with cat-like intensity.

"What is it you think you see?" Loki's voice modulated into a sibilant note and turned his final word into a hiss.

"I see that you're skittish. Keeping your distance physically and relying on illusions when you can't..." Stoic detachment settled over Jake. He stated facts and watched his opponent squirm.

"I suppose you've analyzed my behavior and drawn conclusions utilizing your vastly superior intellect..." Loki threw out the taunt like a gauntlet.

"I have." He allowed himself a small smile but otherwise refrained from reacting. "Want to know what I've discovered?"

"Sure, let's hear it. This should be amusing if nothing else." The Trickster grinned but little things betrayed his unease—the color of his irises and the tension in his lips. His wolfish features restored to elven.

"Fifteen of my hunters were MIA after Tucson. I didn't know where they were or what had happened to them but I owed their families answers," Jake said in a slow, unhurried manner. "So I did something I hardly ever do anymore and opened my second sight."

"I'm surprised you're not catatonic," Loki snapped in a churlish tone.

"Your greater form is still imprisoned. This—" Jake swept his fingers up and down to indicate the other's appearance. "Is just a fragment, and a weak one at that. So I'm wondering..."

"What?" The Trickster's teeth snapped together with an audible clash.

Smiling dangerously now, Jake made his old friend wait before he answered. "If I kill this avatar will you finally go away and leave me alone?"

Bright anger flared in the Trickster's eyes and he bolted

upright, ready to fight or flee. Glee and satisfaction flooded Jake, because he knew at a glance that he was right. Loki may as well have just confirmed it aloud.

"I'd go away now if you'd only listen." Loki's lips pressed together. Shaking, he shrank in on himself. For a time, he gave the impression of being on the verge of changing shapes, perhaps to a fly or a hawk. Jake wondered if he'd take off, leaving the whole inane conversation without resolution.

Yet minutes ticked past, and the Trickster remained. Whatever the god of lies had to say, he must think it was important to be so damn persistent.

A resigned sigh escaped Jake. "Speak your piece."

The silence stretched, pressure building, until the Trickster looked ready to burst. Then, all the sudden, his face twisted into a grimace as though something bitter filled his mouth. He stumbled into speech. "I don't want to do this anymore, Jake. I've run the scenarios through my head a million times. It always ends the same. Your sons are your only real vulnerability. I go after them—"

Real, gut-curdling fear slammed Jake. His rigid hands locked Loki's forearms and dug into the hard muscles beneath his fingertips, broke skin, drew blood. His voice shook. "Loki, what have you done?"

Loki's head jerked in denial. He licked his lips. "Nothing. I had a plan but I called it off—"

A child's piercing scream shattered the serenity of the house. Michael's cry struck dread into the depths of Jake's soul. His heart stopped. He ghosted within a hair's breadth of stepping out of his mortal body to assume his full glory and supremacy as a god.

Shouting in pure rage, Jake threw his arms wide. A burning blade manifested in his hand, a thick haft that fit perfectly to the span of his palm. Jake acted without hesitation. His hands locked about the hilt, poised directly overhead. The knife swept down in a swift stroke. The point pierced Loki's breastbone, sliced clean through, and serrated his heart.

Arms flung wide, the Trickster screamed in agony while the dagger seared his heart to ash. His head jerked back, throat fully exposed, and he convulsed. Smoke rose in curling columns and the room stunk of charred flesh. A writhing serpent-like ribbon peeled off Loki's arm and dropped to the floor, followed by another and then another. Until his entire body collapsed into a pile of wriggling colorful bands that dissolved into a sparkling shower of confetti.

An illusion.

Funny little tingles traveled the length of Jake's fingers. Like the opening chords of a song, the melody resonated throughout this being. The strangest emotion transferred into him—forlorn longing.

Having passed through the Trickster's construct, the blade of his dagger struck the seat of the chair, setting the wicker on fire. A conflagration claimed the whole thing in seconds. Cursing, Jake swept his arm before him and incanted the runes.

The fire went out.

From down the hallway, the boy's yells ceased abruptly.

Wielding his tattoo dagger, Jake sprinted from the room. He met one of his sons in the hallway. The seventeen-year-old carried a rifle and stood outside of Michael's room, holding the firearm with the muzzle aimed toward the ceiling.

"Michael's fine, Dad," JD said. "It was just another nightmare."

Calm suffused Jake. His anger cooled as quickly as it had

ignited. He would have sworn his heart resumed beating. "He's okay?"

"Yeah, he's fine." JD offered a lopsided smile. He titled his head. "Gage's with him."

"Thanks. Go back to bed. I've got this." He turned sideways as JD stepped aside, and entered the room that used to belong to his firstborn son. Loki had arranged Daniel's murder in early December of the previous year.

JD sat on the edge of the queen-sized bed. His hand rested upon the middle of Michael's back. The six-year-old lay on his stomach, arms folded over his head, face buried in his pillow. He cried steadily, the sobs muffled against the cushion.

Rascal stretched across the foot of the bed. The dog's head rested on his front paws. He whimpered as Jake entered.

"Good boy." Jake placed his hand on the dog's large head in a reassuring pat.

Rascal wagged his tail and replied with a sorrowful whine.

"He had another bad dream." Gage looked up and met his father's gaze, biting his lower lip.

Jake tilted his head toward the door. "I've got this. You and your brother should go back to bed. Get some sleep. It's a few hours yet before you have to be up for school."

JD and Gage exchanged a long glance, the sort of unspoken communication shared by twins and soul mates. "We're not tired," Gage said. "I think we'll stay up for a bit."

Jake gave a curt nod to signal his assent. His sons were close enough to being men to make their own decisions. In a movement so smooth it could have been choreographed, he and his son traded places. He settled on the edge of the mattress and laid the flat of his palm against Michael's back.

His hand from pinky to thumb spanned the width of the child's shoulders, a powerful reminder of how young and fragile the boy was even in comparison to the twins.

The boy drew a final stuttering breath and his sobs ceased. Demonstrating laudable courage, Michael rolled onto his side, dislodging Jake's hand. Wide, red-rimmed eyes blinked away the wetness that clung to long lashes.

"How're you doing, kid?" A fierce protectiveness swept him. He couldn't help thinking about what could have happened—so many awful possibilities and dangers. Loki had already orchestrated the death of his oldest son. He wasn't so foolish as to think the Trickster would spare the youngsters.

The boy swallowed so his throat worked. "I had a bad dream."

"Was it about the beast that killed your mother?"

Michael licked lips visibly dry and cracked, and then shook his head. "It was different. There were huge icemen. We were someplace in the mountains—a cabin or a cave. Gage and JD were there. They wanted to kill us..."

Stony silence settled over Jake. Deep down, magic throbbed, the runes rising beneath his tanned skin, writhing and crawling. Dread curdled his gut. "Was there anything else?"

Michael hesitated. "There was a wolf."

"Did the wolf want to harm you or help you?" His voice was hushed. Awareness of their audience fed his unease. He would've preferred the twins not hear any part of the conversation, but it was already too late.

Michael blinked. His small teeth bit into his lower lip and his fists clenched. "I don't know. It wasn't a white wolf."

"Not Victoria then." He glanced to the opposite side of

room. On a silken thread, a tiny black spider hung suspended from the windowsill over the toy chest.

A dozen crayon pictures decorated the wall, pinned so closely together they overlapped. The images formed a nightmarish collage—a black two-legged goat beast, crying children in cages, drums filled with black liquid. Blood in trickles, trails, streams, and pools. A white wolf attacked the monster. A decapitated beast and joyful children running from open cages.

The art would have given a teacher or school psychologist fits, but it fairly represented the child's ordeal and salvation. Jake and Michael had a deal—the boy was free to display whatever he wanted on the walls of his own room, so long as he drew bright, cheerful images for his educators and anyone else who wasn't a member of their family.

"I'm thirsty," Michael said in a rough voice. Then he sat up, tucking his knees against his chest, and extended his arm toward his dog.

Rascal surged toward his master. Tail waving, he pushed his nose against the boy's hand, licking furiously. His antics coaxed a strangled giggle from the Michael.

"Come on, Champ. Let's get you a glass of water." He stood.

"Okay." The boy nodded and scooted off the edge of the bed. The dog jumped down also, sticking to his master's side.

The four of them sat together in the family room for a time, talking in low voices. During such family gatherings, Jake experienced the loss of his wife most acutely. His gaze strayed to the empty spot on the couch where she'd often sat, and he caught the twins following his gaze. Their faces mirrored the heavy sorrow he carried in his heart. Only Michael, who'd never met Sarah, remained untouched.

Eventually, JD and Gage went back to bed, and Michel

fell asleep on the couch with his arms wrapped around the dog that doubled as guardian and pillow.

Jake sat up the rest of the night, standing guard. Loki didn't return.

As DAWN BRIGHTENED THE SKY, the twins emerged from their rooms and chased morning pursuits—competing for the shower and trying to locate their discarded shoes. Exhausted from his sleepless night, Michael dozed on the couch beside Rascal.

Jake wandered out to the kitchen. He started breakfast—eggs, bacon, pancakes, and fresh-squeezed orange juice—enough to feed an army, or the four Barrett men, anyway. The morning meal was always a time when he most acutely felt the loss of his wife. Sarah had always been the better cook. Jake's food passed muster, but no one had ever rolled their eyes heavenward and settled both hands over a swollen stomach with a gluttonous moan of satisfaction.

As the first batch of bacon came off the press, Gage surged toward the counter. He loaded his plate high with crispy strips and then thrust it out, gripped between both hands. "Dad, are the eggs done yet?"

"Yep." Jake seized the handle of the frying pan. Using the spatula, he dumped about half the frying pan of scrambled eggs onto his son's plate and scraped the rest onto the platter. JD was still in the shower, but he'd emerge soon enough.

"Thanks." Gage sat at a stool on the breakfast bar. Gripping his fork in his fist, he dug in with gusto. The boy shoveled food into his mouth, chewing no more than twice between bites. He ate like a wolf.

"If you don't slow down you're going to choke," Jake cautioned.

"Sorry." Gage stuffed his face and made a show of chewing with his mouth closed at least six times before he swallowed.

"Your mother would have a fit."

"Mom's not here." The teenager grinned around a mouthful of chewed bacon and yellow eggs.

"Don't be so damn sure of that," Jake intoned ominously.

Gage choked on his food and grabbed for his juice. He gulped the entire glass before he recovered. After that, he slowed down.

Under the pretext of cracking more eggs for a second batch, Jake turned away to hide his smirk of satisfaction. Served the boy right for being so damn smug...

"Dad?"

"Yeah?" Jake asked without turning. He cast an empty eggshell into the sink, turned on the water, and pulsed the garbage disposal. When he whisked the eggs and the milk together, the mixture came off just a shade too light to be right so he reached for another egg to balance it out.

"Is Mom the reason the apple is back in the fruit bowl?" Gage asked.

Jake's hand clenched, crushing the raw egg. Bits of shell bit into his flesh but none of them sharp enough to penetrate his callus-toughened skin. The cold, slimy insides seeped through his fingers into the bowl. His mouth twisted into grimace. He cast the whole mess into the sink and washed his hands before he turned back to his son.

Gage sat with his elbow propped on the counter, fingers spread to support the fruit balanced on the tips. The apple glowed—glossy and golden—as fresh as the day it'd been plucked from the tree of life by the Norse goddess, Iðunn.

Jake's gaze locked on the apple. It possessed the mystical properties of tremendous rejuvenation—healing, fertility, and youthfulness. When Sarah's cancer had been discovered, he'd pulled strings on earth and in the heavens to obtain the miraculous curative.

"Son, put that back."

"Okay." Gage shrugged and plunked the priceless piece of fruit back atop a stack of oranges. The boy's voice conveyed a decidedly injured note. "But I just wanted to know why it's out again. It's been in the safe since just before Daniel died."

"He's worried someone else is gonna die," JD said from the entryway to the kitchen. His tone was pointed and accusing, decidedly more aggressive than his brother's.

"No one else is gonna die." Jake faced his son square on.

"The apple only comes out before someone in our family bites the dust." JD stood with his shoulders squared and arms lifted, brawling for a fight. His hands clenched to form fists.

"JD, don't—" Gage said.

"We're entitled to answers!" JD all but shouted.

"Quiet down before you wake up Michael." Jake set down the order and both his boys fell silent. He kept quiet for a long while. He stroked his beard while he contemplated. The bristles had grown too long and wooly. In a self-conscious gesture, he stroked his hand over his head, confirming his hair was getting shaggy. Time for a trim.

"Dad?" Gage's forked clattered on his plate.

He focused on his sons, appraising them with thoughtful regard. The twins had good reason to be anxious. He owed them an explanation but the trouble was... Jake wasn't quite sure why he'd removed the apple from the safe and returned it to the fruit bowl.

"You both know I get premonitions even though I keep my second sight closed," Jake drawled, speaking slowly so he had time to compose his words. "Sometimes it's real specific, sometimes it's just a gut feeling..."

"Yeah? What is it this time?" JD asked.

"Just a gut feeling. And it ain't got nothing to do with either of you boys."

JD huffed, deflating, but Gage remained alert. He'd always been the more perceptive of the two.

"What about Michael?" Gage asked. "Is he gonna be okay?"

Jake looked his son straight in the eyes. "I'm going to do everything in my power to keep that boy safe. You have my word."

"Okay." The tension eased from Gage, a testament to his faith in his father. It was a heavy burden, one Jake damn well hoped he would prove worthy of.

"I've got a parent-teacher conference with Mrs. Ricardo at ten." Jake sought to restore a sense of normalcy. He needed to roust Michael soon. The boy needed to eat and shower or he'd be late to school. "After that, they need me on Red Butte. Can you see to it that Michael gets picked up from school?"

"Sure. No problem." Gage nodded.

"Lucy will be by later this afternoon. She had a doctor's appointment this morning. She's supposed to be making cupcakes for the senior class fundraiser." Jake stroked a finger over his mustache. Lucy was their part-time housekeeper and an old family friend. She often checked in on the boys when he was away.

A grin cracked Gage's face, accentuating the teenager's rugged good looks. "So make sure JD and Michael don't eat all of 'em. Check."

"Hey!" JD took a lazy swing at his brother and missed.

"You sure it's okay?" Jake heaped too much responsibility on the twins, and he worried. He should request Sawyer, another of his sons, return home, but pride prevented him from asking.

"It's fine." Gage waved him along. "Dad, seriously. Go."

Jake left the room and made it halfway to the family room before he remembered what he'd missed. He backpedaled and stuck his head into the kitchen, catching Gage in the process of pulling a gallon of milk from the fridge.

"Break a leg out there today."

Gage looked over and smiled. "Thanks, Dad."

"I might not be able to make it to the theater tonight." More than just regret edged his apology. A poignant, bittersweet sorrow hung over Jake. Tonight was the closing night of his son's play, but he had missed a lot more than that down through the years. The birthdays, ball games, holidays, and weekends when he'd been away were too numerous to count. In less than a week, the twins would graduate from high school and then they would make their own way in the world as grown men.

"It's okay. You've got to save the world," Gage assured him without a hint of sarcasm. "We understand."

"Go," JD waved his hand, echoing his brother's sentiment. "We've got this."

CHAPTER FOUR

When first Freya met Arik Koenig, he'd turned her head. He won her favor and rose to power in her hall at an unprecedented rate. Looks, intelligence, and a silver-tongue were a dangerous combination in a man. Upon occasion, the long shadow of doubt hung over her and she questioned— had she made a mistake? Thus far, he'd proven remarkably adept in every task she'd assigned to him, from oratory to military.

Yet while he'd been in her bed and her service for only a few months, already he'd lasted far longer than all his predecessors. The man was a complete contradiction. Refined and intelligent on one level; primitive and primal on another. He owed his animalistic aura to being a wolf shifter, one of Loki's descendants, but that fact alone came nowhere close to explaining his complexities. Most perplexing—his austerity. He made almost no effort to please her, though his skill as a lover paralleled that of many gods. Toward, her, **Freya,** the most desirous of all goddesses, he was often cool.

Indifferent. It drove her mad and acted as an irresistible impetus upon her determination to conquer him.

Just the fact that her cats had accepted him so easily struck her as another piece of the puzzle that comprised the man. As a rule, Tregul and Bygul were standoffish with anyone other than their mistress...if not outright hostile.

She voiced her bewilderment aloud now, "Your rapport with them is astounding. I confess, I had no idea they'd take such a liking to a wolf."

He chuckled. "Obviously, Tregul and Bygul are superb judges of character."

"Obviously," she said but frowned. "You're covered in fur."

"Aye." He took a useless swipe at the sleeve of his coat where a thick layer of fuzz clung to his suit. Despite Freya's chiding, the contrary man persisted in donning the clothing that had been familiar to him during the tenure of his mortality—a tailored, pinstripe navy suit paired a linen shirt and silk tie. And while he wasn't dead...he should have left those things behind when he entered into her service.

Without so much as a "by your leave", Bygul decided that she'd had quite enough of Arik's attention. The tigress bounded off into the thick vegetation surrounding the patio. The man she abandoned only grinned and laughed.

"Ah, cats are such fickle creatures." Freya hid the pleasure she derived from the female cat's cold-shoulder treatment of Arik. She acknowledged her pettiness but she'd always been jealous of her creatures...and she hated sharing.

SIERRA PINES, *California, on the western shore of Echo Lake*
The savory aroma of cooking bacon and the cacophony

of many competing voices greeted Victoria Storm when she ventured into the hallway outside her bedroom. On cue, her stomach issued an embarrassingly loud rumble and her unborn child fluttered in her womb as if to echo the sentiment. If she had been shifted to her wolf form, she'd have tilted her muzzle skyward and let loose a joyful yodel while thumping her tail in sheer delight.

While human, she retained a tad more decorum. Still, hunger urged her onward, but her innate caution overrode her baser desires. Where once she would have charged headlong into potential danger without so much as a second thought, now she hesitated. Dropping her hand to the side of her stomach, Victoria pressed her palm to the swell of her baby bump. At almost six months along, her body had begun to experience alarming and unfamiliar changes, making it impossible to forget even for a moment that every decision she made impacted her unborn daughter.

She had no idea why the kitchen of her lakeside home was full of strangers but the general mood of the bustle didn't sound contentious. Head cocked, she listened intently, assigning names to voices. Ah, there was Morena's bright girlish laughter but the man who addressed the teenager defied easy identification. Then, her keen hearing caught Sawyer Barrett's husky baritone and the last of her concern dissipated.

The pad footfalls upon tile announced someone's approach. A second later, Sylvie Thornton rounded the corner and stopped upon spotting Victoria lurking in the corridor. The Native American woman had a tall, strong stature. Her gray hair was pulled back into a neat ponytail.

"Good morning." Victoria mustered a self-conscious smile, aware of how ridiculous she must appear to her friend. She opened her arms and they traded a quick hug.

"Good morning." Sylvie flashed an easy smile. "I was just coming to see if you ever intended to get out of bed." As Victoria's second-in-command, the older woman held the rank of Beta within the Storm Pack. She also acted as their Skald, the keeper of tradition, and was a devout follower of Freya, the Norse goddess of war and love.

On cue, Freya's aggrieved voice filled Victoria's thoughts. *Once, you were also a devout follower of Freya, My Priestess.*

Victoria flinched at the harsh condemnation and reached out with her prayers to the deity. *I am still your priestess, My Lady.* She lacked the nerve to dare label herself devout. While she possessed many faults, hypocrisy wasn't one of them.

Silence served as Freya's criticism.

Wincing, Victoria looked to see how much of the unspoken exchange Sylvie may have perceived. A worried frown pinched the older woman's kindly face, so she wasn't unaware. Also, Sylvie knew the circumstances that had driven a wedge between priestess and goddess.

Thankfully, Sylvie offered no comment.

"We have company?" Relief swept through Victoria. She wasn't ready to field any uncomfortable questions. These last several months had been wearing. She barely knew where she stood with her goddess anymore, let alone what to say.

"I've been holding your breakfast but fending off hungry hunters, and Morena is becoming onerous." Sylvie waved her hand.

"Hungry hunters—haha. Very funny."

"I thought so," Sylvie said, tongue in cheek. "Are you going to come eat?"

"I'm already fat enough. I'm never eating again." She grimaced because she wasn't kidding. Not entirely. Her entire life, she'd been athletic and slender. A ballerina's build and a werewolf's appetite were a great combination. She'd eaten whatever she wanted and had never gained an extra pound.

Not anymore. Those days were done.

"Of course you're not. Come along." Chuckling, the Skald turned and headed back from where she had come.

Victoria followed. "Are *all* the hunters here?"

"Yup. All three of them." Sylvie's ironic smile wasn't lost on Victoria.

The trio of hunters belonged to a group of hardened soldiers who owed their loyalty to Jake Barrett, the Hunter King. They were currently "on loan" to the Sierra Pines area. Sawyer Barrett, Jake's son, was their leader. Up until then, the hunters had done their duty, patrolling the area, but had kept their distance from the Storm Pack. In December of the prior year, her pack and the hunters had clashed in a brief but bloody war that had left many people—wolves and hunters alike—dead. If someone had told her back in January that they'd all be sitting down to breakfast together in just a few short months, she wouldn't have believed it possible. In fact, Victoria would have sworn that she and Sawyer were far more likely to kill each than ever achieve a truce, let alone an alliance.

Walking side by side, the two women entered the spacious kitchen—the true heart of their home. Rays of morning sunlight shone through the massive bay windows. The atmosphere resonated with bright, positive energy. Laughter and jovial conversation merged with a buzzing ambient aura full of primary-hued swirls. The fragrant aroma of happiness filled the room. Victoria inhaled long and slow, savoring the scents of bacon and eggs, golden pancakes, and maple syrup, which set her mouth to watering.

Stopped within the kitchen entry, Victoria scanned the room and performed a quick head count. Just as Sylvie had said, the three hunters were plunked about the kitchen. The French doors leading to the enclosed patio stood wide open. The pack's four gray wolf members, mother Sophia and her three half-grown pups, were strewn about the area.

The hunter known only as DNR perched upon a stool at the breakfast bar. The young man was in his early twenties with sandy blond hair shorn high and tight, and warm hazel eyes. The initials had never been explained, but his companions always said "DNR" with the air of it being an in-joke.

Morena, a seventeen-year-old wolf shifter, sat at the counter beside DNR. The whip-thin teenager was already taller than Victoria. She had flawless brown skin and black hair, the product of an ethnic heritage of more Hispanic blood than Norse. She wore her short tresses in several ponytails bound with multi-colored bands. Gold piercings studded her ear lobes and cartilage. Her appearance was foxlike, but her pedigree was one hundred percent pure wolf.

While Victoria watched, Morena slipped pieces of bacon to Mick, the adolescent gray wolf who sat at her knee as attentively as any Lab begging for food.

Bacon. She'd better move fast if she wanted any. Victoria darted past Sylvie to make a beeline for the middle of the room. Cali Kinkaid, a petite woman armed only with a spatula, manned the gas stovetop. The female hunter's lack of arsenal counted as a surprising occurrence in and of itself. Her modus operandi consisted of fatigues, combat boots, and enough weapons to be dubbed a one-woman army. The other hunters, including Sawyer, called her Crazy Cali to her face; she never seemed to mind.

"Good morning, Cali. I almost didn't recognize you without your helmet." Victoria greeted the chef with a friendly smile. She took a plate from atop the stack on the countertop and hungrily eyed the disorderly breakfast buffet laid out on one end of the island.

"It's been too hot." Prompted by the reminder, the female hunter raised her hand to self-consciously wind a lock of her frizzy brown hair around her finger. Biting her lower lip, she tugged. "Besides, no one's shot at us in months."

"Is that a complaint? Things getting too boring for you, Kinkaid?" Sawyer heckled from his seated position at the kitchen table.

"No sir! I'm happy to be here babysitting you on your first job—" Cali's fingers flew in air quotes. "Out of grad school."

Good-natured laughter erupted, and everyone seemed to be having a blast. Even Sylvie wore a pleased smile. While more jibes and insults flew, Victoria loaded her plate with food and made her way to the kitchen table. To say she found their presence surprising would have been an understatement. Yet, here they were eating and laughing as if they belonged... She found she liked it.

Sawyer occupied the head position, facing the patio. The hunter sat with his chair pushed back from the table, his legs spread wide, one short work boot rested atop his knee. No matter what time of day, his dark blond, shoulder-length hair always looked like he'd climbed right out of bed with no more concern for grooming than a quick finger comb. The five-day scruff on his jaw enhanced the hunter's already disreputable air in a strung-out-Hollywood-chic fashion. He wore a short-sleeve shirt that revealed well-defined arms and the stylized dagger drawn in black ink on his right bicep. The symbol was the hunter's mark, a badge of brotherhood and belonging.

Judging from the dark circles under Sawyer's eyes, insomnia continued to plague him. He suffered from frequent nightmares but refused to tell her about them. His tattered leather coat and shoulder harness hung over the back of his chair. The hunter no longer brought weapons to the table as a concession to Sylvie—with the exception of his .45. For whatever reason, he refused to be parted with his last handgun, so he and the Skald had arrived at the compromise—the firearm remained holstered and slung across his chair.

Sylvie was to his left. Sometime in the last five minutes, a crochet hook had materialized in her hand, her current baby blanket project in the other.

Approaching the table, Victoria hesitated while a hot, fast internal debate raged. Could she sit? Did she dare? That morning, she had stuffed herself into her last pair of normal pants which had the dubious distinction of being her favorites because they were the only ones that still fit. Even so, she had the top button undone, concealed beneath the long hemline of her blouse.

"I don't bite," Sawyer said, apparently misinterpreting her reticence.

"But I do." With a quick grin, she plunked down to his immediate right.

The high-pitched rip of fabric was shockingly loud. Victoria's smile vanished when sudden freedom down below told her she'd torn her pants right down the rear.

Horrified, she glanced up, staring straight into Sawyer and Sylvie's blank faces. Oh yeah, they knew. Fortunately, the boisterous camaraderie throughout the rest of the kitchen continued without a break. The others hadn't noticed.

Sawyer's eyes sparkled and his lips compressed, bit from within. The man looked about to burst. His aura pulsated like a strobe light.

"Don't. You. Dare." Victoria locked gazes with the hunter. She glared, challenging him to say anything or laugh at her.

She braced her hands on either side of her plate and rose, thinking maybe she would kill the hunter yet.

Unexpected betrayal came from within Victoria's own pack.

Sylvie devolved into a most unbecoming Muttley-snigger. "Oh. Good grief! Victoria Svana Storm, you must have known this day was coming. It serves you right."

"That's so unfair!" Mouth downturned in wounded pride, Victoria turned a look of askance on her friend. Unfair but true.

"Quick, go change before the others figure it out." Sylvie shooed her. The Skald smiled and pinned Sawyer with a meaningful glance. Then she quoted an Old Norse proverb, "A head stuck on a pike no longer conspires."

"I don't know nuthin'." Sawyer thrust his hands up in surrender.

"You're smarter than you look," Sylvie said to the hunter.

He chuckled. "So I've been told."

Discretion being the better part of valor, Victoria shot to her feet. She grabbed the waistband of her pants with both hands to stop them from dropping around her ankles and beat an ignominious retreat. In her room, she changed into a pair of yoga pants which had—of all things humiliating—a stretchy waistband.

There was no dignity in pregnancy.

In a subdued mood, Victoria returned to the kitchen. The others had already finished eating so she sat down at the table and got straight to the serious business of attacking her food—they didn't call it *wolfing* for nothing.

"Cali, DNR. Head's up." Sawyer called the other two hunters to order. Once he had their attention, he continued, "I want the highway patrolled today. Yesterday, Cali and I saw some grungy-looking drifters over in Broken Bend—"

"Shit. Dems just hipsters," DNR interrupted. "Herds of 'em are passing through from San Francisco for that flower-child, free-love music festival."

"*Capullo*." Morena razed DNR, jabbing his side with her elbow. "Hippy. Hipster. Not the same thing."

"Dewey, watch your language." Sawyer's scowl cowed the lad into silence. "I told you. No swearing while we're guests here."

"Yeah, Dewey," Morena mocked, tongue in cheek. "Watch your language."

"Sorry, Sawyer. Sorry, Mrs. Thorton." DNR dropped his eyes, staring down at his hands. The posture made him look years younger, and so did the spiteful way he deliberately avoided looking at Morena.

"Humph." Sylvie offered no other commentary, but her silent approval shone through the empathetic bond like a sunbeam. Sawyer remained imperviously oblivious to the Skald's reaction. His aura hung over him like a little Charlie Brown storm cloud of doom and gloom.

"This is serious," Sawyer said. "Let's hold the jokes until later."

Finishing the last bite of her eggs, Victoria set her fork on the dirty plate. The food had been cold but tasty. She felt one hundred percent better. She found Sawyer's constant state of depression to be worrisome.

Through a complicated and convoluted series of events, both Jake and Sawyer were members of the Storm Pack. While the Hunter King remained at the periphery of their dynamic, Sawyer had slowly but surely integrated into the core. The hunter was an oddly-shaped peg amongst puzzled werewolves, but he was still, irrevocably, theirs.

Reaching over beneath the table, Victoria laid her hand over his and squeezed. "If Sawyer thinks these strangers are suspicious enough to warrant investigation, then we should look into it."

The weight of multiple gazes settled on her, including Sawyer's. His lips formed a reluctant smile and he mouthed a word—"Thanks."

She tipped her head.

"What was it about the drifters that bugged you?" DNR asked.

"What he's saying is that he figures you'd have a natural affinity for long-haired hippy-freaks..." Cali tilted her head back with a smirk that left much implied.

"Yeah, yeah." Sawyer waved his hand but then it curved into a corkscrew. "There was something... off about them."

"Off in what way?" Sylvia asked. "Were they shifters?"

"I don't know but something was off—" Sawyer bit off his words. "I don't know how to explain it."

"Would you like me to come down to Broken Bend? I have an appointment with my OB-GYN at eleven but I'm free until then." Sliding out her chair, Victoria rose and picked up her plate. She reached over to snag the dirty dish and empty coffee mug in front of Sylvie.

"Can I come?" Morena asked with an eager smile.

"No, you're babysitting the Stanton's boy again," Sylvie said.

"Aww..." The teenager's face fell.

"Yeah." Sawyer offered Victoria an easy smile. "That'd be helpful. Maybe you'll be able to pick up on something I missed."

"Maybe. At the least, I can scent them and check their auras. If they really are just..." She hesitated, debating over what to call regular old, non-supernatural humans in the presence of hunters. Once, she'd considered Jake and his people to be humans-with-magic. Now, she wasn't so sure.

Morena made the distinction as 'hunter-monkeys' versus 'normal-monkeys' but Victoria doubted Sawyer and his people would appreciate the joke.

"Human?" Sawyer grinned as if reading her mind. From his intonation, Morena had already deployed her latest strategy in the on-going game of "Get Sawyer's Goat".

"Yeah, sure. That works." Hands full, she headed for the sink where she discovered stacks of dirty dishes and pots.

"Kinkaid, take Reilly here and patrol Route 50. I'll take Victoria over to check out Broken Bend again."

"Sure. From where to where?" Kinkaid asked.

Sawyer dwelled on the question for a moment before replying. "Full circuit—Strawberry to Tahoe."

Grumbling ensued. The hunters traded another round of snarky jibes about cushy assignments and lazy asses. Tales of great fartery abounded. Smiling to herself, Victoria rinsed the dirty dishes and loaded them into the dishwasher. When she straightened, she found Cali at her elbow.

"You should get off your feet and relax," the female hunter said awkwardly. "We'll get the dishes."

"But—" Victoria began to protest. She'd just climbed out of bed an hour ago, and besides, her fortitude far exceeded that of a typical human, pregnant or not. After thinking about it for a second, she shrugged. She had plenty of battles to fight for things that mattered a whole lot more. Besides, she hated the drudgery of dishwashing so it was no great sacrifice to stand aside.

"DNR, get over here and wash these dishes." Cali turned on the most junior member of the hunter's unit, and with dynamics true of any social group, the shit rolled downhill until it hit the Omega. Grumbling, the lad rose and took up his appointed station as dishwasher.

"How long do you need to get ready?" Sawyer asked Victoria.

"I'm ready now." On cue, her cell phone rang. Her caller ID read "Alpha Finn".

Alertness jolted through Victoria. Alpha Finn was the leader of the White Mountains Tribe of Arizona, a powerful and influential group made up of smaller packs and war parties. The werewolves and their kinfolk, many of whom were of Native American descent, constituted a scattered population spread out over a wide territory.

"It's Finn. I need to take this." Reaching to answer, she flashed a wary grin by way of an apology.

Sawyer tipped his chin.

Victoria accepted the call and pressed the device to her ear. "Hello?"

"Victoria? It's Finn."

She cleared her throat. "Alpha Finn. What can I do for you?"

Sudden quiet fell across the room, the weight of all eyes upon her. She handled the unwanted attention with poise but conversations between Alphas required discretion.

"Do you have a moment?" Finn asked. "I have news regarding our pet project."

"Oh? Yes, of course. Just give me a moment to get to a place where we can speak privately." Ignoring her audience, she rounded the far side of the table and passed through the open French doors to where Sophia and two of her pups sprawled on the enclosed patio. Beyond, the landscaped area included an in-ground pool and an outdoor kitchen. No fences bordered the spacious back yard. Only a two-foot retaining wall constructed from rough river stones separated the plot from the surrounding woods.

Even though it wasn't yet past eight, the sun already

shone with the intensity of what would certainly be a hot summer day. Light glittered off the surface of the lake, strikingly pretty and inviting. She'd have loved nothing more than to shed her clothing and go skinny-dipping, but it wasn't the right time. Maybe tonight...

"Are you alone?" Impatience sharpened Finn's tone, quite an uncharacteristic departure from his usual calculated deliberation. Oh, the male wolf always wore a sheep's cloak of coy smugness, but his disguise overlaid toothy cunning. She considered him the most dangerous of all Alphas.

"I am now." Approaching the shallow end, Victoria kicked off her flip-flops and dipped her foot in to the water. It lapped at her ankles, and a sigh of pleasure eased from her chest.

"Good. The Alphas of Yosemite and Roanoke have agreed to attend a gathering to discuss a new alliance with the hunters—"

"Roanoke? The Lost Tribe?"

"Apparently they were in New Jersey this whole time, of course it wasn't New Jersey, then."

"Huhhh..." She stroked her chin. "Who'd've thunk it?"

"Not I." His snicker soared on a lyrical note, then cut short.

From behind Victoria, a high-pitched *craaa* accompanied the beating of wings. Foreboding, a great weight, pressed down upon her so she couldn't breathe. Her carefree mood of just moments before dissipated. She turned toward the sound as two large ravens landed on the roof of the single-story house. The mated pair had a nest constructed atop the master bedroom's unused fireplace.

"Odin is watching us, Finn," Victoria advised in a dark voice. "I've got ravens nesting on my roof." The duties and obligations assigned to her were more than she could bear.

A pause, and then the other Alpha inhaled. "Yes. I've observed unkindness seems to follow me around."

She managed a delicate snort. "An entire flock of ravens? Impressive. I only warrant a pair."

"Don't assume more to be a favorable portent," Finn replied with a perfect blend of self-deprecating humor and cynicism. "**He** watches me more closely because he mistrusts my loyalty."

"Maybe." Thanks to a certain prophecy, Victoria doubted the White Mountains Alpha was right, but she preferred to let him hold onto his misconceptions. Still, she wondered... On the verge of asking forbidden questions, Victoria bit her tongue. A dozen times, she and Finn had flirted with the prohibited topic, exchanging verbal thrusts and parries. She was 95% confident he knew Jake Barrett's secret but retained enough doubt that she didn't dare take the risk.

Sawyer appeared at the entryway to the patio. He stopped just inside the house and stood with his muscular arms crossed over his broad chest. The intensity of his gaze stroked her; as palpable as a touch. Victoria lifted her open hand, reaching for him. He returned the salute but didn't come any closer. The hunter's presence offered her real comfort. Sawyer wasn't another watchman sent by his father to monitor her activities, but rather a protector. He belonged to her pack—*to her*—an odd outlier within their mostly female family, but *theirs* nonetheless. She didn't count on many people but she had increasingly come to depend on him to have her back.

"My unkindness of ravens aside..." Finn grumbled.

She snickered. "We got off topic. As you were saying?"

Finn's tone took a dour turn. "Yosemite and Roanoke bring our total to thirty packs who have agreed to a moot. Of those, only twenty are able to attend a gathering. Three will vote by proxy."

She greeted the numbers with silence, mentally calculating the average strength of the packs. Even with the impressive might of the White Mountains Tribe which boasted four war parties—

"It's not nearly enough."

"I know it's not enough." Finn bit off his words with thinly veiled impatience. "But it's what we have so we will have to make do."

"You're right." She softened her tone, not wanting to alienate her only real ally amongst the packs. "What of your scouts? Have they had any luck locating any of the other missing packs?"

"San Diego and most of Southern California has been overrun by vampires, and according to rumor, Los Angeles won't last much longer. It would already have fallen, except the Governor declared martial law, implemented a curfew— for all the good it does against these so-called Daywalkers— and brought in the National Guard—"

"I saw that on the news."

"Every scout I have sent into those areas hasn't returned. It is too dangerous to send more."

"What of the hunters?" Victoria asked, even though she had the reports both Jake Barrett and Sawyer had given. Her robust sense of caution, however, thought it wise to do some fact checking.

Finn paused, and she could practically hear the wheels in his crafty head turning. No doubt he understood her reason for asking. She imagined him calculating, weighing odds, deciding what to disclose. Advantages gained or lost by keeping her in the dark. Or he might acquire useful new information...

She heaved a heavy sigh. "I'm profoundly tired of guessing games. Tell me what you know and I'll confirm or deny what I know. No holding anything back."

"I have your word?'

"You have my word. On my honor and my pack's honor, and I'll swear on a stack of Bibles too, if that will help."

Finn snorted. "That's not necessary. What I know is this. The hunters made their last stand four nights ago on Tumamoc Hill. Jake called out the Necromancer to appear and face him in a personal duel, but the coward ordered an assault on the city instead. Thousands of vampires descended upon the civilian population. The roads leading into Tucson are closed and thousands have fled by whatever means is available, including crossing the desert on foot. The city is still on fire. A great black cloud hangs over it."

"That matches what I know," Victoria admitted. "Jake has ordered his people to fall back to Phoenix. They've dug in and are preparing for an assault on the city's civilian population."

"They're defending their asses."

"They're defending their families. You can't blame them."

"Yet, just months ago, Barrett chastised me for doing the same." Finn's tone provided new dimensions to the term sarcasm. "*Ironically*, the Phoenix area hasn't been attacked in weeks."

"Finn..." She hesitated, reluctant to divulge, but she had promised. Gathering her resolve, she took the plunge. "Barrett lost almost nine hundred men in Tucson."

"Thor's Hammer. Nine hundred..." His shocked disbelief stretched.

"Convene the gathering, Finn," Victoria urged. "I'll host it in my territory—Desolation Wilderness. Our numbers are low and it may already be too late, but our people cannot be allowed to sit out the fight any longer. Perhaps if we join the war as a united force, the others will hear and come out of hiding."

Victoria's territory extended for miles to the north, including all of Desolation Wilderness, and to the east, encompassing the whole of Echo Lake. The most familiar areas were those close to the town. Primal magic resided within the pristine wilderness, hers to command. The entire area had once belonged to Arik Koenig, her mate. A few months before, in February of that year, a Norse winter witch had killed Arik during a blizzard battle.

"I will do so, but be aware—you will face opposition." Finn's voice rumbled deep in his throat, reverberating on a stifled growl, a wolf's innate response to threat. He softened his voice before he continued. "There are a great many who do not want to listen to the so-called 'Female Alpha'... Especially one in your delicate condition, whose reasoning is addled by hormones and grief over the loss of her mate..."

Anger surging, Victoria snarled. She stepped out of the pool and stalked barefoot about the perimeter. Her disgust and rage at such rigid machoism fed her determination to crush those who opposed her. As a rule, she respected tradition but not when it led to stagnation. She yoked her anger; rage was exactly what Finn wanted to prove his point, so she imposed icy self-control on her hot temper.

"I will strike dead anyone who dares repeat such rubbish to my face," Victoria said in a low, dangerous voice. "Male chauvinists are morons."

"Ah, they may be morons, but they are the morons that we need fighting with us." Maddeningly smug, Finn played at the devil's advocate.

"Let me worry about it. I can handle myself and them. I'll teach them a lesson they won't soon forget, so help me..." She ground to an abrupt stop, on the verge of vowing in Odin's name—an unwise choice, at best. Such oaths were not made casually, and the gods had been known to become downright persnickety when promises weren't kept.

"I'll convene the gathering. If nothing else, it will be worth it to watch you reduce my idiot Beta to a quivering pile of—"

"Call me as soon as it's done," Victoria interrupted, not wanting to listen to another word about Tarak, Finn's second. "Tell them we're meeting in seven days on the night of the full moon. I expect every last one of them to be here by moonrise."

Finn's hesitation was profound. "That's a tall order."

"Odin wants this." Victoria used the All Father's name as a hammer, driving her point home. "I brought you in on this because I thought you were capable and wielded authority among the packs. Was I wrong?"

Finn exhaled, the fuming heat so palpable it scalded her through the phone. "Consider it done. We'll convene the moot on the full moon in Desolation Wilderness."

"Good." She bared her teeth in a wolf's smile. If she had offended Finn, she didn't care. His annoyance was worth the satisfaction derived to finally be doing something after long, frustrating months of *nothing*.

They said their goodbyes and ended the call. Victoria's restless pacing had brought her to the pool's deep end. She turned, intending to head back inside.

Yelling arose from within the house—multiple voices elevated in anger. It sounded like every single hunter must be shouting at the top of their lungs.

And a familiar presence, as disruptive as a rogue lightning bolt, lanced through the pack bond, turning it inside-out and upside down. She recognized the signature chaos—and an involuntary grin lit her face. She enjoyed a heartbeat of stunned pleasure because Logan had finally come home.

A gun fired.

"Logan!" Victoria sprinted for the kitchen, praying to whatever god would listen that she made it in time to prevent a slaughter.

CHAPTER FIVE

Freya dropped her gaze to Arik's lap where Tregul sprawled belly up, an enviable position, to say the least, for any woman or beast. The enormous cat weighed a ton but Arik showed no sign of discomfort. While Arik Koenig had been a lawyer in life, he was also an Alpha werewolf—an extraordinarily powerful one at that. Now, he served and serviced Freya, a general to her army, a position of vast influence and authority.

"You mean their affection is given freely? Are these sweet kitties promiscuous?" He placed a definitive emphasis on the final word. Arik stroked his finger along Bygul's arched back and lingered at the base of her tail, rubbing her lick spot.

Freya's chest tightened. Odd, she'd never heard him sound so...judgmental. She wasn't sure what disturbed her more—the hint of disapproval or that she cared what he thought of her.

Delicately, she cleared her throat. "To what do I owe the

pleasure of your visit, Arik? I thought you would be in the field with the troops."

He looked up, an insightful gleam in his honey-brown eyes, and stared straight through her. "An urgent matter has come to my attention."

"Urgent? Is something wrong with the army?" Freya demanded.

The disposition of the army was always her greatest priority because it constituted the true basis of her power. Centuries ago, Freya, and her brother, Freyr, had been mere war hostages—exchanged following the Aesir-Vanir War. A conflict Odin had started because he coveted *seidr*, an old and powerful type of sorcery, developed and practiced exclusively by the Vanir up until then. Knowledge, particularly knowledge beyond his tenure, had always been Odin's greatest weakness. He pursued the acquisition of such at any cost and valued it more than anything else, including objects and power. When the war ended, Asgard's walls lay in ruin but the All Father had been none the closer to acquiring the mystical arts that elven kind had fought and died in legions to protect.

In the aftermath, Freya had gone to Odin and offered to teach him *seidr* even though her own brother urged her not to, and her father forbade it. Thanks to her shrewd negotiations, Freya elevated her status in Asgard from prisoner to commander of the Valkyries and one-half the military forces. Additionally, she acquired her own hall, but far more importantly, she gained freedom for herself and Freyr.

Her father cursed her but it mattered not. She was autonomous.

"No, the troops are fine," Arik said.

"Good." She exhaled in relief. "What is it then?"

Sierra Pines, California, on the western shore of Echo Lake

Time dilated and everything slowed. Her awareness narrowed to a specific focal point—the fight in the kitchen. Victoria ran, but pregnancy made her heavy and slow. Before she made it, loud cracks sounded in rapid succession—a .45 unloading on full auto.

Victoria burst into the house. Sawyer had his back to her, facing into the kitchen, but his stance told her at a glance that he was the gunman. He clicked empty on the ninth shot and ejected the clip, already reaching for another. She launched airborne and landed square on the hunter's back, her knees dug into his sides.

The impact knocked the hunter down, giving her a clear view of Logan. He rested slumped against the wall, upright in spite of the enormous bloody splotch on the front of his shirt. He was already halfway into the classic wolfman form often depicted in horror movies. It looked like he'd been shot mid-change; his injuries had interrupted his transformation. He'd taken a massive amount of damage, enough to keep him down and out for a while until his regeneration kicked in.

Sawyer grunted as he collided with the ground. Clinging to him, Victoria fell, too, but his powerful body cushioned the force of her landing.

"Victoria! What the hell?" He lifted his head, expression thunderstruck when he saw it was she who had tackled him. His gaze slid past her. Twisting, she spotted the .45 beneath a kitchen chair. He reached for it.

"I can't let you kill Logan." Victoria slithered off his back and lunged. She knocked the handle beyond his fingers and then snatched it up. The weapon's smoky discharge smelled only of gunpowder. Not silver—which was lethal to werewolves.

"He attacked me." The hunter threw in a curse for good measure. The dagger tattoo on his upper arm glowed white-hot, just like hers.

"I'm sure he started it, too." She shot upright and craned her head, scanning the room to mark everyone's locations. Thankfully, Sylvie had already driven the gray wolves out onto the patio. Cali Kinkaid crouched near the gas range, but she didn't see DNR anywhere.

"Over here! I'm clear." Morena jumped up and down on the far side of kitchen, waving her arms. Victoria lobbed the gun to the teenager who caught it out of midair. Snatching open the freezer, the girl tossed the firearm inside and slammed the door shut.

"It's on ice!" Morena flashed two thumbs up.

"Good job!" Victoria laughed despite everything else going on.

Problem number one dealt with, she whirled to confront the next. A maelstrom of masculine anger assailed her through the pack bond. Sawyer tore at her from one side, Logan the other, forcing her to maintain a death grip on her own explosive temper. A thick fog of fear, adrenaline, and rage clogged the air.

A thunk from behind alerted her that Sawyer had regained his feet. She offered up a silent, fervent prayer to whatever god was listening that the hunter would hold back and allow her to manage the situation.

"That's enough. No more violence. We're all friends here." Employing an Alpha's trick, Victoria infused her voice with raw power, creating resonance as she attempted to impose order on chaos. For a second, she got on top of the storm.

Logan hadn't recovered from his injuries yet; the others were suspended in an amber moment in time.

It didn't last.

"Victoria. Get behind me before he hurts you." Sawyer seized her upper arm and yanked her out of the way. A yelp of indignation escaped her, but before she mustered a protest, the hunter had gotten in front of her again.

"He'd never hurt me." She snarled in frustration, certain her assurance would fall on deaf ears. She had a clean shot at Sawyer's back. For a split second, she contemplated crippling the hunter to express her displeasure, but he only wanted to keep her from danger.

Clearly, Sawyer would've preferred she'd obediently stepped aside like a good damsel-in-distress. Too bad for him, she considered herself a self-rescuing princess. But no matter how annoying and overbearing his attitude, his protectiveness pleased her. She detested his machoism and reveled in it all at once.

Sawyer's raw determination poured over her. Drawing his bayonet, he settled into a wide stance, arms and legs spread, shielding her with his body. He advanced toward Logan, clearly intending to decapitate the felled werewolf.

"No!" Terror jolted her back into action. Victoria dodged to the side and took advantage of her short height to pass beneath his guard. She seized hold of his elbow and jerked his sword arm down.

"Fuck. Damn it, Victoria. What the fuck are you doing?" Face contorted, he rounded on her, catching hold of her arm with his strong hand. He checked himself, hampered by his unwillingness to harm her, just as she was reluctant to hurt him.

"Is it such a mystery? I'm stopping you." They jostled for

the upper hand, a back and forth exchange not at full strength or ability, but it was definitely a real competition.

"Why?" Incredulity spiked Sawyer's voice.

"Because—" Victoria sputtered. Her agitation defied a composed and articulate explanation. On a primal level, her she-wolf harbored the answers. Logan—*friend*. Logan—*pack*. Logan—her dead mate's misguided, rebellious, socially-inept son whom she was obligated to protect... even from himself.

On a primal level, instinct urged her to step aside and let them have at one another. Neither was directly challenging her authority as Alpha. Wolf etiquette dictated that competing males should settle their differences with fangs and claws. The most dominant male would emerge victorious—the loser would roll over—and the pack would be stronger for it.

Sawyer wasn't a wolf, though, and therein was the crux. The hunter didn't know the rules, wasn't equipped for a proper fight, and had no concern for pack status. So far, Sawyer had retained control, but his explosive temper was a wild card. He killed as easily as he breathed. It hadn't been so long since they'd been at each other's throats that she'd forgotten.

The hunter scowled. His regard locked on her; he searched her face, seeking answers. A frozen moment but they achieved connection. The pack bond resonated with a glimmer of concord which slowly crystalized—

The snarl of an injured, angry werewolf shattered their unity—Logan awakening.

The hunter's head jerked toward the threat.

In grim desperation, she tightened her grip on his sword arm. She would prevent Sawyer from attacking Logan but she wasn't prepared to hamper him if he needed to defend himself. Her loyalties were wretchedly, painfully divided.

Should her effort to prevent a fight fail, she didn't know what she would do.

Sawyer's eyes betrayed his decision to act in the split second before he moved. The blasted man claimed to be left handed but the reality was closer to ambidexterity. As nimble as a baton twirler, he set the knife to spinning and flipped it neatly from one hand to the other.

Victoria made a blind grab for his wrist, expecting him to be one place, but she miscalculated, and her hand closed on the blade of the knife instead. The edge sliced clean through her palm, and her sharp hurt lanced through the pack bond. Gasping, she opened her hand. Hot blood gushed from the wound.

Sawyer met her gaze—surprise lit his eyes and dismay parted his lips.

Giving a violent shake of his head, Logan rose onto his hind legs. The visage of a wolf stared at her—ears thrust to high points atop his head and jaws that formed a bold muzzle. His mouth hung open, revealing dagger-sharp teeth that glistened with strands of saliva. He swayed on his feet. Blood dripped from the wound on his chest and then smeared across the tile. As he healed, bullets popped from the injury. When he stepped toward her, iron-hard muscles rippled beneath plush black fur, and a visceral thrill of feminine admiration shot through her. His change occurred as swift and smooth as a riptide; his body poured itself into the mold of an enormous black wolf. Most wolf shifters required a minute or more; Logan took seconds. As his mass doubled, black fur burst through rent seams and the claws on his feet ripped through his shoes.

Fully transformed, Logan dropped to all fours and shook off the tattered remnants of his clothing. He stood with his head angled forward, his bristled tail flagged. His jaws parted in threat. A deep, rumbling growl reverberated in his throat.

"Stop." Victoria set down a flat command, reinforced through the empathic connection, seeking to instill obedience even though she expected to fail. She tried anyway; she was desperate. Logan had a hard head and a stubborn streak to match. At best, she hoped to distract him long enough to diffuse the situation.

Teeth bared, Logan lunged at Sawyer.

Simultaneously, Victoria's peripheral vision caught a blur from the left. With a shrill cry, Cali Kinkaid came to Sawyer's defense. The female hunter charged straight toward Logan with her arm raised.

Their combined bodies blocked Victoria's view but a horrified vision flooded her mind, so clear and real she perceived it as prophecy—a decapitated wolf shifter and a murdered hunter. Images swirled in her head, a crazy whirlwind, and a view into a brachiated future. Multiple paths led to the same awful, inevitable conclusion. The enormity of it sickened her.

The wolf-hunter war would resume.

Her stomach heaved. Helpless, Victoria doubled over, fighting the urge to puke. All she could do was watch the train wreck, unable to look away. Cringing, her frame stiffened, joints locking as she braced for the worst. Logan's momentum allowed the female hunter to blindside him.

A strangled scream caught Victoria's throat despite her best attempts to give it voice. She struggled to force her vocal cords to work, but all she could do was squeak. Then, all the sudden, a shout of warning tore from her throat—

"No!"

Both hands locked on the handle of her weapon, Kinkaid swung her arms over and down. The hot bottom of the skillet clobbered the side of Logan's head. A solid clonk and a gruesome sizzle recorded the impact. The burnt stench of seared flesh inundated the air.

Roaring, Logan wheeled on Kinkaid, his jaws parted wide to strike. At the end of her arc, Cali attempted to bring the hot pan up for another blow, but her reflexes were no match for a wolf's—and he already had the advantageous position. Her attack left her wide open.

"Logan, no!" Victoria lunged even though she would be too late.

The black wolf dove toward the hunter, his jaws bared for a throat grab. He shot straight past her clumsy guard and dove for her jugular. His teeth were ever so big and white— more than capable of biting off a grown woman's head.

"Enough. These people are our guests. You dishonor our pack." Sylvie slid into the slight gap between wolf and hunter. She blocked his bite, shoving her forearm between his jaws, and shoved the hunter aside. When Logan's teeth sank into her flesh, the Skald's pain blossomed through the pack bond.

Victoria ground to a sudden halt, and Sawyer collided with her from behind, knocking her right off her feet. His hands locked on her shoulders and stopped her from going over. Unless he'd grown a third arm, he must have sheathed or dropped the knife; she couldn't spare the attention to check. Her gaze remained locked on her pack mates. For a horrified instance, she feared Logan would turn on the Skald.

Logan opened his jaws, releasing Sylvie's arm, and his uneasy regret spread through the empathic bond. It constituted an admission of wrongdoing and an apology. He edged back a stride, his posture defensive, and his wary gaze shifted between the hunters.

"All right. That's it. I want all hunters outside. My

apologies and it's nothing personal, but we need to create a cooling-off zone." Victoria raised her volume, taking control of the situation. She spread her arms wide and stepped back, bulldozing Sawyer away from Logan and toward the patio.

Victoria and Sylvie traded a silent look of understanding, and the older woman positioned herself to cover Kinkaid, edging the female hunter toward the far entrance to the kitchen. Morena hadn't moved from guard duty on the freezer. DNR emerged from behind the breakfast bar where he'd apparently been hiding.

Kinkaid and DNR remained rooted in place, looking to Sawyer for verification. Victoria couldn't see the hunter's face, but she sensed his tightly-repressed anger, a mirror to her own. At the moment, she was thoroughly pissed off, especially with the idiot males who were to blame for the current fiasco.

"DNR, head out through the patio exit and circle around. Meet me out front." Sawyer issued the order with steady confidence.

"Yes, sir. I'm already gone." DNR shot to his feet and hit the ground running, following the proscribed route.

"I think the lad pissed himself." Sawyer shook his head. "And you, Kinkaid—what were you thinking, attacking a werewolf with a frying pan? That has to be the most dumbass thing I've ever seen anyone do." With a touch of offbeat humor, Sawyer deescalated the strain further. A burst of nervous laughter swept the room—even Logan huffed, sides heaving.

"Technically, it was a skillet." She paused. *"Sir."*

"No one's going to stop calling you 'crazy' anytime soon," Sawyer said.

The female hunter cocked her head and flashed a shit-eating grin. "I sure as hell hope not."

Nervous laughter skipped through those gathered. Victoria allowed her arms to fall to her sides, and eased toward the center to assess the female hunter's condition. She deliberately positioned herself between Logan and Sawyer as a buffer. If either tried anything, they'd have to go through her first.

Logan's gaze burned a hole in in her back; his molten anger stewed like a volcano pending eruption. In a pure fit of annoyance, Victoria grabbed raw power and whacked him through the pack bond, delivering the equivalent of a sharp smack.

The black wolf huffed, but offered no other response. Foreboding of another explosive confrontation brewed in Victoria's gut. Logan's restraint worried her, precisely because it wasn't like him at all. More than anything, he was a creature of impulse and passion. She wondered if he'd changed that much in the months since she'd last seen him, and more than anything, she hoped not. She really liked the stupid jerk as he was... sarcasm and all.

"Cali, are you injured? You have blood on your arm." Belatedly, Victoria realized Kinkaid had nowhere to retreat —she had Morena at her back, Sylvie beside her, and Logan in front of her. She lifted her hand and beckoned Morena to move aside to clear a path. The teenager hesitated, but then edged over toward the sink, placing the island between them.

"It's not mine." Kinkaid swiped her hand across her forearm, wiping off blood she then flicked to the tile. The female hunter glanced about, noting Morena's position and the open path. She hesitated as if considering her options, and then carefully set the skillet down on the stovetop.

"Thank you for defending me. I'm sorry you were hurt doing so." Cali addressed her words to Sylvie, speaking in an apologetic tone.

"You're welcome." Sylvie offered a gracious smile. "I am already healing."

"I dented your pot. Thank you for inviting us for breakfast." The female hunter ran a hand through her hair, appearing more nervous with social pleasantries than she had going into combat armed with a skillet.

"I'm sure it'll be fine," Sylvie said. "And you're welcome. Hopefully, next time, things will go more smoothly."

"Next time." Cali tipped her chin. Head held high, shoulders square; she marched past Victoria toward the back patio exit. Maybe it was just to be contrary, or she wanted to prove her courage. Whatever the case, Victoria kept her mouth shut, especially since she landed squarely in agreement with Sawyer—Crazy Cali more than deserved her moniker. Once Kinkaid reached the courtyard, she lingered beside the patio table, keeping an eye on Sawyer.

Victoria didn't blame her in the least; she admired the woman's loyalty. Hoping to diffuse the tension further, she turned to Sawyer. She stared into his grumpy face and tried for a light, teasing tone. "Are you still here?"

"You said hunters outside, pack inside. I'm confused. Am I supposed to stand on the threshold?" Sawyer arched an ironic brow, making light of the matter though his underlying attitude conveyed skepticism and challenge.

"Sawyer, for all your faults, you've never been pissy. Don't start now."

"I'm not leaving you alone," Sawyer said, frowning.

Victoria smothered a smile, once again rather stupidly liking his assertiveness when the smart reaction dictated the opposite.

Thankfully, Sylvie stepped up to offer a neat reply. "She is not alone. I am here."

"Me too!" Morena piped up, ambling closer. True to

character, the teenager refused to be left out of any important event. The girl had the enthusiasm of a hyperactive five-year-old and the energy to match.

"I'm not leaving." Sawyer crossed his arms.

Men. They were both so damn stubborn. Neither would give even an inch. She couldn't win. Victoria stretched her neck to one side, trying to alleviate cramped muscles. For a frustrating minute, the impasse appeared insurmountable. Faced with no other options, she would have to choose between Sawyer and Logan. Keep one, boot the other. Not a decision she wanted to make. Quite selfishly, she preferred to retain both of them. The pack needed strong males to aid its recovery.

Sylvie caught her Alpha's gaze. The Skald rolled her eyes heavenward and pressed her palms together, pantomiming prayer. She mouthed, "Goddess help these poor, pathetic creatures. Blessed be."

An involuntary chuckle caught Victoria unprepared. The worst of her frustration dissipated, and her disposition improved dramatically. Sylvie was right—they were only males, in desperate need of both her patience and her guidance. The guys might not like it, but she would figure out a solution.

Logan's claws scraped on the tile. His hot breath struck the small of her back, and her frilly blouse stirred and was then sucked against his nostrils when he inhaled. She twisted to face him and pressed her palm to his wet nose. If she had been in her wolf form, they'd have bumped muzzles. Instead, she curled her fingers about his snout to complete the ritual affirming their bond. They were still packmates, despite his six-month absence, no matter how contentious their reunion.

As though bidden, Logan's anger rammed its way through

the empathic connection; unmistakable and impossible to ignore—and aimed completely at her. Protectiveness overlay his displeasure. Unfortunately, it rendered his shitty attitude completely acceptable to Victoria's wolf. Her beast preened and luxuriated in the heat of his regard, accepting it as her due.

Images imbued with potent emotion traversed the link, more effective than words. Set to a rhythm, deep bass drums would've pounded out a primal song. His grievances were many and the wound to his ego egregious. Here, he'd returned to discover his home invaded by strangers. The females of his pack surrounded by hunters. When he'd jumped to their defense, he'd been shot, assaulted, and insulted...

"I'm going to stop you right there." She blocked his magic, exerting her own. "You're comparing being territorial to guardianship. Those aren't the same thing. Not by a long shot."

Logan snorted, blowing a spray of spit. He got right in her face, huffing hot, citrusy breath. Glowing amber eyes locked on her accusingly, the prettiest eyes she'd ever seen on a man. Too bad he always seemed to regard her with such hostility.

"Knock it off. You're drooling on me." Victoria's fist flew up. She bashed Logan on the nose. His eyes narrowed but he backed off. "I understand you're upset, but you were gone for months. You said you were leaving and never gave an indication you'd be back. As Alpha, I made Sawyer a member of this pack. Normally, I wouldn't care about a male pissing match for rank so long as you took it outside. But he's a helpless human and it wouldn't be a fair fight."

"Helpless." Sawyer muttered beneath his breath.

Victoria shot the hunter a narrow-eyed glare warning—*Shut up.*

Logan rumbled his disagreement. He shifted—his paw to a claw, his front leg to an arm. Elegant, precision shape changing, unlike anything Victoria had ever witnessed before. He scooped up a handful of the fired bullets littering the floor, shoved his open palm beneath her nose, and then cast the metal aside with an eloquent grumble—*helpless, his furry backside.*

Victoria bit the insides of her cheeks to kill a smile. "Look, we can't talk while you're like this. Shift back. We'll pretend this never happened and start over. I'll make proper introductions and you two can shake hands."

Rearing his head, Logan grunted. His long, low moan sounded suspiciously like "Noooooo."

"Fine, be that way." Victoria edged toward Sawyer. She wrapped her arm about his waist and gently nudged the hunter toward the patio exit. "Are you injured? Do you need healing?"

A shadow moved across his face. "Nah. I'm fine. Just some bruises."

"Good." She scented no hint of deception on his part. Relief haloed her. She'd feared she'd broken ribs when she'd jumped him and knocked him down.

"How's your hand?"

"Already healed." She flashed her palm, flexing her fingers.

"Good." His approval warmed her like sunshine.

Amazingly, charm worked where reason had failed. Sawyer cooperated with her attempts to herd him toward the patio. He only stopped to retrieve his coat and shoulder harness from the kitchen chair.

Victoria laid her palm over his heart. "Give me a couple

minutes, then I'll meet you out front. We can check out those drifters in Broken Bend, okay?"

"Yeah, all right." He sounded like he hated the idea but at least he was cooperating. He tipped his head toward the refrigerator. "I want my gun."

Seconds ticked past loud enough she heard each and every one. She hesitated to return his firearm, but he wouldn't leave without the .45. It all came down to trust.

"Morena, get the man his gun." Victoria gestured with her hand, urging speed. At her back, Logan grumbled his displeasure, but she made a point of ignoring him. Her patience with macho posturing was done.

"Riiight. One gunsicle comin' right up." A bound and a stride carried Morena to the fridge. She jerked open the door, rooted around within until she located the firearm, and then slammed it shut. The teenager deftly flipped opened the gun, checked to be sure the chamber was clear, and then closed it. Grasping the barrel, she offered the handle to Sawyer.

The hunter accepted the .45 and holstered it. His shuttered gaze scanned the room one final time, lingering on each of them in turn. He pointedly failed to acknowledge Logan while the black wolf's unwavering gaze smoldered with loathing.

"I'll be outside. Waiting," Sawyer drawled.

Their eyes locked. The unspoken message came through loud and clear. If she took too long, he'd return, guns locked and loaded.

CHAPTER SIX

Arik ceased obliging Tregul's persistent demands for affection and lowered his hand. The tiger growled to protest the neglect, but it earned him little more than a summary pat.

After a considerable delay, Arik said, "I'm concerned for Victoria."

"Victoria?" Freya floundered, caught off-guard by the direction of the conversation. A coarse, alien feeling filled her... jealousy? No, impossible! A goddess was above such trivial attachments to a mortal man. And just the mention of her disgraced priestess burned her blood. Victoria—whom she'd favored above all others, indulged and spoiled, only to have her generosity rewarded with disobedience and betrayal.

"Yes, Victoria. My mate and the mother of my unborn child." A cool facsimile of a smile played on his lips. Even pinned beneath Tregul's massive bulk, the man was too damn composed to be believed.

She quelled the reflexive desire to correct him. Victoria Storm was his *former* mate. Arik belonged to Freya now. The urge to tell him so, to put him in his place, was great. Right there on the tip of her tongue. But a twinge of intuition urged her to caution.

"What about her?" Freya asked instead.

Arik's brow rose. "It's come to my attention that there's a proximate threat—not only to my wife and daughter but to my entire pack."

"You agreed to sever all earthly ties when you entered into my service." Haughtiness crept into her manner, her tone as piercing as the head of a spear.

"I'm a Philadelphia Lawyer. I know what we agreed to."

Sierra Pines, California, on the western shore of Echo Lake

"You're pregnant!"

Wincing, Victoria turned and found Logan right behind her. Face contorted, he loomed over her; his bare chest in her face. The musk of male aggression permeated the air. He held his clenched fists at his sides, stance rigid and his voice seethed. He'd completed the transition from wolf to human in a handful of seconds, so smoothly she hadn't even noticed.

"Thank you, Captain Obvious."

"Why didn't you tell me, Vic? Why is the only reason I'm finding out because I walked in and caught you red-handed —" He bit off the accusation but it was too late. No mistaking the distrust in his eyes or the hardened suspicion in his voice.

"Caught me red-handed doing what? Being pregnant?"

Infuriated, Victoria thumped Logan right on the breastbone, nailing him with two fingers. "You want to know why I didn't tell you? It's none of your damn business—"

"My dad's been dead less than six months and you've already shacked up with a fucking hunter. Is he the father?"

Shocked silent, Victoria's mouth quivered. His verbal assault thrust a dagger of hurt straight through her heart. His cruelty cut her to the quick. Tears flooded her eyes, spilled down her cheeks, and dripped onto her lips. In the single most humiliating moment of her entire life, she choked on a sob.

Logan got a good look at her expression, and his face blanched. He shut his mouth. Quicksilver emotions crossed his face, mirroring his internal conflict. His voice emerged raw. "Vic, I—"

A blur moved behind Logan, and a chair busted over the top of his head. Solid hardwood shards exploded, flying everywhere. He dropped to the ground like a sack and landed flat on his back. Stunned, Victoria blinked her blurry eyes into focus and gaped in astonishment at Morena. Breathing hard, the teenager lowered her arms.

The silence thundered.

Twisting around, Logan tilted his head to gap up at the girl. "Morie?"

"*¡Tu eres un pendejo!*" Bending, Morena berated him, heaping verbal abuse on his head. She switched to English once her tirade sputtered out. "I can't believe I thought you were so fucking great."

"Okay, got it. You're pissed. You've made your point on my skull." Flat on his ass, he lifted his hand to gingerly touch the injury.

"Asshole." Morena spat on the ground beside him. Then

the teenager sprinted through the French doors. Sophia and the three half-grown adolescent gray wolves followed right on her heels.

"Wow." Astonished, Victoria stared after Morena, wanting to say thank you, but the teenager and wolves were already out of earshot. Just the fact of her Omega's defense took the worst sting out of her hurt. Her pack loved her and would defend her even if this one stupid jackass said whatever thoughtless thing popped into his mouth.

"I don't think I've ever been as proud of that girl." Stepping close, Sylvie pulled Victoria into a sisterly hug. "Are you all right, Victory?"

"Yes, I'm fine. Thank you." She pointedly ignored Logan, as did Sylvie.

Muttering, Logan climbed to his feet and marched from the room. "I'll be back—with pants!"

Even though she swore she wasn't going to look, Victoria stole a quick glance. The male werewolf was long and lean, his build sinewy, and she critically noted he appeared to have shed pounds he could ill afford to lose. He was already too thin, and his broad shoulders and big hands and feet enhanced the impression of an adult male who'd not yet achieved his full growth. Logan had a tramp stamp across his lower back—a tattoo of an Ouroboros serpent, a snake devouring his own tail. He didn't appear to have acquired any fresh ink, at least not on this side. He had the ass and thighs of a swimsuit model.

"Humph." Sylvie's snort spoke volumes.

Victoria grinned and shrugged. "It'll be a while before he's back unless he's willing to wear maternity pants. All of his clothes are bagged and shoved to the back of the closet."

"I'll help him... if he asks." From the severity of Sylvie's tone, it would take an apology to earn her assistance.

Well, tough. It served him right.

"That was Finn on the phone, before all this, this..." Victoria waved her hands at the disheveled room in general. "Before it got out of hand."

"Oh?" Sylvie lifted her brow.

"Finn says things are getting worse." Taking a deep breath, she brought Sylvie up to speed on her conversation with Finn.

"Are you sure it's wise to bring outsiders into our territory?" Sylvie asked once Victoria petered out.

"Maybe not wise, but it's happening." She shrugged.

Sylvie snorted. "What about Logan?"

"Better to keep him out of it, at least for now. Don't tell him what's going on or he'll find some way to cause trouble." Victoria fidgeted, casting an uneasy glance in the direction Logan had gone. She spoke in a hush, wary of being overheard.

"Agreed. Why on earth are you squirming like you've got ants in your pants?"

"Sorry." Victoria forced herself to be still. "Right now I just want to get out of here before Sawyer decides to come looking for me." Or worse, Logan. She imagined he'd be annoyed when he found out she'd been living in his room instead of the master suite that had belonged to Arik.

She panned the kitchen and trailed off. The area was a disaster. Overturned and destroyed furniture, blood on the floor and walls, spilled food and ceramic shards from a dropped plate, not to mention the dirty dishes people had abandoned.

"Go. I'll clean this up." Sylvie shooed her.

"But I should help." Victoria bit her lower lip, debating her desire to go versus her duties to remain.

"Morena and Logan will help. I'll see to it." The Skald

waved the Alpha away. "Go. If Sawyer has truly detected intruders in our territory, then you have bigger concerns than these."

"Okay." Victoria capitulated because she lacked any real desire to argue. Deciding to follow the route all three hunters had taken, she crossed to the French doors which still stood wide open. Hesitating, she looked back. "Sylvie..."

In the act of gathering coffee mugs from the table, the Skald paused and looked up. Her brow rose in silent question.

"Thank you."

"You're welcome." The Skald tipped her chin.

Hurrying her steps, she passed through the courtyard and turned to head around the house, but then remembered her phone. She'd been holding it when the commotion had started and must've dropped it. Worry niggled at her that the device had fallen into the water so she retraced her steps and breathed a sigh of relief when she spotted it on the concrete beside the pool.

The phone was face down, a yard from her forgotten flip-flops. Pausing, she wedged her feet into the sandals and then bent to scoop up the device. Intense irritation ran through her when she turned it over and discovered a shattered screen.

"Damn it, Logan, you're buying me a new phone." She fumed, heaping the blame on the male werewolf. At the same time, her topsy-turvy pregnancy emotions tilted her toward intense sorrow. To the point where she wanted nothing more than to find a man's strong shoulder to lean on and have herself a good cry.

A man's strong shoulder... The most awful joke yet. **She** did not cry on shoulders. Male or otherwise.

"Goddess, no one warned me pregnancy was the same as

being certifiably insane," Victoria said aloud, addressing the words to Freya, the Norse goddess of love and war who she served as priestess.

Actually, we did warn you but you chose not to listen. Freya's tone was scathing and it stopped Victoria in her tracks.

A tremor ran through her. She blinked rapidly to prevent the tears that stung her eyes from falling. Months ago, Victoria disobeyed Freya's will and explicit instructions when she had resurrected Sawyer Barrett from the dead. Broken faith was bad enough, but she had consorted with another Norse god to accomplish the feat.

Disobedience and infidelity.

She ached from body to soul. Oh, how she missed the rapport she'd once shared with her goddess. Not so long ago, their conversations had been full of lighthearted banter and affection, laughter and joy. Now, Freya made her censure known through both her silence and scornful comments on those rare occasions when chose to speak. Freya's anger was justified—a goddess commanded; a faithful priestess submitted. Once that trust was broken, could it ever be mended?

Victoria blamed herself; the dishonor belonged to her alone. She'd apologized countless times already and would do so however many more times her deity required.

My Lady, please. My heart is broken. It was wrong of me to disobey you. Please, set a task before me. Grant me an opportunity to make amends. Victoria closed her eyes and clasped her hands together in prayer. Her deity had to take priority— Sawyer could wait a while longer.

Freya's silence served as her answer, just as it had the other times Victoria had begged for an opportunity to do penance. She released a thin sigh and opened her eyes.

Any task I set before you will be difficult as befits the offense you have given.

Her heart leapt to her throat, lifting on a surge of hope. Tears spilled down her cheeks. *Please, Goddess, I'll do anything you ask!*

Anything? Freya asked in the severest tenor.

Yes, anything. Victoria's blood ran cold but she had no choice but to promise. She dared not refuse the first glimmer of forgiveness she'd seen in months.

I will contemplate it.

SHE ROUNDED the house and found Sawyer had already backed her car out of the detached garage. The hood was up on the 1970 Chevelle SS 454, and the denim-clad ass and legs of the man bent over the engine were visible. The convertible's top was down, and its glossy red paint glowed in the morning sunlight, as did the pristine white leather interior. The motor idled, a steady purr, like a great cat loving the attention lavished on it.

"I might've known," Victoria teased, approaching the vehicle. And yeah, though she was reluctant to admit it, she took the opportunity to admire the hunter's tight back end. Her gaze lingered. Damn, the man was fine. Off-limits, because she had once dated his brother, but a girl could look.

"I've been meaning to check the timing belts." Pulling back, Sawyer closed the lid and stroked his hand over one of the two black racing stripes that ran down the hood. Long dirty-blonde strands hung into his face, so her fingers itched for a pair of scissors. Or, even better, some clippers.

The other two hunters were gone, as was their vehicle.

"I guess we're taking the Chevelle?" Victoria asked, hazarding the obvious. She'd left the keys to the SUV on the key hook in the kitchen, and loathed the idea of going back inside and risking another run-in with Logan.

At times, she wondered why she'd bothered paying for the title transfer and registration that made her the legal owner of the vehicle. Sawyer spent as much time behind the wheel as she did. Not that she blamed him. Before he'd given Victoria the Chevelle to settle a debt owed, the convertible had belonged to Daniel, Victoria's lover and Sawyer's older brother. The car held enormous sentimental value for them both. She preferred to share. Cutting Sawyer off from the tie to his brother would've been petty and spiteful.

"Do you want to drive?" Sawyer asked. At a glance, he appeared relaxed, but underlying tension defined the set of his shoulders. Notes of aggression and unease overlaid his base scent, which was clean and musky. Her hyperactive olfactory sense noted the recent use of an offensively powerful soap and aftershave.

Her nose twitched, and then she sneezed.

"God bless you," Sawyer said.

Squinting through watery, itchy eyes, she waved a hand while battling another sneeze. "Please, I don't need that sort of complication."

Sawyer laughed, and then walked around to the passenger side and opened the door. For an instant, she assumed he wanted her to drive but he just stood there—waiting. Confused, she hesitated. What manner of misplaced chivalry was this? Was he seriously holding the door for her?

Under her stare, Sawyer's cheeks turned pink, but he stubbornly stood sentry. At last, to end the awkwardness as much as to spare them both further embarrassment, she entered the car, and fastened her seatbelt. She cast a glance over her shoulder and confirmed the location of the hunter's folded coat and holstered .45 on the backseat.

"You're not wearing your gun? Don't cha feel naked?"

"It's hot." Grinning, he rounded the vehicle, and got in on the driver's side. Before he put the convertible into gear, he settled in and adjusted the radio to a rock station.

Listening to music, they rode without talking while he backed the car out of the driveway and navigated the narrow private road that led toward town. The tension failed to improve until Victoria could stand it no longer. Reaching over, she laid a hand on his forearm. At her touch, he glanced down and then up, a question in his chocolate-brown eyes.

The empathic connection flowed at a trickle instead of the full-blown rush she shared with most of the pack, but it was enough to permit a glimpse of his mood—a vital blend of protectiveness and possessiveness. Even though he wasn't a wolf shifter, Sawyer had all the right instincts to make a good Alpha. While she counted his hotheadedness as a mark against him, he was only twenty-six. Time and experience would cool his molten temper and forge a steel-hard resolve. If he turned out even half the man his father was…he'd be heroic.

"Thank you. I'm not used to anyone opening doors for me." She offered a tentative smile which he returned.

"Especially me?" His tone was rife with irony but his attention returned to the road as they navigated a sharp turn. Sawyer drove in the same manner as he approached everything else—brashly, without a hint of fear.

"We've come a long way since the last time you tried to kill me." She infused her tone with sarcasm. "Though, we need to reset the clock to less than an hour since you tried to kill a member of my pack."

His jaw hardened. "He started it."

"I don't have a doubt he did." Victoria's familiarity with Logan extended to his exceptional talent for provoking even the most levelheaded people. The guy possessed an almost preternatural gift for being a jackass.

"For the record, I wasn't trying to kill him either. Just neutralize him." A great cloud of sullenness hung over the hunter.

"I'm sure you exercised the utmost restraint."

He shot her a shrewd glance that slid sideways across her face, but she read his look—he wasn't in the mood to be humored or teased. *Well, too damn bad.* Victoria sucked in her cheeks and slapped on her angel face.

"You're cute when you do that," he said, chuckling.

"Yeah, thanks." Scrunching her nose, she lifted her lip in a sneer.

"Do you want him taken care of?" His brief amusement evaporated. The hunter's face set into a stoic mask—dead serious. His brown eyes turned flinty, and an uncanny resemblance to his father overtook him.

He wasn't kidding.

A thrill and a chill shot along Victoria's spine. Stark fear filled her, not for herself, but for what this man was capable of. At the same time, his willingness to kill for her empowered her and her pack, granting them a more secure life. As the Hunter King's son, Sawyer had the resources of the entire organization at his disposal. If she asked, he'd eliminate Logan.

"No, absolutely not. Logan is a member of my pack, and so are you. We need to get past this thing where you keep threatening to kill—" She bit off the accusation because it wasn't fair. Sawyer never threatened the female members of the pack or the pups. In fact, she relied on him to keep them safe... And that realization jarred her. She wondered when in the last several months she'd crossed the trust line. She sighed. "Thanks, but no thanks. Please don't kill anyone for me... Well, maybe unless I ask."

Sawyer produced a sound between a grunt and a snort. "Who is this Logan guy, anyway?"

Victoria hesitated. Fuck, talk about awkward situations that defied ready explanation. No easy way to say it, so she launched into a rambling response. "He's my mate's son and legal heir. When Arik died, Logan inherited everything—the house, the land..."

"You got nothing?"

"It wasn't like that. There was no prenup or anything... In fact, there was no wedding." Her face heated, although, she would have signed one if Arik had asked her to do so. Her interest in his financial security had begun and ended with his fitness as an Alpha, his ability to protect and provide for her pack. "I can't believe Morena hasn't told you any of this..."

Sawyer stabbed the radio power button, silencing it. "Morena's told me some, but I'd rather hear it from you. Anything she tells me is suspect."

Victoria snickered. "She likes screwing with you. Just to see if she can get a rise out of you."

"Yeah, I get that but some of her stories are so preposterous, I'm never sure what to believe. For instance, last week I took her bow hunting, and we killed a buck. I was going to bring it over but she discouraged me. Said I should be careful about bringing over food or I might wind up in a whirlwind werewolf courtship..."

Victoria stiffened and fell silent.

He cast a glance over, caught a glimpse of her face, and his smile dropped. "She wasn't kidding?"

"No, she wasn't kidding. It's an old custom. Among my people, a man offers food as a gift to the she-wolf he desires. The more impressive the gift, the more status he's accorded. If she accepts, he has gained her consent and may court her, including the right to challenge his rivals."

"Rivals being the other suitors?" Sawyer's inflection was frustratingly neutral.

A bitter smile touched her lips. "Correct."

"And if she rejects the gift."

"He's SOL." Victoria turned her head to stare out the window at the passing scenery. Thick copses of trees bordered either side of the road, but they were almost to town. Once they passed through Sierra Pines, they'd head south toward U.S. Route 50. Broken Bend was another ten minutes. Thankfully, the ride would be over soon.

The hunter offered no response, so Victoria decided it was high time to change the subject. "Logan allowed us to stay at the house while he's been away. We owe him."

"Owe him for not throwing a pregnant widow, an old woman, and a teenage girl out on the street? Yeah, he sounds like a real prince."

She flushed hot with anger, not embarrassment. Her face jerked toward him. "He didn't have to. He could've kicked us out and sold the house. And don't let Sylvie catch you calling her an old woman. She'll smack you upside the head."

"Yeah, probably, but this isn't about Sylvie, is it? Where the hell has this jackass been all this time?"

"I don't know." Her hands shook.

"Where was he when you and my father were still at each other's throats?"

"I don't know!"

Yanking the wheel to the right, Sawyer slammed the brakes. The Chevelle fishtailed but he compensated and brought her to a smooth stop. With a quick stab, he hit the release on his seatbelt and twisted around to face her. His aura formed a solid wall of male aggression; anger rained down upon her.

"What *do* you know?"

"How is any of this your damn business?"

Victoria snarled in the face of his wrath, refusing to be cowed or intimidated. Unwilling to remain restrained when he was free, she undid her own seatbelt.

"I'm a member of this pack. You made me." His teeth ground together, creating a nerve-grating crunch. "He left you undefended. You're carrying his sister, right?"

"Half." She winced. "Arik was Logan's father."

At the moment, she had no appreciation for the hunter's bluntness. Sawyer had a talent for going right to the soft underbelly and eviscerating the gut of the matter. Nothing, absolutely nothing, having to do with Arik's death or Logan's abrupt departure was easy for her. She wore nonchalance and confidence as armor, but a surface scratch beneath, her emotions were raw.

"Doesn't he have some sort of duty to protect you?"

"It's complicated." Her hands clenched to fists.

"I don't get it. Why are you defending this asshole?" His hard eyes burned holes in her soul. No mercy. No understanding.

"It's complicated." Biting her lower lip, she looked away again.

"You're defending him. Why? I don't get it. *You* of all people. Are you afraid of him? Did he threaten you?" His hands locked on her shoulders.

"No. None of this is his fault." She shook her head. Tears

blinded her, and her heart raged. She resented his timing and questioned his motives. Why couldn't he just leave her alone with her scars and her trauma?

"Damn it, Victoria. There's something you're not saying. You're swimming in guilt. I can feel you drowning in it—"

Seriously, who was *he* to lecture anyone on guilt? Back in December of the prior year, in the aftermath of Daniel's murder, Sawyer had succumbed to a murderous rage. He'd come after Victoria and almost killed her...a couple times. People had died in the crossfire, including members of her pack—*Rand.* Although he refused to discuss it, she was convinced the guilt was the source of his depression.

"Amazing you can perceive anything beyond your own guilt—"

"Low blow."

"Sorry." Victoria ducked her head. He was right—it had been a cheap shot. He had her on the defensive or she wouldn't have resorted to such pettiness. Time to get this conversation back on track. "Look, Logan comes across as abrasive at first but he's actually a good guy..."

Oh wow, she sounded lame even to her own ears.

"A good guy," Sawyer repeated in a flinty tone.

"He's got good reasons to be angry with me."

"Yeah? What's he got on you?"

She compressed her lips, stubbornly silent, and hunched beneath her onerous guilt. She didn't wallow the way Sawyer did. She had done everything in her power to make restitution. But so long as Logan blamed her, she harbored regret.

"Victoria, I can't protect you if you're not honest with me. Tell me the truth, or I swear the next time I see that bastard, I'll put a silver bullet right between his eyes." His piercing gaze locked with hers, boring into her soul.

"I got him killed! Me. He died. My fault." The furious words bust from her in sheer defiance of her will. Her hands fastened on his shirt, twisting knots in the cloth, as she hauled him toward her. She got in his face to complete her confession. "He fought his own father because of me. Arik murdered his own son while I just stood there and watched. Logan's blood is on my hands."

Consternation etched his face. "I don't get it. He's alive."

"I brought him back from the dead. Just like I resurrected…"

Sawyer paled, and the unspoken resonated between them — *Just like I resurrected you.* In the months since his death and rebirth, they'd never actually discussed the matter. Averted, ignored, skirted, and circled; a grand old game of pussyfooting around.

"I admit. I'm having trouble with this..."

"Why? I healed your father. I healed you. Lately, it's how I deal with all my problems. Get someone killed—bring 'em back." Bitterness poisoned her voice.

"What god—"

"Freya. I'm her priestess, remember?" Victoria closed her eyes, took a deep breath, and then opened them. How could Sawyer, of all people forget that?

"Oh, yeah." His mouth puckered as if tasting something sour.

Freya's disapproval brushed Victoria's mind. *He and his father would prefer that you forget me.*

My Lady, I could never forget you. Victoria scrambled to offer assurances of her fealty. The goddess had good reason to doubt her priestess. Guilt ate at her insides. She had no one to blame but herself for the awful divide separating her from her deity.

Odin desires to estrange us. Watch and wait. Soon enough, he will press you to choose sides again. Smog of darkness accompanied the goddess's displeasure.

"Are you talking to Freya?" Sawyer asked.

Victoria's startled gaze flew to him—total attention restored. She mouthed "How?" even though the dreamy, distant look on her face must have been a dead giveaway. Sometimes, she even talked out loud.

"Can I help?" Sawyer extended an open hand, palm up.

She started to reach for him but hesitated. If his father hadn't been a god, Sawyer probably would've been an atheist. He simply couldn't understand her commitment to her goddess. Being a priestess was more than a profession or a calling; it was her heart's passion.

"Look—" She pressed her palm to his chest over his breast. Heat and strength radiated through the soft cotton. Solid muscle and a fierce heart; steadily beating, strongly beating. The throbbing rhythm of the man's life. Hidden beneath his shirt, Sawyer's chest bore a silvery handprint. The indelible mark she had left upon him.

"What?"

"Logan's got the same scar right here," Victoria said. "My hand print."

"Okay, you brought him back." Sawyer managed to make the confession sound skeptical. Victoria pressed her lips tightly together. She got how he managed to get under his father's skin. "He's alive," Sawyer continued. "What's the problem?"

Her frustration mounted, and with it the overwhelming desire to cry. She gasped, shoving her grief down deep, struggling to get the lid back on the bottle. But too late... A whimper escaped from her. "Damn it, Sawyer, haven't you listened to a word I've said? I got him killed. Fighting a challenge with his own father over the right to become my mate."

"He's alive. It's stupid to feel guilty. Let it go."

"I could say the same to you. You cling to guilt with both hands." A sob strangled her throat. Pain, but no tears.

"Hey, don't cry." Sawyer seemed torn, unsure of what to do. Then his arms closed around her, hands against her back. He hauled her against him, a rough and uncalculated motion. When he lifted her, the gear shift struck her thigh hard enough to elicit a grunt from her. It hurt to the bone but wasn't worth even mentioning; it would heal faster than she could take her clothes off to check it.

"I'm not crying." She made the denial in a strangled voice, and she spoke the truth. Her cheek settled against the thick swath of muscle across his shoulder. His chest supported her. He settled her atop his lap, wedged between his chest and the steering column, but his arms sheltered her from the wheel. If not for her petite size, her tummy would've gotten in the way.

"You cried in that ruined gas station—where my brother died. It's the only time I've ever seen you cry. Before or since." His open hand buried in her hair, fingers threading through loose locks. For the first time, she became aware how many strands had come free from the plaited braid.

"Alphas don't cry. Leaders don't show weakness." But she wanted to—more than anything. She ached for the outlet.

"There's no one here but you and me. I'm not going to think any less of you." In other words, he accepted her as his leader. Her insides turned all warm and fuzzy, and the last glimmer of distrust she harbored toward him dissipated. Amazingly, that didn't matter to her. Sawyer wasn't a threat but rather an ally.

A friend.

"I know. I want to. I do." But she couldn't. A cork bottled up her emotions, and the pressure built. Sooner or later she'd explode without release.

She turned her face into the thick cotton of his shirt. She inhaled hard so the material was sucked against her nostrils, drinking in the comforting heat and tang of his body. Male. Virile. Once, she'd scented him and automatically equated him to his brother, but the space of a few months had granted her a period of mourning. Sawyer wasn't Daniel, and she no longer confused the two men.

Intensity and tension abided between them. Air thick, humming. A vibrant splash of primary color through their blended aura. Desire hardened his body, and she hungered for him in return. The one kiss they'd shared lingered in her memory. Oh, she questioned everything. The right. The wrong. This man, this hunter, Jake's son, Daniel's brother... He wasn't—

Not for her.

Still, she wanted him. She would already have consummated their mutual attraction if it weren't for the myriad complexities: One, she'd loved his brother. Two, it wasn't fair to Sawyer to use him as a substitute for Daniel. Three, it wasn't fair to her either.

And four, Sawyer wasn't Daniel.

She breathed in his scent, earthy and inviting, uniquely Sawyer, and luxuriated in the marvelous rarity of being held. *Safe.* Five, she no longer confused them or needed to. Maybe...

Sawyer's warm lips pressed to her forehead, and his arms tightened in a gentle hug. "I'm here if you need me."

"Thank you." She accepted his decision to end the embrace before things escalated beyond their control. It was the right choice. Their relationship—whatever *this* was—

would progress at a natural and comfortable rate. Sawyer had to have reservations about becoming involved with a pregnant woman, especially since the baby wasn't his or his brother's. She sighed. Pragmatism dictated nothing would ever come from their mutual attraction.

It wasn't right—but it wasn't wrong either.

CHAPTER SEVEN

Sessrúmnir, Freya's hall in Fólkvangr

Freya frowned. "I don't know what a 'Philadelphia Lawyer' is."

"No, you wouldn't... I agreed—" He cocked his head and continued in an eminently smooth delivery. And he quoted the words he'd spoken on that frozen February night a few months before, "To sacrifice my mystical bonds to my mate and my pack. My mate and son will be allowed to assume I died in the fight with the witch, Hrafnar. I will accompany you to your hall and serve you in any and all capacities you deem appropriate."

"I know what we agreed to! Why are you repeating it word for word—?" Her frown deepened to a scowl. She wondered if his verbatim recitation of the vow she'd extracted from him was a clever ploy meant to irritate her. Could the man truly be so pedantic that he engaged a devil's regard for adherence to the letter of their verbal contract?

Arik spoke over her, ignoring her interruption. "In

exchange, you promised to protect my mate, my children, and my pack from future supernatural threats."

"As I stated—I know what I promised."

"I've kept my end of the deal. It's time for you to keep yours."

The man's audacity annoyed her, but Freya parsed her patience. It sounded as though he believed his concerns to be valid. Honor dictated that she listen to him and take whatever action was necessary. She drew a deep breath, using the space to reassert her poise.

"What is the nature of this threat?"

He nodded as though accepting her capitulation but at least he didn't smirk. Rather, his demeanor was markedly severe. "There's a hunter, one Sawyer Barrett, who's gotten close to Victoria. He's a threat."

"How is he a threat?" She pursed her lips, silencing her skepticism. She was well aware of Victoria's budding romance with Sawyer. While Freya didn't approve, she hardly considered the man to pose a valid danger to the Storm Pack. Clearly, Arik was jealous—plain and simple.

"Sawyer Barrett fired the first shot in the war with the hunters that decimated the Storm Pack and he tried to kill Victoria multiple times." His fist smacked his palm. Arik backed each word with the force of his personality. For the first time, his impenetrable exterior cracked, revealing molten rage at his core.

SIERRA PINES, *California, on the western shore of Echo Lake*

"We should get going. Can't sit here all day..." Sawyer's voice had a gruff burr that originated in his throat. Too much emotion...

"You're right." She loathed losing the intimacy of their embrace, but it was time to move along. Twisting, Victoria eased from his lap and back into the passenger seat. An awkward silence settled over them while they fastened their seatbelts again. Sawyer pulled out onto the road.

"There's an interview coming up at nine I wanted to hear," he said, reaching for the radio dial.

"Yeah?" Victoria awaited further explanation. When he didn't offer anything else, she shrugged—easier to wait than to pry information when he got tight-lipped.

Sawyer settled on an a.m. talk channel and cranked up the volume. The host's obnoxiously boisterous voice boomed from the front speakers—

"...morning Sierra Pines! This is Straight Talk with Johnny Straight! It's 8:46 a.m. on this beauuu-ti-ful June morning. The forecast today is sun, sun, sun with a high chance of fun! Coming up at nine I'll be bringing you the daily news update. Now, here's a word from our sponsor."

"Do you have a flea problem?" a woman asked. *"Keep those pesky—"*

"No." Victoria dialed the volume down so it was barely audible.

"A little too close to home?" Sawyer snickered. "I wanted to listen."

"Tough," Victoria mouthed.

"I can't hear."

"Turn it back up when the show comes on then."

He grunted.

She hesitated, considering what to say next. She really didn't want to discuss Logan anymore. Changing the subject seemed like a good idea. Oh, more of that conversation was certainly coming, because Sawyer needed to hear the entire story, but she needed a break. Doling the saga out in small doses was easier than all at once. Besides, she wondered how much of the tale Morena had already shared. It seemed the questions he hadn't asked were as telling as those he had. For one, she appreciated being spared having to explain how Arik and Logan had wound up fighting over her in the first place.

"We should talk shop. This is as good a time as any to catch up."

"Yeah, you're right."

"What did Finn want anyway?"

"Oh, yeah." Surprise washed over Victoria, followed by embarrassment. How had she forgotten about *that*? She composed her thoughts and launched into a detailed summarization of her conversation with Alpha Finn that kept her talking for the next five minutes.

"Next week is sudden. That's not much advance warning—"

"Sorry, but it's time. We've delayed too long already."

"I'll have to call my father and catch him up..." Trailing off, Sawyer cast a questioning glance. "Unless you want to?"

"Nope, you do it. I'm pressed for time." She offered up a wolf's smile, showing her teeth. "Besides, I communicate with your father just fine, whereas *you* could use the practice."

"Gee, thanks." He bared his teeth, returning her grin.

"You're welcome."

Sawyer slowed the vehicle to the lower speed limit. Sierra Pines, California, located within the heart of the Sierra Nevada Mountains, had a small-town, big-money feel. The exclusive alpine community clung to the western shore of Echo Lake. Miles of pristine alpine forest full of deer and elk and other small prey extended in every direction, including the remote and rugged Desolation Wilderness. Fallen Leaf Lake and Lake Tahoe lay to the north.

The downtown district consisted of a picturesque Main Street lined with small businesses and city government buildings. The commercialized section wasn't large but it contained all the usual suspects—a grocery store, a few retailers, and even a dilapidated old theater. A small collection of historic homes clustered about the only elementary/middle school and the adjacent high school. Despite a modest population, Sierra Pines also boasted a ski resort and a state of the art medical facility. Housing was just ridiculously expensive, and the priciest properties were those located on the lakefront.

The stray thought served as a sharp reminder to Victoria that she and the pack owed their residency in one of the most expensive zip codes in the country to Logan's generosity. She couldn't afford to rent a place for herself, let alone house Sylvie, Morena, and the wolves. Given his attitude, and what he'd said to her, she had to wonder if they'd be homeless once the dust settled. The prospect filled her with anxiety. She needed stability—craved it. As her pregnancy progressed, desire to nest preoccupied her more and more.

The 9 a.m. show came on the radio and the enthusiastic voice of Johnny Straight returned. When Sawyer turned up the volume, Victoria grimaced but kept her mouth shut. She figured the hunter had his heart set on listening to some sort of sports interview. All the Barrett men were huge baseball fans.

"I'd like to welcome my guest today, Dr. Kevin Danbury, wildlife biologist with the Federal Department of Natural Resources. Kevin, welcome to Straight Talk."

"Thank you, Johnny. It's a pleasure. Thank you for having me." Kevin Danbury's voice was mature but hesitant. To the practiced ear, he sounded smart but shy.

Lips parted, Victoria tilted her face toward the driver's side. Had he known...? From the intent set of his jaw, her answer was an unequivocal yes.

"No, the pleasure is mine. We're excited to have you." The host released a counterfeit laugh. *"Now tell all about the return of gray wolves to the Echo Lake area. I understand this is quite a momentous event?"*

"Indeed, it is." Kevin cleared his throat. *"As you may know— or not—gray wolves were once indigenous to California, including the Sierra Nevada mountain range."*

"WOW!" Johnny exclaimed. *"What happened to them?"*

"Well, no one can state their fate as a definitive answer. There was a combination of contributing factors—habitat displacement and hunting. It's believed the last gray wolf in the wild was killed in 1924 as part of a government-funded extermination campaign."

"The species is protected under the California Endangered Species Act?" Johnny asked. *"Is that correct?"*

The interruption set the biologist back. The resulting pause turned into dead air until he grunted and made a sudden recovery. *"Yes. Yes, that's correct."*

"But wolves have returned, haven't they?"

"Um. Yes. Er. Well, we haven't yet sighted particular members of the species but their presence has been confirmed via other markers."

Johnny chortled. *"Confirmed. Well, that's one way of putting it. I'll tell you, I recall that spectacular night back in February when all of Sierra Pines heard the pack howling for the first time. So eerily haunting. Sent shivers up my spine..."*

Tilting her head back, Victoria stared up at the clear blue sky and sighed. She'd long suspected that night would come back to bite her in the ass. Doom confirmed.

"We do have definitive evidence to support the presence of a pack in the Echo Lake area," Dr. Danbury said, talking fast as though trying to regain control of the interview.

"And that would be?"

"Well, we've collected paw print castings..."

"What's that? Plaster of Paris?"

"Yes, and, um. DNA testing of spoor samples—"

"Spoor samples—as in poop?"

"...identified the samples originated from an adult female and three adolescent gray wolves..." Dr. Danbury's mumbles were barely distinguishable.

"A mom and her pups. Isn't that amazing?" Johnny smacked his palm against a hard surface and continued, allowing no response to his question. *"Folks, I do apologize but we're running out of time. I'd like to thank Dr. Kevin Danbury for visiting with us today. We're about to take a break but when we return, we'll be discussing the disaster in Tucson. This is Straight Talk with Johnny Straight. Now, a word from our sponsors."*

A commercial for a local chiropractor came on. Victoria gave the volume control a quick twist, lowering it again to an inauspicious volume. She asked Sawyer, "Do you know what this means?"

Following a delay, he said, "Unwanted attention."

"Men with guns who consider wolves a threat to their livestock or land—"

"You can skip the euphemism and say 'hunters'."

She slanted a glare in his direction but otherwise ignored

the wisecrack and continued her rant. "Worse, assholes after a trophy kill. Government agents. Rabid conservations. Curious hikers." Victoria threw up her hands. "They'll come in swarms armed with rifles and traps, hidden cameras and binoculars."

"Victoria, calm down. Don't you think you're over-reacting?"

"No, I'm not. How can you not take this seriously?" She pinned him with a disbelieving look.

Sawyer grinned. "You'll look cute in a radio collar."

"I'll collar you," she muttered, brandishing her fist.

"Look, Southern California is going to hell in a hand basket. How much trouble do you suppose this can cause? Calm down. It'll be fine." Sawyer laughed but his smile had the suggestion of subterfuge. No matter what he said, he'd worried enough to tune into the radio show in the first place. Obviously, he wanted to offer her reassurance.

"I hope you're right." She crossed her arms over her chest and slumped into her seat, brooding on the matter. Call her a pessimist, but she couldn't help entertaining worst-case scenarios when it came to humans being aware of her pack's presence in the Echo Lake area.

She sat up straighter as the Chevelle reached the end of the downtown district, passing through the last stop sign. As soon as they cleared the intersection, Sawyer stomped on the gas pedal to get back up to a reasonable speed.

Next stop—Broken Bend.

"What can you tell me about these drifters?" Victoria asked.

"Nothing, really. There was just something... off about them." Sawyer pursed his lips. He started to say something, but then shook his head, and tightened his hands on the wheel. Suspicion crystalized his aura, and nuanced his scent.

Obviously, he doubted his instincts or he'd have said more. Or maybe he hadn't managed to put a finger on it yet.

"Why were you in Broken Bend yesterday?" While he watched the road, she studied him. Maybe asking a few questions would jog something free in his mind.

"I took Cali to lunch at the Broken Bend Café."

"DNR wasn't there?" She kept her tone bland on purpose. Tightness coalesced in her gut. Cali was a few years older than Sawyer—in her early thirties—but it was not a consequential gap. She could see how they'd be attracted to one another, especially since dating options for hunters were limited.

"Nah, he had something else to do." He sounded distant. Preoccupied.

"Did you see the drifters at the café?"

"They were over at the Fireside Inn."

"Oh? You took Cali to *that* dump?" Her tension upped to the point where she didn't bother keeping the bitchy/judgmental note out of her voice.

Sawyer's head jerked toward her so suddenly that the motion traversed through his arms to the wheel, causing the car to swerve right. He corrected, but not before she caught the blankness on his face. Then understanding and a wry grin replaced his surprise.

"We're not like that. I was just showing her around to help her get familiar with the area. I think she thinks I'm Jake Barrett's idiot son and she's stuck with babysitting duty."

"She calls you 'sir,'" Victoria countered.

He laughed, loud and carefree. "She calls me 'dumbass' and 'tenderfoot' too. I try not to let it go to my head."

Ten minutes later, they reached the truck stop community of Broken Bend, which consisted of a couple gas stations, a diner, and sleazy motels. The towering Northern

Sierra Nevadas dominated the landscape and US Route 50 bordered the town on one side, a steep, pine-studded mountain on the other. The community's economy relied entirely on commuter traffic traveling through the pass.

Sawyer turned into the parking lot of the Fireside Inn, though if Victoria hadn't known the name already, she couldn't have deduced it from the sign. The only letters remaining were "F R S E I N" in large block letters across the top. Beneath that, a wooden cabin was interposed over a bright red flame, a combination that inspired the impression *firetrap* rather than the homey association that was no doubt intended.

Gravel crunched beneath the Chevelle's tires and they rolled to a stop in front the shabby front office. While she watched, Sawyer removed his .45 from its holster and tucked the firearm into the back of his jeans beneath his shirt.

They left the convertible's top down and approached the wobbly steps that ascended to a rickety wooden porch. The motel complex consisted of the main building and seven dilapidated A-frame cabins tucked in the woods. It did the majority of its business in the winter, catering to skiers. The parking lot was deserted.

"Watch that second step. It's rotted," Victoria warned. Sawyer held his foot positioned to descend. She reckoned the step would hold under her weight but doubted it'd support the hunter's greater bulk.

Reflexively, he raised his arms to compensate and tested its soundness. Sure enough, the board creaked and buckled. He skipped the stair, as did she.

"Thanks," he said.

"You're welcome."

When he lingered at the top of the staircase, she stopped in front of him. Curious, she tilted her head and stared into his face. His basal scent, like his expression, registered tension. She asked, "What's up?"

"When we question this guy, I need for you to do your lie-detector thing," Sawyer said in a husky voice. Stray bangs covered his left eye.

She quirked her eyebrows. "My lie-detector thing?"

"You know what I mean." He blew those offending strands of hair aside but they immediately fell into his face again.

"Yeah, I know what you mean." Fingers twitching, Victoria closed her eyes and shifted her attention to the metaphysical plane, and opened them again. On some level, she was always aware of souls and spirits. However, the deliberate choice to gaze deeper produced a marked alteration in perception. Breathing through her mouth, she centered herself, using Sawyer's aura as her focus—

Vibrant reds turned reddish orange overlaid a dark marine core. Nothing unexpected or unusual there. The man radiated strength and passion, always one step away from dangerous anger. He was smart and loyal; distrustful and suspicious. The canvas of his soul would've been beautiful if not for the dark streaks of gloom and guilt metastasized throughout. Those negative emotions even affected his scent. Beneath the musky and rich aroma that reminded her of autumn, he carried mossy notes of nostalgia.

"You've got angry eyes," Sawyer said, using his term for wolf eyes.

Startled, Victoria blinked because she hadn't consciously chosen to undertake even a partial shift. She dropped her gaze to his chest, willing herself back to normal. "I'm sorry. It must be being pregnant that has me off kilter." She looked up. "Better?"

"Nope."

"Damn it." Looking away, she flexed her hands in

frustration. Sunglasses would've been nice to have right then but in her haste, she'd left them back at the house.

"Don't get upset. It's not a big deal. I'll do the talking, okay? Just pay attention to whether he lies and about what. And try to avoid looking straight at him."

"Yeah, fine." Grumbling, she followed. She was annoyed with herself, not him.

The hunter crossed the porch and opened the front door. A bell sounded within and he stood aside, allowing her to go first. This time, his chivalry didn't catch her off-guard. She took it in stride and passed through the entry into the office.

Long fluorescent tubes, half of which were burned out, bled through cracked acrylic panels, and cast the interior in yellowish light. Prints of dogs playing poker in chipped oak frames decorated the plaster walls. Tattered green swathes of Astroturf covered the floors, but the sour stink of mold was so pervasive that Victoria would've bet good money that the original soiled carpet remained beneath.

Sawyer's nose scrunched and his mouth contorted in a sneer. Sheltering against the initial onslaught, he buried his face in the crook of his elbow. "Ugh."

"You don't know the half of it." Her acute wolf senses painted pictures in Technicolor compared to his grayscale olfactory intellect.

"For once I'm glad for my stupid-ass nose."

He ducked his head and dropped his voice, speaking only to her as he passed. He had his hand on his back pocket, in the act of extracting his wallet.

"Good morning. How can I help you folks?" The squat, portly form of the office manager rose from behind the waist-high reception desk. The pungent perfume of sweat and whiskey clung to the man. A thatch of graying hair formed a half-moon about his crown. Thick jowls and a triple chin. His wide gut overhung his belt.

"I'm Sheriff Barrett with the Maricopa County Sheriff's Department." Sawyer flipped his wallet open. A cop's gold shield shone bright. He tipped his head toward Victoria. "This is my partner, Deputy Storm."

Victoria sucked in a sharp breath but then clamped down on her surprise before she blew his gambit. Hurt stuck her heart, a dagger's blow. The only reasonable explanation for how Sawyer had a badge with his surname on it was that the shield had belonged to Daniel.

To cover her reaction, she turned toward a side table and fabricated an interest in the guestbook. Victoria flipped the guest log open and turned the pages until she reached the last one. She ran her finger down the list and stopped beneath the final entry.

"Maricopa County..." The manager's face pinched. His gaze darted to Victoria and then returned to Sawyer. "That down in Arizona?"

"Yeah, that's right," Sawyer confirmed. "We're here as guests of El Dorado County's Sheriff Department, following up on a crime that crossed state lines. What's your name?"

"Donald, Donald Hines."

"Donald, we'd like to ask you a few questions."

"Sure thing, Sheriff, what about?" Donald asked. To Victoria's perceptions, the manager remained guarded but truthful.

"We're following up on some persons of interest that were seen in this vicinity yesterday—one woman and two men. They were grungy. Long hair. Disreputable-looking."

The fat man chortled. "You mean like you?"

Sawyer had his back to her but the thump and snap of his aura said it all. He snorted, "Yeah, like me."

"You two undercover—cause you're two 'o the most unlikely-looking cops I ever seen."

"That's confidential. I'm unable to discuss the case."

"Heh, sure." Donald slapped his palm against the desk with a sharp crack. "M'kay, some fellas matching that description came through here a couple days ago. I seen 'em around."

"Did they stay here?"

"No, sir." Deceit lit the man's aura like a solar flare, so obvious that Victoria didn't even need to note the souring of his scent, marking the lie.

"You know their names?"

"No, didn't speak with 'em," Donald said, lying still. "Old Sal across the street at the Chevron may've sold 'em some gas."

"Thanks, I'll check that out." Sawyer removed a business card from his wallet, and slid it across the desk. "Here's my card in case you think of something else."

"I'll do that." The manager spared it a brief glance and clutched it in clubbed fingers. As they left the office, he called out after them, "You officers have a nice day!"

In the lead, Victoria turned her head toward Sawyer when the hunter settled his hand against the small of her back. His breath stirred her hair. "He was lying?"

"Yes, but you already knew that. You expected him to lie." She skipped over the uncertain stairs rather than risk them, and landed lightly on her feet. "The only cabin that was rented in the last couple days was number three."

He copied her method of descent. "Was that in the guest book?"

"The maid staff marks the edge of the page with the cabin number and their initials to indicate they cleaned it." She smirked and held up her hand to show off the master key she'd snagged while the office manager had been preoccupied.

They reached the car and stood shoulder-to-shoulder facing it. The convertible shone ruby-red in the mid-morning sunlight, as bright and beautiful as a budding rose. She stuck out like a sore thumb on the uneven gravel lot. No way even a boob like Donald Hines could miss it. If the drifters returned while they were inside the cabin... the potential complications abounded.

"Yup, I'll move the car," Sawyer drawled.

"I want to walk the perimeter of the property and see what I can smell."

"Sounds like a plan."

Victoria rode with Sawyer to the driveway and then hopped out. "I'll meet you at cabin three."

"See you there." Sawyer gave an offhand salute, too sloppy to be construed as anything more than a parody. Unlike his father and older brother, he had never served in the military or law enforcement. Oh no, not Sawyer; the family rebel who was a doctoral student at MIT, currently on leave.

She watched him pull onto the road before she left. Crossing the lot, Victoria kicked a loose stone, sending it shooting toward an overgrown patch of bushes, and worked her way to the motel's border. Ambling, she skirted the outer edge, stooping periodically to sniff for scent markers.

Fifteen minutes later, she hooked up with Sawyer in front of cabin three. In lieu of a greeting, he asked, "Find anything?"

"Nope." Not worth mentioning anyway. She doubted Sawyer had a particular interest in the squirrel population or the comings and goings of the deer herd that lived in the area.

Victoria had the master key so she once again assumed

the lead. The front door opened to reveal a main room with stone fireplace, and a tiny eating nook and galley kitchen. The interior of the cabin was just as she remembered—dark, dank, and dingy. Her nose scrunched and her stomach curdled. She gagged her mouth and nose against her hand to muffle the stench.

"Whew." Sawyer coughed and mimicked her gesture. "Didn't think it was possible but this place reeks worse than when I stayed here."

"This place is such a dump. It's no wonder the worst element always winds up here," Victoria said in a cagey tone.

Sawyer's mouth curved in a sardonic smile, but he refused to be baited. No doubt, he thought she meant him. Well, she did, but Victoria and the pack had stayed in Cabin #7 when they'd first arrived here back in February. She smiled at the irony but didn't share it.

"It doesn't look like anyone's here now." Leaning over, she inhaled, breathing through her mouth so air passed over the sensitive glands in the roof of her mouth.

"Do you smell anything?"

"Humans. One woman. Two men." She wuffled, tasting the air. "One of the guys is ill or abuses cherry-scented cough syrup. Another has new boots. The scent is five or six hours old since they were last here." She rose and shrugged. "That's all."

He chuckled. "That's all? You can't tell what they had for breakfast?"

She rolled her eyes. "They left before dawn so they hadn't eaten breakfast yet."

They spread out to explore; Victoria branched left toward the kitchen; Sawyer went right. The interior showed signs of occupation: the waste can overflowed with empty beverage and fast food trash; an open bag of potato chips sat on the counter; and the fridge contained four sodas and three beers. Plenty of miscellany, but nothing personal or consequential to testify to the nature of the men who had stayed there.

The silence was awkward.

"Your deadline for fall enrollment at MIT is coming up fast, isn't it?" Victoria asked Sawyer who stood beside the mantle.

"Yeah." Sawyer's mouth pulled at the corners. His face contorted into a grimace. "Next week, as a matter of fact."

"Have you decided whether you're going back to Massachusetts?" Unease filled her. She'd come to depend on the hunter. While she hated the idea of losing him, she understood he had a life back east, including his educational program, friends, and even a girlfriend he'd left behind. He wasn't so much a hunter by vocation or preference, but simply as a matter of birth.

"Nah. Dad's told me to do whatever I want, but I feel like it'd be wrong to leave. Especially with Daniel gone..." Grimness and grief hung over Sawyer. He turned away from her, settling his handle upon the broad mantle.

"Do you want to leave?" Victoria asked, narrowing her eyes to stare at his hunched back with a shrewd gaze. Thanks to the empathic connection between them, she thought maybe she understood his emotions better than he did.

Right up until he said, "No, but I'm not sure I can stay."

"What? Why not?"

His teeth ground together with an audible crunch. For a second, it seemed he wouldn't answer, but then he released a forceful breath. "He doesn't think I have what it takes to be a hunter."

"I'm sure that's not it." Victoria wasn't sure whether her reflexive protest came in Jake's defense or Sawyer's, and maybe it didn't matter. Her instincts compelled her to defend both men from and to each other. She rushed from the kitchen, moving close to the hunter.

"That is it. He told me so." He hung his head, long hair hiding his face.

"Sawyer..." She exhaled his name, thin with impatience. So far as the Barretts went, Jake and Sawyer were two of the most stubborn men she'd ever known. When they got into it, the confrontation resembled two rams butting heads. Over and over and over.

"Let's check the back rooms." He lurched into motion, heading down the narrow hallway which led to two bedrooms and a bathroom.

Determined to keep up, Victoria followed right on his heels. When he opened the first door, his bulk blocked her view of the room but distinctive musk hit her nostrils. She doubled forward, hands clutched protectively about her gut.

Sawyer whirled. His hands closed about her shoulders. "What's wrong?"

"I smell wolves." The scent was stale. Dead. Combating the urge to retch, she wondered why she hadn't detected it before until she glimpsed the shapeless pile atop the double bed. Lashing out, she hit the wall switch.

Pale illumination filled the room. A heap of wolf skins perched atop the mattress.

Sawyer sucked air through his teeth, a wet slurping sound.

An angry growl rumbled in her throat. Gagging, Victoria pressed her lower face against Sawyer's arm but her horrified gaze was riveted upon the hides of her murdered cousins. Gray wolves from the coloring of the pelts, their heads still attached. Three pairs of fake marble eyes stared at her with intent accusation. Tears flooded her eyes and throat so she gasped for breath. She leaned into Sawyer, allowing him to support her.

"Don't look." Sawyer nudged her toward the entrance but she refused to yield. The hunter's aura engulfed her, a dark red shroud.

"Did you know about this?" Victoria asked in a ragged voice. She dug her fingers into the unyielding muscle of his bicep. His magic, her magic—it burned. Both dagger tattoos blazed with supernatural fire. She couldn't tear her eyes from the horrid spectacle.

"No, I swear to—" He cut his words short and swallowed. "I'd *never* expose you to this on purpose."

"You suspected something, Sawyer. I know you well enough to judge when you're withholding something." Victoria hung onto her humanity—and her human form—through sheer will. She inflicted the brunt of her revulsion to Sawyer via touch and the pack bond. Her nails broke his skin, drawing drops of blood, but the real burden he bore was that of her anger and accusation.

"Okay, all right." He nodded and turned so his chest blocked her. Not that it mattered. When she closed her eyes, she found the image etched indelibly on the insides of her lids.

"Go on."

"Yesterday, the drifters who caught my attention. They were suspicious but nothing too out of the ordinary except—"

Powerful emotion flooded their dual bond of wolf and hunter, conveying mental pictures—a woman with hair as black as the feathers she wore woven into her braids. At the base of her throat, she wore a silver wolf's cross... An amulet cast in the shape of Mjölnir, Thor's hammer, but with a wolf's head at the bail where it hung suspended from a rawhide cord. The vision entered her mind so clearly she could *see* it.

"How are you managing this level of detail?" Victoria asked in wonder. "The pack bond doesn't—" And she bit off her words upon the realization of the obvious.

"I'm using hunter magic. You'll learn it," Sawyer murmured. The images changed to two men who accompanied the woman. One of the men had stringy hair and ancient Norse runes inked on his forearms. The words, big and bold, solid black lines...

"His tattoos said, 'Hail Odin,'" Sawyer grated. "Hail the One-Eyed."

Her heart heaved against her breastbone, seeking escape. "I hadn't realized you'd studied the runes."

His voice, like his scent, tasted bitter. Regret and sorrow, but his were not the words of a liar. "Considering who my father is, is it really that much of a shock?"

"No, I guess not." Victoria eased away from him, and at last yielded. Moving in concert, they backed into the hallway. She breathed easier once they were clear of the bedroom.

"I had to investigate further," Sawyer said, his tone urgent. "But you have to believe me—I didn't expect *this*."

"I believe you." Victoria exhaled, relaxing her fingers so her punishing grip on Sawyer lessened. Righteous anger overrode her revulsion, but not an iota was aimed at him. "The bastards who committed this atrocity *will* pay."

"They will. I'm with you." Through their empathic connection, he made unspoken promises which resonated as clear as thunder. She took him at his word—a man of honor, just like his father.

"Thank you."

"Wait here." The hunter's movements were jerky. He shoved open the second bedroom door, spent about thirty seconds or so within, and then returned. "From the looks of it, these guys haven't checked out yet. I'm going to call Cali and DNR. We'll set up a stake out to catch them when they return. All right?"

"I've got a doctor appointment this morning." As much as she wanted to help out, she had to keep her prior commitment. She already had too much on her plate—first the gathering of the packs, and now *this*. "I need to call Sylvie and warn her to keep Sophia and the pups close."

"Do that and don't worry. You don't need to be here. I'll handle this, okay?"

"Okay."

"Let's get out of here." He edged her toward the exit.

Victoria hesitated. "Sawyer, will you bring the pelts? Please? They deserve a proper burial." The skinned animals probably hadn't been shifters or kinfolk, but she wanted to honor their spirits.

"Yeah. I'll take care of this. Go wait outside."

Victoria left, accepting Sawyer's protection, no longer ashamed to do so. The world was too full of villains for her to waste energy fighting her own.

CHAPTER EIGHT

Freya stared at him in astonishment. He hadn't revealed any secrets she didn't already know. The real question was—how had he found all this out? What was his source? Did she have a mole within her own hall?

"The war with the hunters is over," she said, adjusting her stance.

"The war with the hunters hasn't even begun!" Arik growled; the wolf in his eyes. His ferociousness—pure and primal. The bones in his hands crunched and ground, marking their transformation to claws.

Startled by the sound, Tregul snarled and bristled. The tiger leapt from the wolf's lap and stalked off, his flagged tail straight behind him like a bottle brush. The cat's indignity commanded the attention of werewolf and goddess, an unexpected intermission in the drama. Staring, they watched the great cat stalk off before looking at one another again.

Exhilaration coursed in Freya's veins along with marked

desire. *This* unrestrained passion beneath implacable austerity—his fervor set her blood on fire.

"Come now, Arik. You're letting your emotions get the better of you. Victoria and Jake have made peace and shaken on it. I do believe Sawyer may even have been part of the settlement. There was talk of the hunters paying a blood price in the form of an arranged marriage. Jake Barrett only has sons, you know...and Victoria *is* single again."

"I'm not jealous."

"Are you sure?" Freya concealed a smirk but she couldn't resist baiting him. It served him right for daring to cross her.

"I'm sure."

*P*HOENIX, *Arizona*

Premonition always tasted sour.

Obeying his gut, Jake turned his SUV off the road into the parking lot of a grocery store. He pulled into the first available slot. The driver of a white compact to his right had done a crap job so the front end of the little car hung several inches over the line. Jake centered neatly within his space, even though doing so left a gap of only a few inches between him and the other car. He thought about reparking, but then rejected it. Screw it. Asshats who couldn't park straight in shouldn't be allowed to drive in the first place.

He trusted his intuition but a premonition that *something* was wrong wasn't worth a hill of beans. Still, it was enough to stop him from traveling any farther until he figured out the source of his unease. Ten minutes ago, he'd dropped Michael at his private elementary school. The parent-teacher conference wasn't for another hour-and-a-half so he'd headed home afterward.

He opened the car door and stepped into a broiler oven. Heat poured over him. The prior day's rain shower was nothing but a faded memory and the temperature seemed to be making up for lost time. The sun shone big and bright overhead. Not even a hint of a breeze stirred the air to provide the slightest relief.

Squinting, Jake adjusted his Cardinals baseball cap, tugging the rim down over his eyes. He'd forgotten his sunglasses on the kitchen counter. The twins teased him unmercifully about being so old he couldn't remember his own name. Sawyer, being Sawyer, took it one step further and trotted out even more scathing observations. "Geez, Pops, are you worshipped as the god of senility, too?"

Grumbling, he attributed his absentmindedness to a lack of sleep, which conveniently allowed him to blame Loki. An Old Norse correlative to the modern Murphy's Law held: *When something goes wrong, Loki's to blame.*

Loki this, Loki that. Lately, the Trickster's name preoccupied his thoughts far more than he liked. The prolonged conflict with the undead required all his consideration. He couldn't afford distractions at a time when missing something important could cause his people their lives.

Tilting his head back, he scanned the clear sky. He lifted his hand to his mouth and let loose with a sharp, loud wolf whistle. The sound rose and carried high and far. Cocking his head, he listened. Within seconds, a female raven's distant *craa* flew to him on a mystic wind. She answered his call—*on our way.*

As he settled back to wait, his old-school flip phone rang. He fished the device from his pocket and opened it. Contrary to the modern culture of upgrading to a newer "smart" device every six months, Jake preferred to trust what he knew. So he'd used the exact same make and model phone for over a decade. They got destroyed every now and then, but he had over a hundred stashed away in a storage closet up at Red Butte.

A glance at the screen ID'd the caller as Sawyer.

"What's up?" Jake asked, bypassing the preamble of a greeting. His sons didn't expect one from him and wouldn't have known what to do with a pedestrian "Hello, how are you doing?" from their father.

"Dad?" Sawyer began, sounding like he had no idea what to say. Or maybe he did but hadn't figured out how to word it.

"You expectin' someone else to answer my phone?" Out of habit, Jake assumed his gruff hard-as-nails, don't-take-no-shit attitude. His relationship with Sawyer stood about a world removed from the one Jake shared with Michael.

Sawyer all but growled in reply. "No. Look—"

"Sounds like something's gotten under your skin." Based on his son's apparent agitation, Jake envisioned Sawyer running his hand through his hair, shoving those too-long bangs out of his eyes.

"Something has," Sawyer bit off and then fell silent.

Ever patient, Jake glanced down and noticed his short nails had a dark layer of grime beneath the edges. He wedged his phone between his face and shoulder. Then he drew his belt knife and used the point of his blade to clean them while he waited.

"It's nothing I can't deal with."

"Okay," Jake said in easy agreement. He respected his son's judgment as an adult...for the most part. But sometimes when his notoriously hot temper, impulsive nature, and rebellious tendencies combined, Sawyer was prone to terrible lapses in judgment.

Well, father and sons often had issues.

"Dad, do you have any worshippers up here in the Sierra Pines area?" Sawyer asked out of the blue.

Jake's lips parted. His initial inclination was to request clarification, but there was really no mistaking the implicit meaning. "I have worshippers far and wide. Not as many as I used to, but they're still around. But you know I'm cut off from my greater form while I'm human."

"So you're not aware of any of your specific followers being here." A solid thump, Sawyer's hand striking a hard surface, reinforced the demand.

"No. What's this about?"

"Nothing I can't handle. That's all I needed to know." Sawyer once again chose to play the independence card.

"All right." Jake rolled his eyes. As the twins said— *Whatever.* He could have pressed for more information but it would only lead to another argument.

The sleek shape of a raven circled overhead. Two males flew escort; her wingmen. Their calls had already attracted the attention of other birds from miles around. Via his kenning, Jake sensed the brooding unkindness.

"I called to tell you that Victoria has given Finn the go-ahead to schedule the werewolf conclave," Sawyer said, cutting to the point at last. "It's happening on the next full moon in Desolation Wilderness."

The news caught Jake off-guard. The tip of his knife slipped, slicing the pad of his finger wide open, and a stream of blood gushed from the wound. "Damn it," he muttered, and yanked the blade away. A few more drops of blood splattered the pavement before the wound healed.

"Should I tell them to wait?" Sawyer asked, misinterpreting his father's curse.

"Nah, that ain't it." Jake wiped the knife clean on the leg of his jeans and sheathed the weapon. "I trust Victoria's judgment. I just wasn't expecting this to happen so fast."

Though, he supposed, he should've. The damn gathering of the wolf-shifter packs had been months in the making. Even with Alpha Finn's help, they'd encountered one obstacle after another. Entire packs gone MIA—displaced or destroyed by undead. Stubborn, small-minded Alphas concerned with their own selfish priorities. Bickering. Suspicion. Herding werewolves was even more aggravating than herding cats.

The timing sucked. Couldn't have sucked worse. His people were reeling from their devastating losses in Tucson. They needed him close. Throw in Jake's enemies, Loki and the Norns, who were just circling, looking for an opportunity to strike. He dared not leave Michael unguarded. As much as he hated to admit it, he needed help and only Sawyer possessed the right ability, knowledge, and status to render it.

Jake swallowed his pride. "Son, you'll have to represent me at the werewolf conclave. Things are bad here. I can't get away."

Dead silence, and a beat passed.

"Ah, sure. No problem," Sawyer managed in stunned response.

Jake exhaled, and a tension boulder rolled off his chest. "Thanks."

"If things are that bad, should I come home?"

"No, I *need* this alliance with the wolves to happen. We need to catch a break, Sawyer. Every time the Necromancer strikes a civilian populace, the size of his army swells..." Jake trailed off. His son was a smart man; Sawyer didn't need the obvious spelled out. While the hunters were magically enhanced, they were still human. When his soldiers died, Jake couldn't simply call bodies forth from the grave to re-enforce their ranks.

"I'll take care of it, Dad. Consider it done. You have my word." Sawyer sounded so damn much like Daniel that Jake's heart hurt. At the same time, he had never been as proud of his rebellious son as he was in that moment.

Jake dropped a brusque nod. "Keep me informed."

"Will do." Sawyer ended the call without farewell. *Like father, like son.*

Raising his arm, Jake loosed another whistle. He held out his arm. The female raven swooped toward him and alighted on it. Her sharp talons bit into his bare flesh, securing her roost. He stroked a tender hand over her sleek black feathers.

Bending his head, he conspired with his pet.

CHAPTER NINE

Arik's eyes narrowed and his hands reverted to fully human in a quicksilver recovery. His voice was as smooth as fine whiskey. "Do you remember that kid in Albuquerque—the one who died?"

Her face slackened. All humor drained away. She clipped her answer. "Yes. His name was Jasper."

Freya recalled the incident in question only too well. December, the prior year: In the wake of the massacre in Phoenix, the surviving members of the Storm Pack had fled Arizona to New Mexico. They'd arrived in Albuquerque with Jake Barrett and his men right on their heels. In the ensuing conflict, fifteen-year-old Jasper, a teenage werewolf, had been captured and murdered. It remained a sore bone of contention even in the ensuing peace.

"Sawyer killed Jasper. He shot the poor kid square in the back." He dropped a lawyerly nod and folded his arms across his chest. "But then you already knew that, didn't you? When you made Victoria swear herself to justice rather than revenge—you knew."

The atmosphere crackled with hostility and division. Freya held herself rigid. Her first instinctive response was to issue a vehement denial and progress straight to tears. She possessed an exceptional talent for deceit. She opened her mouth; the words perched on the tip of her tongue. But then she hesitated. Something about Arik's impassive stare convinced her lying was the wrong strategy.

Instead, she rolled her shoulders. "I didn't *know* anything for certain."

His eyes narrowed in keen appraisal. "But you suspected?"

"Yes, I had my suspicions." The confession parted from her with the difficulty of yanked teeth.

Arik continued, relentless and cruel. "Jasper's soul is damned to the rest of eternity in the frozen wasteland of the underworld. Suffering because he died a coward's death."

"He was only a child," Freya whispered, succumbing to tears. She still mourned the boy. A star had gone out of the sky when the teen perished.

"So Sawyer murders a child and gets a free pass. And you lied to Victoria—" He crafted air-quotes. "For her own good."

"Don't you dare judge me! I did what I had to do to protect Victoria and her pack. If I'd told her, she'd have gone after Jake Barrett and she'd be dead too."

*Phoenix, **Arizona***

A raven sat on a street lamp and gazed down upon the world.

The bright, clear morning bustled with activity. Teachers hurried to open their classrooms before the first bell sounded. Parents escorted rambunctious youngsters to the Kindergarten corral. Vehicles dropping off students crowded the surrounding streets, and pedestrians flowed toward the school like a living river. On the playground, a pack of boys chased past in a game of tag. The persistent squeak of rusty chains marked the back and forth of the swings while other children swung from bars and tumbled down slides.

A lone six-year-old boy played amidst the motion, and a lone watcher observed.

"Ladies and Gentlemen! Look up! Ten thousand feet up, and you'll see The Magnificent Michael as he balances on the world's thinnest tight rope! Without a net!" Arms held straight out to his sides, he placed one foot in front of the other and moved steadily forward along the wide brim of the raised planter.

Beyond the fence surrounding the play yard, Loki adopted the identity of Benjamin. Hooking his fingers through the chain links, he leaned back, tilting his head to stare down the two-lane residential street. The Trickster noticed things mortals missed. He marked the lengthening of shadows upon a particular section of the road and turned his ear toward the ground, listening to whispers emanating from deep within the earth. Voices only he heard.

Oh, and that damn bird on the lamp.

Prescience slapped the back of his mind—a brilliant

strobe light. Pain and knowledge. Loki turned the brown eyes of Benjamin Hustler toward a silver Mercedes SUV a quarter of a mile down the road as it zipped past the *Slow—School Zone* sign, doing double the posted limit. The driver had a cell phone tucked between his face and his shoulder. He drove distracted—engaged in an avid discussion with his wife over the aggravation of having to submit yet another round of refinance paperwork to their mortgage company.

The strobe flashed again.

Loki's gaze shifted to a white bungalow house directly across the street from where he stood. A seventy-year-old woman wobbled toward her white Toyota sedan and then gingerly climbed into the driver's seat. She was on her way to the pharmacy to pick up a prescription for her arthritis; every movement produced pain and required a great effort on her part.

"Wait! What's this! Oh no!"

The boy's shout grabbed Loki's attention, snatching it away from the woman.

"Michael the Magnificent has lost his balance!" The boy's foot lifted, flung far out to the side, and his arms windmilled while he acted out the scene conceived in his imagination. "Will he fall? Will he plummet to his death?"

"Hey, Michael! Over here!" Loki rattled the chain link fence to add emphasis because he had to be sure to catch the boy's attention.

Hopping on one foot, Michael swung toward the call. Upon spotting Ben, his face lit with a grin of recognition.

The strobe flashed, providing another image of events beyond his perception. Loki winced, wishing the foresight to be gone, but the onslaught continued. Across the way, the Toyota's backing lights came on and the vehicle began a slow roll toward the bottom of the long driveway.

"Hey!" Michael called. His high wire act seemingly forgotten, he placed his second foot back on the edge of the planter and turned toward Loki. "Do you go to school here?"

"Hey!" Ben surged against the chain link fence, hooking his feet into lower rungs. "Yeah, I'm in Mrs. Riding's third grade class. What grade are you in?"

"First." The discrepancy in their elementary status brought a frown of displeasure to the boy's face. He jumped down from the planter. "But I'll be a second-grader when school lets out in a week."

"I'll be in fourth." Ben smirked in boyish one-upmanship, and rattled the fence.

"Yeah, well, maybe I'll skip a grade," Michael said, determined not to be outdone, as he came over to the other side of the fence from Loki.

The driver of the Mercedes performed a rolling stop at the four-way intersection and ignored the energetic reprimand of the crossing guard to get off his phone. He remained intent in his outrage over the injustices of the banking process. A persistent buzz broadcast over the school's auditory system marked the first bell, prompting motion across the grounds toward the buildings. Students had five minutes to reach their classrooms or be marked tardy.

"Shoot, I'd better hurry or I'll be late." Ben dropped to his feet and headed toward the closest break in the barrier, a gate on the far corner of the playground. He dragged his feet for a split second.

"Want to hang out at lunch today?" Michael asked, assuming a course parallel to Ben's.

"Sure. Do you buy or bring?" Ben cast a quick glance over his shoulder just as the Mercedes sped past the driveway of the backing vehicle.

The sedan rammed into the side of the SUV. The shear tore the Toyota's rear bumper from its frame. Within the Mercedes, the airbags deployed and smacked the driver who cranked the wheel and smashed his foot down on the gas.

With a startled yelp, Michael jerked toward the sound just as the SUV plowed into the chain link fence. Groaning, the steel posts bent. The stressed section of fence toppled. The vehicle shot forward. It collided with the planter, demolishing the barrier before coming to a full stop.

Loki had always thought nothing was quite like the silence that followed in the wake of a tragedy—the dramatic intermission between life's acts.

"Whoa!" Michael's mouth hung open. He grabbed Ben's shoulder and clung. "You coulda been killed!"

The Trickster opened his mouth to retort—*So could you.* But he stopped before voicing the words aloud. He thought it better to remain silent. Michael already suffered from nightmares. Why risk making the boy's PTSD worse? Especially when there was nothing to be gained from it. Besides, Ben and Michael were supposed to be friends.

"C'mon. Let's get out of here before we get into trouble." Ben urged Michael to run. On flying feet, the boys shot off down the street, their backpacks bouncing on their backs.

THE TALL ROCKET ship in the center of the small park afforded the boys refuge and a vantage point from which to spot the vigilant truant officers on the prowl for delinquents such as themselves. Drought-resistant bushes and trees grew at infrequent intervals. At the center of the open range, play structures stood atop a cushy surface made of recycled rubber; a volleyball court at the center of an emerald patch of artificial turf.

With more than a touch of smugness, Loki supposed the rocket ship wasn't a bad hideout at all... If only his partner in crime wasn't a nervous wreck.

The six-year-old moaned in misery. "I'm going to get into trouble."

"You're not. Stop worryin'."

"I am. I just know it. My dad's gonna find out."

"Balderdash." Still wearing the guise of Ben, Loki rolled his eyes and cracked the tab on a one-hundred-percent-pure-cane-sugar cola. The can was ice-cold; moisture beads clung to the shiny surface. None of that crappy high-fructose corn syrup—only the best for the God of Lies. Tilting back his head, he chugged the entire twelve fluid ounces.

"Balder-what?" Michael squawked his distress.

"No way Jake's gonna blame you for playin' hooky." He emitted a long belch and flashed a self-satisfied smirk. "If he does, then blame me. If he gives you a hard time, blame me and cry. The old man's a sucker for the water works."

Frowning, Michael settled his hands on his hips. "How do you know my dad's name?"

"Long story. Trust me, kid. If you blame me, your dad won't question it for a second." On the playground below, a green trash barrel was located beside a bench, more than sixty feet distant. With an overhanded throw, he heaved the can into the air. As soon as it left his hand, a gust of wind caught and swept the container across the playground. The breeze died as suddenly as it'd sprung up, dropping the empty soda into the receptacle.

The world might paint him as evil, but Loki cleaned up his own messes.

"We're going to get caught." Michael paced in tight circles

—the only passage the narrow cone of the playground rocket permitted.

"We're not going to get caught." Dangling his feet between the protective bars enclosing the rocket's nose, Loki dug into his bright red backpack. His head bent so unruly dark curls tumbled into his face while his agile hands worked magic, conjuring a feast of candy and gum, chips and soda.

"But what if we are!" Michael ground to a halt and threw up his hands.

"Good grief, Charlie Brown." Rolling his eyes, Loki tilted his head and stared into the cloudless sky, watching the dozen or so ravens circling above.

"Who's Charlie Brown?"

"Who's Charlie Brown? Are you kiddin' me?" Loki glanced over and registered Michael's blank expression—complete and total confusion.

"Yeah, who's Charlie Brown!" Michael stomped his feet.

"Wow, your generation lives in a cultural wasteland." Loki dumped a pile of saltwater taffies onto his lap. He opened candies and stuffed his mouth until his cheeks threatened to burst. Chocolate on one side; strawberry on the other. Good separately but awesome together. As the wrappers fell from his hands, they followed the same flight plan as the soda can straight to the trash.

"Boy, you're weird." Michael simply stared at him.

His mouth was too full for speech. Loki chewed furiously, mashing the two flavors together, and swallowed a gob big enough to choke a snake. "Yeah, I get that a lot."

The boy frowned.

Loki thrust his hand into his backpack. He passed a fistful of chocolate and licorice to his friend. "Here. Maybe some sugar will calm you down."

Long-faced, Michael accepted the stash. He heaved a long

sigh and plunked down beside the Trickster. The two boys sat with their feet dangling, staring out over the empty playground while they devoured a mountain of junk food. When Loki set his legs to swinging, his companion took up the rhythm.

"How do you do that?" Michael asked as the breeze whisked a Doritos bag through a roller coaster of loop-d-loops before dropping it into the bin.

"Magic." Loki rolled the word off his tongue out of respect for the mystery. Everything about the modern era was trite and clinical; scientific explanations devised to undermine the wonder of true mysticism. They lived in a cynical era, full of cynical people. Charlatans and con men deceived unsuspecting fools. Magicians performed tricks, and then revealed their secrets.

"Coooool. Can you teach me?"

"Maybe. It depends."

"On what?" Michael asked.

Lips curved in a secretive smile, Loki glanced over at the boy. "On you."

"You sound like a damn fortune cookie," Michael grumbled in a near perfect imitation of what little boy Jake must've sounded like.

Clutching his sides, Loki chortled and fell over and succumbed to a paroxysm of laughter. Michael stared in bewilderment, but then a giggle erupted from the boy. Not just one but a fit. Lolling on their backs, they laughed themselves weak.

"Where'd you go the other day? Was that magic?"

Pleased with the prospect of an attentive audience, the Trickster chose to indulge the questions. "I turned into a bird and then a bee until a willow flycatcher tried to eat me, so I—"

"What's a willow flycatcher?" Michael interrupted.

"A bird." He opened his mouth to continue the story.

"But it's called a flycatcher. Why would a flycatcher wanna eat a bee?"

Exasperated, Loki cocked his head. "Do you want to hear the story or not?"

"Yeah. I do." Michael nodded with enthusiasm. "Yes."

"Then shush." Loki waited to confirm the child's silence, and then resumed his tale. "And so I became a cat."

A short pause followed. Finally, Michael cleared his throat. "And?"

"And what?"

"What happened next? Did you eat the flycatcher?" Michael threw up jazz fingers of impatience, like ten small exclamation points.

"Nah, after all that I was tired so I took a cat nap." Tongue in cheek, Loki rolled his head to the side and observed the lineup of avian silhouettes alighted across the top of the swing set. He counted three sets of three—ravens to the nine.

Nine—a number of power.

"That's a stupid story." Michael fell to pouting, but his own irrepressible nature proved his undoing. His sullen brooding didn't last even a minute before he cracked. In a plaintive voice, he said, "I'd like to learn magic."

A smile tugged at the corners of Loki's mouth. "Okay, I'll teach you a trick so long as it's reasonable."

"What's reasonable?"

"Reasonable—something not too big. For instance, I could teach you to fly but not to become a fly." Loki wiggled his fingers, waving at the ravens.

"You could teach me to fly?" Awed, Michael gaped at the Trickster.

"Sure. Flying is easy. All it takes is a magic feather and

faith." Technically, the magic feather was optional but even Dumbo had required a crutch the first few times. "So what is it, kid? One super power—you gotta choose."

"Gee, that's tough. I don't know." Michael chewed on red licorice while he thought on the matter.

Loki waited, bursting with impatience, and squished the temptation to badger. Frankly, the boy's answer interested him a great deal. Just the fact that Michael gave the matter such thorough consideration struck the Trickster as unusual. He expected children to make easy and obvious decisions.

"Okay, I know what I want." Michael nodded to himself, confirming his choice in his head before speaking it aloud.

"Yeah?" Loki prompted, damn near ready to burst into a cat, so compelling was his curiosity.

The boy took a deep breath. "I want to not be afraid anymore—of anything."

He triple-blinked. "Fearless is a super power?"

"My dad's not afraid of anything. I want to be like him."

"You want to be like Jake?" Oh, now there was irony to be savored.

"Yeah, that's what I want." Michael's resolution solidified, growing palpable.

"Okay, I can do that, but I don't do favors for free. You'll have to trade for it."

"Trade for what?" The boy's brow pinched. He glanced down, chewing his lower lip. "My stomach hurts."

"Nerves," Loki deduced authoritatively. He thrust a lollypop toward the boy. "Here. Sugar will make you feel better."

"What do you want to trade for? I don't have anything." Misery on his face, Michael accepted the sucker. The aura of worry about him intensified.

The Trickster shifted, uncomfortable in his own skin.

Weird. Usually, he savored the moment when his mark succumbed to anxiety and second-guessing, but the boy's discomfort brought him no pleasure. Rather, a sickness of guilt swirled in his gut and it wasn't the copious amount of candy he'd consumed either. He'd once subsisted on nothing but jelly beans and marshmallow chicks for an entire month just to win a bet. A pound of processed sugar was child's play.

"Information," Loki said, but his answer elicited nothing more from the kid than a blank stare. "Tell me about your monster—the one from your nightmares."

"I don't want to talk about that." Color drained from the boy's face, and fear soured his scent. A tremor swept the youngster's body. Pulling away, Michael tucked his knees against his chest and wrapped his arms about his drawn legs.

"Talking about what scares you takes away its power to scare you," Loki employed a cajoling tone but the boy shook his head. When Michael remained stubbornly silent, the Trickster extended a tendril of power, eavesdropping on the boy's thoughts.

A jolt of pure terror slammed through Loki, and he glimpsed something enormous and malevolent lurking in the basement of Michael's psyche. No clear images, only bits and pieces, flashes—burning red eyes and black fur, horns and hooves. A musty odor and the sickening scent of blood. Something familiar about the beast nagged at him so he delved deeper, taking care to ensure his spying left the child unharmed. It took a moment but then a sad little Christmas tree appeared in the mish-mash.

"Ahhh." Loki snapped his fingers. *Krampus*—one of Loki's descendants via his daughter, Hel. An unpleasant creature with unsavory appetites, but then most monsters failed the Niceness check.

A stifled sob tore from the child, and his conscience drop kicked Loki's gut. "Hey, don't cry. Please? I'm sorry I asked. Forget about it, okay—"

"I don't— I don't— I don't—"

"Take it easy, kid." Panic seized Loki. Uncertainly, he patted Michael's back in a clichéd *there-there* fashion. While he'd been a parent countless times over, his offspring tended to be terribly resilient, not to mention downright scary.

The boy stiffened and nosily inhaled snot and tears. Making a concentrated effort, he said, "That's the trouble. I can't remember her and I want to. I can't see her no matter how hard I try—"

"Her?" Loki seized on the word. By itself, the pronoun didn't make much sense but he had limited access to Michael's thoughts, and thus shared the child's profound sorrow and loss. The boy's heart longed for the person who'd loved and cared for him his entire life.

"My mom." Tears squeezed past the boy's tightly-shut eyes. "I've tried and tried but I can't remember her face or her voice or anything." His hands opened and closed. "Nothing."

"You don't have a photo of her?" Sympathy ate at Loki's insides like a cancer. The fun had gone out of the adventure. Damnation, but he'd miscalculated, and in a truly epic fashion. He'd been wrong-headed thinking the boy could be manipulated to his advantage or used to gain leverage over Jake.

In that moment, Loki's self-disgust exceeded even his monumental ego.

Michael's tears coursed down his cheek. Snot ran from his nose over his upper lip. He gave a hard shake of his head.

Mildly disgusted, Loki fished Kleenex out of his red knapsack. He ripped open the package and thrust a fistful of tissue into the boy's hands. "Here. Blow your nose."

While the kid snorted snot, nosily, Loki tumbled into a hasty conclusion—responsibility for the boy's trauma was pretty much his fault any way he looked at it. Guilt didn't sit well with him. It made him itchy and nauseated, and intolerably uncomfortable. Impulsively, he decided to fix the child.

"Michael, you don't remember your mom because of the monster?"

"I can't see her face or hear her voice in my head..." Swinging his arm, Michael threw the wad of used tissue through the bars of the rocket cone. This time, the trash followed its natural course and plummeted to the ground because the Trickster's attention was focused on the twisting, turning passages of the boy's subconscious.

"You haven't forgotten your mother. The trauma you experienced has blocked her from your memory." Loki wasn't a healer but he was a thief. Circling the ordeal, he set to studying it to determine the correct approach. He had a crystal clear view of the traumatic experience which had happened last Christmas, just six months ago. No wonder the poor kid was such a mess. "Tell me what happened so I can figure out how to help."

"The monster hurt my mom to punish me," Michel said, slow and reluctant in his confession. "I was bad. I stole a fire engine—"

"The Matchbox?" Loki hissed, unable to constrain his anger. *All this over a fucking 99 cent toy...*

The boy plowed forward with his confession. Words poured forth as if once started, he was unable to stop. "It hurt her and took me to a dark place that smelled bad. There were other kids there too. A girl—her name was Margaret—and a boy but I don't know his name. It drowned them. And there was a girl Crystal and a baby who didn't talk. The monster took all of us because we were bad. It was going kill me next."

"Jake killed the monster?" Loki surmised without the benefit of telepathy. The foregone conclusion was obvious.

"Victoria," Michael said, jerking his head to the side. "She came first and fought it and tried to help us. Jake got there later."

"*That* I'd have loved to see," Loki said with so much irony the metallic tang coated his tongue. He had a firm grasp of the remembrance now. "Do you want your memories of your mother back?"

"Yes, more than anything." A true survivor, the boy backed up the assertion with an adamant tone and a remarkably strong will.

Loki's eyes narrowed in shrewd consideration. "Do you want to remember what happened but without the fear?"

"You can do that?" Michael stared with wary, red-rimmed eyes, and although he didn't voice his preference aloud, the thought ran quicksilver through the boy's mind.

"I'm magic." Loki's voice resonated as he concentrated on hollowing out his insides to make room for the child's monstrous misery. He laid cool fingers on the back of the Michael's feverishly hot neck. Reflexively, he lowered his body temperature even farther so his hand grew ice-cold.

"That's what I want," Michael whispered.

A raucous ruckus arose from the unkindness of ravens as they signaled the approach of their master. Time grew short and yet his work required precision. Perspiration beads proliferated on Loki's brow, stung his eyes, and dripped onto his cheeks.

Swiping his lips with his tongue, Loki tasted the salt of his sweat. He concentrated until his magic acquired a deep, narrow focus. With a deft touch, the Trickster swiped the boy's fear. Acquiring the emotion without taking memory of what had caused it challenged even his considerable skill as a thief but he managed. A huge lump of terror passed down his throat and settled in his gullet, an unsavory meal he'd be long in digesting.

He hesitated, on the verge of withdrawing then and calling it even-steven, but something niggled at the sense of decency he would have flat-out denied having if called on it. Nothing ever boiled down to just one feeling, especially not the sort of ordeal Michael had endured.

Shaking from head to toe, Loki reached further. Michael suffered from PTSD. With an effort, Loki pulled the nausea into himself. He removed only the *memories* of pain associated with the trauma—scrapes, bruises, cramped muscles, suffocating heat, cold steel. Like an anaconda swallowing a bison, the Trickster stretched and strained to internalize the child's agony; his entire being twitched and writhed. He left behind a recollection stripped clean and sanitized.

The boy exhaled a long, slow sigh and breathed easier.

"You're not afraid anymore," Loki murmured. "From now on there's a special place inside you where fear doesn't exist. If you need to not be afraid then say—*No fear.* Envision the safe place."

"No fear," Michael parroted. The boy's soul shone brighter, twinkling like a wishing star. He retained sorrow and self-blame, especially with regard to his mother's death, but nothing approaching the affliction Loki had removed.

Loki *almost* swallowed the youngster's guilt as well even though the burden would've left him too bloated to escape. He considered the act of kindness, of self-sacrifice, and came *this close* to absorbing that enormous emotion too. His sense of self-preservation proved too strong.

Ravens screamed.

"Get the hell away from my son." Jake Barrett descended larger than life, an avenging force come to his son's defense. A burning blade sliced through the steel bars that formed a protective cage about the rocket ship's cone.

"Sorry, kid. Gotta fly." The heat seared the hairs on the back of Loki's neck. Flinging out his arms, he burst into a cloud of gnats. The dagger cut a wide swath through the swarm before it struck the fiberglass platform.

Loki's agonized shriek echoed for miles. Hundreds of gnats perished but thousands survived, and so the Trickster endured but just barely. Clinging to his existence with his remaining strength, he scattered his particles even farther and shape changed into pollen spores, sinking his essence into particulates carried on the hot desert wind.

CHAPTER TEN

Freya's breathe rasped, incalculably loud in the quiet of the catio. She wanted to scream, to hurl insults. To call Arik a hateful liar. However, the truth had weight and mass, and possessed inescapable inertia. It crushed her. Her defense remained a justification that sounded weak even to her.

Anger swept her, swift and sure. The goddess leveled an accusing stare at the man she'd thought she'd known, at least on some level. Now, she perceived how she'd fallen into his trap—a complete stranger. "I won't apologize for my actions or justify them to you! How do you know all this? Who told you?"

Arik shrugged. "I know. Does the how and why of it matter?"

"Yes, it matters. Tell me where you learned these terrible secrets that have burdened my soul," Freya commanded with the resonance of divinity in her voice. "I haven't spoken of my doubt to anyone—not a single word. Yet, you are privy to the worst fears of my heart."

When Arik refused to answer her question, Freya's determination underwent a transformation to diamond-hardness. She marched straight up to him, fists clenched, ramping up for battle. He slid to his feet, brushing thick clumps of tiger fur from his jacket.

"Tell me." She seized his lapel.

Arik smiled, wide and hungry, a ravenous wolf. "I know the same way I know that *you* held back a piece of the unbreakable ribbon that imprisons Fenrir. You had it made into *Vanadium*, the only weapon that can cut the binding."

Freya stopped breathing; horrified realization dawned. Her hand rose to her heart—*no.*

"Although, I'll grant: that one's a gimme." He kept speaking, damning her and himself with each word. "No one but you, Freya, would be vain enough or dumb enough to name the weapon that'll bring about Odin's death after yourself."

It couldn't be. Couldn't.

She mouthed a denial—*"No."*

"I have all your secrets, doll." The smug bastard dropped a wink. "I know you're diverting all the souls of wolf shifters to your hall—in violation of the agreed fifty-fifty split you have with Odin. Just like you know who I am."

"No!" She stared at him, unable to rip her gaze from his face.

"Say my name."

"Loki."

PHOENIX, *Arizona*

The magical dagger vanished from Jake's hand, and reappeared on his forearm as a tattoo at the center of massive burn scars. The nasty stench of melted plastic permeated the air, potent enough to curl his nostrils and curdle his stomach. Waving his arms to clear the air, he leaned into the rocket's cone, taking care to avoid the red-hot ends of the severed rebar cage.

Michael sat on the platform with his knees drawn to his small chest. His arms wrapped about his knees, and his head bent while he cried. His sobs were great and piteous, torn from the depths of despair, a child suffering. Otherwise, he appeared to be physically unharmed.

"Michael? Are you okay?" He bent and placed his palm on the boy's slender back. Worry sickened him, anxiety that manifested physically from the cramped muscles of his shoulders to sharp knots in his abdomen.

"Jake?" Michael's voice quavered as he lifted his face to look up. Tear tracks streaked the youngster's face—a naked sorrow that hurt to look upon. The boy grabbed hold of his guardian's bicep and scrambled to his feet.

The boy's suffering injured Jake, and he ached for his son's anguish. Loki was slime, using an innocent child in his twisted games. Loki would pay, but later. For now, Michael needed a father to offer comfort.

Jake gentled his voice. "I'm here, Champ. It's going to be okay. Let's get you down from here. Can you stand up for me?"

"Sure." Michael wiped his eyes with both hands, leaving

dirty streaks on his cheeks. Then he turned his face into his sleeve, smearing snot on the cotton.

He conducted another subtle once over, double checking to ensure the boy wasn't suffering a physical injury. When Jake sank down, something crunched beneath his knee. He glanced down and discovered an odd curiosity in the form of an open box of Kleenex.

"Here, use these." He offered the boy the all-too-convenient box of tissues. Its presence struck him as incongruent, especially since the rest of Loki's artifacts, including the bright red backpack, had vanished along with the Trickster. The discrepancy bugged him.

"Thanks." Michael grabbed a wad and blew, and then wiped off his face. He glanced down toward a trash can and his hand moved in a subconscious gesture as if he intended to try for the impossible throw.

"Let's get down from here." Jake scooped Michael up and held him with one arm, snagging the boy's blue backpack as well. He surveyed the damage he'd caused to the play structure with regret but it couldn't be helped. Once he found the time and opportunity, he'd look into having it repaired. The top of the rocket was about twenty feet high, a short though challenging climb with only one free hand.

"I can walk. Put me down." Squirming, Michael asserted his independent streak as soon as they reached the ground.

"All right. Stop fussing." Jake swung his son down and released him. Trying not to be too obvious about it, he hovered while Michael took his first shaky steps.

"I need to throw this away," Michael said, holding up the wad of used tissue. Instead of heading toward the receptacle, though, he detoured beneath the rocket ship to where a piece of refuse lay in the tan bark. He scooped up another tissue.

With his narrow shoulders squared, he marched over to the green barrel and dropped the trash inside.

Out of more than just idle curiosity, he glanced into the waste bin. A cynical snort escaped him when it proved just as he'd suspected—empty soda cans nestled amid torn foil candy wrapper.

"Just how much of this junk did you eat, Son?" He appraised Michael again, and the pinched look on the boy's face took on a whole new dimension of meaning.

"No-ne..." Michael sputtered out a clumsy lie. His throat worked convulsively so his Adam's apple bobbed, and his hands clutched at his belly. "Not much. I had some, but Ben ate a lot more."

"I'm not surprised." Despite everything, Jake's lips twisted into an unwilling smile once his fear for Michael's safety started to fade. Scolding the lad served no useful purpose. Some lessons were learned the hard way or not at all. "Is Ben that other boy's name?"

"Ben is my friend."

"I'm not so sure about that."

"Jake, I want to go home," Michael said in a plaintive voice. Tears brightened his eyes, and his complexion retained its ruddy hue.

"C'mon, kiddo, my car is this way." He jerked his head to the side. "Are you sure you feel up to walking?"

"Yeah, I'm fine." Arms crossed over his abdomen, Michael shuffled toward him. He made it three feet when a tormented groan tore from his throat. "I don't feel so good."

"What's wrong, kiddo? Can I help?" Jake laid a hand on the boy's forehead and found his temperature was flushed and feverish. Whatever Loki had done, the symptoms were worse than just an upset stomach.

"I think I'm gonna be sick." Moaning, Michael doubled over and puked all over Jake's boots.

"I'd say that's a given." Jake held the boy's head for a couple minutes, and then picked him up and carried him from the park. Michael was a small, precious weight in his arms. He rested his head against his guardian's shoulder, so quiet that Jake's concern steadily deepened. He took his son home rather than return Michael to school. Until Jake figured out what Loki had done to the boy, it was better to keep a close eye on him.

"Ahh im tble?" Michael mumbled around the thermometer in his mouth.

"What's that again?" Jake gave up on the boy being still to have his temperature taken. He removed the device and checked the digital display. It read 98.6, confirming what a forehead check had already told him—Michael wasn't feverish.

"Am I in trouble?" The six-year-old pushed off the bathroom counter and dropped to the ground, landing squarely on both feet. At Jake's insistence, he wore pajamas but it was under protest.

"For playing hooky from school, hiding out at the park, and eating enough candy to give your dentist apoplexy?"

Unrepentant, the boy grinned. "Yeah, that."

Jake doused the end of the thermometer in rubbing alcohol to sterilize it and returned it to its place in the medicine cabinet. "Do you think you should be?"

"Ben said I should blame him."

"Did he?" He grew still, the hunter in him intent.

To Jake's utter exasperation, Michael trucked right on out of the room to where Rascal waited for his master. "Yeah. He said I should cry and some other stuff, too." Boy and dog shot down the hallway toward Michael's bedroom.

"Hey! What else did he say?" Irritation prickled his skin like a heat rash. He hurried to catch up with the two-and-four-legged terrors.

At the intersection of the hall and the kitchen entrance, Michael skidded in a smooth circle, looked back, and flashed a cheeky grin. "He called you a sucker."

A rusty chuckle rattled his chest, and he felt like a man who'd forgotten how to laugh. Slowly, the hard block of fear in his chest was melting, but even indulging amusement struck him as inappropriate. Although Michael seemed to be fine following his encounter with Loki, appearances were all too deceptive, especially when the Trickster was involved.

Jake walked into the kitchen and inhaled, breathing in the aroma of fresh-baked chocolate chip cookies. Hearty warmth permeated the atmosphere from the oven. Tasting the air, he identified toasty cinnamon and rich brown sugar, and the bittersweet note of dark chocolate. The scents set his mouth to watering and his stomach to rumbling.

Cooling cookies formed neat rows atop paper towels on the countertop. Lucy Ketteridge, his housekeeper and the only solid female presence in their household since his wife's passing, buzzed about the kitchen. Despite being slightly arthritic, the woman was a dynamo—a baking whirlwind. Her extensive and colorful resume included hippie, monster slayer, and a trauma nurse. Her experience had prepared her well for her current position in his employ. Lucy knew how to handle the boys and she understood the nature of Jake's calling.

The lush apple of Iðunn sat in the fruit bowl atop a stack

of oranges. An unripe banana bowed before the glowing fruit that looked more a replica cast in pure gold than an edible thing. It drew the eye and captured attention; impossible to overlook.

Stretching out his arm, Jake plucked the apple from atop its perch. He gripped it in the palm of his hand and considered it while his mind traveled back through the years to when Sarah had first been diagnosed with breast cancer. His initial reaction had been absolute shock and denial—gods simply did not suffer earthly ailments.

Unthinkable and unacceptable.

Following the first chemo treatments, Sarah's hair fell out in clumps that clogged in the drain. She put on a brave front for her husband and sons, but she cried in the shower, using the hot spray to hide her tears. The treatment made her nauseous until she all but stopped eating. The paler and gaunter she grew, the worse Jake's turmoil until he finally couldn't stand it anymore.

Jake pulled strings on earth and in heaven to obtain the apple which was a cure-all for any and all sicknesses and diseases. In doing so, he broke every rule he'd set for himself as a mortal man. Until then, he and his mate had lived human lives along with all the associated inconveniences and infirmaries. Together, they bore children and built a life but he, Odin, the All Father, the mighty and powerful king of the gods hadn't been prepared to accept the death of his beloved spouse.

He chose a Friday night when all the boys were out of the house to present it to her. Discomfort made him brusque. He thrust the apple toward Sarah and growled a command. "I want you to eat this."

She stared at the apple long and hard, until his outstretched arm ached from the strain of holding the same position. Then, with a sad smile on her lips, she lifted her face toward him. "No, my love, I cannot."

"Why not? It's right here in front of you. Not eating it doesn't make any sense." He all but shouted for the world of frustration and anger shredding his heart.

Sarah spoke with serenity that destroyed him. "Because this is what we chose together. A mortal life with an inevitable mortal end."

"I can't accept that."

He'd never been able to accept the limitations or live within the boundaries as Sarah had done. He aged but he refused to surrender the runes he secreted within his soul even for a short lifetime. Thus, he cheated and retained remarkable strength, stamina, and regeneration. Kept his weapons. Allowed one fatal flaw capable of ending his human existence. And not once had his beloved wife ever questioned or criticized his decision.

"I'm sorry, but it's not your choice. It's mine. If mortal medicine cannot cure my mortal body, then I'll accept my death. I'm grateful for you and our four amazing sons and this life we've had together." She framed his lower face within her hands, pressing her palms to his beard, and brushed a sweet kiss to his lips.

"If you won't do it for me then do it for our sons. They need their mother." He shook in the grip of devastating sentiment. His monumental anger was great enough to destroy worlds.

Pain twisted her lovely face but he was too much of a selfish bastard to apologize and retract the spiteful words. Sarah drew upright, a queen in her bearing. "No. Our sons must learn the difficult lessons of life, and death of a loved one is the hardest of all. It is fitting."

His shout carried for miles, shaking the ground. He

slammed the apple down on the kitchen counter before her. "It'll will be here when you change your mind."

She shook her head, adamant in her decision. "I won't change my mind."

And so the apple sat in the fruit bowl on the kitchen counter of their Arizona home—a glaring reminder of their marked disagreement. Months passed. Jake wasted more than half their remaining time together on anger before he stumbled into the awful realization that Sarah meant it. He scrambled to make up for loss but it hadn't been enough. Not by a long shot.

She died on a fine spring morning in April, cradled in his arms. She left and took her light and love and laughter with her. His wife—gone more than two years now. Not a day passed that Jake didn't mourn her and miss her. His sons suffered in her absence and, for a time, their family hadn't experienced joy or celebration.

A couple months after Sarah passed away, Jake locked the apple away in the safe and there it had remained until the weeks prior to Daniel's sudden and violent death. There'd been no opportunity to save him. Once again, Jake sealed the apple away—until now.

"I want a cookie!" Michael's insistent voice intruded on Jake's reverie.

Jake blinked, forcing his attention to the present.

"Why can't I have a cookie?" Michael donned his puppy dog face and clasped hands with the shameless determination of a skilled beggar.

"Because young men who have eaten so much junk food that they puked should not have cookies." Lucy used her spatula to add emphasis to her point, aiming it toward the boy like a wand. Although her expression was schooled to sternness, her deep blue eyes shone with good humor. She wore her dishwater-blonde-going-gray hair confined in a neat bun, and a fluffy yellow apron protected her clothes.

"Ooohhh, that's not fair," Michael moaned.

"Life isn't fair." Her face relaxed into deep smile lines.

"Can I have a cookie?" Jake asked, already reaching for one.

"No." The spatula tapped his knuckles hard.

Undaunted, he stole a cookie anyway. The hot dough burned his callused fingers, but not enough to deter him from popping the whole gooey goodness straight into his mouth. Chewing, he reached for another one.

"These are good."

"Jake Barrett, you're a bad man. You know that?" Lucy looked askance at him and issued a firm warning. "I'm making those for the bake sale. I'd better not turn around and find out you've eaten the entire batch."

"Yes, ma'am." Jake mumbled around a mouthful of cookie. Michael and Rascal looked on in pure jealousy while he downed a third. Neither boy nor dog could have one, and for good reasons, so he didn't feel the least bit guilty about eating in front of them.

"I let you get away with murder."

"Yes, you do." He flashed a shameless grin.

"This doesn't look like a young man who should be home sick with an upset stomach." Shaking her head, Lucy eyed Michael with the critical eye of a mother suspecting illness fraud.

"Trust me. I was there when he got sick. My boots paid the price," Jake said, offering assurance. In fact, his boots were sitting on the front porch waiting a thorough cleaning before they'd be fit to wear again. "Thanks for agreeing to watch him, Lucy. I'm sorry you had to cancel your doctor appointment."

"Not a problem at all. I don't like that doctor anyway. I swear, the man is a moron." The corners of her eyes crinkled, matching her smile. She rinsed her hands and dried them on a towel. "Is he allowed to watch television?"

"Later, after he's taken a proper nap," Jake said, evoking a groan of protest from the boy. "I mean it. That nightmare had you up last night for a couple hours, so I know you didn't get a good night's sleep."

"But—" Michael began an automatic protest.

"No arguing." Jake addressed Lucy. "I'll see him to bed so you don't have to deal with the fuss."

Hands on her hips, Lucy harrumphed. "All right. Though, I'm sure I could handle one little boy..."

"I'm sure you could too." He threw up his hands to signal his surrender on the issue, but then dropped them to herd the boy from the kitchen.

"I'll lie down but I'm not tired." Michael sprinted toward his bedroom.

"Fine. Then just lie down." Jake wasn't in the mood to argue technicalities. Besides, he suspected once the boy's head hit the pillow, sleep would soon follow of its own accord.

When he arrived, Jake found the boy in the middle of ripping his drawings from the walls. All the artwork depicted images from Michael's traumatic encounter with the monster that had murdered his mother and kidnapped him the prior Christmas.

"Whatcha doing, Champ?"

He leaned his shoulder against the doorframe. As he watched, Michael dumped an armful of pictures into his waste bin. A few escaped, swishing and sliding on the air, scattering in random directions. One landed at Jake's feet.

When he bent to retrieve it, a sinister brown spider

sprinted across the carpeting. Jake's skin crawled. Reacting rather than acting, he smashed his boot down on top of the arachnid. He lifted his foot but found no bug juice smear. Just a long, wriggling leg as it vanished beneath the baseboard.

A cursory inspection of the drawing in his hand revealed a painting of children imprisoned within oversized birdcages. As always, anger and protectiveness churned within Jake, but to no avail. The beast responsible had long since been slain. His wrath had no outward target to lock onto.

"I'm getting rid of all this. I want them gone so I don't have to remember." Michael deposited pushpins into the top drawer of his desk, and returned to taking the macabre artwork from the walls.

"How come?" Standing around didn't suit him, not when there was work to be done. Jake targeted some of the higher pictures, leaving the lower tier for the boy to deal with. Once white space appeared on the wall and the small waste bin neared capacity, he realized just how many of the damn things there were; drawings and watercolors had been tacked in overlapping layers.

"Because." Michael offered only the single word and nothing else.

With a shrug, Jake accepted the answer. Sometimes, a man had to put his thoughts in order before he was ready to share them. Instead, he helped Michael clear every last troubling reminder of his traumatic experience from the room. Once they were done, the two of them stared at the overloaded waste bin and the stack of papers that hadn't fit.

"Can we take these out to the big can?" Michael asked.

"I have a thought," Jake said. "That might be more satisfying than throwing these out."

"Yeah. What?" Michael's small face gazed up, curiosity bright in his eyes.

"C'mon. I'll show you." Jake tipped his head to the side, inviting Michael to accompany him. Given the remarkable development, his son's nap could wait a while longer. He wasn't quite sure what to make of the sudden improvement in the boy's condition—if it truly constituted advancement for the better.

Together, they made their way to the backyard where Jake constructed a small pyramid from charcoal briquettes, applied lighter fluid, and lit a match. Standing opposite each other, the man and the boy fed drawings to the fire and watched them burn. Thick smoke rose in a column, adding its heat to the broiling atmosphere.

"Ready to talk yet?" Jake asked, testing the waters. He had to leave in fifteen minutes or he'd be late to the parent-teacher conference.

"Yeah, I think so." Across the flames, Michael held Jake's gaze. Square shouldered, the boy stood straight and proud but then he frowned. "What're we talkin' about again?"

His mouth carved out a hard smile. No matter what, the boy wasn't a slouch. The kid understood the art of evasion, though his technique could use some polish.

"You were explaining why we're burning all your art."

"Oh yeah." Michael thrust another drawing into the fire. Hungry flames licked at the edges which curled inward as the fire ate toward the center. The boy took a deep breath and began to speak. "My mother's name was June, June Fraiser. She was thirty-two years old and she had pretty brown hair that curled at the ends around her shoulders. She smelled like flowers. The perfume she wore was her favorite. She used to say it was her mom's favorite and it reminded her of Grandma. I never got to meet my grandma because she passed away before I born. It was always just Mom and me. We were a team. We didn't have any money, and I know she loved me..."

A tear streaked the boy's cheek, running in a swift stream to his jaw. Others followed, painting his cheeks with the tracks of his sorrow.

"You remember your mom?" Jake asked carefully, striving to keep his voice neutral though his emotions formed a messy mix of joy and relief. For months, the boy had been unable to recall anything about his mother aside from the barest facts—her name and age, their address and phone number, but nothing personal. Nothing intimate. At last, the barrier to his memories of her appeared to have vanished.

The convenience left him wondering. As a rule, he put no faith in coincidence.

Jake added another handful of papers to the grill.

Michael nodded and a smile brightened his young face despite the tears streaking his cheeks. "I can remember now. I can *see* her face again and what she used to look like when she smiled."

"Do you know what happened to change things so you could remember?"

The child's head rocked up and down, and he hugged himself. "Ben helped. I don't know how, but he helped. It doesn't hurt anymore. I still feel bad. If I hadn't stolen that toy, then mom would still be alive and none of this would've happened."

"We've talked about this," Jake said in a gentle voice. "What happened wasn't your fault. The Krampus was a monster that fed on guilt and targeted helpless children. None of its victims were to blame."

"I know." Michael bobbed his head, and a rain of tears fell from his face. "I still feel bad."

"Guilt takes time to work through, but you're going to get better. It's a sign of improvement that you can remember your mom."

"Ben said I couldn't remember her because of the bad stuff. Now I can so I must be better," Michael said, implementing a child's simplistic logic with cutting effectiveness.

"Ben, the boy on the play structure?" Jake asked in a voice thick with skepticism. He had to be sure—no room for doubt. It wasn't often Loki got accused of doing something helpful and even rarer that it proved to be true. He'd hate to simply accept such an account at face value without asking questions or trying to discern the Trickster's ulterior motives.

"Yeah. Ben's my friend." Michael looked his adopted father straight in the eyes. "He took away all the stuff that was scary and that hurt."

"But you can remember everything that happened?"

"I can still remember it, but it's like I watched it all on TV." Michael dumped a thick swath of papers onto the grill, freeing his hands. "Can I go back inside now? I don't want to take a nap. Maybe Lucy will let me play video games."

"Sure, go ahead, but I wouldn't count it." Jake stared after the boy in perplexed silence while his mind worked to analyze what he'd just learned. None of it made any sense or fit with what he knew to be true.

Son of a gun—what game could Loki be playing at now?

CHAPTER ELEVEN

SESSRÚMNIR, FREYA'S HALL IN FÓLKVANGR

For an eternity, Freya stood shock still, unable to think or muster words. Stomach-turning sickness curdled her gut, nausea unlike anything she'd ever known. It couldn't be...it musn't. But the terrible truth of him stared her right in the face...and he smirked.

"C'mon, you can do it." He coaxed with his hands as though she were a child.

Bile filled her mouth. She'd fucked the bastard. She wanted to puke. She *needed* to scrub her skin raw. Instead, she regurgitated his ugly name. "Loki."

"Good. Now breathe. Keep calling me Arik. It'll make it easier to perpetuate the ruse when we're around others."

Freya gasped and shot straight past panting to hyperventilation. He thought—he *thought*—she'd help him continue his masquerade. Well, did he have another thing coming! She turned from him so she wouldn't have to look into his face any longer. Reaching up, she wrapped her hands about the back of her head and moaned. "Impossible. This has to be a nightmare."

"Afraid not. It's real."

She swiveled on her heel, poised on the precipice of despair. "But I saw you..." Her throat worked. "Arik was asleep in my bed when..."

"Loki." He nodded encouragement.

"Loki visited."

"Ah, that." He wove a spell with his hands—ribbons of magic swirled and formed clouds that rained a shimmering sparkle. When the pretty light show faded, two identical versions of Arik stood side by side.

"Illusion," said the Arik to the right. His twin took a stage bow. "An old trick but still one of my most effective."

*Phoenix, **Arizona***

Like the twins, Michael attended a private elementary school. A fence enclosed the main campus and private security guards were part of the staff. A construction crew had already assembled to repair the damaged section. While school was in session, the gates were locked to prevent trespassing. Visitors had to sign in through the front office and were then escorted to their destination.

After he checked in, Jake followed a plump Hispanic receptionist down a hallway of white subway tiles. Bright bulletin boards provided pops of color against the beige walls.

"They're waiting for you inside, Mr. Barrett." She held open a faded orange door.

"Thank you." He entered and the door shut behind him.

He stood inside a small room that held an oversized table. It dominated the entire space, leaving little in terms of walking area to either side. On the far wall, vertical blinds covered the tall single window.

Three women sat at the far end—ominous in demeanor, possession-marked auras hinting at the elder world. One was youthful and pretty, one middle-aged and stern, and one elderly and bitter. Three eldritch witches come a callin', dressed in mortal disguises.

Foreboding hung thick, a blanket of smog in the air. The hairs on the back of his neck and arms stood on end. Jake stopped. The muscles of his face hardened to a stoic mask, and he summoned his magic to him, double-checking to be sure all his wards and shields were in place. Anger percolated deep in the core of his being.

"Mr. Barrett, thank you for coming." Vera Ricardo, Michael's first grade teacher, was an attractive Hispanic woman in her mid-twenties. Quite understandably, Michael had something of a crush on his pretty teacher. When prior social occasions had brought them together, Jake found her to be articulate and pleasant, though a tad naive. Her intuitive empathy and gentle nature allowed her to relate to children in a way well beyond his capacity, so she had his respect.

"It's a pleasure to see you again, Ms. Ricardo." Jake offered a bland smile and tipped his chin to the foul creature that wore Vera Ricardo's body as her disguise.

"Mr. Barrett, I'm Cecelia Mallory, the principal. I don't believe I've had the pleasure of making your acquaintance before." The austere administrator, a woman in her mid-forties, ruled from the head of the table. She wore a dark gray pants suit cut in an ascetic style. Her features were sharp and narrow. Her silver hair slicked flat against her skull, revealing a widow's peak, and pulled into a tight top knot. Her eyes were hard, glittering diamonds; her tinny lips belonged to a joy-sucking vampire.

He didn't just dislike her. He despised her.

"I'm afraid you're mistaken. We have met." Jake settled into a wide stance, arms crossed over his thick chest, feet planted firm. He'd have preferred to wield his burning dagger, but he settled for a dangerous smile.

Uncertainty flickered over the principal's face which then wrung into a scowl. He used the opportunity to study the final woman who bookended the set. Her identity was unknown to him. The matron had sharp black eyes set within a gaunt face. The canvas of her skin pulled taunt over the prominent bones of her face. Severity enhanced her chronic mien. Spidery fingers clutched the thick spine of a book; yellowed nails dug into the cover. The novel lacked a dust jacket and the pages appeared jaundiced with age.

The silence grew brittle.

"Mr. Barrett, are you sure you wouldn't like a seat?" Mallory gestured to the lone chair at the foot of the table again.

"I'd rather stand." As Jake expected, the women's gazes riveted upon his tattoos.

"When is it you believe we met?" Mallory asked.

"We spoke on 'back to school' night."

"Oh. Oh, yes." The principal rubbed her eyebrow. "I'd forgotten." After a short pause, she gestured to the eldest of the three women and offered an introduction. "This is Dr. Doris Noma, the school psychologist. She'll be consulting with us today regarding Michael."

"I see." Jake stroked a hand across his jaw. He didn't see, not really, but he understood how the Sisters Wyrd operated well enough to be on his guard. Whatever their motives, these harpies meant him and his son no good. His enemies were closing on him from all sides—first the Necromancer, then Loki, now the Sisters. Fear chilled his blood, not for himself, but for Michael. These ruthless villains had no qualms about targeting a child to get to him.

Somewhere above them on the roof, an air conditioning unit rattled and clanked, and then warm air blew through the air vent above the door. An irritating high-pitched buzzing came out of nowhere and intensified. A tiny tear in reality appeared above the principal's head. A writhing black leg shoved through the fissure and hung suspended upon the dust-laden air. A black bot fly pulled its fat body through the crack and whizzed through the air on furious wings.

Mallory ducked and took a reflexive swipe at it.

"I know you were only expecting a parent-teacher conference today to discuss Michael's progress," Ms. Sanchez said. "However, recent events have caused me to become concerned, so I thought it best to invite my colleagues."

"What recent events?" Since he found her less objectionable than the others, Jake centered his attention on Sanchez.

"Truancy is a serious matter, Mr. Barrett. Michael played hooky this morning." Placing her hands flat on the tabletop, Mallory cast the long-stare down her straight nose in an attempt to intimidate. The fly zipped past her face, ruining the effect.

Jake sealed his lips, suppressing a snort. Loki was a damn nuisance when he set his mind to it. It was a pleasant change of pace to *not* be the target of the Trickster's antics for once.

"Michael wasn't truant this morning, Ms. Mallory. He's home sick. Poor lad's been sick to his stomach. I'm afraid it's entirely my fault the absence didn't get called in. I'm a single father with three boys living at home. Sometimes the little things get away from me." Jake offered the expert lie with an apologetic, aww-shucks smile. Loki might be the God of Lies, but he wasn't the only one skilled in deception. Jake had learned a thing or two during their long association.

"An unexcused absence isn't a little thing." The principal's face flushed. Anger shone in her eyes.

"The school day isn't over yet. I'll call as soon as we're done here." His tone darkened, daring further challenge. "Now, do we have any further business here? I'd like to get home to my son."

"There is no need to call. We'll mark today as an excused absence. However, there is the original reason for the meeting." In an attempt to make peace, Ms. Sanchez offered a wan smile that failed to reach her eyes. "Michael is a delight to have in class but I must admit, I do worry about how closed off he is. He is a hard worker and polite, but he does not participate in classroom discussion. At lunch and recess, he is always alone on the playground."

Miss Sanchez glanced across the table to the old woman seated across from her, an action that implied a passing of the baton. Up until then, Doris Noma had remained silent and in profile to Jake. She shifted toward him in an uneven stop-and-go motion that reminding him of rusty clockwork.

"Mr. Barrett, prior to your adoption of the boy, Michael suffered extensive trauma. When I interviewed him, he stated his mother was murdered and he was abducted by the killer. Most interesting perhaps, he claimed that *you* rescued him." Gleaming raven eyes menaced him. The psychologist's thin lips parted to yellowed teeth and her knuckles tightened on the book in her hands.

She paused and stared at him in obvious expectation. Jake raised his eyebrow. He remained stubbornly silent. The determined fly shifted its focus from the principal to the psychologist. It hovered about the older woman's head, zooming toward her ear and then out again when she released her death grip on the book to strike at it.

Noma huffed in annoyance and resumed. "Upon review, his file contained no record of such a traumatic incident having occurred."

"Is there a question?" Jake raised a challenging brow.

Emitting a high-pitched whine, the insect lighted upon Dr. Noma's cheek. Its legs and antenna worked furiously as it crawled toward her mouth.

"There were a great many questions I was unable to find answers to." Dr. Noma swatted at the fly. Her face was like curdled milk as she smacked her cheek, but the fly escaped into flight again.

Jake bit back a grin. *Loki—God of Irritation.* How apropos.

Principal Mallory glowered across the room. "We are concerned about Michael's future—whether he will even have one."

The stilted threat got to him. White-hot anger burned through Jake. Clenching his teeth, he clamped down tight on the reaction before the tattoo dagger on his arm acquired a molten glow. In spite of his best efforts, he sensed the magic intrinsic to his soul pushing toward the surface. It writhed in his breast, pulsating like a living thing.

"Michael's future is my concern. Not yours," Jake replied in a voice deceptive for its softness but in that moment he was at his most dangerous. The potential for violence built with each passing second.

"We must disagree. Our role in his life is paramount—far reaching beyond even your considerable influence." Sanchez kept her face turned from him. Her speech hiccupped, a product of uneven cadence and uncertain delivery.

Principal Mallory's gaze impaled him as a spear,

penetrating and designed to deliver a deep wound. "We will play an instrumental role in the boy's future, so I am sure you understand our interest."

"I don't. Why don't you spell it out for me?" He choked his righteous anger, checking his temper. Those three women were innocents. They weren't responsible for what they said or did while possessed, and ending their lives wouldn't have done any good. He could slay a thousand people and Michael wouldn't be the least bit safer.

Mallory's smile embodied death. "What fate will befall him resides in our hands. Should misfortune take the boy's life, you will know the manifestation of our wrath."

The tattoo dagger on his arm lit up like a star. Jake reached for the hilt, intending to draw, but a tremendous clamor arose from the fly, more like the roar of a lion than the drone of an insect. It shot forward, a swift blur, and blazed the shape of a sigil into the air with its flight. The rune—*Hagalaz*, the hailstone. It shimmered, shedding sparkles.

Without missing a beat, Jake took up the Trickster's suggestion. He removed his belt knife from its sheath instead of *Stakhla*. At the flash of steel, the three women hissed and reared like cobras. He employed a short, swift stroke and sliced his palm open with the point of the blade. Ruby droplets rained upon the tabletop.

He traced the rune in his own blood and incanted its true name. Vast energy flowed—objective confrontation—past patterns. Stinging hardness. Repulsion. Shadow elements expelled—invading spirits cast out. Ironically, it represented in part the inevitability of fate, but Jake rotated *Hagalaz* to accentuate the restoration of victim consciousness—waking up the minds of the possessed.

In unison, the three women threw back their heads.

Banshee screams tore from their throats. They writhed and convulsed as the magic manifested.

Mallory doubled over, claw-like hands locked about her throat. Gagging, her face turned dark red. A huge spider dropped from her gaping mouth. It hit the smooth wood and scuttled away. More arachnids poured from her ears, nose, and eyes—the essence of evil expulsed.

Talking over each other, the other two women slapped Mallory on the back but within seconds the runic restoration overpowered them also. Ms. Ricardo collapsed to the floor, vomiting spiders. The hairy creatures formed a living river upon the floor of the conference room.

Dr. Noma succumbed last. Wriggling black legs thrust from her nostrils and between her lips but the Past Norn hung on with sheer obstinacy. She gritted and marshaled her will—pushback. She lifted her spidery hand, reaching for him. "Wodan, I curse you!"

"Out, witch! Get out!" Jake snarled and placed both his hands upon the smooth wood, sketching more sigils from the Elder Futhark in blood. Their quintessential magic—fundamental to the fabric of the universe. His to command. The magic clashed, immense and primordial, the essence of conflict.

Jake discovered he had help from an unexpected quarter. Loki's sneaky, subtle magic worked in parallel with his own. Undertow, undetectable beneath the water's placid surface, was nonetheless deadly. The assassin's hidden blade. The scorpion's unexpected strike. Old allies come together, unified to a common purpose.

Noma shrieked and toppled. At last released, a tarantula disgorged from the older woman's mouth. It dropped and landed atop the mass of its smaller brethren that had already been driven from the other Sisters Wyrd. The circulating spiders located the air duct on the wall and poured through the slits in the cover. The conference room emptied with remarkable swiftness.

As the exorcism of the other two women neared completion, their convulsions ceased. They lay where they'd fallen, groaning in sickness. Abruptly, Jake faced a problem of a whole different nature—discovery. The whole fucked-up situation promised to be difficult to explain, and impossible to cover up.

Loki appeared, taking on the form of the black-haired boy. He waved his arm. "I'll steal their memories of this. Meet me outside."

"Yeah." Jake spun on his heel and yanked the conference room door wide open.

As he passed the front desk, the receptionist glanced up at him, surprise plain on her face. Then she contorted her face, and she spoke in a voice not her own. "You can walk away from us, All Father, but there's no escaping. The hour of your curse is upon you."

Jake kept going. Flattening his palms against the office's glass door, he shoved it open and emerged into the bright, hot afternoon. Free, he breathed easier.

Well, hell. The shit had just hit the fan. Michael wasn't ever coming back to this school.

Ever.

Halfway to the parking lot, Jake stumbled into an unnerving realization. He had just worked with Loki against their ancient foes as though he and the Trickster were still faithful allies. He hadn't hesitated, doubted, or questioned.

He'd trusted.

A boy, wearing a red baseball cap perched atop unruly black locks, waited in the parking lot. Loki, in his guise as Ben, employed the bumper of a car as a bench. As Jake approached, Ben's chin lifted and their gazes met. A knowing gleam shone in the Trickster's dark eyes.

Jake didn't question the Loki's presence or speed. The god of deceit had always had his methods of moving swiftly from one point to another, short cuts and secret passageways, so skilled in burglary that no stronghold could keep him out.

Settling into a gunslinger stance, Jake stopped ten paces from his old rival. Instead of reaching for his dagger, recent events had left him more inclined to listen than attack. So instead, he waited.

Loki pushed off the bumper, bouncing to his feet. "It's a dagger of the mind—a false creation."

A typical, ambiguous Lokism.

"It's real enough," Jake retorted, marked disagreement in his tone. He shouldn't engage the Trickster. Yet, even as he cautioned himself against falling right back into old traps and bad habits, curiosity got the better of him. "I believe the Sisters Wyrd have sent a *dís* after Michael... What do you think?"

Dísir were undead female agents of Fate that caused misfortune.

"I think—we're screwed if it's a *dís*," Loki said in a strong, clear voice. Although he wore the body of a child, he comported himself with confidence well beyond his apparent years. "Deadly accidents will keep befalling Michael until one of them kills him. Even with my help, his luck will run out sooner or later... There's no escape."

Grim-faced, Jake offered only silence. Deep down, he seethed. He hated it when Loki was right. He despised helplessness even more. As a god, he was more than a match for even the most powerful *dísir*. Lesser and greater Norns, including the Sisters Wyrd, fled before his wrath.

"I don't get it," Loki mused in a seeming random tangent to what they'd been discussing.

Jake wasn't fooled. The Trickster didn't make unrelated inferences or leap to illogical conclusions. If something he said or did appeared disparate, it usually meant one didn't yet have all the puzzle pieces. He decided to indulge Loki and see what it got him.

"What don't you get?"

"Why didn't you kill them all? They flat-out threatened the boy. You're well within your rights to wipe them off the map." Loki's arm waved in a gesture that encompassed not only the administration building but the entire school. Maybe even the whole world. "I could tell you wanted to, but you went to the trouble to exorcise them instead of killing them."

"Those women are innocent of any wrong doing." Jake shook his head. Cynicism was in his heart. He'd been tempted to do just as Loki said. And, in fact, the exorcism had come at the Trickster's promoting. He had no regrets. The Norns may have chosen the trio as temporary conduits, but the women themselves were mere puppets. He could no more hold them responsible than the sun could be held accountable for shining.

"What do you care for human life?" Loki's lips parted to reveal a delicate array of sharp canine teeth. He fidgeted, giving every impression of anxiety, or maybe simply having too much pent-up energy.

"Let's turn that around. What do you care for the life of a mortal boy?" He pinned his old rival with a flinty stare.

"I don't!" Loki spat the word on the blistering sidewalk and then jumped up and down. "All right, that's a lie. I do care—even though I shouldn't. The kid has a certain charm. I've got to hand it to him. He's got some serious backbone to have gone through what he did and not have turned out a jabbering mess. I *like* him..."

"I could spend the rest of eternity shifting through your lies. Unfortunately, the world hasn't got all that long, and I don't have time to waste." Jake shifted, intending to continue on to his car.

"Earlier today, I wasn't trying to hurt the boy." With a bold stride, Loki blocked Jake's path.

"You abducted Michael from the school yard. What was I supposed to think?"

"Bah." The Trickster produced a disgusted sound deep in his chest. "The Norns made another attempt on his life. Maybe, like you said, it was the work of a *dis*. Whatever the case, *I* saved him from being crushed by that car. *I* used magic to make him harder to find until you were able to come get him." He thumped his chest. "Meeee..."

Jake opened his mouth to argue but Loki's verbal barrage continued unchecked.

"Oh, and don't go claiming to not know what I'm talking about. There was a raven watching when those cars crashed. Ravens followed us to the park. Your eyes and ears—present every step of the way." Loki pinned him with a venomous look of accusation. "You knew and you still tried to kill me—"

"What I see and what I know aren't the same," Jake grated out. "I can't perceive intention. Maybe you meant for him to die that accident."

"Fuck you." Loki sneered, the expression made all that much uglier for his youthful appearance.

"A few months ago you boasted of being behind Daniel's murder. It's not a stretch to believe you're capable of killing another of my sons." He clenched his fists, crushing the urge to grab Loki's shoulders and shake him until his teeth fell out.

"I've no desire or intention to harm the boy. If I'd wanted Michael dead, he'd have died at the park when the bony fingers of fate rose through the water."

"What?" Jake stopped cold.

"Urðr made a grab for him at the park." Loki's arm wagged dismissively. "Look, that isn't relevant—"

"When?"

"I dunno. Yesterday. Before the baseball game. Will you stop interrupting and *listen*. None of that matters!" The child-sized Trickster waved his hands in a dance of frustration.

"You tried to help him without an agenda." Speaking softly, Jake tilted his head, but Loki seemed oblivious to his rival's scrutiny.

"Damn it! It's like I tried to tell you last night—right before you tried to kill me again—this thing between us is out of control and I want it to stop—" Loki pounded his palm with his fist. "It's one thing—you and I going at each other. It's even sorta fun. But now thousands of mortals —*children*—are dying."

"You're right."

"Of course I'm right! I'm always right!" Loki ground to a full stop. "Wait! What? You're—*agreeing* with me?"

"This thing is out of control. It's gotta stop."

"Oh. Oh..." The Trickster pantomimed extreme shock. "Could I be hearing this correctly? This must be a sign of the apocalypse— The dead rising from the grave! Human sacrifice, dogs and cats living together..."

"Mass hysteria!" Jake chuckled.

Loki missed a beat.

"What? You think you're the only one who's kept up with the times?" Jake snorted to convey his derision.

"Well, yeah." Loki's look said—*Duh.*

"Maybe you're even right about this morning. Maybe I took a cheap shot at you when you were doing your best to help Michael." The admission stuck in Jake's craw, but he was determined to make a valid effort.

Parodying a cartoon character, Loki used one finger to close his hanging jaw. "Is that the best you can do?"

"Thanks for looking out for my son." Jake pinned the Trickster with an unyielding gaze. "That's the best I can do. Don't expect an apology."

Too much bad blood existed between them for that to ever happen.

"I can live with that, so long as you stop accusing me of malicious intention toward Michael." Loki sounded more like a lawyer than the child he appeared.

"You fed the boy a crap load of sugar. He puked on my boots." Jake let his stare do his talking—he wasn't a fool. "You pulled the same stunt with Thor when he was a boy."

Loki smirked. "Well, I always was more the fun uncle than responsible father."

"Daffy Duck would've made a better parent."

They shared a laugh that ended all too abruptly, and the ensuing silence was even more pronounced and uncomfortable—a poignant, painful reminder of what they'd once had and lost. Long ago, before bitterness and betrayal divided them, the two men had been as thick as thieves.

"If you kill the *dís*, it won't stop the curse," Loki mused once their mirth petered out. "Another will just take its place."

"I'm aware of that." He dropped a brusque nod and considered continuing on his way. His to-do list wasn't getting any shorter and the hours kept slipping away. The afternoon heat put a nasty edge on his already foul mood, and his sweat-soaked clothing and parched throat aggravated his discomfort.

Loki chewed his thumbnail, deep in thought. "The only way to escape a *dísir* curse is for the jinxed person to kill her."

"Michael is six. He's hardly up to the task."

"And the only thing that will kill *dísir* is a weapon that's been touched by Fate." Loki eyed him. "Those are few and far between."

"I'm aware of that too." Ironically enough, Jake's own weapons were not equal to the task. With fastidious precision, he protected his tattoo dagger and his spear with runic wards.

"Don't go getting surly. I'm just thinking aloud."

"So you say." Jake fixed his fierce regard on Loki. He wasn't sure what, but he didn't need second sight to sense something momentous about to happen. The atmosphere between them was round and heavy, pregnant with collusion. The whole thing possessed an intense intimacy. Untold times, he'd stood with his head bowed, voice lowered, engaged in tight conspiracy with the Trickster. It had the feel of familiarity and comfort, like an old pair of slippers.

They complemented each other well. Jake possessed a mastery of short-term tactics implemented in pursuit of long-term strategies. Loki excelled at subterfuge, conspiracy, espionage, and assassination.

A voice in Jake's mind whispered he should be on his guard. At the same time, his determination to protect

Michael was taking on a desperation that could prove his undoing. Originally, he adopted the orphaned boy out of a sense of duty and obligation, and as a means of restoring sullied honor. But over the last six months, Jake's attachment to the child had deepened. He loved Michael.

And now, enemies targeted Michael to get to him. He'd be a fool not to consider that Loki might be working the same angle. Jake asked, "Aside from you supposedly liking Michael, what exactly is your interest in him?"

"Consideration," Loki spat out the word as if it were a curse. "I figure the kid is my chance to prove to you that we could work together." His eyes narrowed. "If I help you save Michael from the *dís*, that should be enough to at least earn your consideration of my proposal. Am I right?"

Jake smiled grimly. "You're not wrong."

"To help you, I need more than I've got."

"What are you asking me for?'

"Information." The Trickster bit off the succinct word. Boyish arms raised skyward, crossed at the elbows, and he grasped his own hands. He twisted about. "There's too much I don't understand. Why is Michael important to you? Why are they stalking him instead of going after your older sons? It was Sawyer who cheated death."

Flinty-eyed, Jake kept his expression guarded, concealing his inner turmoil. Loki already had a firm grasp of the fundamentals. Sawyer had cheated death—thus defying the Norns—when Victoria had resurrected him. The Trickster had the pieces to the puzzle; he just didn't know how to put them together.

Loki pinned Jake, an accusing look. "When that poor she-wolf cheated death, the Norns ripped her to shreds."

"I fought for Lenna." Bile pushed into Jake's throat.

"You failed her," Loki hissed. "Because you're clinging to

mortality—" His hand swept up and down, indicating Jake's human form. "Like a drowning man. Except, you have an ocean of power at your fingertips. None of it makes a lick of sense."

Balanced on one leg, Loki tipped to the side, windmilling his arms to maintain his balance. He continued to conjecture in his childishly high voice. "I figure you've used magic to guard Sawyer and the twins—something that affords them some sort of protection. But that you can't use on Michael because he's not your son by blood."

The whole situation made him queasy. Damn Loki for being right *again*—Michael was the most vulnerable of his sons. He glanced over his shoulder at the school. Maybe the Norns knew it too. More than anything, Jake disliked uncertainty, whether it stemmed from lack of conviction or ignorance. He preferred fortitude and forthrightness in pursuit of a goal, even if such an endeavor were ultimately doomed. Better to try and fail than to sit on one's ass and never accomplish anything. And another old axiom suited the situation perfectly. *The enemy of my enemy...*

Casting doubt aside, Jake made his choice. He wasn't ready to strike a deal with Loki, but it was high time to entertain possibilities. On a gut level, he perceived a potential benefit that could damn well prove worth the risk. Such involvement required a minimal degree of cooperation and trust. He drew a deep breath.

"You're correct. The magic I used to shield my older sons won't work on Michael," Jake said in a gravelly voice. He found sharing his closely-guarded secrets more difficult than he'd have thought. Suspicion stuck in his throat. "The boy is human. In the greater scheme of things, he doesn't matter."

"Except to you." Loki eyed him.

"Except to me." Jake tipped his head in a curt nod. "And a few others."

"One more thing." A quizzical expression hung on Loki's young face.

"What?"

"Are you protecting the boy because Krampus once served Odin, or is your love for him genuine?" Loki's clever tongue cut as a two-edged knife.

"Both." Jake gave the blunt answer without the slightest hesitation. Loki had to be looking for a chink in his armor, a place to slip the knife through, but the hunter refused to provide his foe with shame or a cowardly denial. "I understand and acknowledge my culpability in what happened to Michael. If it's your intention to turn that against me, you're only going to hurt him."

Loki's fingers wiggled in dismissal. "I'm not assigning blame." He flashed a lopsided smile. "I just wanted to know if you had the backbone to own up to it."

"I'm not a coward."

"No, you've never been that." Loki eyed him. "One more thing..."

"No. you already had your 'one more thing'."

"Tell me why you're here—in Midgard—living as a mortal."

"None of your damn business."

The Trickster shrugged and grinned. "It was worth a try."

"Loki, I swear, if I'm telling you all this and it doesn't produce a viable plan from that devious mind of yours..." Jake backed up the intimidation with his hands, threatening to wring the Trickster's throat.

"I'm thinking. We need to locate a weapon touched by fate that will enable a six-year-old to slay a *dis*. It's not exactly a simple problem." The corners of Loki's mouth skewed in an ironic smile.

"What about your dagger?" Jake asked.

Loki possessed a wooden knife carved from a branch of the World Tree. Aeon ago, the Trickster crafted the weapon specifically for use against Norns—on the notion that since Yggdrasil had been touched by fate, any weapon made from it would injure the Sisters Wyrd and their agents. Jake didn't know whether the theory had ever been put to the test.

"I've lost it." Loki shrugged.

"Have you?" Jake's jaw tightened. His suspicion remained hard and intact despite their alignment. Ingrained mistrust was more natural than cooperation.

"Temporarily misplaced." Loki tugged the brim of his cap down, hiding his eyes. "Listen—even genius of my magnitude requires cultivation. I'll find a weapon we can use against the *dís*..." Loki sidestepped, attempting to go around.

"Don't be too long." Jake moved crosswise, blocking the Trickster's path.

"Or what? You'll imprison or slay everyone I've every loved? Oh wait, you've already done that." Throwing out the taunt, Loki ducked low and sprinted past.

Jake turned around, but the boy was gone. A red-tailed hawk rose into the air and soared on spread wings.

SESSRÚMNIR, FREYA'S HALL IN FÓLKVANGR

Summoned, her spear and shield appeared in her hands. Freya hefted the weapon, aiming at one of the twined Ariks. She didn't know whether it was the correct one, but she had a fifty percent chance of being right.

"You won't get away with whatever it is you're planning," Freya said, a ringing declaration.

"I won't? Why won't I? Please, tell me." The brows of both men arched, mirror images of skepticism. They lifted their hands in a gesture of surrender. Then one of the Ariks dissolved into a cloud of glimmer before it went *poof*.

"I'll stop you."

Arik snickered. "You will? You're confused, Freya. Do you have the mistaken notion that you're one of the good guys? We're playing on the same team. I'm your ally, remember? "

"You duplicitous eel," she seethed. "An ally doesn't trick his friends—"

He pulled a face of distaste. "Friend is a strong word.

Conspirators would be more apropos, I think... You and I, the villains in this grand comic farce."

"You have violated the terms of our agreement." Her grip tightened about her spear. Oh, so tempting to run him through.

"I have—how so?" He arched his brow. "By assuming the role of your general?"

"Without my knowledge!"

"Pah. All I've done is place myself in an advantageous position which benefits us both. As soon as I obtained useful information, I brought it to your attention."

SIERRA PINES, California, on the western shore of Echo Lake

The reception area of the obstetrician's office was long and narrow; adjoined stainless steel and threadbare, cushioned seating took up every free inch of wall space. Additionally, another row of chairs ran straight down the middle of the room so the walking space that remained formed a squished oval.

Perplexed, Victoria gripped the clipboard the receptionist had handed her. She panned her gaze, surveying the room which was empty except for her and one other exhausted-looking woman who had a screeching toddler in her arms. The boy was in the middle of a full-fledged melt down, shrieking at the top of his lungs and flailing his limbs. In all, she counted thirty chairs—a number that seemed disproportionately large for Sierra Pines' tiny population. The office would've been better served by the addition of a play area for the energetic older children of the pregnant patients.

"You can have a seat anywhere," Laverne, the brunette receptionist said in a voice that was stiff with ill-concealed superiority. She sat behind the rise of the front desk as though it were her personal fortress.

"Does Dr. Ellis know something the rest of us don't?" Victoria pinned the woman with an unflinching stare.

Ever the coward, Laverne averted her gaze.

Sighing, Victoria shrugged and chose a seat located in the corner furthest from the wailing child. A vague sense of guilt hung over her, but the boy's piercing scream was an assault on her sensitive wolf hearing. Was she a terrible person? Odds were good she'd find herself in that poor woman's shoes a year or so from now. It made her thankful that her daughter was still contented—*and quiet*—in utero.

The vantage point also satisfied her innate caution, though, permitting her to watch the entire room. Clicking the pen, the crossed her legs and perched the clipboard on her knee. For reasons unstated but not unsurmised, the receptionist insisted that Victoria fill out the damn application anew for every single appointment. Maybe the woman expected the answers to change overnight. The spaces for *Father's Information* would no longer be blank or *Insurance Company and Plan Number* would say something other than "Cash".

Her breath expelled as a thin hiss between her clenched teeth. She needed a job. She hadn't worked in a month; not since her baby bump had finally become too obvious to hide any longer. The prim owner of the dance studio where Victoria had worked part-time as a ballet instructor had ever so kindly suggested that the physical demands of the job were simply too much for a pregnant woman to handle. Translation: the upper-class mothers of their students wouldn't abide an unwed mother near their precious daughters.

The other pregnant woman and her sobbing child were finally called and led away. Victoria heaved a deep sigh of relief.

She hadn't been too broken up about the loss of the low-paying job which had served as a placeholder while she was struggling to get back on her feet. Just a few months ago, her life had been in shambles. The war with the hunters left many members of the Storm Pack dead and the few survivors homeless. When she'd lived in Arizona, Victoria had worked as an emergency room RN in a Phoenix hospital. She was already in the middle of updating her credentials so she could obtain a license to work in California. The Sierra Pines Medical Facility had several nursing openings on their website for which she was qualified.

The door to the reception area swung open and a male voice summoned her—"Victoria Storm!"

She shot to her feet and crossed the room. The nurse who'd called her stood in the entrance. She'd been seeing Doctor Ellis for months but she didn't recognize him. He had to be new. He looked about her age, mid-twenties, and of average height and build. Freckles speckled his nose and cheeks. He wore medical scrubs, but underneath he had on a turtleneck; an odd choice for June attire. He held what she assumed to be her medical chart.

Magic tickled her nostrils—the sharp cleanness of pines. Victoria's stride hitched. She hesitated, almost stopping, but then forced herself to keep walking. Approaching the nurse, she proffered the clipboard.

His head bowed and he spared the half-complete form a

brief glance. His lips compressed to a tight line. "Has anything changed, Victoria?"

"No." She inhaled, sampling his scent, and detected nothing out of the ordinary. He was human—except for that mystical evergreen shimmer.

"We don't need this then." He yanked the paper free of the clip, crumpled it, and then plopped it into a round file container with a one-handed toss. With that simple act, he gained her liking if not her complete trust.

"Hi, Emanuel Luce. Please feel free to call me Manny. Obviously, I'm new. This is my first week with Dr. Ellis." Tipping his chin, he offered a knowing smirk.

"Hi, Manny. It's a pleasure to meet you." Victoria smiled in return.

"Dr. Ellis just called in that he's going to be late—"

"Did he get caught in a sand trap?"

"Quite possibly." His gaze glanced over her. His interest was detached and clinical. "I'm a registered nurse. I'm qualified to conduct your checkup. Are you okay with that?"

"Sure, it's fine." She nodded.

"Great. Come this way." Manny escorted Victoria to the scale, and she endured the humiliating weigh-in with stoic forbearance. Head bent over her chart, he led the way to the exam room. She trailed him, duly impressed with his ability to walk and read at the same time.

"You've only gained eleven pounds since your first visit with us back in March. This is the middle of your second trimester." Manny hooked the edge with his foot and bumped the door with his butt. She noticed how he left it open a few inches.

Ah, how it must suck to be a male nurse in this litigious culture.

"I'm almost six months along."

The added privacy afforded her the opportunity to look him over again more closely. At a glance, everything about him appeared unremarkable except for little things such as the collapsed Mohawk worn in a ponytail. Empty piercing holes punctured the cartilage of his ears. The edge of a tattoo collar on his throat peaked out from his turtleneck. She suspected he probably had matching bracelets inked on his wrists.

Victoria closed her eyes and then opened them, focusing her attention on the spiritual world. When she took a closer look at Manny Luce, she perceived his innate magic—a palette of tranquil sea tones from aqua to cool blue streaked his aura. Here and there bright yellow starbursts sparkled with gemstone intensity.

"You're not gaining enough weight. You need to eat more." Still looking down, he wrote something in her chart. "Let's get your blood pressure."

"I eat like a wolf." She chuckled and hopped onto the examine table, seated close to the wall-mounted blood pressure monitor.

"So, Vicky. Can I call you Vicky?" He reached for the armband attached to the device and pulled it down, shaking out the curly cord.

"Vicky. Sure, if you're feeling lucky. We are in a hospital so it's a short walk to the ER."

"Oohh, touchy. Victoria, then." Chuckling, he looked up straight into her eyes. His mouth dropped open and then he jerked away from her with a fearful start. His invigorating scent acquired a moldy, rotted wood tang. Without a mirror, she couldn't be sure but his reaction suggested her eyes had gone wolf-wonky again.

"Shit." Slightly panicked, Victoria double-and-triple-blinked in an attempt to return her eyeballs to normal.

Losing control in front of Sawyer was one thing. The hunter was a member of her pack and had witnessed her shift shapes to a wolf many times. She trusted him with her secrets.

A stranger like Manny Luce, however mystically inclined, was another matter. He constituted an unknown...and hence, a threat to both her and her pack.

A startled cry arose from Manny. Stumbling over his own feet, he backed toward the closed door. Victoria hopped off the exam table. She sprinted and ducked around the nurse, reaching the exit first, and put her back to it.

"You're a werewolf." Manny spun to face her. Upon realizing his escape was cut off, he retreated toward the exam table. His fixed stare locked on Victoria. Once his back hit the wall, he assumed a defensive stance that suggested he'd had martial arts training. More alarmingly, the air crackled, pregnant with magic as he summoned power.

Victoria quelled her own reflex to respond in kind. She didn't want this to escalate and turn into a mystical showdown. So far, Manny hadn't succumbed to yelling. She took that as a good sign. Maybe he could be reasoned with.

"Look, I don't want trouble. I'm here for my checkup. That's it. Dr. Ellis is the only obstetrician in a twenty-mile radius who will see me without insurance. I really don't want to have to switch doctors." Victoria held up her hands, a calming gesture.

"You're an actual, real-life, fucking werewolf." Manny stared at Victoria as though seeing her for the first time. He gave her the thorough up-down, obviously trying to figure her out. His regard held zero sexual interest, confirming Victoria's earlier suspicions. Not every man wanted her, but the vast majority of healthy, heterosexual males found her attractive. Pheromones never lied.

"Right." She took a deep breath, rolled her eyes, and summoned patience. "I'm a werewolf, and you're a witch. Look, I know werewolves and witches don't always mix—"

"Druid."

She raised her brow. "Pardon?"

"I'm a druid."

"Tree-hugger or the bloodthirsty kind?"

He stared at her from beneath hooded eyes. Okay then—bloodthirsty druid.

"Even better." Victoria reached for her own magic but only used it to boost her own innate charisma. Her voice acquired resonance—soft and soothing.

"Why is that better?" That pleasant pine-fresh scent restored. He cocked his head and loosened his stance, curiosity edging out caution.

"Environmentalists get wiggy about wolves. This is already awkward enough as is it." Victoria judged he had calmed down enough not to bolt, so she eased aside, clearing the path to the door once again.

The room was small. They engaged in a cautious, shifting ballet and circled clockwise. In the end, she wound up back on the exam table where she belonged. Manny remained silent while he took her blood pressure and added another note to her chart. Figuring he needed time to adjust, she waited.

He returned the blood pressure monitor to the wall. "I'd heard there was a pack of gray wolves in the area..." He scratched his chin. "Is that you?"

"They're part of my pack. I'm the dominant female."

He frowned. "What is that? You're the pack domme?"

"I'm not a domme." She frowned. "I'm dominant. There's a difference."

"Right. Not a domme at all." Manny's drawl implied otherwise.

He didn't know the language of wolves—she rephrased it. "I'm Alpha."

"It's okay. I'm in the lifestyle. Nothing I love more than watching a skilled domme at work." Manny dropped a wink. The smile that lit his face elevated his looks from average to cute. A natural flirt.

"Are all druids such hams?" Victoria looked askance at him.

"Dunno, are all werewolves so damn serious?"

She sighed. He had a point. Severity was one of her great character flaws. Lightning up would probably be for the best. The druid had proven remarkably resilient—transitioning from cautious to curious in a matter of minutes. He had not only taken her being a werewolf in stride but also tried to ease the tension with his quick, albeit, corny humor.

"Are you doing an ultrasound today?" Victoria indicated the machine.

"I can. Are you comfortable with that?"

"Yes."

A knock sounded on the closed door to the exam room. In unison, they turned toward the entrance, and a second knock followed. Manny answered it, pulling the door open halfway to reveal the brunette receptionist. Laverne frowned and fidgeted, biting her lower lip.

"What's up?" Manny asked.

"The Sheriff is here—asking for *Miss* Storm." The receptionist aimed a condemning glare toward Victoria. In her mind, the law officer had no doubt come to arrest their petite blonde patient.

Manny's quizzical gaze settled on Victoria.

She smiled in reassurance. "It's okay. He's a relative of mine."

"Ah, okay." His aura buzzed with curiosity, and doubt marred his scent. Regrettably, his ease of moments before was gone.

Victoria departed the exam room and passed through the office area. Manny and the brunette trailed her, making no attempt to conceal their rubbernecking curiosity. Before she reached the reception area, the door swung open to reveal a man wearing an El Dorado County sheriff's uniform and badge.

Sheriff Mike Trash, the brother of Arik's murdered first wife. In his late-forties to early fifties, he had a rectangular face, ears that stuck out a bit, and a receding hairline. Victoria considered his piercing, intelligent brown eyes to be his best feature. Not quite handsome, but cute. He stood a handful of inches taller than her and was in good shape. His solid aura embodied stability and strength. Though human, he was a medium capable of perceiving spirits. His awareness of the supernatural and his law enforcement position made him a powerful and influential person.

"Mike." She greeted him with an uncertain frown, wondering what he wanted. While he wasn't the last person she expected to seek her out at a doctor's appointment, he didn't make the short list. Maybe she needed to revise that list.

"Victoria, I'm sorry for disturbing you." Mike crossed his arms, radiating tension.

"It's okay. What's up?" With an effort, she schooled her expression to a polite smile. Brow arched, she looked to the sheriff, more than happy to let him make the call on how to proceed. Doubtless, Mike didn't want to divulge his secrets in front of strangers, especially if it involved police business.

"Damn!" Manny expressed shock and amazement at a shout. His pheromones spiked, signaling spontaneous arousal. Victoria and Mike both turned toward the young man but he remained oblivious to their curious regard. Instead, his stunned gaze was directed past the sheriff and out the open entryway. Following his initial outburst, he dropped his voice. "Hot damn."

Craning her neck, Victoria spotted Logan lurking in the waiting area. He slouched against the opposite wall, close enough to overhear everything they said. Just the sight of him set her blood to boiling. Her ire rose; a snarl contorted her mouth and trembled in her throat.

"It's urgent. I would appreciate your help." The sheriff cleared his throat, edging closer. He extended his arm, creating a barrier between her and his nephew, but didn't touch her. Good thing too because her emotions were out of control to the point where she was reacting instead of acting.

"Sure, I'd be happy to help if I can. What's it about?" Taking a deep breath, she reined in her temper.

The sheriff cast a significant glance toward their audience. Fortunately, Manny picked up on the subtle hint. Catching Mike's gaze, Victoria turned toward the humans.

"Laverne, get back to work." Manny turned a stern glare on the receptionist who flushed and retreated to her station.

"Thank you," Victoria said.

"No problem. I'd love to wait in the lobby." Manny ducked his head and stepped toward her. His voice dropped to a conspiratorial whisper. "Is the hottie straight?"

"He claims to be straight..." A mean smile played on her lips. "But you know, I've wondered that myself. Mostly, I think Logan is just horny. And slutty."

"I can work with that." With a spring in his step, Manny headed into the reception area. Oozing confidence, he strolled up to Logan, looked him straight in the eyes, and said, "You're so beautiful that you made me forget my pickup line."

Logan's jaw dropped and his mouth hung open. Victoria wasn't sure she'd ever seen the smart-mouthed jackass at a total loss for words.

It was a beautiful thing.

A shout escaped Logan, alarmingly loud, and easily mistaken for anger. Then, howling with laughter, he collapsed against the wall. Manny succumbed to chuckles also. Amid the din, Logan said something short and pointed to Manny but his words were lost.

Victoria glanced back to the sheriff, and found him watching her. "What can I do for you, Mike?"

The sheriff cleared his throat. Frustration and foreboding wafted off him, so thick his scent blended with his aura like wet paint. His hand rose, beckoning to her. "It's complicated... I need to show you."

"Is it urgent? I'm right in the middle of a prenatal checkup." Reluctance led her to dig in her mental heels.

A sharp shake of Mike's head vetoed the suggestion. He leaned toward her and spoke in a low voice. "I'm sorry, this is urgent. There are bodies. I want you to accompany me down to the morgue."

"Bodies?"

The sheriff gave a curt nod.

Dry-mouthed, Victoria gulped. Bodies probably meant spirits... Spirits were her calling. "All right then. That settles that."

Victoria marched into the hallway to where Manny and Logan were engaged in witty, flirty banter. The sheriff trailed her, but remained silent. The two men stopped talking and looked toward her.

She tensed when Logan's hooded amber eyes settled on her. His gaze dropped and lingered on her all-too-visible baby bump, but his face remained set in an impassive mask. His aura was equally inscrutable, closed off and awash with dark, swirling colors. Victoria pointedly gave him the cold shoulder.

Following an uncomfortable pause, Manny asked, "What's up?"

"I'm sorry, but I need to cut the appointment short. It's an emergency," she said, mustering a smile.

Manny frowned. His confused gaze darted from face to face.

Common decency compelled Victoria to offer at least a cursory explanation. "The sheriff needs my help in the basement."

"I see..." Eyebrows skewed, Manny stared at her. "Isn't the only thing in the basement the morgue?"

Both Mike and Logan tensed and shuffled their stances. Deciding to trust her gut, Victoria waved them off. "I'm sort of an expert in spirits. I'm a medium."

"You're a seer? Like a psychic?" Quizzically, Manny cocked his head. She could see the young man's thoughts on his face while he sorted it out in his head. And while she had no idea what a druid could do, she suspected their basic abilities might not be too divergent.

"I'm a priestess," she corrected. "To Freya..."

And sometimes Odin, Freya said in a catty little aside only Victoria could hear, but that caused her to wince anyway.

"Okay, cool. Good luck."

"Thanks." She hesitated and crossed mental fingers. She desperately hoped she wasn't going to have to find a new obstetrician. "Can I call back to reschedule my ultrasound?"

He smiled, warm and welcoming. "Absolutely."

"See you." She headed out, expecting Logan and Mike to follow her. And indeed, they did.

"Damn, gorgeous. I'm just going to stand here and watch your fine ass walk away," Manny called out after them.

"Yeah, you do that," Logan shot back, waving his arm. "You're not going to see any finer."

Ducking her head, Victoria hid her grin behind her hand.

"THIS WAY." Mike took the lead through dungeon-esque passages of the basement that stank of dust and mold. The dimly lit corridors seemed to stretch forever. They met in irregular intersections, and took inexplicable turns. An extraordinary number of ghostly whorls wisped past. Victoria always expected to encounter spirits in a hospital, but this was more like a cemetery. Disturbingly, the wandering souls looked like they'd died centuries before, which left her wondering who they'd been and how they'd died.

After what must've been five minutes of walking, she became convinced they were going in circles. She was confident she could follow her nose to backtrack their path, but otherwise she'd have been hopelessly lost.

Logan voiced her thoughts. "This place is a fucking labyrinth."

"It smells like standing water." Her nose crinkled in involuntary disgust. When they'd first entered the basement, the air had been damp and musky, but now the aroma of pungent rot offended her well-being. Queasiness swam in her gut like goldfish in a bowl.

"The foundation is old," Mike said, leading the way. "The

hospital was built on top of a much older structure. Water seeps in. When it gets bad, they bring in sump pumps. If you stay out of the east end, you'll be fine." The sheriff's posture radiated unmistakable tension.

"I can't believe the amount of money Dad sank into this place." Logan waved a hand in a flourish that indicated the whole of the building around them.

Victoria's brow furrowed. Granted, Arik had been an attorney but he'd only practiced family law. Her gaze swung toward Logan and a question formed on her lips, but the sheriff rounded a corner and stopped, which halted her question as well. A sign over a set of double swinging doors proclaimed MORGUE.

"Your father was a pillar of the community." Mike shot Logan a forbidding frown.

"Can we at least try to maintain a semblance of honesty here?" Logan rounded on his uncle. "Mike, you and Dad didn't even speak in the two years before he died. Now you're making him out to be a fucking saint?"

"Your father wasn't a saint, but he deserves respect. For all our differences, I always respected your father." Mike fell into silence. "Wait out here for a minute. I want to be sure the area is clear before we go in. The staff is supposed to be at lunch."

"Yeah, sure. Whatever." Logan exhaled a dismissive huff.

Mike stared at his nephew for a long moment. His jaw worked and he looked about to speak, but then his lips compressed. "Wait here."

"Aye, *capitan*," Logan dropped a sloppy salute.

The sheriff shook his head and plowed into one of the hinged doors. It swung wide enough to admit him and then dropped shut with a pronounced thunk, leaving Victoria and

Logan completely alone for the first time since his unexpected return home.

All their issues reared like the ugly hooded visage of a cobra. An exaggerated, uncomfortable silence suspended between them. Logan stood with his shoulders hunched and regarded her with a smoldering gaze that set her teeth on edge.

"Why are you here?" Victoria asked.

"Mike came by the house looking for you. Sylvie made me scrub the kitchen and it looked like she was getting into her head to give me another project, so I decide to get while the getting was good."

"You better have helped her clean up the mess you made." She snorted in disgust.

"Hey, it wasn't just me making the mess."

Victoria harrumphed in exasperation and changed the subject. "What are you doing back?"

"In Sierra Pines?"

She gave a curt nod. "The last I'd heard you were off 'finding yourself.'"

"Consider me found."

"So you're back? Just like that?" Larger than life, imperiling the delicate balance of her entire existence and the stability of her small pack. His motivation for his abrupt return remained a mystery, one that tight-lipped Logan appeared unwilling to resolve. So she was left with worry and fear.

"In spades. Well, for one, I live here. This is my home. Two, I don't have to explain myself to you. My father was Alpha. This whole territory was his. Now, it's mine." Aggression defined his underlying scent. The same assertiveness bled into the orange-red hue of his nimbus. His tension put her on edge to the point where Victoria's wolf strained against her control.

That wasn't how it worked—Alpha status was earned, not inherited. Victoria opened her mouth to protest but then closed it. She didn't stand a snowball's chance in hell against him in a fair fight. He was strong enough to take everything she valued from her—and she sure as hell didn't trust him not to do so out of spite.

Logan confronted her with unshakable confidence, and her spirit sank. All these months spent dreading the inevitable challenge to her influence, for her status and her territory, but always she'd thought the threat would come from outside her pack. Of course, Logan had always been a potential rival but she'd naively hoped his apparent lack of interest in power would persevere.

At a loss, Victoria struggled to formulate a diplomatic reply. She inhaled and decay struck the over-sensitized olfactory glands in the roof of her mouth. *Undead.* A growl rolled from her throat and she turned toward the threat, instinctively placing her back to Logan. In unspoken cooperation, he assumed a guard position, facing outward.

Around them, the shadows flowed in a river of darkness, running across the surface of the walls. Puddles devoid of light pooled on the floor. It prickled her sense of familiarity. She'd seen this before; she just couldn't quite remember where.

"Hey, Logan. It's me, Evan. Call off your friend, okay?"

"Evan?" Logan, demonstrating truly questionable judgement, dropped his guard and slouched. When she continued to bristle, he waved a hand in her general direction. "C'mon, Vic. Knock it off. Evan is harmless."

"Evan is disgusting and unnatural, and there's no such thing as a harmless revenant." Fuming, she nevertheless swallowed a snarl and forced her wolf to subside. Logan's terrible taste in friends aside, Evan had never threatened her and he'd actually proven helpful at least once in the past.

"Geez, it's a good thing I'm not sensitive or my feelings would be hurt." The breathy, childlike voice registered in the falsetto range and emerged from the limber shadows. The smell of decay accompanied it. But the dead thing remained hidden from direct view, more like a ghost than a ghoul.

"I want to kill it," Victoria muttered, clenching her fists.

"No." Logan snapped his tone and his fingers. "N. O."

"Logan, I don't have long so you have to listen," Evan ran his words together, clearly sensing his peril. "You shouldn't be down here. It's dangerous. The morgue is a gateway to the underworld. Oh, and I was sorry to hear about your father."

"Wait. What? Back up. The morgue is a gateway to what?" Logan asked.

"The underworld. Realm of the dead. Niffleheim. Helheim. Whatever the Hel-hick it is your people call the frozen wasteland on the other side."

"Do you mean Canada?" Logan snickered.

"Hardy-har-har. Very funny. Not. Look, no kidding, you should leave."

"Oh, this is ridiculous." Victoria shoved one of the heavy swinging doors to the morgue open and peeked in. Nothing beyond but a sterile looking front office. "See, nothing here but—"

"The Master is coming." Evan vanished from plain sight.

"How does he do that?" Victoria stared at spot where the ghoul had stood.

"Beats me." Logan shrugged.

Victoria cast a glance over her shoulder in the direction they'd come from. She wanted to leave. The scrape of Logan's shoes on the concrete floor sounded remarkably loud. With a burst of annoyance, she wished he'd cease his restless shuffling and just stand still. The basement was spooky enough on its own. Evan's surprise visit and bizarre proclamations upped the creep factor by a hundred.

Logan's gaze shifted. "Hey, Uncle Mike. Are you the Master?"

An uneasy quiver shot through her gut. Victoria turned. Sheriff Trash stood within the morgue's reception area.

Mike frowned. "I prefer 'sir' but you can call me Uncle Mike, Son."

"Gee, thanks." Logan rolled his eyes.

"C'mon in." Mike beckoned them with a wave of his arm. "The coast is clear."

CHAPTER THIRTEEN

Sessrúmnir, Freya's hall in Fólkvangr

Freya's head spun—she was unable to think straight for her rage. The Trickster talked a good game but this had to be a con. She just couldn't see the trap for the web of lies he wove, obfuscating the truth.

"Whatever you're up to, I won't allow it. I'll expose you first." Irrational, foolish anger fueled her thoughts but her inner-serenity had been thoroughly fractured.

"Expose me, expose yourself. I might fall, but so will you, and you have so much more to lose than I do. So please, be my guest." He gestured—*ladies first.* "It will be entertaining. How will you explain your complicity to Odin? You've been stealing Valhalla's rightful share of wolf warriors for months now."

She glared and dismissed him. "An oversight—easily corrected."

"Perhaps, you may even get away with it. But what is your defense against having made Odin's sworn enemy the commander of half his army?"

MELISSA SNARK

"I'll say I was tricked. It's embarrassing, but it's also the truth."

"And I'll say you knew all along. I may not be believed. You may win, but it'll be well worth your public humiliation when it comes out that you took me to your bed."

Freya's spine grew ramrod stiff. Anger thrilled through her. Incensed, she tightened her grip on her spear. "You're disgusting. So help me, if you try to touch me again, I'll strike you down where you stand!"

He snorted. "That won't be a problem. I've had my fill. Just remember Freya—betray me and consider our deal nullified. I'll abandon you to your fate when Ragnarök tears the nine worlds apart."

Freya loosened an infuriated shout, seeking to release the enormity of her emotion. Unflinching in the face of her wrath, Loki only smiled. She seethed, wishing nothing more than to strike him down, but the maddening voice of practicality insisted she do no such thing. As the weasel had pointed out—she was stuck with him. She released her grip on her armaments. They vanished before they hit the ground.

Sierra Pines, California, on the western shore of Echo Lake

The morgue's reception area resembled a prison more than a hospital. A lonely desk sat in one corner; the surface sparsely populated with an old curly-corded phone and a canister of pens next to a neat pile of paperwork. The rolling office chair stood empty. No one appeared to greet them, and someone had printed "Back at 2" in red marker on a white board on an otherwise bare wall.

"I sent the staff out to lunch." Mike answered her unspoken question. He escorted her and Logan through another swinging door, down some twisty corridors, and then into a refrigerated chamber. An ominous row of steel doors lined the far wall where, presumably, bodies were stored. The stench of bleach and formaldehyde burned at her nose and set her stomach to churning.

The air was cold enough to store meat... the random thought made her wince when she realized it was pretty much a statement of the obvious.

"I should warn you, bad smells have been making me queasy." Victoria dragged her feet, swallowing saliva in an attempt to quell the nausea. During her medical training to become an RN, she's never been squeamish. No, that hadn't happened until she'd gotten pregnant and her body had rebelled.

"Thanks, I'll keep my feet clear. Hold on, I'll get you something to help with the odor." Mike headed straight for a rack of metal shelves and removed a small stack of blue face masks. He passed her one along with a small vial of essential oil. "I've only got peppermint. Hope that's okay. You know how this works?"

"Peppermint is fine, thank you." Victoria thought it odd the sheriff had essential oils on his person but she kept the observation to herself. She uncapped the vial, applied a drop to the tissue, and then pulled the mask over her head and down about her throat until she needed it.

Logan turned over the mask he'd been handed in apparent cluelessness. With a huff, Victoria caught his wrist and held his arm steady while she squirted oil across the inside of his mask.

"This goes over your nose and big mouth. Do you need help?" Victoria asked in a saccharine tone.

"Thanks, I think I can figure it out." He flashed teeth in a fake smile.

"In here." Mike passed through an open entrance to a smaller area set to serve as an autopsy room. Here, the sickly-sweet perfume of death pervaded the atmosphere, distinguishable even over the disinfectant and the peppermint. A dark green sheet covered something big atop one of the metal tables.

Victoria's unease grew. She no longer wanted to be there. She would have been only too happy to hightail it out so fast none of the series of swinging doors would've stood a chance of hitting her in the ass. Whatever the sheet concealed, the mound exceeded the dimensions a person. It had to be an animal...or it concealed more than one body.

She sensed Logan's looming presence behind her. His aura shifted from threatening to protective. She had no idea how anyone could be so damn annoying one second, and reassuring the next, but she was glad he had her back. Bracing for the worst, she grabbed the edge of the sheet and yanked it off—and wished she hadn't. Her breath exited her lungs in a horrified expulsion and her stomach somersaulted even as her mind struggled to process the macabre sight laid out before her on the cold stainless steel.

The body of an adult male wolf lay on its side, a sad caricature of the magnificent predator it had once been. His fur coat had been skinned from nose to tail, exposing veins and muscle, greyish and bloodied. In death, he curled into a fetal position which enhanced the impression of an aborted fetus. Beside the wolf, the corpse of an adult man rested on his back—skin intact. A severed jugular appeared to be the cause of death.

Victoria recoiled in horror. She sucked in a shallow breath, afraid a deep one would make her puke, and closed her eyes. She reached behind her back, and Logan latched onto her fingers. Through the warmth and intimacy of joined hands, their auras collided and merged. Primal verve rushed through her, intoxicating and unexpected, and her head spun. Logan's strength startled and terrified her. More lone wolf than team player, he always held himself apart. He was a force of nature—unpredictable, always a threat to the stability of her safe little world.

An imperative overrode all other concerns—she had to check on her pack to ensure their safety. Within the shelter of Logan's arms, she turned away from the carnage, rested her forehead against his chest. Once she recovered, she pulled her mask down and summoned her personal power.

"What are you doing?" Logan asked, also yanking his mask aside. The question reminded her of his inexperience with pack magic. Potential wasn't the same as knowledge or ability.

"I have to make sure the others are safe."

"How do you do that?"

"Watch. It's easier to demonstrate than explain." She summoned the energy and channeled it to serve her will. By focusing, she extended her awareness through the metaphysical connection known as the pack bond that bound the members of the Storm Pack together—wolves, wolf shifters, and hunters—and also formed the foundation of their magic. As a rule, it worked best at proximity. Lately, Victoria experimented with pushing the boundaries of what was possible. Her limits continued to expand.

"Uh-huh. Cryptic response. About what I've come to expect." Logan clicked his tongue against the roof of his mouth.

"Oh hush." Victoria found those closest to her—Sylvie and Morena. A hazy, dreamlike image of the two women formed in her mind. Both were inside the lakeside house, but in separate rooms. Without disturbing them, she brushed past and cast a wider net until she located the four gray wolves sacked out on the floor of the living room. They were well.

Sawyer proved harder to isolate. Victoria reached for him and came up empty-handed. Frowning, she tightened her search, pouring more energy into the effort. While the hunter belonged, he didn't quite fit—the square peg on a board of round holes. To make matters worse, he possessed an uncanny talent for stealth.

"Who're you looking for?" Logan asked in an edgy tone. "Sylvie, Morie, Sophia and the pups..."

His aura roiled with territorial aggression; he knew who she was searching for.

Like Sawyer, Logan didn't conform. He occupied a far-flung point on the periphery of their group; a part of and yet apart from the dynamic. Unlike Sawyer, Logan was disruptive to their stability.

Exhaling heavily in exasperation, Victoria gave up. A phone call would settle the matter easily enough, and besides, the man could take care of himself. Licking her lips, she pulled her attention back, easing out of the spell. Her thoughts flashed to Jake Barrett, and she wondered whether she should she check on him too.

But no—the omnipotent Hunter King could...

I can what? Jake's gravelly voice boomed through her mind.

Take care of himself. Victoria responded with cultivated grumpiness. *And stay hell out of my head.*

Jake chuckled. *You reached for me, girly.*

Correction: I thought about you. There's a slight difference.

"Who the hell are you talking to?" Logan stirred, and his alarm crashed through the pack bond. An unexpected huff of hot, citrus-scented breath blew across her face, and she jumped. Her eyes popped open, and she discovered Logan hunched over so his face was in hers. He held both her hands in his own.

"Praying," Victoria said aloud, hoping to sooth Logan's fear. "It's something I do sometimes—"

"I thought you worshiped Freya," Logan interrupted. "That's a man's voice."

Victoria faltered in the grip of sudden doubt, and then stumbled into worry. Her lips formed words but she had no idea what to say. Logan shouldn't have been able to eavesdrop on her conversation with Jake.

The pack bond was empathic, not telepathic.

Victoria, is something wrong? Do you need help? Jake manifested within her mind; rumbling thunder and flashing lightening marked the coming of the storm. His offer was genuine. If she asked, he'd come with his magical dagger and his undying ferocity, and quite possibly a crew of hunters. He would obliterate everything and everyone who opposed him.

She swallowed, trying to eliminate the lump in her throat and fear froze her heart. While having the Hunter King as her enemy had been terrifying, counting him as an ally was only slightly less scary. She had loved his oldest son with all her heart; a part of her died with Daniel. She respected Jake and, against her better judgement, loved him as a father. Despite all that, she worried about the potential for friendly fire...and only a fool would dismiss the possibility of real conflict breaking out between wolves and hunters. It'd happened before. It could happen again.

Her silence went on too long.

Victoria? Jake prompted.

"Vic, what the hell are you hiding?" Logan spoke louder

than was necessary, and Mike Trash shifted and mumbled something that may have been cautionary. Her anxious gaze raked Logan, and she contemplated all the things that could go wrong if his rebellious attitude ever clashed with Jake's authoritarian rule. TNT—an invitation to disaster. She had to keep Logan safe which meant keeping him as far as possible from the hunters.

"I appreciate your concern but I'm able to take care of myself," Victoria employed her most assertive tone, speaking to both of them in a no nonsense manner.

Following a beat, Jake chuckled and somehow his inflection implied an eye roll. *I'm here if you need me, kid.*

Thank you. Without staying goodbye, Victoria cut the psychic connection. Maybe it was abrupt but the last thing she wanted to do was fall into the habit conducting an internal dialogue with Jake. Especially since Freya already had more than enough reasons to be angry with Victoria. No sense in giving the goddess more. She tilted back her head and looked straight up into Logan's smoldering gaze.

From the granite set of his jaw, he seemed determined to have it out with her. His grip shifted from her hands to her upper arms, and he cast his uncle a furtive glace. His volume dropped to a hiss. "Damn it, you're talking to *him*, aren't you?"

"Who I pray to is none of your concern." Victoria's brow rose. She wondered just who it was he assumed she was praying to. The list of potential deities wasn't all that long.

His handsome face contorted in a grimace. "You're making a big mistake even talking to him..."

"Him who?" She studied Logan, coolly, and then belated realization overcame her. The worst speculation she'd indulged in crystalized a horrified certainty. Somehow, she *knew*. She just *knew* the truth in her gut. Her hands locked on

Logan's arms hard enough to leave bruises and she whispered in the hopes none of the gods would overhear.

"Logan, have you been talking to Loki? Is he your..." Soul sick, she couldn't finish the question.

"I'm an atheist, Vic. I decided the whole priesthood thing doesn't work for me. I can't keep vows or my pants zipped, and my taste in partners runs more to dumb blondes than young men, by the way." Logan bared his teeth in a cryptic, contrary show of defiance. He would offer nothing further, helpful or otherwise.

"I'm not dumb," Victoria protested without thinking.

His smile widened dangerously. "Who says I was even talking about you?"

Oh, burn. Smarting from the sting, she turned back to Mike. "I'm sorry for the interruption. I had to make sure my pack was okay."

"I understand. Are you ready to proceed?" Mike indicated the autopsy table.

"Yes." She preferred to leave but the sheriff had asked for her help in solving this crime. And besides, the skinned wolf must be the handiwork of the drifters who had cured wolf pelts piled high on their bed over at the Fireside Inn. The guys Sawyer suspected of being Odin's worshipers... Just the whole line of thought made her ill. She recoiled from the logical conclusion, and wondered if a no-holds-barred conversation with Jake was in order. But she needed more information first. Immature suspicions... Poor word choices... Misunderstandings... She refused to risk her alliance with the hunters over an unlikely coincidence and unproven suspicion.

She pulled her mask back into place and approached the dead wolf first. Robbed of his fur, nothing remained of his face but his teeth and eyes—brown eyes full of misery. Even his nose had been stripped away in the skinning process. Ichor clung to his pale flesh; not a living creature. A macabre mannequin.

Bursting with unshed tears, Victoria bent toward his rear legs. Sleeves of fur remained on his ankles and the tops of his paws. Victoria touched the pad of the paw, turning it for inspection, and discovered a distinctive star-shaped scar. She rubbed her fingers over the deep points.

"His soul's moved on. Thank the goddess." She fervently hoped and prayed the poor animal hadn't suffered. Fortunately, the souls of animals seldom lingered. Well, except for cats—lazy, contrary creatures.

"Where do the souls of animals go?" Logan asked. "Is the whole 'rainbow bridge' thing a metaphor for Bifröst because — Shit, I never made that connection before."

Leaning over, she checked the wolf's teeth. "He was full grown but not very old. I'm guessing about three years."

"Close. He turned three last month," said the man suddenly standing beside Victoria. A chilly blast accompanied the manifestation of the spirit. Fog congealed out of the air around them, forming a thick bank that swirled about their ankles, and frost formed on the bodies and autopsy table.

"Sounds like you knew him." Victoria tilted her head, deliberately keeping her motions slight and her voice soft. Sprits tended to be skittish and ephemeral, and terribly shy. Often, they lacked self-awareness, little more than lingering echoes of the soul that had already passed on. Loud noises and bright lights as well as unpleasant revelations, such as the bad news of their own death, could startle a ghost into destabilizing.

"His official designation was OR-41, but I called him Malfoy." The spirit's pattern seemed stable—exceptionally so.

Whereas many ghosts faded away at mid-thigh or waist, he had solid feet encased in a pair of brown hiking boots. The rest of his attire matched the hiker motif from his tan vest to his khaki pants. Not designer, name-brand attire either, but rugged clothing that had a lived in look to it.

"Why was that?" She turned toward him more fully. The ghost's appearance was the same as that of the dead man on the table, right down to the gaping cut across his throat. He was Caucasian and in his mid-forties with black hair and gray blue-eyes. She judged him to be physically fit.

A sad smile touched his lips. "Malfoy was born in the Cascade Range, but he was a wanderer. At about a year and a half, he left his pack and moved steadily south through Washington and on into north Oregon. He got into constant trouble—chicken coops, trash bins. Hell, a couple times he even robbed fast food drive thrus—snatched the sacks right out of folk's hands. He had no fear of people. His ability to evade detection was uncanny. No one ever caught him on camera but his star-shaped paw print was always found at the scene of the crime."

"Was he one of us?" Logan asked, and Victoria winced, more than half expecting the ghost to vaporize in reaction to an unexpected voice.

"One of who?" A quizzical look on his face, the man turned toward Logan.

"A wolf shifter," Logan said but when the ghost stared at him, he clarified. "Was he a werewolf?"

"No, of course not! Werewolves don't exist..." A bark of laughter escaped the spirit but then he trailed off, frowning. "Do they?"

Blankness dropped over the spirit. His profile thinned and he wavered like a sheet on a windy day. Frantically, Victoria waved Logan off, but she really wanted to smack him. She had to get the conversation under control before the ghost destabilized.

"We're about as real as ghosts." Victoria murmured. "What's your name?"

"Kevin. Kevin Danbury," he said without hesitation. His form gained substance, returning to three-dimensional solidness.

Victoria bit her lower lip. She recognized him now.

"I'm a Wildlife Biologist with the Federal Department of Natural Resources..." Kevin's voice grew stronger the more he talked.

"I heard your interview on the radio this morning." Victoria had spoken with dozens—hundreds—of spirits through the years and Kevin impressed her. His stability was exceptional, as was his influence over their environment, judging by the thick blanket of fog that hung at knee level over the morgue floor.

Mike Trash cleared his throat. "That's impossible. He was murdered sometime last night. The coroner places the time of death at between six and eight p.m."

"The interview was recorded in advance." Kevin noticed the look on Victoria's face, and he mustered a wry smile. "Is something wrong?"

"You." She shrugged. "You're amazingly lucid and cognizant for a spirit..."

"This morning, a hiker found the bodies about ten miles north of here on the edge of Desolation Wilderness. I was one of the first officers on the scene but Kevin here refused to speak with me and Logan..." Mike aimed a reproving glance toward the ghost.

"You're not nearly as cute as she is." Kevin returned a cheeky grin.

Victoria snickered, and Logan echoed her amusement.

"Once I understood the killers might constitute a threat to the pack, I realized I ought to involve you," Mike concluded, addressing Victoria.

"Thank you. I appreciate that." Relieved to have the mystery solved, Victoria dipped her head in a show of courtesy. Frankly, she wasn't used to having another spirit speaker around, let alone two. It freaked her out a little. Given the circumstances, the sheriff's decision to bring her in on it made perfect sense.

"Kevin, please continue," Victoria prompted the ghost.

Kevin opened his mouth and hesitated as though reviewing where he'd left off. "OR-41. Malfoy had way more than three strikes against him. Our only choices were to move him or put him down. When an unmated adult female with pups appeared in the Echo Lake area, it was heaven sent. We decided to relocate him to a protected area within Desolation Wilderness."

Victoria bit the insides of her lips, quelling the impulse to advise the man that Sophia wasn't unmated—she was widowed. Only such a distinction wouldn't make sense to this man, so she tried to regard Kevin's motives as they were obviously intended—well-meaning, if misguided.

The biologist exhaled. "Look, I'm not a fool. I hold a doctorate degree in Biology, and I've dedicated my entire life to studying wolves. I understand it was a shot in the dark, but frankly, it was the only chance Malfoy had. Besides, it was necessary to introduce a genetically unrelated gray wolf to the area to reduce the risks of inbreeding. There aren't any other documented wolf packs for hundreds of miles from here. We're not even sure where the Echo Lake Pack originated."

"Storm Pack," Victoria interrupted with a knit brow. Golly, but the man was long-winded and she couldn't help wondering if he'd worked as a lecturer or a used car salesman at some point.

Kevin blinked. "Excuse me?"

"We're the Storm Pack." Logan said with a sarcastic inflection.

Bristling, Victoria spared him a sharp look. It wasn't what he said but how he said it that set her on edge. His tone made her wonder if maybe he thought the pack should be called something else—the Koenig Pack, maybe? The thought riled her because the renaming would've been a likely outcome if Arik had lived. He hadn't though. He'd died before they even had a chance to discuss it.

Logan held her gaze, and cocked an eyebrow, sprouting that smug smirk of his that always, but always, made her want to clobber him. With an effort, she forced her attention to the biologist.

"Oh. Right. You're wolf shifters? Werewolves?" He hesitated until Victoria offered a nod of acknowledgement. "Sorry, I suppose I seem slow on the uptake. Must be part of being a dead guy and all..." His laughter broke in the middle and his form wavered again. A section of his arm vanished at the elbow, leaving his unconnected hand floating in midair.

"Actually, so far as the newly dead go, you're refreshingly lucid. Please don't get upset. I know this is a lot to process all at once. You're doing remarkably well." Feeling sorry for the poor guy, Victoria laid a reassuring hand on his forearm. Her abilities extended to touching spirits as well as speaking with them, but she always did so with caution. The moment she touched him, his elbow reappeared. His flesh was ice cold.

"Right. What an incredibly nice way of saying, 'Get a hold of yourself, man!'" With an awkward laugh, Kevin threw his hands up to show he'd pulled himself together.

"Beats a sharp slap." Logan's tone implied that's how he'd have handled things.

"Do you always have to be such a jackass?" Releasing the ghost's arm, she turned her irate displeasure his way but the spirit actually intervened on Logan's behalf.

The biologist waved her off. "Nah, it's fine. He's right."

"Kevin, do you mind explaining?" Mike asked. "It'd be helpful if you could elaborate."

Visibly disturbed, the spirit rocked on his heels. He exhaled a stream of vapor that formed wispy fingers adjoined to a frail palm. The spectral hand drifted across the autopsy table, grasping for something just beyond reach before merging with the fog bank still roiling about their feet.

"Malfoy was released three days ago up near Eagle Lake. He wandered for a bit and then headed southwest. I followed him on foot—"

"Was he wearing a radio collar?" Victoria asked.

A wry smile twisted Kevin's lips. "Yes. When the Department relocates an animal, it's standard practice. Malfoy only had his on for about five hours before he managed to slip the collar. After that, I had to track him the old-fashioned way." His sorrowful gaze flitted to the wolf's skinned corpse, then darted away as if the sight were too painful to linger upon. "Houdini would've been a fitting name for him too."

Damn near bursting with impatience, Victoria nodded. She didn't want to disrespect the poor man or trivialize his feelings, but she would've preferred a more succinct account. The killer—or killers—presented a real and present threat to her pack.

"Yakkity-yak. Enough already," Logan interrupted in his

typical abrupt manner. "Let's cut to the chase. Who murdered you? Who skinned poor Malfoy here?"

Victoria winced, a reprimand on her lips, but she bit her tongue. In truth, Logan's abrasiveness worked in her favor this time. He had the candor to say what she longed to, and suffered none of the compunctions of politeness.

The spirit offered a heavy nod. "It was almost dark when I came upon the hunters—"

"Hunters?" The sharp, involuntary interruption tore from Victoria. If she hadn't already been standing, she'd have shot to her feet. Her hands clenched and her entire body stiffened. She stopped breathing. For one awful second, she believed in her heart that *her* hunters must be involved. Sawyer reverted to his former ways, or hunters gone rogue. Jake's second-in-command wasn't called Skinner for being bald.

Through the pack bond, Logan's anger rolled like the swells of a coming storm, and tension delineated every inch of his long frame. His amber eyes acquired a burnished glow like old gold, cutting through the fog that still thickened the atmosphere. Beside him, Mike Trash looked every bit as wary.

Then her common sense asserted itself with a vengeance, leading her to bitch-slap her own lack of faith in her allies. *Of course,* Sawyer and Jake weren't involved. Kevin had to mean *hunters* in the generic. If he didn't know about werewolves, how could he know about Hunters.

"Yes, hunters. There were three of them." The biologist's face twitched. He registered their reaction even if he didn't know the reason for it. "They'd already killed Malfoy and had hung his body from his hind legs. They were in the process of skinning him when I stumbled into their camp. Of course, I wouldn't have let them know I was there if I'd known what they were up to but by the time I realized..."

"It was too late?" Victoria felt awful for him but she was glad he was finally sharing the important information about the enemy.

"It was too late." Kevin spread his hands to communicate his loss and frustration. "The big guy came at me with a knife. It's embarrassing because I didn't even react to defend myself. He was that fast. All I remember is his face... Pain."

"I'm so sorry. You didn't deserve this. Neither did Malfoy. I'll do everything I can to help you cross over once we're done here." Victoria laid a hand on his arm again, offering the only comfort she could. The interrogation was unfortunate but necessary; especially if Kevin needed assistance in crossing over. A spirit's most likely reasons for remaining were revenge or unfinished business. It sounded like he desired both.

"Can you describe the hunters?" Mike asked in a professional cop-voice, neutral but authoritative.

The spirit bobbed his head in agitation but remained coherent. "There were two men and a woman—all Caucasian. The guy who attacked me was in his mid-twenties, long dishwater blond hair. Scruff." With an absent motion, he stroked his jaw. "The woman was the oldest. Thirty-something, frizzy brown hair. The other guy was younger, maybe twenty, not very memorable except I recall the woman calling him DNR which I thought was weird, but I was too sickened by what they'd done to Malfoy to think about it..."

Surreal paralysis seized Victoria, rendering her unable to speak or move. Each second spent listening to Kevin's account—each damning detail—moved her farther off-center from her conviction until she hit another crisis of faith that left her scrambling for something to cling to. She thought she might die at any second—cease drawing breath, her heart still in her chest, and her spirit would step neatly out of her body.

"Was there anything distinctive about them?" Mike asked in his maddeningly dispassionate manner.

Kevin's face slackened and his chin dropped to rest against his chest. His entire posture altered, the animation gone, and the spirit lost his two-dimensional aspect. He grew paper thin. "I-I..."

"It's okay if you don't..." Victoria managed in a strangled voice.

"No, I do." The spirit's hand rose to touch his upper arm, tapping a specific spot. *Too specific. Damningly so.* "They all had the same tattoo of a dagger right here. I remember noticing it because they glowed as if they were enchanted."

Victoria's heart broke and she reflexively grabbed her upper arm that bore the exact dagger tattoo Kevin had described. The hunter mark. The sleeve of her shirt concealed it, but she could feel it there through the thin cotton—buzzing with raw magic.

"I *knew* those fucking hunters couldn't be trusted!" Logan's rage surged through the room, as palpable a force as a volcanic explosion. The spirit's pattern wavered, filling with lines of static when the werewolf's outburst disrupted his coherence.

A slight movement at the periphery of her vision marked the sheriff's retreat from the center of the room. The human was smart enough to realize he didn't want to be standing too close to angry werewolves.

"Logan! Stop! Let me handle this." Victoria shouted to compete with his sheer volume. Common sense urged her to speak in a soft voice in an attempt to calm him down, but her instinctive reaction to the male werewolf was *never* reasonable or measured. She fed on his excitement.

Worse, he provoked her.

"It was." Logan slammed his fist against his palm and glowered at her. He paced with furious energy, a destructive force seeking release. "I bet it was that Sawyer guy. He has stone-cold killer eyes."

"He's not like that." She rushed Logan, seized hold of his forearms, and all but stood on his toes to close the distance between them. He grabbed her in return, probably hard enough to hurt but she only registered pressure. No pain. Her passion burned white-hot, obscuring any sense of caution or compunction.

"You're blind if you can't see it. He's described their tattoos." He got into her face and shook her hard enough to rattle her teeth. Their auras clashed, setting the atmosphere ablaze with a light show to rival the aurora borealis.

"Logan..." Victoria licked desert-dry lips, scrambling for any sort of balance. Serenity had never been in her nature, but never giving up no matter how many times she got knocked down—*that* she excelled at in spades. "Sawyer wouldn't have done this. None of them would've. Not Cali and not DNR."

"How do you explain this then?" Releasing her, Logan swung his arm wide in pure disgust.

"I don't. I can't."

Logan's mouth curled in disgust. Glaring, he backed away from her. "I'm going to kill them—starting with Sawyer. They're a threat to the pack. I can see that even if you can't."

"No." Infuriated, she lost her grip on reason. A red patina washed over her vision, tainting everything with its fiery glow.

"No?" Narrow-eyed, Logan glared at her in challenge and open rebellion. Yet caution edged his regard, as if he wasn't quite sure about her.

"I forbid it."

"You... Forbid it?"

"I forbid it." She tilted her face, forced to look up to hold his gaze.

"And just how do you intend to stop me?"

"I'm Alpha."

"Alpha." He mocked her.

"That's right—Alpha." At least until he deposed her.

"That's contestable," he returned with an ugly smirk.

Time to play her ace.

"I'm going to remind you that you owe me." Victoria laid her hand upon Logan's chest over his heart, in the mark she'd left on his flesh. To her immense satisfaction, he lost that arrogant smile. "I believed in your innocence when all the evidence damned you as guilty. I believed in you and I fought for you... And I want you to consider the irony of *you* being ready to act as judge, jury, and executioner based on the word of one spirit..."

She'd apologize to Kevin later for impugning his testimony. At the moment, her main priority was talking Logan down. If she had to play every IOU in her possession, she would. Even so, touching on events of the prior February was tremendously difficult. Yes, she'd helped the Koenig family, but she'd also made a terrible mistake that cost Logan, one which neither of them had ever forgiven her for. But there was nothing gained by dwelling on past blunders.

"I'm right and you damn well know it. So I'm forbidding you to go off half-cocked and attack a man who is more than capable of turning you into a wolf skin rug." As soon as she uttered the joke, she wanted to retract it. Her gut churned and all she could think of was that pile of wolf hides she and Sawyer had found.

"Ahh, geez, Vic. You're fighting dirty." Logan's handsome

face pulled into a grimace. His hand rose to rub behind his ear. Oh boy, he looked pissed and chagrined all at once. An impossible combination, but he pulled it off brilliantly.

Her mouth curved into a slight smile. "I think we've already established that I'll do whatever it takes to win."

Logan huffed and puffed his way into a concession. "Okay, fine. But I'm not placing blind faith in that asshole's innocence. We'll investigate, prove he's guilty, and then I'll kill him."

"Of course we'll investigate." She rolled her eyes, but she had feeling it was the best she would get from him. The important thing was obtaining Logan's agreement to wait. Hopefully, Sawyer could provide an airtight alibi for all three hunters' whereabouts the prior evening.

"Glad you two got that sorted out. Now can we get back to the investigation and stop dicking around?" Mike asked with no small amount of sarcasm. In unison, Victoria and Logan turned toward the sheriff who stood at the far side of the room, about as far as one could get from them without leaving.

Kevin had vanished.

"Logan's tantrum was more than the spirit could handle. Kevin winked out. He may reform once things settle down," Mike volunteered before Victoria could ask.

"Sorry," Logan mumbled sheepishly, ducking his head.

"I hope he comes back. I wanted to help him cross over." Victoria spared the dead man's body a pensive glance. She experienced a twinge of guilt that all her initial sympathy had been for Malfoy. It made her feel a bit bigoted.

"I'm sure you'll get another chance." In his take-charge manner, the sheriff assumed command of the investigation. "I'm going to take Logan out to the crime scene and see if his werewolf super sniffer can pick up any scent markers. Better to do it before any more time passes. It's a ways north of here so we'll be a few hours."

"Yeah, that's a good idea," Logan agreed with lukewarm enthusiasm.

"If there's nothing else I can do, I'd like to get home." She winced, imagining the unavoidable conversation she and Sawyer needed to have. The irony just about killed her, but she figured she could at least count on the hunter to be more reasonable and levelheaded than Logan.

The sheriff used the sheet to cover the bodies and then led the way out of the morgue at a brisk pace. Preoccupied with her troubled thoughts, Victoria dragged her feet and followed. After a minute or so of walking through the labyrinth like hallways, she became aware of Logan beside her.

Tilting her head, she stole a sideways glance and found him watching her. From the glittering intensity in his eyes, he had probably been observing her for a while. The judgmental look on his face angered her all over again. She hadn't forgotten what he'd said to her back at the lake house. Hadn't forgiven him either. He'd all but called her a slut, but more offensively, implied she'd been disloyal to the memory of her mate.

"Tell me one thing," he said. "Are you fucking that Sawyer guy?"

Victoria blinked. For a split second, she considered slapping him. She wanted to, but a cooler head prevailed for once. Then she backed off and opened her mouth to inform him it was none of his damn business, but the devil inside her led her down a far more tempting path.

"Nooo..." She grinned and winked. "Not yet."

Logan growled and his posture tensed. "Do you care about him?"

"He's a member of my pack." Her shoulders rolled in a shrug.

He snorted, grinned in derision, and shook his head. "That's not an answer. I'm a member of the pack too, in case you've forgotten."

"I haven't forgotten, but you're the one who left us, Logan." Victoria waited to give him an opportunity to speak, to explain his inexplicable absence and return. His jaw pulled but he remained stubbornly silent. Her nostrils flared as she exhaled in profound exasperation.

"I had to," he mumbled, and then sealed his lips.

"I care about you too, *asshole*. It's nonexclusive." Gathering herself, Victoria sprinted to catch up with Mike, leaving Logan behind her where he belonged.

CHAPTER FOURTEEN

Resignation helped numb the worst of Freya's ill temper, though the wound to her ego would fester for a long time to come. "Your games are tiresome. Why have you pressed me about Victoria? Tell me what you really want."

Arik regarded her, a cool appraisal. "As I previously stated, I want Victoria and my children kept safe. That means Sawyer Barrett hell and gone from Sierra Pines."

"I don't understand why you're dragging me into this," Freya said in an aggrieved voice. "I've warned Victoria to be wary of Sawyer many times. Does she listen? No."

"Which brings us to another point of concern..." He sounded thin with stretched patience nearing its end. "You're losing all influence over Victoria."

"She's disobedient."

Arik's smile was a scythe. "Victoria's smart enough to question authority. No, this mess is entirely your fault. You've allowed your ego to compromise your judgment,

Freya. Your petty, snotty attitude is driving Victoria straight to Jake Barrett."

She pinned him with an astute look. "I was right—you're jealous. Except this is about the father and not the son, isn't it?"

He looked askance of her. "You're a stupid cow, but you're what I have to work with. My concerns are strategic. Odin knows Victoria has the only weapon that can free Fenrir. Obviously, he's manipulating her—driving a wedge between you."

"I've had the same thought myself." Freya forced the admission out though it stung her pride. And she loathed giving Loki anything he could use against her.

Fortunately, he zoomed right in on the obstacle facing them both. "Right now your priestess refuses to obey you in even simple matters. How do you plan to convince her to cut my Fenrir's bindings, knowing it will bring about Odin's death?"

"I don't know." The concession was bitter.

The last time we spoke, you swore she'd obey you because she loved you so much. Do you still believe that?"

"No," she said in a voice thick with tears. "I don't."

SIERRA PINES, *California, on the western shore of Echo Lake*

The rugged peaks of the Sierra Nevada formed irregular juts beneath the orange and the red, an ocean of rock stretching toward the setting sun. Nighttime arrived hours sooner in the mountains than it did in the desert. Phoenix in June—dusk stretched long and thin, the bony fingers of light gouging the sky for hours. At a few minutes past six p.m.,

Echo Lake already lay beneath a blanket of black velvet and starry twinkle. Victoria had lived in Arizona her entire life before her abrupt arrival in Sierra Pines less than six months ago. Her new home—when she dared to call it such—was still strange and new. She couldn't help comparing and contrasting the two places.

After the morgue, Victoria returned to the lake house and conducted a quick powwow with her own pack to bring everyone up to speed. Then she spent the next several hours fielding queries from Finn and other werewolf leaders. With Morena's help as her computer advisor, she distributed mass emails containing times, dates, and directions. Speaking sweetly, she offered advice couched as suggestion for the sake of Very Fragile Alpha Male Egos. At one point, she even attempted to translate the incoherent babbling of a Scottish man with a thick brogue... Thankfully, the call had dropped.

Victoria loitered on the boat dock, a vantage point that granted a clear view of the lake and surrounding forest. She held the cell phone she'd borrowed from Sylvie to her ear.

Alpha Finn droned on in his deep, rumbling voice. "...I'll distribute the GPS coordinates we've agreed upon to the other packs, with the expectation that we'll gather in Desolation Wilderness on the night of the next full moon."

"To keep our numbers manageable, each Alpha will be permitted an entourage of two companions—one enforcer and one advisor," Victoria reminded him. No doubt, the sharpness of her tone betrayed her apprehension but she had good cause for concern. Strange wolves, a number on the magnitude of sixty males, would soon enter her territory— every last one a potential challenger and threat to her sovereignty.

"Agreed. I am bringing my Beta, Tarak, and the priest, Bodaway," Finn replied but the exact meaning of his response was ambiguous, at best. His inflection suggested sardonicism.

Victoria tilted her head as though the angle might enable her to intuit his thoughts. In the past, Finn had made stilted statements about both Tarak and Bodaway. He never came right out with bold criticism, but his dissatisfaction with both men was impossible to miss. She very badly wanted to ask why he would choose such disreputable companions for such an important meeting. She hesitated, biting her lips until prudence won out. If he wanted her to know, he would tell her.

"Of course, that's your decision."

He released a burst of laughter. "Unfortunately, it is. Be grateful for your small, close-knit pack, Victoria Storm. I am a warrior; ill-suited to politics. But I see more infighting within my own tribe than actual battle. The petty rivalries. The backstabbing. Much more and my head will split. By the will of Thor—I will soon be rid of such burdens."

"Godspeed."

Silence stretched. Then Finn resumed the recitation of things they'd already gone over and agreed to. Victoria crossed her fingers, hoping he would find satisfaction in the second repetition because she doubted she had the patience necessary to endure a third.

"A suggestion..." Finn's voice hissed, a sly insinuation.

Picking up on his tone, Victoria snapped to alertness. "Yes?"

"I'm aware you have hunters patrolling your territory."

"What of it?" Suspicion crystalized in her gut. Her wolf bristled and she bared her teeth. What were Finn's sources— was he spying on her pack?

"Peace, we are allies," he said, easy and soothing in

cadence. "Barrett has made it widely known he has hunters stationed in Echo Lake."

"He has?" Taken off guard, she licked her lips. Conflict and confusion formed a flurry in her thoughts. On the one hand, she was grateful but on the other...

"Barrett has made a point of acknowledging you as betrothed to his son. When he names you daughter, his eyes are obsidian. His voice crushes stone. His gaze burns through a man's soul..."

Victoria gulped and her heart palpitated. Never mind. She had no objections.

"You're quite the poet, Finn, for one of Thor's followers," she quipped for lack of a profound reply.

"Thank you." Finn snickered and continued boldly. "Since the entire point to this gathering is to negotiate a treaty, another skirmish between wolves and hunters—"

"Would spell disaster," Victoria concluded. Renewed hostilities would doom a renewal of their alliance, and render their efforts pointless.

"Precisely."

"I'll warn the hunters that strangers will be arriving at my express invitation." Victoria wrapped things up and bid Finn goodbye. She shoved the cell phone into her pocket and turned to stare out over the lake.

Doubt and worry plagued her. The first pack was due to arrive in less than five days, which left her under the gun to put her house in order. She needed to locate and deal with the men who'd left the wolf hides at the Fireside Inn. Presumably, they were the same assholes that had murdered poor Kevin Danbury and skinned Malfoy. Identifying and locating the killers should resolve the accusations the ghost had brought against Sawyer and his crew. Unless—

Unless Sawyer and his people are the killers. Freya touched

Victoria's mind, an unwelcome intrusion, giving voice to her deepest fear.

Victoria faltered for a second but then found the path to trust. "It wasn't Sawyer. I was with him when we found those wolf skins at the inn. He was as upset as I was. He couldn't have faked his reaction and fooled me."

Conviction strengthened her declaration. Okay, sure, her initial reaction in the morgue had been born of raw horror but even a few hours to think on it had granted her perspective. Not only was Sawyer *not* that good of a liar—but she didn't believe him capable of such heinous crimes. He could be a dangerous hothead at times, but he was also decent and kind.

You are blind to his true nature! Sawyer is a murderer and a liar. Freya thundered her disapproval. A sharp crack split Victoria's eardrum and she winced.

"It's far more likely that one of our enemies is attempting to sabotage the moot—to prevent wolves from once again allying with the hunters," Victoria argued.

Enough. Stop making excuses.

"Goddess, please. Be reasonable."

No more. And with that, Freya ended their communion.

Shoulders hunched, Victoria perched on the edge of the dock and stared down into the lake that had taken her mate from her and almost claimed Sawyer. The water's surface was smooth and placid, sucking up the surrounding light. *Black water.* Once, not too long ago, she harbored no phobias of darkness or deep water but now... Irrational dread. Ever since she'd gotten pregnant, she worried about the myriad things beyond her control. Was it caution or cowardice? She didn't know. Maybe her fear wasn't so unfounded or unreasoning. Either way, tonight she intended to forego the midnight swim she'd been anticipating.

A draft of chilled air pulled down from the snow-capped peaks gusted across the lake. Shivers coursed through Victoria, but she wasn't cold. Within seconds, tremors shook her body so hard her teeth clattered. She wrapped her arms about herself and strangled on a sob—scared and weak when she couldn't afford to be. People counted on her to be strong. Alpha to the Storm Pack. Freya's priestess. Valkyrie. And now, the leader who would unify her fractured people and guide them back to Odin. Far too much responsibility for a twenty-five-year-old woman who was recently widowed and pregnant. She struggled to come to terms with how her body was changing from day-to-day. Soon, her life would change forever and she could barely comprehend the magnitude of it. A child was the most profound responsibility she could conceive of, and she had to adapt to handle all that and more. Whatever the future held...

The burden crushed Victoria.

CHAPTER FIFTEEN

Arik considered Freya, his surprise evident in the part of his lips. "I didn't expect you to it admit it so easily."

Freya closed her eyes, fighting tears. Easy? There was nothing easy about it. Victoria's treason had broken her heart. But, as Loki had pointed out, she and he were in a partnership for survival. So for her own good, she acknowledged the truth of her priestess's betrayal.

"What would you suggest I do?" Freya asked, though she loathed seeking advice from the worm. Obviously, the Trickster had something in mind or he wouldn't have revealed his true identity. And while she despised both him and his methods, there was no denying that his plans worked.

"Test Victoria," he dictated in an even tone. "Present her with the truth and then push her to choose between you and Odin. Should she side with you, then all is well."

"And if she doesn't?" The question tasted sour enough to turn her stomach.

Her self-proclaimed Philadelphia Lawyer spread his hands. "If she fails, then take away *Vanadium* and cut her off. You don't need a priestess who can't and won't obey you."

SIERRA PINES, *California, on the western shore of Echo Lake*

In the stillness of the night, sound carried. The rumble of the car's engine reached the boat dock even though it was located more than a quarter mile from the two-lane road. The house and its heated in-ground swimming pool were positioned on a rise overlooking the lake. The property was miles from their nearest neighbor and the northernmost settlement before the stretch of federally protected land that composed Desolation Wilderness. The entire territory, all the way south to U.S. Route 50, belonged to her pack.

Victoria had more than enough warning to pull herself together. She rubbed her hands over her eyes, wiping away evidence of the tears that had threatened to overwhelm her. Weakness wasn't an option. Not for an Alpha. Not for her. So she mastered her emotions, shoving them down deep, and reached for the vast wellspring of wild magic below her feet. She connected with it easily, just as Arik had taught her, although she possessed only a fraction of her deceased mate's skill. Near as she could tell, the source was without limit; the only restriction to what could be accomplished was truly a matter of talent.

Police lights flashed, red and blue strobes, just for a couple seconds but more than enough for Victoria to identify their visitor. The few times he'd been out to the house to visit, Mike Trash made a habit of announcing his presence. In his words—*"Startled wolves are worse than startled cats. And a hundred times more dangerous."*

The vehicle rolled to a stop, the passenger door opened, and one person climbed out. Even from a distance, Logan's lanky form was easy to identify. He and his uncle exchanged a few words in farewell.

Once the patrol car turned around and departed, Logan marched down the hill toward Victoria. His stance screamed readiness from the square set of his shoulders to his solid gait. Logan, who typically personified laziness, had a spine straighter than a ruler. His posture communicated superior status—a message aimed square at her.

As he drew nearer, Victoria braced in anticipation of the confrontation to come. In her heart, she actually didn't want to fight with him. As much as she dreaded it, she refused to shy away from it and she wouldn't back down. As Alpha, she had to defend her territory against challengers or lose it, especially since she hadn't won it fair and square in the first place. Following Arik's death, Logan had left almost immediately. But as the Alpha's son, he had a valid claim to the territory. Worse, he also owned the lake house. She and her pack lived there at his discretion.

"How did your visit to the murder scene go? Did you find anything?" Victoria asked once Logan came within speaking distance. She hoped talking would diffuse some of his tension.

"The scene was overrun. I caught over a dozen distinct scents."

"What about Sawyer?" She hated the necessity, but she had to ask.

"Nah." Logan swiped his hands together as though angry with the admission. "Near as I could tell, the other two hadn't been there either."

"Good."

"That doesn't clear them."

"No, but it doesn't condemn them either."

Once he reached the dock, Logan sped his pace, racing toward her way too fast for comfort. His footfalls thudded against the wooden planks. From the weight of each step, she expected him to stomp right through one of the boards. His aura was more wolf than man, and within seconds he could complete a full transformation—many times faster than it took her.

Fear fed her unease. She fought it, tried to hide it, and failed. She'd clung to the belief that he wouldn't hurt her no matter how they fought but the last twelve hours had eroded her faith in that conviction. In an involuntary reflex, the skin on her arms rippled in precursor to a shift. Her she-wolf, bursting with maternal instinct, was already riled. His blatant masculinity only made it worse.

"Stop. That's close enough." A growl of warning tremored in her throat. He possessed every physical advantage: size, strength, and speed. In a challenge, her survival depended on her getting to *Vanadium* before he could reach her.

Logan pulled up short. His gaze dropped to her hands which were covered in the snow-white fur of her wolf, and his eyes narrowed. His scent grew muskier, marking heightened aggression. The atmosphere was explosive.

He looked up—his stare penetrating and his tone sarcastic. "Seriously, you're challenging me? Did I miss something? Is the witch back?"

"I'm not the aggressor here. You are." For fuck's sake, she was the one who was cornered. She had the lake at her back and sides—nowhere to go unless she wanted to risk the dark waters closing over her head and pulling her under forever.

"Me?" His voice spiked on an incredulous note. "I've got

news for you, sister. You're nuts. I'm just standing here. You're the one making like Lon Chaney Jr."

"We both know how fast that can change."

"Right. Because I'm just a rabid dog that needs to be put down." He smiled but it was a parody of niceness. Enough testosterone to bust balls ripened the air.

"Damn it, that's not what I've said. I told you to stop. To give me some space. All you've done since coming back is push and push. You didn't even call before you came home."

"It's my house. I wasn't aware I had to call ahead." He bared his teeth, flashing incisors, and his false smile lost all resemblance to a friendly expression.

"It's your house." She ground her teeth over the difficult concession, and strove to remain impassive while anger percolated in her gut. Logan's name was on the deed, but as a wolf, Victoria regarded the territory as *hers*—and therein was the great conflict.

"It's my house. My land. My territory." His bold gaze never wavered from her face. "Everything that belonged to my father is mine."

Shock crashed over her. For a second, she assumed he meant her too but she dismissed the possibility out of hand. *That* way nothing but the folly of ego. No, he meant the property and the territory. And honestly, she'd expected Logan to give her a hard time, but his complete reversal caught her unprepared. He'd invited her and the pack to remain in the house. He'd chosen to leave.

Victoria stood to lose so much more now than she would have then. A new baby required stability. And it wasn't just her. Sylvie considered the lakeside house home now. Morena had enrolled in the local high school and started to make new friends. Sophia and her pups roamed the forests along the lakeshore. So why would Logan assert his inheritance rights just as she'd started to feel comfortable?

It baffled her but worse, her heart ached. Home...she'd only just started calling it that and now she might lose it all.

"Are you telling us to get out? Out of your house? Or out of your territory?" She swallowed a snarl. Instinct dictated she fight him. Throttling him possessed innate appeal; a simple solution to her problem.

"What if I am? What will you do? Run? Take the pack on the road again? What if I want to be Alpha and keep the pack? What then?" His expression was inscrutable. For the life of her, she didn't know what he was thinking.

Losing her pack...her worst fear.

"I'll fight—to the death if I have to." *For her pack. For her territory. And yes, for her title.* Rooted in place, Victoria acknowledged his birthright even as she came into the bitter acknowledgement that she would not accede to him. The land was bonded to her, and she to it.

"You'll fight me? Considering I'm your ordained champion, this could get damn convoluted." Logan's nostrils flared and his mouth compressed. Amusement and disgust crossed his mobile features.

"I'll fight you if I have to. I refuse to lose *everything* again." Victoria stood rigid, stubbornly proud, scared to death, and thoroughly confused. How could he make jokes at a time like this? How dare he!

"Damn it, Vic. You love your precious pack more than anything. I *know* that. Do you really believe I'd do that to you?" Logan backed off, withdrawing from the fight. His shields dropped and a thick, miserable fog engulfed his aura. "I thought we were past the point where you automatically assumed the worst of me."

"I don't." A reflexive denial escaped her lips, but it had the ring of falsehood. Belatedly, Victoria realized she'd been played. Logan had said just enough to evoke her deepest fears. He'd stood by while she'd jumped to the worst conclusions possible. Shame filled her because that too was an unjust attempt to divert blame entirely onto him. She had to own her own chunk of it.

"I think you do. I spent two years enslaved to my Alpha, and every day I wanted to die. In the end, it killed me. No one believed in me except you. You saved me. I owe you everything. So how can you think I'd do that to you?" His head hung and his grimace lingered.

Damn it all to hell! Maybe she'd misread the situation. Obviously, she'd hurt his feelings but how had this wound up being all her fault? She rallied against the awful unfairness of the accusation. "Hold up. That's so damn unfair I don't even know where to begin. Logan, you're the one who burst into the house without so much as a word of warning—"

"I texted."

She stared at him blankly.

"This morning. I texted I'd be home in about an hour."

"Oh." She pressed her palm heel to her forehead and dragged it down her face. Her eyes lit in sheer determination. "Which reminds me—you owe me a new phone."

"Do not." He frowned. "How do you figure?"

"My screen got smashed when I dropped it by the pool."

"How the hell is that my fault exactly?"

"You started the fight."

"Did not. The long-haired psycho shot first."

"Sawyer said you shifted." Talking fast, Victoria cut off Logan's next interruption. "Besides, who acted first is beside the point."

"What's the point?" He arched his brow.

"The point is you burst in, started a fight, got everyone amped up, and then called me a slut and a liar." The reminder riled her up. She surged toward him, all fear forgotten, and punched Logan's side to add emphasis to her displeasure. *"Asshole."*

"Oh. Yeah." He bowed his head and his shoulders shook. For an awful second, she feared he was crying, but then he threw his arms wide, braying laughter like a jackass. His huge hand slapped his knee. *"That's* what I meant to apologize for—*oomph.*"

"That's for implying Arik isn't the father."

"Yeah, okay. I'm sorry and I apologize. I'm an asshole—" Logan positioned his arms to protect his ribcage against future assault.

"You don't say." She pantomimed shock, hand to her throat.

Tension etched lines in his handsome face. "When I'm caught off guard, my knee-jerk reaction is to say something asinine. Why didn't you tell me you were pregnant? Do you have any idea what it felt like to find out like that?"

Victoria opened her mouth to offer a neat reply but found herself at a complete loss for words. Logan deserved more than a cavalier answer, but the truth hurt. Sighing, she gazed out over the lake because it was easier than meeting his eyes.

"I didn't want to drag you down with me."

"Ah, okay..." Logan scowled, his bewilderment plain on his face. "No, not okay. I don't get that at all. You're having my sister. I have a responsibility to help. It's my duty to protect you."

"Responsibility. Duty." Victoria shook her head in adamant denial. "That's precisely why I didn't tell you. You'd have felt obligated to stay. After Arik's death, you couldn't get out of here fast enough. I wanted you to be free."

And happy...

"So you were protecting me, huh?" He looked askance at her.

"Yeah, I guess." It sounded pretty stupid—and selfish—when she looked at it from his perspective.

"Aren't we a fine pair? I suppose it's my fault you turned to Ken-doll for protection." With a sardonic chuckle, Logan ran a hand through his hair.

"Don't call Sawyer that." Victoria choked on a wet giggle.

"You've thought it yourself or you wouldn't be laughing." Logan crossed his arms. His brow arched in question. "So, is it? My fault?"

She inhaled sharply. "*No.* You don't get credit for that too. My involvement with the hunters goes back to before we met. And, I'll have you know, I managed to work out all my troubles without your help."

He watched her from the corner of his eye. "So, you're saying you don't need me? Maybe I could stick around for a while, anyway? I've been having trouble with the magic you showed me. For one, I can't get the damn rainbow bridge to open. I could use a few pointers."

"Ha! Now your true motives are coming out."

Logan eyed her but refused to take the bait. "Are you going to give me a hard time if I want to stay?"

"That depends." Her lips twitched, but she suppressed the smile, playing the hard line. "Are you going to evict us?"

"Nope." He ducked his head. "The pack is welcome to stay in this house, and on this land, for the rest of their lives. But I want to be part of it. I want a place where I belong."

Happiness percolated in her heart, bubbling upward. Victoria sank her teeth into her lower lip to keep from smiling and schooled her expression to sternness. "Are you planning on challenging me for Alpha?"

"Oh, hell no." He huffed, expelling a puff of citrusy breath. When he shifted, his arm jostled hers. "I don't want that sort of headache."

Victoria inhaled through her mouth, drinking in his odor, which she fully expected to change on the utterance of a falsehood. She suspected him of dissembling for her sake, except she failed to detect so much as a hint of deception. Come to think of it, she'd never caught Logan in even a white lie. Logan continued in a husky voice. "That doesn't mean I'm going to submit to your control. I can't live like that again."

"Will you at least try to work with me?" Victoria pursed her lips and kept her tone strict. She put on a damn convincing display of primness, if she did say so herself.

"Translation: you want me to do what I'm told when I'm told to do it."

"No." She paused and grinned. "Yes."

Logan rolled impertinence in his mouth. His smile split his face. "Depends. Will you be wearing black leather and high heels?"

"No."

"You hesitated."

"No, I didn't."

"Did so."

Sighing, Victoria rolled her eyes. The devil on her shoulder urged her to be naughty. "I dunno, Logan. I don't think this is gonna work."

He lost his smirk to a worried frown. "What?"

Victoria set her face as sternly as she could, not an easy task since she was dying to laugh. "You have to go."

"Why?" Logan blurted out, a streak of panic coloring his voice. "I thought you trusted me—"

"It's not that." She cut the air with her hand.

"Aww, c'mon. Don't get rid of me, Vic. I'm a keeper. I'm housebroken and everything." Logan looked fit to be tied, and as though he might jump out of his skin on a second's notice. Few and far between were the instances when the smartass didn't know what to say.

She savored his vexation and remained silent.

Logan gave her an up-down appraisal. "You have that 'I'd rather stick needles in my eyes' look on your face. If memory serves, you're about to call me an idiot and then punch me."

It hurt not to laugh but she managed. Taking a deep breath, she wrung her hands and rushed her confession before he mouthed off again. "I'm not going to be able to resist trying to squish you. Every time you mouth off, I'm compelled to try. I can't help myself..."

"So... I'm just too damn squishable."

"Yeah, that's right."

"You lay awake all night, just thinkin' about me. Don'tcha?" Logan rolled over and just about died laughing.

"Not even in passing." Victoria wheezed, ruined the effect, and lost her cool. She succumbed to the same fit that held him in its grip. Clutching her sides, she fought it but tears leaked past her squeezed lids, and damn—it felt good.

"Next time you have a go at squishing me, can we grease up first?" Logan wagged his eyebrows and puckered up.

Without warning, the baby moved and nailed Victoria in the kidney. She sobered up fast, still holding her side but for different reasons. "Oh. Oh, that hurts."

"Is the baby kicking?" Logan sat straight and wide-eyed. He reached for her abdomen. "Can I feel?"

Surprised by his enthusiasm, she withdrew but then stopped. In fairness, Logan had a vested interest in her child. Bracing, Victoria took his wrist and guided his open hand to the spot on her stomach where the baby was kicking. She remained still and silent so he could experience the determined flutter.

"That's so fucking cool." A big grin spread on his face. His hands were huge and hot on her abdomen, and more than mild adoration shone in his eyes.

When he looked at her like that, she got scared that his feelings for her exceeded horny affection. Her heart ached, a wound to her soul. She didn't love him—never would. Not for lack of desire, but because she was damaged goods.

His embrace was good and safe and right—and oh so wrong. Logan was an unstable foundation; she dared not build her house here. With bittersweet regret, she stepped away. He made no attempt to restrain her.

Logan watched her retreat and his smile waned to a cynical smirk. He licked his lips and asked, "What're you doing down here anyway?"

"Oh, just thinking." She hedged on purpose. She had to tell him about the planned werewolf gathering and the treaty negotiation with the hunters. First, though, she needed a couple minutes to compose her thoughts and figure out what to say.

"I'll bet you were thinking about my father, huh?" Logan seized his tangent with both hands and ran with it. "Wondering if Dad pulled a Disney Villain Death?"

"Uh." She tilted back her head and gazed at him, thoroughly perplexed. She had no words. She swore she wasn't stupid, simply weary. Heavy thoughts weighted her mind, leaving her unprepared to navigate Logan's obstacle course of mixed pop cultural references. And what he'd just suggested about Arik's demise stopped her cold. Icy fear swirled in her gut.

They'd never recovered his body from the lake's arctic depths.

"I do it too," Logan continued, lapsing into what sounded suspiciously like a confession. "Sit and stare at the water, expecting to see his head break the surface. For him to come walking—"

"Knock it off, jackass." She jabbed his ribs, blustering to hide her disquiet. He had her so freaked out, her skin was crawling.

Logan caught her wrist in a steely grip and held on.

"We both loved Arik. Losing him hurt—" Her voice broke.

He stiffened and lifted his head. His tone was severe. "Last time we talked, you denied loving him."

She flinched. She found confessions difficult, but Logan deserved the truth. "I was lying to protect myself. So many people I loved had already died... When my pack arrived in Sierra Pines last February, we were on our last leg. Arik was a godsend. He was everything we needed. He saved us."

He saved me. She swallowed around the lump in her throat, struggling to keep going. In many ways, Arik embodied Victoria's ideal mate: strength, stability, and generosity. Even his flaws were traits she admired, because a contrary part of her liked difficult males.

Logan snorted. "Dad isn't the saint you're making him out to be, Vic. You don't know him the way I do."

"I don't want to argue, Logan. I'm trying to explain why I denied my feelings. This isn't easy. It's taken me a long time to accept..." She trailed off, struggling for the words to explain how truly damaged she was, but they were all inadequate. It wasn't until she finally acknowledged her denial and owned her devotion to Arik that she'd finally been able to mourn him.

"Don't. I get it."

"Good." She preferred not to explain, especially if it meant dissecting her psychology. She and Logan were both taciturn types when it came to their feelings.

Logan's hand dropped to the front of his pants. For a second, she thought he was about to do something incredibly inappropriate. And yeah, a tiny, stupid part of her hoped he would. Frowning, she cast a sharp glance down. He had paired fingers and his thumb wedged into his front pocket, fishing out a container of Tic Tacs.

"Get your mind outta the gutter, Vic."

"I swear, you're an addict." Victoria laughed and her mood lifted. With a touch of envy and a definite craving, she watched while he pried open the top and tossed back half the contents.

"Want some?" Crunching, Logan proffered the candy with a mocking flourish.

"Yeah." She palmed the box, polished off the remaining mints, and ground them to powder between her molars. Shiny pops of orange zest exploded on her tongue. "Just so you know—we're not courting."

"Oh, snap." Logan fingers produced a crisp break. "I forgot—and here I swore to never fall into your Tic Tac Trap again."

"I didn't think you were smart enough to understand alliteration."

"Well, I showed you." He paused. "What's alliteration?"

"Bigger than your IQ."

"Ha." He exploded with a shout of laughter. His grin grew fearsome. "Sounds like you're back on your feet, so whaddya say? Ready to ring the bell and go another round?"

His casual acknowledgement of the verbal sparring that was their norm put Victoria at ease. She liked this Logan, her antagonistic friend, so much more than the angry stranger from earlier. Eventually, they needed to sit down and talk, but for now she had more urgent priorities.

"Not yet. Please." She laid a hand on his arm. "I'm right in the middle of a huge mess, and I can't handle anything else. I'm brooding on boat docks. One step away from a country western song..."

Amber irises glimmered in the dark. He held her in a long look. "You want my help?"

"I *need* your help."

An odd intensity overtook him. He thumbed his chest. "You can count on me."

"Good," she said, nodding.

"So, what's the mission brief, V?"

She grinned and adopted his flippant attitude. "Whaddya say we resurrect the crime fighting duo of Storm and Koenig?"

"Wanna break into the morgue?"" He dropped a wink and a nod.

"Maybe. I thought we'd start by following up on the guys I believe are the real killers. Earlier today Sawyer and I checked out some drifters over at the Fireside Inn."

Logan snorted. "That claptrap? How does the plot always bring us back there?"

"Dunno, don't care. These guys—whoever they are—had a pile of wolf skins draped across the bed, Logan." She shushed him with a wave, and her voice rumbled with the fierceness of her anger.

He lost his smile, and his face hardened into harshness. "Why didn't you tell me about this earlier?"

"Haven't had the chance." Victoria shrugged, deliberately

choosing the dodge. "Does it matter? I'm telling you now. The hunters are over in Broken Bend on stakeout. I'm heading over there to check in with Sawyer."

And, with any luck, the boys could start fresh—a handshake instead of a firefight.

"I'll go get the Mystery Machine. Let's roll, Scrappy." From a standing start, Logan sprinted along the dock toward the shower.

Pregnancy made her slow but she gave the chase her all. "Call me that again! I dare you."

CHAPTER SIXTEEN

SESSRÚMNIR, FREYA'S HALL IN FÓLKVANGR

A long, uncomfortable silence ensued. Freya stared at Arik in complete and utter disbelief. End her relationship with Victoria—absurd. Or at least it would've been six months before. And though she hated even owning to it, Freya had harbored similar thoughts herself more and more as of late.

His proposal contained a certain incontrovertible logic, but it was also heartless and cruel. The spiritual bond between a goddess and her priestess was intimate and integral. Severing that connection would be akin to cutting off a limb, or two, or three...

"She'll be hurt—egregiously so," Freya protested. "You claim to care for Victoria and your child with her. Yet you're willing to casually subject her to torture."

"No, not casually," he said, shaking his head. "But better she endure a grave wound now than whatever torture Odin will visit upon her later. By removing *Vanadium* from her possession, I'm actually protecting her. Surely..." He smiled. "You, of all people, can understand that."

"You're assuming she'll fail." The realization shocked her. She supposed it shouldn't have. Loki was a deceitful, cynical creature at his core. A friendless fiend could hardly conceive of a scenario where others exceeded his worth.

"Yes, I am. Odin already has his claws sunk too deep—"

"Fine, I'll do this despicable thing for you. But in return, we're through."

"Through?"

"All our deals are null and void." She crafted an adamant gesture, cutting cords. "You will vacate your position as my general and leave my hall—never to return."

"Are you sure? You'll be alone."

"I'm better off alone than with an ally like you," Freya asserted harshly. "Additionally, I'll have your word. No more extortion or blackmail..."

He cocked his head. A war of indecision, conflicted desire, played brief upon his face but at last he growled. "All right—fine. You have my word. I'll leave; never to return. No more extortion or blackmail..."

"What do you suggest I do?" Freya asked. One final time, she would lower herself and roll in the muck with pigs. After this, she'd be free.

His features sharpened, foxlike in his slyness. "I'll tell you exactly what you're going to do. This will work like a charm so long as you follow my instructions to the letter..."

Broken Bend, *California on U.S. Route 50*

The SUV's headlamps lit the pavement right in front of the speeding vehicle as they banked into a sudden turn. The road was a blur. The lights didn't pierce the darkness beyond the guardrail where the pine forest was dense. Victoria gritted her teeth and braced as they slipped through the curve. She bit her tongue to stop from nagging Logan that he was driving too fast.

Taking a deep breath, she resumed her explanation, providing Logan with a recap of the complex political situation she found herself embroiled in. She questioned the wisdom of involving him. Logan was a hothead and uninitiated to the cultural traditions of their people. Before meeting Victoria and the Storm Pack, he'd been raised in isolation and had never known wolf shifters other than his father. Given his return, she had no choice but to include him. Certainly, he was bound to notice when dozens of strange wolves arrived in the area.

"Sooo..." Logan rolled the syllable off his tongue. He slanted a sideways glance. "Let me see if I've got this straight."

"Go on." Victoria nodded.

"You've invited sixty-something strange wolves representing twenty-something packs *here*." He aimed his finger at the ground beneath the speeding car.

"Yup."

"They're arriving in a few days *en masse* for a massive werewolf jamboree."

"Yeah." *Jamboree*—she liked that. It sounded fun.

"For the stated purpose of uniting the werewolf packs. To the express end of signing an alliance with the hunters. Who we've been at war with for months. A war that *you* started no less—"

"It's more complicated than that." A sharp twinge bent her. She silenced a defensive protest—the blame for the mess should be spread around. The majority went to the Necromancer—and thus Loki—but Sawyer owned his fair share.

"Wanna explain that too?"

"Nope."

Logan muttered something acerbic and explicit beneath his breath. "And with this alliance we'll attempt to defeat a huge-ass undead army commanded by some self-stylized jerkoff who calls himself—" He took his hands off the steering wheel to make air quotes. "The Necromancer."

"I've never actually met him so I don't know if that's what he calls himself. But yes, that's what he's known as."

"And—" His voice rang, a note of buildup. "The Big Boss at the end of this game is Loki." He released the wheel to punch the air. "We go all fists of fury on his ass. End Game. World saved. Top score!"

"I wish it was that easy." Victoria exhaled a thin sigh.

"The whole thing sounds like the plot to a corny movie."

"I admit, it's far-fetched. But yeah, that's about the sum of it."

"Huh. So, those are your plans for this month. What're you gonna do in July?"

"Lame." She groaned but then giggled. But then she was wistful. Glancing down, Victoria wrapped her hands protectively about her baby bump. "I'm so sick of being pregnant. What I'd really like to do is just have this baby. Fuck all this: werewolves, hunters—"

"Loki," Logan said with a weird note in his voice.

"Um, yeah." That hadn't been what she planned to say, but it worked.

Logan fell silent, brooding on—whatever went on in that mysterious male mind of his. No doubt, he needed time to think. The whole thing was a lot to swallow, especially in one dose. Despite having known for months, she still experienced surreal moments when she wondered whether she'd gone nuts or was dreaming. She kept expecting to wake up, but never did.

Victoria held her piece and engaged in some worrying of her own. Her mind returned to the morgue visit, replaying the scenario over and over again. Nothing about it sat right, starting with the brief but disturbing visit from Evan. She'd never given the ghoul's origin much thought; never had a reason to before. But all reanimated corpses from ghouls to zombies to vampires were revenants—owing their very existence, and thus their allegiance, to whoever happened to be pulling the strings. So who was the master Evan had spoken of with such urgency?

Her intuition insisted Kevin Danbury hadn't been right either. The spirit's exceptional stability and coherence deviated from the norm. His description of his supposed killers had been dead to rights specific—calling out details that made the hunters immediately identifiable. She could only conceive of one explanation that covered both ghouls and lucid ghosts: necromancy.

A chill ran down her spine; gooseflesh rose on her nape and across the backs of her arms. She gulped and spoke without premeditation. "Logan?"

"Mmm, yeah?"

Victoria's lips trembled, a long-held suspicion on the tip of her tongue—*Do you follow Loki?* She struggled to spit the question out but her vocal chords were paralyzed. She feared the loss of Logan.

Deep down, she was terrified of the answer he would offer. Therein, her truth resided. At least if she didn't ask, he couldn't lie to her. Or worse, confirm her worst fear. This way, she retained plausible deniability and the ability to indulge in soothing self-comfort. She was paranoid. Silly. Unworthy. Always assuming the worst of Logan—a bad habit she should break. He deserved better.

"We're here." Logan's announcement struck the frozen surface of her dark deliberations, fracturing them into a million pieces.

He slowed as they approached Broken Bend. The tiny community consisted of a cluster of buildings situated to either side of the state road. The old saying applied—you could miss it if you blinked.

"Pull in here." Victoria indicated the entrance to the packed parking lot of the diner which was directly across the road from the Fireside Inn. Although Logan's SUV was less conspicuous than the Chevelle, she preferred to err on the side of caution.

Logan turned off and parked around the side of the restaurant. The Broken Bend Café wasn't much to look at from the outside but it served the best food for miles around. The size of the dinner crowd gathered in front testified to the quality.

They joined at the rear of the vehicle and walked toward the busy highway that cut through the center of town. As they approached to cross, Victoria snagged Logan's elbow and tugged. He stopped and glanced over, quirking his brow.

"It might be best if I went ahead and warned the hunters you're here." Victoria intended for Logan and Sawyer to make a fresh start. She was determined to see it happen—if she had to clang their heads together like coconut clackers until they saw things her way.

"Dickless is easily startled, I take it?" Logan radiated superiority.

"Sawyer," Victoria enunciated distinctly. "Has an itchy trigger finger." She clenched her fist and started counting —*one...*

"Yeah, I figured him for a quick shot."

"*You.* Stay put." She nailed his chest with her knuckles —*two.* Shoulders squared, she looked both ways and marched out onto the road.

Logan sang out after her. "You know, there's no Norse god of premature ejaculation but I hear one's coming fast!"

"You're an idiot."

"You know you love me."

Midstep, she hesitated and smiled, but only because he couldn't see. She resumed walking and safely reached the other side. The shoulder embankment was steep; the climb surprisingly challenging. She tackled it head on, slipped and almost fell, but caught herself. Her flip-flops lacked traction but she couldn't wear her normal shoes because, like every other part of her, her feet had taken to retaining water. She struggled and crested the hill, but only after an embarrassing amount of exertion. Flushed, Victoria hunched, panting for breath. Damn her changing body, her screwed-up balance, and her fat feet.

Victoria glanced back. Amazing, Logan had stayed put. He stood on the other side of the highway, watching her, and she suspected, laughing his ass off.

A raven's *craa* caught her attention. She tilted her head back, gazing up at the big black bird perched above her on the branch of a pine tree. Its shiny black eyes gleamed and it croaked a harsh gurgle.

"Cut me some slack. I'm doing my best."

Odin's pet gargled in scratchy counsel.

"I'm sorry, I don't understand—don't speak raven."

The bird's rude reply flew right over her head.

Heaving a sigh, Victoria returned her attention to the motel property. She stood on the perimeter. A thick copse of trees separated her from the cabins but she could glimpse the buildings through the brush. Most likely, Sawyer would be watching from the cover of the tree line so to find him she just needed to—

A wolf's furious howl punctured the night. A shotgun blasted. Wings flapping furiously, the raven screamed as if to say, *"I tried to warn you!"*

A burst of excitement seized Victoria. Her heart labored from the rush of adrenaline, catapulting her to battle readiness.

She and Sawyer shared a dual bond—wolf and hunter. The tattoo dagger on her arm glowed white hot, burning with its arcane magic. Too bad she had no idea what it meant. More familiar, the pack bond combusted, fueled by his anger and agony. Certainty without knowledge; Sawyer was in danger, under attack by that strange wolf who'd invaded her territory.

A savage shout formed in her throat. Her weariness of moments before was forgotten as she plunged through the copse of trees toward the combat. Victoria ran without seeing; her vision narrowed to a tunnel. Her wolf guided her steps, just as her instinct to protect her packmate governed her actions.

Behind her, Logan shouted her name. Ahead, the wolf and shotgun roared in unison. More gunfire—the steady, repetitious burst of a pistol. The voice of a second wolf, also an intruder, called out a challenge.

An unearthly growl, weightier and brassier than that of any wolf, resounded with rage. Victoria's blood froze. She'd never heard anything so visceral or so horrifying. She wasn't one hundred percent certain, but she though it came from a—

Bear?

A slick patch of pine needles sent Victoria skidding. She compensated, surfing the debris until she found traction in the rough dirt again. Normally, she would have changed to her wolf form but her advancing pregnancy made even partial shifts hazardous. Instead, she reached overhead, seeking the mystical dagger that hovered over her shoulder, always invisible until drawn. As soon as her hand closed on the silken hilt, *Vanadium* appeared in her hand. The weapon murmured in welcome, warmth rather than words.

As light as a feather, as swift as the wind, as bright as moonlight on water. The magical dagger was the product of Dwarven craftsmanship, a sword of prophecy said to be able to cut through anything and with good reason. Its blade was a piece of *Gleipnir*, the ribbon that bound the great wolf Fenrir, made from six impossible things. A gift from goddess to priestess, Victoria wielded the weapon the same as her mother and her grandmother, going back over many generations. Someday, Victoria would pass *Vanadium* on to her daughter. Someday, but not today. Today, she would use the dagger to kill.

Gripping the hilt, blade aimed toward the ground, she raced between two cabins toward the conflict. She meant to slow but misjudged the distance. She plunged into the open, straight into the thick of the fight. Bullets sprayed overhead. Sulfur and silver metastasized in the air, a toxic fog.

Combatants all around.

Not knowing friend from foe, Victoria dropped and slid

on her side. The bottom of her foot wedged on a rock and brought her to a halt. Panting hard, she rolled to a crouch and scanned her surroundings.

Cali Kinkaid and DNR, both armed with guns, stood with their backs against the side of a cabin. Two pony-sized creatures, as large as the average shifted werewolf, faced the hunters. Wolves in form, but *wrong* in substance—facsimiles of werewolves, but a different breed. The product of the foulest magic. Gray fur matted with mange, tattered with age. Flaps of skin, just bits and pieces, dangled from the underside and limbs, resembling an ill-fitted suit. They stank of grime and grease, and the note of mothballs. Even so, their claws were long and wicked, and their fangs sharp and fearsome.

Kinkaid fired her pistol—hit one in the head. The wolf staggered. Shouting, she unloaded her clip and advanced toward it, not a hint of hesitation or fear.

The second wolf leaped toward DNR. The young man jerked his weapon, tracking the moving target, but his shots missed. He threw up his arm. The wolf descended and bit the hunter, sinking its teeth into his forearm.

DNR's agonized shriek split the air.

Victoria started to the hunter's aid, but then pulled up. Now that she had her bearings, she sensed Sawyer's location to be in the opposite direction, on the other side of the cabins. The pack bond pulsated with the hunter's red-hot rage but also conveyed his pain. He'd been injured.

The bear rumbled again.

The attacking wolf ripped a chunk of flesh from DNR's arm. Blood sprayed. The hunter went down beneath his attacker. Her breath gusted from her lungs and she made the selfish decision—she chose Sawyer. She swiveled, reversed direction, and charged across the yard. As soon as she emerged from between the buildings, she came upon the scene.

Sawyer lay on his back, covered in blood and dirt, pine needles matted in his hair. Even messed up as he was, the maddening man aspired to a higher standard. The man made fucked-up-beyond-all-recognition look sexy as all hell. He gripped his shotgun against his chest, cradled like a lover. As grim as a reaper, he reloaded the weapon with steady hands.

A few feet away, an enormous grizzly reared on its hind legs. Gunshot wounds covered its body. Blood splattered like graffiti on its hide. Wrongness defined the bear, the same as the wolves. Scabrous brown fur, lumpy in the gut but loose in the thighs. It stank; a repugnant cologne of astringent chemicals and decay. Vile magic.

The bear would reach Sawyer before he finished reloading. Shouting to attract its attention, Victoria rushed at the grizzly. She closed from the side with the intention of distracting it until the hunter reloaded and recovered his feet.

The ruse worked. Still standing, the bear swung around and advanced toward her. It swayed with each step, the result of its injuries, comically resembling a drunken sailor in gait. Deliberately, she retreated but slowly, her voice lifted in challenge. She heckled the grizzly and lured it until her back came up against the side of a building and she could retreat no further.

The grizzly towered over her, and she fell into its shadow. Victoria grasped the dagger's hilt in both hands and held *Vanadium* out before her. The bear's boulder-sized paw rose skyward and hovered, eclipsing Victoria's view of the sky. Wicked claws glistened like the points on a maul, daggers coated in Sawyer's blood. Fat droplets fell from the tips and splattered her face.

The grizzly's arm dropped; certain death descending. Victoria braced and held steady. Her sword was her shield. The shimmering blade caught the bear's paw. *Vanadium* rippled and shimmied, a faint vibration traversed its length.

The bear bawled in agony. The severed paw struck her chest and a fountain of blood caught her full in the face. The hot fluid hit her open mouth. A wolf at her core, Victoria gulped and hungered for more. Blinded, she made an opportunistic snap for the bear's stump but her jaws closed on empty air.

She glimpsed motion in the corner of her eye—her only warning. The bear's remaining claw walloped her shoulder, long claws gouging severe lacerations. She got knocked off her feet and thrown through the air until the A-frame roof of a cabin stopped her flight. The impact knocked her senseless. Her world tumbled, head over heels. The ground rushed to greet her.

Blackness engulfed her.

She had no idea for how long she lost consciousness. Maybe seconds, maybe minutes. Her awareness of intense physical injury returned before her vision started to come back. Light and darkness; no color. Everything was smooth and round, lacking distinct lines and sharp corners. All edges resided within her—jagged discomfort and stabbing aches.

The blurry bulk of the grizzly lumbered over her. Thick huffs of musky breath pouring from wide nostrils, regular puffs as though produced from a laboring steam engine. It heaved toward her, and her wolf's survival instincts kicked in. An adrenaline surge jolted her back to cognizance.

Panicking, Victoria flexed her fingers but her hand was empty. When dropped, *Vanadium* vanished and returned to its astral sheath. She thrust her arm over her head, groping for the dagger's hilt. Her reflexes were beyond sluggish and she feared there was no way could she reach her weapon in time.

From out of nowhere, a gale-force furry comet descended from the sky. Fully wolfed out, Logan slammed into the bear, burying all four claws in its back. He snarled and sank his teeth into the thick throat. Yowling, the grizzly reared and twisted, attempting to reach the werewolf.

Rallying her wits, Victoria rolled onto her side, tucking her limbs to safeguard against getting trampled. Nausea slammed her. Bold, deafening in her head, hazing out coherent thought. Swimming queasiness in her stomach—retch in mouth seasickness. She longed to vomit but wasn't strong enough for even that.

Back on his feet, Sawyer fired point blank. A crimson blossom appeared dead center on the bear's chest. Squalling in agony, it stomped its huge feet and tilted, undertaking another abrupt change in direction. Logan rode the grizzly, zealously digging into his target with fang and claw. Chunks flew through the air, discarded clods of flesh and fur. Squalling in agony, the bear bucked and dropped, dislodging the wolf from his perch.

Molten silver seared her nostrils. Victoria gasped and coughed, struggling for air. Her eyes burned, tears splashing down her cheeks. She dug her fingers into the packed dirt, clawing for purchase. Self-recrimination ravaged her confidence. She *knew* better than to enter into combat while pregnant. The risk of severe injury, the threat to her life, but more importantly, her child's, was substantial. Peril she couldn't afford. The odds were good her presence presented more of a liability than an asset. Trouble was—always—that it went against her nature to stand aside while others put their lives in jeopardy.

The fight moved away from her—passage marked in

guttural resonance. Snarls and growls. Gunfire—the roar of the shotgun and then then crack of Sawyer's .45. An inane motion whizzed through her mind and she strangled on a giggle. How ironic was it that her intimacy with the hunter extended to identifying his guns by their voice?

With a heroic effort, Victoria got herself upright, kneeling in the dirt while the world performed crazy loop-d-loops. She hurt from head to toe. Queasiness unabated. Groaning, she settled on bent bare toes. She'd lost her sandals somewhere. She rapid-blinked her vision into focus. She grabbed for raw power, drawing from the wild magic of the land, and used it to boost her own regeneration.

On all fours, the infuriated bear barreled straight at Sawyer. It ran with a limping gait, favoring its injured limb. The enormous creature gathered slow but unstoppable momentum, bearing down on top of him. Unwavering, the hunter fired steadily and stood his ground. The grizzly rammed Sawyer and knocked him over. He smashed to the ground, flat on his back. The bear trampled him. A huge paw smashed his chest and Sawyer's limbs flailed. Wicked claws raked terrible gouges.

Sawyer's anguish screamed along the empathetic bond he shared with Victoria. A shout of rage and denial tore from her throat. She summoned power, healing magic. Brilliant light flowed from her palms, haloing her hands. Her first steps wobbled but she plowed onward, determined to reach him at any cost.

The bear's course had carried it far past Sawyer. It still faced away from them and its movements were ponderous. Prominent injuries littered its mangy hide. Blood puddled in its footprints.

Sawyer was as still as a corpse, mutilated beyond recognition. His throat was a meat mash. Her stomach somersaulted and she averted her gaze, unable to look at him. He still lived—she sensed his vitality within the dual bonds.

"Not again, buddy. I'm not resurrecting you again." Victoria fell toward Sawyer, dropping to her knees. She placed her hands on his chest over the severest wound, channeling raw healing magic into him. No finesse, only brute force.

The grizzly's rumble grabbed Victoria's attention. She looked up in time to witness its plodding turn as it swung toward her and Sawyer again. A fresh adrenaline spike reduced her to a quaking mass.

"Logan!" She howled his name—demand and appeal, expectation and need.

He answered in the primal call of the wild, the storm's thunderous boom, a protracted song proclaiming his supremacy and prowess. He promised protection and vowed the obliteration their enemy. Wolf song resounded with epic dominance—harkening to their ancient ancestor, a beast borne in legend, Loki's son, Fenrir. His cry resonated from somewhere above, resonating high and wide as though he were in flight.

The bear paused. Lifted its head skyward.

Excitement electrified Victoria. Her wolf ascended, overtaking her psyche. She threw back her head and joined her voice to Logan's, a triumphant ballad heralding him. Magic surged, flowing like a raging river. As Alpha, Victoria was the nexus—drawing energy from her pack, the land, and even the far-flung hunters who were connected to her through Jake Barrett. She stood before the flood, the dam and the gatekeeper. She channeled the primal verve, transformed and refined, and slammed it all into Sawyer.

Odin's son convulsed beneath her touch.

Great black claws seized the roof ridge of the cabin. The head and shoulders of a great black wolf appeared over the pinnacle of the steeply-sloped roofline. Amber eyes shone brilliant-bright. A gaping mouthful of fangs; thick ropes of saliva dripped from his jaws. The boney knob of his shoulder joint glistened, covered in slick red, at the center of a gaping wound. Fur and flesh missing.

Yodeling a challenge, the grizzly reared onto its hind legs and rose to a height equal to the roof. Logan snarled, his lip curling to reveal even more tooth and blood-red gums. Dagger-length talons tore into the slate, ripping out a shower of shingles. He leapt straight into the bear's one-armed embrace, splayed jaws going straight for its throat.

The pair toppled.

Trust was a capricious thing that Victoria had struggled with her entire life. She gave it cautiously, grudgingly, often in half-measures, and only after excessive soul-searching and deliberate, conscious choice. She doubted everyone: herself; her deceased parents; her goddess; her murdered lover; her lost mate. She even mistrusted the All Father himself.

Victoria looked away from the struggle between wolf and bear without a question in her mind that Logan would win. Confidence flowed, as did magic. Her gaze dropped to the man beneath her hands, appraising his injuries not only with the educated mind of a trained medical professional but also, the regard of a talented healer. She lost her connection with the physical world, and submersed herself in the hunter's faded life force. At a weird space in reality, the corporeal and the spiritual intersected.

Black slashes disrupted the passionate tones of Sawyer's aura, overlying the actual injuries on his chest. Sawyer had a gaping wound on his throat. Not just a cut; all soft flesh ripped out. More damage: lacerations and deep punctures, riddled his abdomen. Broken bones—multiple ribs, a shattered pelvis, and fractured femur. He wasn't breathing. His heart was an inert lump in his chest.

Dead.

Dead—no wonder the deluge of rejuvenating magic wasn't making any difference. Resurrecting a dead man exceeded her abilities. She knew because she'd tried before. She couldn't do it, not without divine assistance. The odds were nil to none that Freya would agree to help Sawyer. The goddess had already refused once before. All the energy she channeled into the hunter went to waste but even faced with that futility, Victoria couldn't accept defeat. She kept trying because denial raged in her heart.

The jerk couldn't be dead. He just couldn't. *Not again. Damn it.* She cared for him, an ambiguous affection that was unclear and undefined. Maybe as a friend or brother, but quite possibly he meant far more. They hadn't had enough time together for her to figure it out. But in her heart, she knew with certainty and conviction that she couldn't stand to lose him. He belonged to her and she refused to give up.

"Freya, please. Help me. Help him." Victoria turned to her goddess in prayer and as a priestess, opening herself to act as a divine channel. To her shock, she slammed headfirst into a wall.

Victoria, he doesn't require your help, Freya said in a severe tone.

"He doesn't?" She bent over the hunter, looking at him more closely. At last she identified that nagging inconsistency at the edge of her awareness—dead men didn't have living auras. Yet his flame burned bright; his spirit powerful and persistent.

He does not.

He's changed somehow, My Lady. I've never seen this before.

Oh, but you have. Look closer.

Obeying her goddess, Victoria stared deeper and gave the phenomenon serious consideration. Slow dawning realization came over her. Yeah, okay. She had seen this before. Jake Barrett, Sawyer's father, healed all wounds he sustained. Severe enough injuries knocked him down, but he always came back with a vengeance. Only a fatal blow to the heart could destroy him.

She used her hands to remove a clotted layer of blood and dirt from Sawyer's chest, scraping clean a patch of skin, and flicked the gore from her fingers. Exposed runes writhed just beneath the surface. Bold but blurred, the arcane symbols danced.

Her eyes rounded and her breath escaped on an awed gasp. Strangling on disbelief, she abandoned her healing spell because it wasn't necessary. Thanks to the runes, Sawyer would recover under his own magic. Blowing out, she rocked back and plunked onto her backside. She couldn't stand not to touch Sawyer, so she scooched over. Sitting cross-legged, she pulled his head into her lap and stroked his long hair.

In her roles as priestess and Valkyrie, Victoria had studied the ancient language of the gods. On paper, she knew the name and meaning of each rune, and understood its inherent power—in theory. Living magic, however, was an entirely different beast. Without struggle and sacrifice, the runes defied comprehension. When her gaze locked on a specific character and her mind reached for understanding, it altered and eluded her.

Freya addressed her again. *Victoria, you have begged me to give you a task. A penance that will allow you to demonstrate your fealty and win my pardon. I have chosen.*

"Yes?" Victoria jumped, too excited with the prospect of

redemption to consider the unfortunate timing. Whatever the reparation, she'd do it. No questions asked. No chore too big or small. She desired nothing more than to go back to the way things had once been between her and Freya.

This is your task—draw Vanadium.

"Vanadium?" Victoria raised her hand but then faltered.

Obey me. The command was flat and forceful.

Blind obedience—*this* was the will of her goddess. Grinding her teeth, Victoria smashed her doubts and reached overhead. She yanked her dagger from its astral sheath. The mystical weapon appeared in her hand, a shimmering ribbon, as light as air, swifter than the wind. Wooziness swept over her and the world spun.

"Now, what do you ask of me?"

Now, I command you. Look at him.

"I'm looking." Victoria said even though she wasn't sure what she was supposed to see—had she missed something related to the runes? Sawyer's head still rested in her lap. A mask of gore concealed the hunter's face.

This is the man who has lied and deceived you, Victoria. Sawyer Barrett is the hunter who murdered Jasper.

Disbelief rang through Victoria's hollow soul. It couldn't be true. Rejection fierce and feral. NO—caught in her throat. No, not Sawyer. Jasper had only been a child, a teenage boy, and his death had come close to so many others. The loss of him had dealt a wound to her heart because he was so young and bright. And the failure—the burden of guilt—*all hers.* He'd died while under Victoria's protection, murdered by a hunter who'd been anonymous.

Until now.

"I can't believe it." Hot tears dashed down her cheeks. Blood roared in her ears. She held up her free hand before her as though to stop whatever came next. The sensation of being taken against her will resonated throughout her being. She didn't want to go—dragged straight to hell. She struggled to wrap her head around the enormity of the revelation.

It's true. I have never lied to you Victoria. I never will. The goddess's anger swept through Victoria, a divine flame that scalded her soul. She whimpered, shuddering at the spiritual assault. Pain burst upon her in clusters, lancing along her nerve endings.

Deep down, in her gut, Victoria knew the truth. She couldn't stand to remain in contact with him anymore—would never be able to touch him again without wanting to kill him. She dumped Sawyer's head off her lap. Off balance, she tipped and thrust her arm back to save herself from falling over. She attempted to release her bone-crushing grip on *Vanadium's* hilt but her locked fingers refused to comply.

Freya pressed. *He must die.*

"Goddess, I can't—" Victoria uttered an automatic protest. Without being told, she understood the purpose of the weapon in her hand. Dreadful was the suspicion.

You can and you will. Freya went on without mercy. *Victoria, you swore on your soul. You swore by my name. Now that we have discovered Jasper's killer that Oath must be fulfilled.*

"I also gave my word to Jake Barrett that this matter was settled." To her own ears, she lacked conviction. In her gut, she *wanted* Sawyer dead. She hungered for vengeance—for blood—exactly what she couldn't have. "I foreswore revenge."

Jake, *the bastard*, had tricked her. But his deception was a matter for a different time and another conversation. She and he would have their reckoning, but not this day and not this way.

You have made promises which now come into conflict. You cannot honor both, so you must choose. As your goddess, I demand that you keep your promise to me. This is justice—Jasper's murderer should die by your hand. Cut out the hunter's heart, Victoria.

"This isn't justice. It's revenge." Victoria could no more harm Sawyer than any other member of her pack who was helpless before her. She thirsted for blood but her overriding instincts were those of a protector.

Then it's revenge. Call it what you will. Sacrifice him—to me and in my name. Then, all will be forgiven. We will be as we once were—priestess and goddess.

"No." Victoria howled in defiance. Red, the deepest shade, hazed her vision.

So be it. You are my priestess no longer. I sever with thee. I take back all I have gifted thee. Upon the proclamation of the decree, Freya cut the spiritual ties that bound them. Simultaneously, *Vanadium* vanished from Victoria's hand— torn from her soul.

Bright agony ripped through Victoria's overworked vocal chords. She screamed, but no sound emerged. Her lungs ached—empty of air. She hoped, she prayed, the torment would end, but it went on forever. She collapsed onto her back, staring up at the screaming sky. A twisting, horrible pain in Victoria's gut—and a piteous wail formed in her mind. The sound of a child sobbing—her baby. A hundredfold more distressing than any torture. She found fury and fear, a fresh infusion of strength to bolster her fading will.

High overhead, furious motion blacked out the moon. Ravens. Their raucous cries were a furious chorus. The thousand—*million?*—avian forms converged into a whirlwind, an enormous tornado that danced against the stars. The raven twister descended and touched down, forming a giant man made of sleek feathers and bristled wings. His single eye and mouth glowed molten steel. His voice boomed—thunder and lightning.

"**Stop.**"

"This is not your concern, Wodan."

"I'll summon The Hunt. I'll come after you, Freya."

The assault ceased.

Victoria collapsed into a boneless heap. She fell for a long time, weightless, free. When blackness caught her, it was a blessing.

CHAPTER SEVENTEEN

Sessrúmnir, Freya's hall in Fólkvangr

Vanadium glowed orange and red, a narrow and intense aura that was close about the blade. Normally, the enchanted blade emanated a cool silver or warm gold, a radiance that lit the entire room with spectacular ribbons of blue and green that danced like the northern lights. The weapon vibrated with furious energy.

Freya turned toward Loki, venomous loathing in her gaze as though she'd like nothing better than to split him in two from the top of his head to his groin. Hidden in the thick foliage, Tregul rumbled his agitation, and then Bygul echoed her mate's sentiment. Leaves shook on their branches, but neither of the great cats emerged from cover.

The God of Lies took a swift step off the edge of the paved patio into a clump of ferns. He disliked putting his back to where both of the tigers lurked but he judged the irate goddess to be a greater threat. The magical charms he'd used on Tregul and Bygul should protect him from attack, but with cats—such fickle creatures—it was always a gamble.

"You're a monster!"

"Am I?" He clicked his tongue. A monster? Yes, he supposed he was. Loki belonged to a long and fearsome bloodline of unnatural beings and had sired more than his fair share. Always, the matter came down to a simple question—what sort of monster did he want to be? Not whether he would be.

"Yes! Only a bastard would do what you did." Freya spoke with fervency but also the sort of slow-dawning realization that Loki expected of her. The goddess was the loveliest creature in creation, and also, one of the dumbest.

He cocked an arrogant brow. "Must I remind you that you agreed to our agenda before we undertook this joint venture? It's hardly fair to cast sole blame on me now."

"You coerced me to hurt the mother of your own child. You disgust me—" Freya frothed at him in an outpouring of rage. She swiped the bottom of her foot across the ground as though trying to wipe excretion from her soul.

"Me—Coerce you? I don't think so. Oh no, you chose every step of the way—for centuries. From the first time you conspired with me against Odin to this travesty." Loki didn't think she'd come clean so easily. He wouldn't either, but he wore gray armor. More grime on his black heart hardly mattered. Oh, he acknowledged his own evil but considered the means worth the end.

Victoria had endured short-term harm, but it was nothing compared to what she'd have faced if she'd remained aligned with Freya, the faithless whore. His tenacious little mate was resourceful and resilient, as she'd proven time and again. She'd come through this trial and be stronger for it in the end. With Freya off the field, the path to Odin was clear and wide open. Should Victoria ever learn of Arik's role in this farce, her hatred for Loki would intensify, but that too was for the best. He couldn't protect her from Jake. No one could but the old man himself.

"You're contemptible." Shudders shook Freya, so great the weapon in her hand vibrated. For a moment, she crossed over to her warrior-aspect, a towering personification of conflict. Grudging admiration filled Loki and he gathered himself, preparing to change shapes and flee should she attack. But then she succumbed to tears and her fierce facade crumbled.

"You tortured your own priestess, sweet goddess. I simply stood by and watched. Tell me, who's really more contemptible?" He shook his head.

Shoulders hunched, Freya sank to her knees on the glossy tile of the patio. She gripped the hilt of *Vanadium* without regard for the magical dagger's immense importance. Tears streamed down her cheeks, crystal clear and bright. The wench even cried artfully—not a hair out of place or a trickle of snot. Her vanity was freaking unbelievable.

Loki gnashed his teeth and fumed. Much more of this and— Damn, too late!

The male tiger growled, resounding through the catio. The thick ferns shook and mighty Tregul emerged from hiding. Bygul followed right behind her mate. Both felines headed straight for their mistress. Their golden gazes fell on the Trickster, considering whether he presented an imminent threat. He tensed but held their stares, unflinching in the face of their potential animosity, and trusted his charms would hold. When the great cats took to restless pacing, he exhaled in relief.

Freya sobbed, piteous in her distress.

Loki shook his head in silent disgust. Reaching into the pocket of his suit coat, he extracted a silk handkerchief. He bent and offered her the hankie. "Here, take this."

"I hate you!" She refused the hankie.

"I hate you too, but let's not make this personal." With a shrug, he returned the handkerchief to its proper place.

"Not personal!" She jerked so her hair flew over her shoulders. Her lips quivered and her chin shook. "This has been nothing but personal. Why? Why do you hate me so much?"

"You don't even remember, do you?" Loki stared at her long and hard, disgusted with her anew. He wondered whether she was so stupid the matter had slipped her mind. Or perhaps she believed him so callous and unfeeling that the persecution and slaughter that befell his family so long ago no longer mattered.

Whether a day or a century or a millennium passed—he'd never forget. Centuries past, following in the chaotic aftermath of Baldur's death, Thor and his followers had hunted Loki. Sigyn, Loki's human wife, and their two young sons, Nari and Vali, had sought sanctuary in Freya's hall. The goddess had sheltered them for a time, but when Thor arrived at her gates, she'd turned Loki's family out. His boys —murdered. Faithful Sigyn joined her husband in his punishment.

The temptation to remind Freya was enormous but Loki bit his tongue. No good could come of dredging up the distant past, no matter how painful. Besides, he'd be handing her ammunition to use against him. "Never mind. It has no bearing on what we did accomplish together today. What's important is you made the right choice."

"The right choice..." She sucked a deep, watery breath. "Is there such a thing?"

"Of course there is," Loki assured her in a smooth voice. "Our alliance, however brief, wasn't founded on camaraderie. It was a product of self-interest. Most importantly, we both want to survive Ragnarök. Regardless of what you think of me, this was for the best. You tested Victoria and she chose Odin over you."

Freya's lovely face twisted; her smile ugly. "It's Victoria's destiny to free Fenrir. Without this—" She hefted *Vanadium*, a clumsy swing that he evaded easily. "Your precious wolf son will never be free."

"Destiny?" Loki flicked his fingers, a dismissal. "Not a fan. I prefer to make my own and besides, it's that pretty little dagger you're holding that matters. Victoria was an implement of Fate. Someone else will take her place."

"Is that what you want me to do—find another priestess to give it to?" Freya asked, but the tautness in her tone suggested she'd do exactly the opposite of whatever he asked even if it harmed her long-term interests. Spitefulness ruled over reason.

Bygul passed within a few feet of Loki, pursuing a circular path that orbited her mistress. He reached, imploring fingers spread, and clicked his tongue. The cat's head swung toward him; her unblinking stare fixed while she considered his worth. He conjured magic and spun it into a twig of fresh catnip clutched between his fingers. Immediately, the tigress abandoned her reticence. She thrust her muzzle into his open hand. Her raspy tongue crossed his palm, snatching away the offering.

Loki stroked his hand along the slant of her nose and dragged his fingers through the luxurious fur, scratching behind her ears. From there it was easy-peasy. He extended his thoughts, connected with her contrary cat-brain, and implanted a suggestion—*Freya needs you. Go to her.*

The cat rumbled in agreement and approached from opposite her mate, so Freya was sandwiched between her pets. It placed the goddess in the difficult position of managing a deadly dangerous dagger in proximity to creatures she cherished.

"We've had our differences in the past, but I'm impressed with what you did to Victoria. Putting a pregnant woman to the press—that took backbone. Guts. I have to admit, I didn't think you had it in you, Freya. Obviously, you've changed. The way you handled it was *exactly* what I would have done." Loki forged reluctant admiration, tarnished with just enough resentment to attain believability. It wasn't difficult. Freya had followed his instructions almost to the letter so the lie wasn't even a real lie.

"I feel sick." Groaning, Freya pressed her face against Tregul's shoulder and sobbed.

"Chin up. The worst is over. You don't need to do anything with *Vanadium* yet. I'm sure once the heat of emotion fades and you have time to reflect, you'll reconsider our alliance. We have time to find an appropriate pawn to wield it. Until then, I suggest you hold onto that precious dagger. Keep it close. Just be careful—you almost shaved off poor Bygul's whiskers there."

"I don't want anything to do with this thing or you!" In a fit of temper, Freya cast *Vanadium* from her. The weapon landed on the tile a few feet away. "You made a promise— now keep it! Get out! I never want to see you again." She threw her arms around Tregul's neck and turned into the tiger's side, burying her face in his fur.

Ah, his prize! Excitement surged through Loki. He damn near released a cry of anticipation which he swallowed whole. As a veteran practitioner of the confidence game, he wouldn't risk tipping his hand. In a swift, smooth motion, he stooped and snatched up the discarded dagger.

Vanadium was nothing within his hand; an enormous burden on his soul. The moment he touched her, Loki sensed the weapon's profound disapproval. It possessed the sentience necessary to grasp his basic shifty character. Perhaps the weapon even understood the role he'd played in separating it from Victoria. Whatever the case, she made her displeasure known—the buzz of an angry hornet touched his mind.

It didn't matter. He only intended to keep *Vanadium* long enough to transport her to where she was needed most. So he stashed the dagger in a convenient fold in space, one of his many hidey-holes, and skipped into the form of a peregrine falcon. He shot straight up, passing from the patio to open sky, and soared high above the uppermost branches of Yggdrasil.

The top of the whole universe—overlooking the entirety of the Nine Worlds. The view was spectacular, but he continued on without enjoying the sight even though it was probably the last time he'd see it for a long time to come. Once Freya discovered she'd been tricked and *Vanadium* stolen, their bridges were burned.

He'd made an expensive gamble. If it didn't pay off, he was screwed.

CHAPTER EIGHTEEN

BROKEN BEND, CALIFORNIA ON U.S. ROUTE 50

Big hands grasped her shoulders and shook her. A big, goofy puppy with its ragdoll. "C'mon, Vic. Wake up. You've gotta wake up."

Her teeth clattered together with the force of the tremors, so hard her jaws ached. Her head pulsated. Bloated. Each throb threatened to burst her skull and spill her brains. Forcing her eyes open, Victoria made a blind grab and wound up clenching Logan's forearm in both hands. On an abstract level, she registered his full nudity but it hardly mattered. As a rule, shifters weren't self-conscious.

"Stop," she grated. "Stop shaking me or I swear you'll be sorry."

"Vic! You're alive." Logan breathed her name like a prayer. He flung his arms wide, hauled her off her feet, and squeezed the life out of her. The pressure about her abdomen was the last straw.

Twisting in his grasp, Victoria wedged her arms between them and shoved. He released her. The unexpected drop dealt the death blow to her traumatized stomach. She landed on her feet, executed a sharp turn, and lurched forward. She doubled over and spewed the contents of her stomach onto the ground. The taste was awful, and the stench even worse.

Logan, *damn him*, was right there holding her head. He supported her physically and via the pack bond, as solid as the Rock of Gibraltar. She stared straight down. Logan's bare feet edged her field of vision. He had nice feet—big but shapely, and covered in a smattering of light brown hair. Trim calves and muscular ankles. She blinked and focused on his toes. His nails needed trimming.

As soon as she mustered the strength, she turned away from the mess. Grimacing, she swiped her mouth across her forearm. She worked her jaws in disgust, unable to rid herself of the aftertaste.

"Here." Logan shoved a piece of unwrapped gum into her face. She bit it, snatching it whole from his fingers. Her molars pulverized the soft candy to its natural chewiness. Juices flowed with saliva, ridding her of the lingering bitterness of bile. She chewed fast and furious while he unwrapped and fed her a second piece and then a third. The intense mintiness helped soothe her nausea

"Thank you." She shoved the entire gob into the corner of her mouth to speak. She leaned against Logan, and rubbed her face against his chest to be rid of tears and snot. Poor guy would have to shower—but he had to do that anyway. She'd apologize later.

"You're welcome." Logan smiled with his voice, warmth and affection, and, she suspected, vast amusement at her expense. She nodded, banging her forehead against his chest, but he didn't follow through with the snarky remark she expected. Instead, he drawled in a nervous tone, "Um, Vic?"

"Yeah?" She had to let go soon, but Logan was big and

solid. An anchor and a shelter. She didn't want to release him because doing so meant facing the real world once again. His scent: conversant, citrusy, and comforting. He smelled like blood too, which made her hungry—an unwelcome need following so close behind her debilitating queasiness.

"Who's the scary birdman?"

She jerked away, so fast her poor swollen head throbbed in protest, but she ignored the pain. Twisting around, she scanned their surroundings. Her gaze skipped over Sawyer who lay where he'd fallen, still dead for all intents and purposes. She couldn't stand to look at him for too long, but based on what she understood of the runic magic, he should be back on his feet within the hour.

"There." Logan pointed, directing her gaze.

Odin's manifestation stood just beyond Sawyer, standing guard over his fallen son. He towered, sky high. The god's body was composed of living birds, glossy black ravens; the embodiment of unkindness. The flock swirled in constant flight, an avian tornado. Tapered wing edges like a thousand deadly blades. A single eye and mouth were fiery red, glowing molten against the darkness. On his crown, he wore a funnel of whirling birds that rose higher and wider to the doomsday flock overhead that blotted out the moon and stars.

It was eerily, deathly silent.

Victoria shook her head. Gods only knew how the mortal population of Sierra Pines would react to the carnage and devastation of the fight. Let alone the appearance of an actual god—who was too big and obvious to miss even from across the highway. And to think she'd worried about the stir caused by last February's Howl...

"Let him be. He's not someone you want to mess with." Victoria pushed away from Logan. Her instincts as a healer and a protector pushed to the fore. She walked toward Sawyer but then faltered, remembering...

"Huh. For once, I think I'll just do what you say."

"You're a smart boy." She patted his back, except her hand dropped low and she wound up spanking his backside. But only twice.

"Vic, does Ken need help? He looks deadish."

A broken laugh escaped her. "Deadish. Is that an official diagnosis?"

"Hey, I'm not the healer here."

"Sawyer's gonna be fine." She didn't dare spare the hunter a second glance or she'd be tempted to kill him...right in front of his father. Freya's revelation had rocked the foundation of her world. She couldn't afford to think about it too hard or for too long.

"Yeah... Not like I actually give a shit anyway." He drew a loud, deep breath through his nostrils. He moved his arm, waving around a torn piece of clothing. Wondering, she scowled at it for a long time before her tired mind supplied an answer—his jeans. For some reason, Logan was carrying around his ripped Levis. At least she didn't have to worry anymore about where he'd gotten the damn gum from.

"I'm sorry. Don't worry about Sawyer. He'll be fine." Which was more than she could say for herself. Victoria stepped back, glanced at Logan, and then performed a double take. "You look like shit."

Severe lacerations—lines in parallel—covered his chest and she guessed his back as well. A gaping wound in his shoulder ran deep, exposing the underlying bone. His arms and legs bore similar injuries—no wonder he smelled like blood. Yet despite it all, he was steady on his feet and propping her up. Instant guilt overcame her. The guy must be in agony. She was so used to Logan's accelerated healing that she hadn't considered his wellbeing.

"Can I heal you?" She reached for him with shaking hands. Her own strength hadn't recovered. She still had unhealed injuries, and was damn close to collapse.

"Nah, I'll be fine." He waved her off, ducking beyond reach.

"What happened to the bear? Did you kill it?" Victoria didn't have the strength to chase Logan, so she let it go. Let him live with the pain for a while. All things being equal, her money was on him to recover his full strength first.

"I think so, but I'm not sure." He jerked his head, indicating some distant point over his shoulder. "I eviscerated the bitch but she kept coming. Fucking unstoppable."

"It's still alive?" Victoria reared back in alarm.

"She stopped moving after I damn near ripped her head off but *fuck*—I've never seen anything like it before in my life."

"Where is it?"

"Over there." He pointed toward where one of the cabins had once been, but no more. A pile of wreckage stood in its place. The A-frame roof had collapsed inward. Two of the structural walls gone; the others propped upon underlying rubble. The stone chimney tipped at a steep angle from the building.

"Wow." Victoria widened her inspection of their surroundings. The hotel area looked like a disaster zone—fallen trees and debris everywhere. A telephone pole had fallen across the front lobby of the lodge. Every cabin within view showed some sign of damage.

Cali Kinkaid and DNR were nowhere to be seen. Neither were the wolves they'd been fighting. Victoria gave brief consideration to searching for them, but then discarded the notion. At the moment, she wasn't feeling predisposed toward helping the hunters at all. If they were in trouble —tough.

"This way." Logan marched off in the direction he'd indicated, leaving Victoria to trail him. He skirted Sawyer, going wide to avoid the god's watchful apparition.

Victoria hesitated and then took the other path that brought her close to Odin. Then, just to up the ante and make the choice truly foolish, she stopped before him. She tilted her head back, staring up into the visage of living ravens. Understatement to say the god had one hell of a poker face at the moment—his aspect was both implacable and terrifying. This wasn't Jake, who she'd come to love like her own father.

A hot gale blasted her shoulders as though the god had exhaled. A tremor shook her. She braced, employing pure gumption. "I kept my word to you," she said in a raw voice. The inside of her throat was dry and cut up as though she'd swallowed razors. "We agreed on a blood price and I swore not to seek revenge on the man who murdered Jasper..."

A raucous cacophony arose from the countless ravens and they were the god's voice. **"Blood price has not yet been paid."**

She hesitated, wanting to ask but not daring to make demands on the omnipotent All Father. Oh irony—the blood price they'd agreed to was the marriage of one of Jake's sons to an eligible she-wolf from the Storm Pack. During the peace negotiations with Jake, Victoria hadn't known the true identity of the teenager's killer. Obviously, the Hunter King had practiced purposeful deceit—he and his murderous son. She acknowledged their betrayal in the coldest, most clinical way because she hadn't had time to process the full implications yet. The two men she'd considered honorable and trustworthy—the allies she *needed* to defend her territory against outside invaders—had proven to be anything but.

Odin said nothing else, so Victoria continued on her way. She joined Logan at the wreckage of the ruined cabin. He stood in the middle of the mess, over an enormous furry heap that bore stronger resemblance to a pile of turd-brown shag carpeting than the grizzly they'd fought. It was rank with musk and decay.

"Where's the bear?" Victoria asked, trading a quizzical glance with Logan.

"This is it. Dunno what happened." He shook his head, equally baffled, and prodded the thing with his foot. The shapeless mass shifted, revealing dozens of holes in the hide. Belatedly, realization dawned and then revulsion struck her —it was a *bear skin.* Just like those wolf skins she'd found in the cabin...

The thing twitched and then jerked.

"Whoa!" Logan rocked back.

"Be careful!" Already on edge, Victoria jumped clean off her feet. Her leap carried her into Logan, so she used her momentum to knock him from harm's way.

Covering her mouth and nose with her hand, Victoria edged closer to obtain a better look. The abomination kept moving about. Blood matted fur thrust and tugged. Someone or something struggling to escape from within. The odor of wrongness—*wicked bad mojo*—was overwhelming. Nothing about it was natural. *Nothing right.* And yeah—there was a living thing under there moving around. It was visible through the slashes, although, Victoria couldn't make out any details.

Both Victoria and Logan bristled and circled, snarling at the thing, reacting as wolves even though they were fully human. In the moment, pack mentality overtook reason and any canine from a Chihuahua to a wolf would've possessed an innate understanding of their instinctive reaction.

The bear skin's head rotated and rose. Dull eyes made of dark glass. It shook in the grip of a severe convulsion and a terrible, gut-wrenching moan emanated from the thing under the skin.

Victoria quivered from her head to the tip of the tail she didn't currently have, and stole a glance at Logan. He was already midway through a full shift: ears pointed and high on his skull, jaws elongated into a muzzle, increased height and mass. Thick, glossy fur covered his body. His fangs—impressive enough to put the big, bad wolf to shame—and his claws the same. He was a healthy, *living* wolf shifter—a marked contrast to whatever the fuck this *thing* was.

"Enough is enough." She lunged and seized the edge of the grizzly hide. With all her strength, she yanked and cast it away. The bear skin flew aside, revealing—

A girl. Taller than Victoria, but then that was true of almost everyone. She had tangled brown hair—some strands plaited, the rest worn loose past her waist. She wore a headdress of sleek black feathers—raven or possibly crow. Her face was young and old beneath an intricate pattern of dark blue lines. She was nude except for the myriad tattoos that covered her entire body. Her figure was firm and full. Not a girl but a woman after all

The woman reeked of bad magic—an unmistakable scent marker that was branded permanently into Victoria's memory. Their enemy was *seiðr*, a Norse witch. According to Sylvie, who loved nothing more than to retell the ancient sagas, the wicked breed hailed from the mystical Iron Woods.

"Well, this is unexpected." Logan edged closer, extending his clawed hand as though to poke at the woman.

"Don't. She's a witch." Victoria snarled in warning. They still had no idea as to the woman's capabilities beyond her ability to change shapes by donning an animal skin. Alarmingly, they didn't know anything about the witch or her people at all. But Victoria intended to rectify that dearth of knowledge—no matter what the cost.

"Witches. I hate witches. Have I ever told you how much I *despise* witches?" Logan pulled back. His grumbling was two degrees shy of a hearty growl.

"No, but I might've guessed." Despite everything, Victoria smiled and then snarled. "*Seiðr*, face me."

"Do you know me, wolf?" The witch swayed on her feet. She staggered but managed to execute a half turn toward Victoria. A silver amulet glinted at the base of her throat. It cast a powerful magical aura so potent the enchantment punctured the veil between the spiritual and physical planes.

Victoria's gaze locked on the brightness. Acting on instinct, she lunged straight at the woman's throat, grabbed hold of the amulet, and yanked as hard as she could. The silver burned her palm and fingers—agony.

The *seiðr's* scream rent the night. She clawed at the Victoria's face, but Logan captured the witch's forearms and restrained her. Even so, his prisoner writhed and shrieked like a banshee, fighting to keep her amulet.

In Victoria's grasp, the rawhide cord grew taut but didn't break. The toxic metal corroded her flesh, and the stench of seared meat flooded the air. Gritting her teeth, she gathered her strength and hauled back with all her might.

The twine snapped; the amulet was hers.

"Give it to me! Give me back the key!" The witch shrieked.

"Tough luck. It's mine now." Seething in pain, Victoria forced her fingers open and ducked her head, squinting to study her prize. The pure silver talisman rested in the cup of her hand, atop blood and blistered flesh. The basic shape was a cross but it wasn't Christian. It was Thor's hammer, Mjölnir, but a variant from the standard form. A wolf's head formed the bail where the piece had attached to the cord. It didn't look like a key but then she had no idea what the lock was supposed to look like—if the witch's raving could be trusted to make sense at all.

"What is it?" Logan asked once the witch's furious struggles subsided.

"It's called a wolf's cross."

"Looks Norse."

"It is."

"Is that what made the bear so damn hard to kill?"

"Might be."

"It doesn't look like a key."

"No, it doesn't."

"My, aren't you a fount of information."

"Sorry." She shrugged. "Wolf's crosses are uncommon but not unheard of." She purposefully left out a relevant detail she preferred not to share with Logan. The wolf's cross was a symbol sometimes worn by Odin's followers—sometimes but not always.

Dread in her gut, Victoria cast a sharp glance toward the silent god. Unflinchingly, enigmatic in his manifestation, Odin stared back at her.

She looked away.

"It's silver. You can't use it but I can," said Logan, who was immune to the metal's toxic effects. "Can I have it?"

"No. It's too dangerous." Victoria desired nothing more than to cast the enchanted amulet away, but doing so would've been too reckless. But her pain threshold had hit its limits so she shoved it into her back pocket. The cotton lining was thin but hopefully it'd insulate her skin from the silver until she managed to find something thicker.

"I hate it when you talk to me like I'm in preschool," Logan complained, maintaining his grip on the witch.

"Then learn to respect what you don't understand." Victoria fisted her hand. Blood seeped from her fist and dripped to the ground, but she was already healing. Unfortunately, silver injuries took much longer than other kinds.

Logan grumbled beneath his breath. If he hadn't been stuck holding the witch, he'd have talked with his hands. She could tell.

Victoria addressed the woman. "What's your name?'

The witch hesitated.

"Talk or I'll snap your skinny neck." Logan jostled the prisoner, who hissed.

"Magdalena." The *seiðr's* voice had unlikely sweetness, and an Old World accent that Victoria couldn't place.

"Magdalena." Victoria tried out the name, twisting her mouth around the foreign syllables. "Okay, Magdalena, do you know who I am?"

"You are a werewolf." Magdalena narrowed her eyes and pursed her lips.

"I'm Victoria Storm, Alpha of the Storm Pack, and the fella behind you is Logan."

"Pleasure, ma'am." Behind the witch, Logan sneered.

"Your names mean nothing to me," Magdalena said coldly. "But I can see from the look on your face, you think they should."

"We helped kill your sister. Last February." Victoria

reached overhead for *Vanadium.* Her hand closed on empty air—*gone.* Cold shock slammed her.

"I don't have a sister."

"No? Her name was Hrafnar." Logan lifted the witch off her feet and shook her.

"Ah, I knew of Hrafnar, but she was no sister of mine." Magdalena twisted to stare over her shoulder at the male wolf. "You, wolf, would make a powerful skin."

Logan roared full in the witch's face.

When Magdalena looked back, a sinister smile twisted her mouth. "Victoria Storm, you and I are sisters in spirit even though I must wear the skin of a wolf to become one."

"I am nothing like you!" Victoria lost her grip, surrendering to anger.

Magdalena frowned. "Ah, but we are. You're willfully blind if you can't see it."

Victoria pulled up short, and took stock of what she'd learned. While they stood there, Logan fidgeted and the witch twisted and turned as much as his grasp permitted. When the *seiðr* found the man made of ravens, an ecstatic fascination lit her face—eerie but also beatific.

"So you can become a wolf when you wear a wolf skin and a bear when you wear a bear skin," Victoria said, seeking confirmation. To her amazement, she sounded calm to her own ears. A miracle considering the anger bottled up within her.

"Yes," Magdalena said in a breathy voice. She gave her answers in a distracted fashion because her attention never strayed from the silent god.

"Any animal? What about a seal?" Logan craned his neck to follow the witch's gaze.

"Only animals that belong to Odin," Magdalena said.

Logan snapped back to Victoria—the lightbulb of

epiphany over his head. Uh-oh. She stifled a groan because she could tell—

"Is that Odin?" Logan mouthed, pointing toward the birdman.

"Yes." Victoria mouthed in return. Dreading the worst, she braced.

"Crap on a cracker." His jaw hung and he stared.

Victoria waited but no Logan-esque explosion arose. Well, that had gone down better than expected. The witch remained in a fascinated thrall, so Victoria formulated a hasty plan to exploit that weakness.

"Magdalena, tell me why you invaded my territory and attacked my pack without provocation," Victoria infused her voice with magic to make the command compulsory. Normally, strong-minded people proved resistant to the persuasion, but the preoccupied witch didn't have her head in the game. Maybe the Alpha's trick would work.

"We came hunting wolves for their skins. We didn't expect to find Loki's children here," Magdalena said. "We didn't attack your pack. You attacked us when we returned from the hunt. We were all tired. The men with the guns ambushed us."

"What about the man you murdered in Desolation Wilderness? His name was Kevin Danbury. Did he ambush you too?" Victoria had to confirm the truth about the biologist's death one way or the other. She no longer worried about discovering the killers had been Sawyer and the other hunters.

"He interfered in our hunt. His death was unfortunate but justified."

Victoria bobbed her head. She found no satisfaction in the truth—only resignation and acknowledgement. Logan leveled an unhappy look her way, but he appeared to accept the witch's confession.

"Who the fuck are you?" Logan asked.

Annoyance penetrated the woman's reverie. She jerked, turning toward Logan. "My name is Magdalena. I've already told you that."

"He means," Victoria said thinly. "What do your people call themselves? Does your order have a name?"

"Ahh. Yes. Long ago, we were known as the *berserkir*—wearers of bear-shirts. And the *úlfheðnar*—wearers of wolf-hides..." She lifted her eyes and addressed the heavens. "Now we simply call ourselves *Den Valgte*—The Chosen."

"The Chosen..." Victoria repeated. The sour words curdled in her mouth.

"Well, aren't y'all special," Logan drawled.

"Odin's Chosen." Magdalena's smile remained blissfully oblivious to Logan's corrosive sarcasm. "We all serve Him as children do their father."

A hush fell. Victoria stared at the woman in absolute affront, afraid to speak for what she might say. Through their empathic connection, she sensed Logan's deep and abiding anger. To hear this horrid woman describe herself as a daughter of Odin was an outrage. She waited and kept waiting for the god to speak up in denial or condemnation.

Odin remained stoic.

Victoria opened her mouth to speak, though she had no idea what to say. From her heated perspective, violence presented itself as a perfectly acceptable option. To start, ripping the woman's head from her shoulders appealed... A white-hot, achingly familiar presence joined Victoria and Logan in the pack bond, and then they were three.

Distracted, Victoria faltered.

The witch beat her to the punch—the verbal one anyway.

"It is why I said we are alike. You are *dís ulfhuguð*—a wolf-hearted woman. Like me, you are also a daughter of Odin—"

"You're no daughter of Odin." An avenging angel, Sawyer stepped into the awful silence. He offered the exact words Victoria had longed to hear—but from the wrong man. The hunter held his .45 aimed at Magdalena's head, but the weapon was pointed also at Logan, who happened to be standing directly behind the witch.

"Don't aim that fucking thing at me!" Logan shoved the witch toward Sawyer and released her. He dove for cover.

Magdalena staggered forward, and flung her arms wide. She shouted, indecipherable words, incanting a spell. Lightning danced about her splayed fingers. The sharp points of quills punctured her skin, growing from within, and cast a ruby spray. The witch shrank and sprouted ebony plumage all over her body. In a wink, she transformed into a raven.

Sawyer adjusted his aim to target the raven-witch. The gun spoke—fire and boom. Lightning arced across the heavens and thunder rolled. Screeching birds in countless number rode on the storm.

The shot missed.

CHAPTER NINETEEN

*BROKEN BEND, CALIFORNIA ON **U.S. ROUTE 50***

The raven-witch rose into the air on beating wings.

"Son of a bitch." Arm extended, Sawyer tilted back his head to track the fleeing bird. The hunter had a steady arm and rock solid stance, but his target was small and swift. Another hundred feet and Magdalena would reach the flock and be lost—another distant dot amongst the thousands.

Movement caught the corner of Victoria's eye—a swift, black blur. A great black wolf, Logan leapt and soared in a high, wide arc. The wolf's trajectory carried him straight toward Magdalena—and brought him into the hunter's line of fire.

"Logan!" Acting on reflex, Victoria lunged toward Sawyer and latched onto his elbow, jerking his arm to the side. The handgun went off, firing a wide shot that missed by a mile. The gunshot boomed and set the entire unkindness to croaking out a storm of protest.

In unison, Victoria and Sawyer craned their necks, straining to see—

Logan's gaping jaws closed, snatching the raven-witch from flight. The sound crunched like a hundred chicken bones snapping. Empty space remained where the bird had flown except for a fistful of stray feathers that drifted on the current.

The black wolf dropped out of the sky—body arched in the middle and legs spread, rather like a cat. He landed on all fours. With a lithe twist, he turned toward them. A row of primary feathers from the raven's wing bristled from the side of his mouth, the gruesome remains of the witch.

"Ugh." Victoria's stomach turned over, and she probably would've puked except there was nothing left. Persistent nausea had its claws in her, and it didn't seem like she'd feel better any time soon.

"At least he didn't swallow." Grimacing, Sawyer returned his firearm to its shoulder holster. He turned to her, covered in grunge from head to toe, but amazingly, miraculously whole in spite of having been mauled to death by a bear.

"Um, yeah," she said in what officially qualified as the most inarticulate response of her life. She deliberately kept her face slanted away from the hunter. She couldn't stand to look at him.

Head high, Logan pranced up to Victoria. His ears formed erect peaks atop his head and his tail lashed side to side with lupine pride. He halted before her and opened his mouth. The lifeless bird body landed on top of her bare foot with a wet splat. The feathers were soaked with blood and wolf slobber.

"Ew, gross." Victoria's mouth contorted in disgust. She kicked the corpse away and shook her foot a couple more times for good measure, attempting to shed the thick, sticky liquid.

A mournful moan escaped Logan. His ears flattened and

his tail drooped. Those beautiful amber eyes beseeched her. Heavens help her—guilt assailed her. He'd gone from being so damn proud of himself to looking deflated. Poor guy. She heaved a heavy sigh and edged around the mutilated raven to pat the black wolf on the head. "It's a lovely gift. Thank you."

Logan perked up. His tail resumed energetic thumping. He thrust his muzzle into her hand, rubbing his wet, warm nose against her palm. A few feet away, Sawyer muttered a disgusted-sounding phrase beneath his breath. He moved off toward where she thought the manifestation of Odin watched and waited. Her gaze flickered in that direction, confirming—

Yep, the big scary birdman was still there. Sawyer conversed with his father in a low voice—his words lost within the rasping of the ravens. Apprehension ate at Victoria's insides. Oh, yeah, this was bad. Gods, especially *him,* didn't just drop by. No, Odin's presence was a bad omen.

She turned away, choosing to ignore Sawyer; the only option open to her. Everything felt surrealistic, as though she were trapped in a nightmare. Absolute exhaustion worsened her warped perception of reality. If she confronted Sawyer, rage and hatred would overwhelm her. Fervor was a luxury she couldn't afford. She had to conserve her strength and the best way to do so was to pretend nothing was wrong.

Tunnel vision narrowed her perception of the world which kept rotating faster than it should. She hurt from head to toe; every single part of her ached. Weakness threatened to knock her knees out from under her. Seeking support, Victoria stuck her hand out and found smooth, cool metal. A glance revealed it to be the ruined cabin's refrigerator which lay on its side. Bowing her head, she leaned against it and reached for her connection with the land. A wave of energy flowed at her summons. The recharge didn't put her back at one hundred percent, probably not even to fifty percent, but it helped. The dull roaring in her ears faded.

"Are you okay?" Logan's big hand dropped onto her shoulder.

"Yeah, I'm fine." She blinked and her regard zoomed in on a solid six-pack of abs and a pronounced ribcage. Too lean—he needed to eat more.

"You don't look okay, Vic. You're pale. Is the baby all right?"

"I'm—" She looked down at herself, taking stock. Her clothing was torn and covered in dirt and drying blood, but otherwise intact. She had a few cuts and bruises but nothing she couldn't heal. When Freya's assault had ceased, her awareness of her child's distress also faded. No, aside from the fact that she was emotionally and spiritually broken, she was just peachy.

"Maybe you should sit down."

"Logan?" She tilted her head and stared into his face.

"Yeah?"

"Go find some pants. You must have a change of clothes in the car."

The corners of his mouth bowed unhappily. "Yeah. I'll do that. Back in a sec."

Logan walked off, relieving her temporarily of the burden of his concern. She acknowledged she was a bitch for resenting Logan's well-meaning consideration. *Fuck.* She was lucky to have him, especially since she couldn't count on Sawyer or his father for the pack's protection. It occurred to her she'd better get her attitude on straight or she risked losing Logan too.

"You okay?" Sawyer asked, edging nearer.

"Yeah, I'm fine." Victoria backed off like he had the plague. At her withdrawal, a fleeting glimmer of hurt and confusion crossed his handsome face. She broke out in a cold sweat for fear he'd press her.

Determined to create distance, she stabbed her finger toward the towering figure of the vigilant god. "Why is your father still here?"

He frowned. "Dunno—he's being oblique."

"How so?"

"I asked and he said—"

"Hey! I need help! Over here!" a woman called out.

Victoria turned toward the direction of the female voice. Cali Kinkaid stood amidst the wreckage of another ruined cabin. She was upright but swaying on her feet and had a nasty gash over her eye. She held her forearm cradled against her stomach.

"Cali! Hold on, I'm coming!" Sawyer charged straight toward his fellow hunter.

Hesitating, Victoria held back. She was torn; disinclined to help the hunters at all, given the recent revelation. However, her resentment didn't hold up long against her conscience. Regardless of Sawyer's iniquities, Cali had always been decent toward the Storm Pack, as had DNR. Taking out her anger on them wouldn't be fair.

Unsteady on her feet, Victoria picked her way through the rubble. Sawyer reached Cali, got a supporting arm around her, and guided her toward Victoria. Their paths intersected in front of what appeared to be the sole standing cabin which was inexplicably intact.

"Her arm is broken and she's sustained a pretty good blow to the head. She might have a concussion," Sawyer said to Victoria. "Can you help her?"

"Maybe. I'm drained pretty bad right now. Have her sit down." Victoria focused on the female hunter so she didn't have to look at Sawyer.

"It's nothing. Hell, I've gotten hurt worse playing lacrosse. Damn it, DNR—" Cali jostled Sawyer, attempting to shake off his help, but she only succeeded in wrenching her arm. She winced and groaned, and her brief struggle ceased.

"Knock that shit off, Kinkaid. That's an order." Sawyer lowered Cali to the ground and positioned her with her back against a tree trunk.

"Go check on DNR. Fuck. Damn it. I'm sure the stupid kid is dead, but there might still be a chance—" Choking on a sob, Cali drew her knees against her chest and rested her injured arm across her thighs. Her posture was tense but not enough to stop her entire body from shaking.

"I'll do that." Sawyer bounded off without waiting for acknowledgement.

Feebleness wasn't a quality Victoria associated with the female hunter who had an attitude ten times bigger than her body. It drove home the startling realization that Cali was only a few inches taller than Victoria. Equating frailty with helplessness would've been pure foolishness.

"May I see?" Victoria knelt before the hunter and extended her hands. She stopped shy of touching the other woman—asking tacit permission.

Victoria's conscience kicked her, and she could only think about how she'd turned away from the pair of hunters instead of going to their aid. DNR might still be alive if she'd chosen them. The bitter irony was that her presence at Sawyer's side made not one iota of difference to the final outcome.

"No, I don't think so." Cali regarded Victoria with hardened suspicion. "Not yet."

Victoria nodded. "Okay. Your call. Want to tell me what happened while you're deciding?"

"We got attacked by two of those drifters we were staking

out. Winds up they were werewolves. They must've caught wind 'cause they got the drop on us." Perspiration dotted the other woman's brow. Sweat dripped into the gash on her forehead, mingled with the blood, and then ran into her eye. It had to sting. She squinted and hissed, rubbing at it with the back of her good hand.

"They weren't from my pack," Victoria said in an even voice. "They weren't even real wolf shifters. Their shape changing abilities were stolen."

"Yeah." Cali's agreement sounded more like an acknowledgement. She paused, considering, and then said, "Ugliest fucking wolves I've ever seen. Their fur was mangy. They smelled rank."

Still, she held herself apart from Victoria.

"Were they hard to kill?" Victoria asked, because she had to wonder whether all the members of *Den Valgte* were as tough as the grizzly. Killing Magdalena had taken her, Sawyer, and Logan—even then it'd been close.

"*Oh hell yes.*" Cali huffed but the sound morphed into a groan. "Me 'n DNR—we filled 'em full of lead. He went down and I reloaded with silver ammo. It didn't make a bit of difference—didn't even slow them down."

"How'd you survive?"

"A big black wolf came out of nowhere. Second I saw him, I thought—for sure we were dead. But the black one lit into the one attacking DNR and ripped him a new one. The fight distracted the wolf after me. Gave me a chance to get away."

"That would be Logan. He's a member of my pack." Victoria composed a quick silent prayer of thanks but then stumbled over a mental block. Tears burned her eyes, and she slid sideways into despondence. She didn't know who to pray to anymore.

"Logan. He's that jackass from this morning?" Cali demanded with obvious skepticism.

Victoria mustered a weak smile. With the way her insides were swimming, she was pretty sure her mouth formed a comical wave. "Yeah. That jackass from this morning. I know it's hard to believe but he's a good guy. He just sucks at introductions."

Face blank, Kinkaid stared. Then, wheezing laughter broke over her. She groaned and struggled, tears on her cheeks. "Sucks at introductions—fuck, that's rich." She waved her good hand. "Okay, yeah. Help me, please."

She raised her open hand, held it level with Cali's forehead. From her training as an RN, Victoria gave the head injury priority even though the broken arm hurt more. A traumatic brain injury could cause death. With a frown, she concentrated on weaving the wild magic of Desolation Wilderness into a restorative spell. It was hard and required immense effort. More difficult than it'd ever been for her, except maybe years ago when she'd first begun studying to become a healer. She hoped it was due to her exhaustion, but feared her severed connection with Freya was to blame.

A faint glow emanated from her palm. Radiant beams bathed Cali's forehead. Slow but sure, the wound closed. When Victoria extended her perception, she detected swelling inside of the other woman's skull which was putting pressure on her brain. "Sawyer was right about you having a concussion."

"Don't tell him. He's already insufferable." Kinkaid grimaced and shifted.

"I won't. Promise."

"Can you fix it?"

"Yes, but I'm not sure about your arm. I'm tapped out already."

"Whatever you can do is fine. I appreciate it." Cali clipped her words, conveying the distinct impression of someone at odds with expressing gratitude.

Victoria mustered a thin smile. She lacked the wherewithal for conversation and magic so she fell silent and concentrated on healing the hunter's head wound. Life went on in the periphery of her awareness. Logan returned, wearing a white t-shirt that proclaimed him "Hot & Tasty" and black leather pants. Somehow, she missed Sawyer's approach. Whether he came before Logan or after, she didn't know. What mattered was the two men were standing around—not trying to kill each other.

"Your head is as good as new."

"Thanks. That's cool," Cali said.

"I'm afraid you're going to have to visit the ER for that break." Victoria ended the healing spell and allowed her arm to fall.

"Sawyer can take me." The female hunter struggled to her feet.

"Always happy to serve as your chauffer, Kinkaid." Sawyer took Cali's good elbow, lending her support until she steadied, and then he released her.

Victoria stood as well and surveyed her surroundings. She hoped to find Odin's ominous presence gone now that she'd healed Cali. With any luck, he would be appeased and finally leave. But no—

The towering figure of Odin kept his vigil. The whirlwind of living ravens rose above him until it merged with the enormous kindness overhead. The flock blacked out the moon and the stars and yet it was hauntingly, unnaturally quiet.

A bad omen for sure.

CHAPTER TWENTY

A hundred feet away, brightness flashed as Bifröst opened a magical portal. The shimmering pathway connected Asgard with Midgard, the world of humanity, and also with the underworld where it opened at the base of Yggdrasil. The rainbow bridge burned with all the colors of fire.

"What the fuck? What is that?" Cali's voice rang with awe.

Victoria opened her mouth to reply but Logan beat her to the punch. He said, "That's Bifröst." And he mispronounced it "by-frost".

"*Bivrost*," Victoria corrected him sharply. Normally, she'd have let it pass but Odin's presence had her wound tight. She *hated* the persistent feeling of being out of control. Her suppressed resentment toward Sawyer percolated on a back burner in her mind to the point she was scared to even speak to him. She daren't say something to him in front of witnesses, especially Logan who was already spoiling for fight.

"Beef-roast," Logan enunciated, incorrectly and beyond a shadow of a doubt, on purpose.

"Oh hey, Valkyries!" Sawyer sounded just like a kid at the zoo seeing lions and tigers for the first time ever.

Victoria didn't even want to acknowledge Sawyer to the extent of even looking, but she had no choice. The situation demanded her attention. The bridge disgorged the figures of six warrior women—all athletic, and carrying weapons that dated to ancient times when spears or swords and shields had been preferred. Firearms weren't forbidden or even unheard of in Asgard's armies, but they were rare.

"Really—Valkyries?" Logan bounced on the balls of his feet. "Cool. I've never seen a real Valkyrie before—*oomph*."

"I'm a Valkyrie." Victoria removed her elbow from Logan's side.

"Oh, yeah. I forgot." Logan's wheezed snicker hinted the opposite.

"Shhh..." Victoria stole another pensive glance at the taciturn god. Abruptly, his reasons for lingering were made painfully clear to her. Oh yeah, the shit had just hit the fan.

Ráðgríðr, the High Valkyrie in charge of all others, headed the procession. The ebony-haired woman stood taller than any other woman in her command, and topped most men. During her apprenticeship, Victoria had heard much speculation about the woman's usual stature. Rumors placed her heritage as a giantess or half-breed. Given her heavy bone structure, giant blood made more sense than elven. She lacked the comely appearance that was the norm among the Fae. Her features were severe and intimidating. A sharp, beaked nose and pointed chin combined with her curved neck to grant her a looming vulture-like presence.

Victoria counted and acknowledged in turn each of the five women who accompanied Ráðgríðr. Hervör Alvitr and her sister, Hlaðguðr Svanhvít, composed the High Valkyrie's personal guard. Beautiful Rota whose name meant *sleet and storm*; she was infamous for her hot temper. Thrud, who was the daughter of Thor and his wife, Sif, was envied by many for her deific heritage. Hildr, the youngest and prettiest, but also the least experienced, had curly flame-red hair.

The procession went straight to Odin first, offering their respect and reverence. Their regards went unacknowledged. The watchful god remained stoic, and Victoria found herself wondering if she was mistaken in her assumption that he was even paying attention at all.

Impatience got the better of Logan. "Okay, so they're Valkyries—so are you. Big whoop-de-do. What's that mean?"

"Valkyries choose the souls of the slain—who goes to Valhalla—" She stumbled and frowned in confusion. "You've been to Valhalla. Why is this news to you?"

"The redhead is hot." Logan averted his gaze, staring at Hildr.

"Are you always such a dick?" Cali asked of him.

He snickered. "No, but when I am, I'm a big dick..."

"Asshole." Cali punched him in the arm.

Logan covered the point of impact with his hand. He flashed a wolf's smile. "Shit, owie... You hit like a not-girl, Kinkaid."

While the pair continued to banter, Sawyer edged closer to Victoria. He nudged her shoulder with his elbow. "Any idea why they're here?"

"No clue, but I'm going to find out." Victoria jerked away from him, tucking her arm against her side. She swallowed around a lump in her throat. A leaden weight parked itself in her gut. Dread spread. She had not a clue why Ráðgríðr and her escort were present, but Odin's manifestation no longer struck her as quite so inexplicable. The All Father must have come to preside over whatever was about to happen.

Taking a deep breath, Victoria squared her shoulders. Determination drove her steps. She approached the entourage and addressed their leader. "Welcome, Lady Ráðgríðr."

Ráðgríðr tipped her chin in the barest nod. "Victoria. I'm pleased to see you're still here. We won't have to track you down."

Victoria stiffened as though overcome with rigor mortis. She noted Ráðgríðr's failure to cite her title. When properly addressed, "Valkyrie" or "Lady" should precede her name. With any other, she would've suspected the omission to be no more than an oversight. But not Ráðgríðr, oh no, not the haughty High Valkyrie.

"Track me down?" Victoria passed perplexed to pissed off in one-second flat. Her jaws clenched so hard she feared her teeth would break. She blunted her tone so it was devoid of all courtesy. "Why you here, Ráðgríðr?"

Ráðgríðr looked down her long nose. Her pencil thin eyebrows arched. "We are here to choose who among the four warriors who fell this day are worthy of being taken to Valhalla—"

"*I* am here. *I* will select those who are worthy and escort them to Odin's hall." Victoria pitched her voice to carry. She stood forthright in her assertion of her rights. By ancient custom, the Valkyrie first on the battlefield did the choosing.

"Indeed, you would be correct." Ráðgríðr's piercing gaze cut straight through her. "If you were still a Valkyrie. However, you are not. Victoria, you have been stripped of your rank and your privileges."

Aghast at the denouncement, Victoria rocked on her heels and almost staggered. Behind her, an angry exclamation and a muffled growl came from the men. Her temper ignited on a long, slow burn. Having Sawyer and Logan witness her denigration was embarrassing. But the real humiliation came from having it happen in front of her sister Valkyries. Her wolf bristled; primal instinct urged her to lunge and rip out the other woman's throat. Exhaustion, of all things, proved to her advantage, slowing her reflex to violence. It enabled her to get out ahead of her anger and cut it off.

"On whose authority are you stripping me of my station?" Victoria demanded point-blank.

"Our Lady of the Vanir has rescinded your status," Ráðgríðr advised her coolly.

"Freya." Her face pulled, contorting with her mixed disgust and anger. It hurt to have muscles working against one another, and she was certain her expression was ugly. "Freya doesn't have the authority."

"I should have you arrested for—" Ráðgríðr kept talking but her words ran together. Victoria couldn't make out a single one over the roaring in her ears.

On the ball of her foot, Victoria pivoted to face Odin. She staggered and stopped before him. She tilted her head back to stare into his inscrutable visage. The thought foremost in her mind, echoing—*So it comes to this?*

Despite her familiarity with Jake, his greater form was a total stranger to her. Odin was austere, enigmatic, and formidable. Those who won his favor often lost it, sometimes for unknown reasons. In the corridors of Valhalla, she'd heard it whispered that the All Father had gone mad. He no longer spoke to his own priests. He seldom addressed anyone but his wife and sons. He brooded for hours on end, keeping counsel with a dwarf's severed head.

"Are you hearing this, Jake?" Victoria shouted at her god.

"Are you going to stand by and allow this after all *the shit* I've gone through for you?"

Dark thunderheads brooded overhead. Ráðgríðr protested, but the cacophony of the ravens swallowed her words. The birds that composed the god's body split into two pillars that flew on furious wings and vanished into the cloud bank. A man stepped from the nexus of the V and squared his shoulders, settling into a wide set stance.

Victoria's breath caught in her throat—*Jake Barrett.*

He wore his sixty-something years on his countenance, and he wore it well. His short brown hair was dappled with gray; his skin tanned and tough like old leather. At six-foot plus, Jake had a dense, muscular physique. Covered in scars and a few select tattoos, he looked more the part of a convict than an athlete. Physically, he was imposing but his true intimidation derived from his implacable magnetism. Mountains took lessons in how to be remote and rugged from him.

The man was notorious among men and monsters. His titles varied from the prosaic to fanciful but he was most commonly called the Hunter King. Rumors abounded regarding his true nature. Some said he commanded powerful magic. Others that he'd sold his soul to the devil. All in all, the truth was much more terrifying than the wildest speculation.

Gale-force winds beat down on her head and whipped loose hair that had escaped her braid about her face. Victoria registered her surroundings in only the remotest, most abstract way possible. The others faded from her awareness as well. Her reality was surreal. Disjointed and disconnected.

When Victoria's gaze locked with Jake's, the most difficult thing to accept was the most trivial. The man had only had one good eye. Over the other, he wore a patch. Of course, it made sense. It stood as common knowledge that Odin had sacrificed his eye to the Well to gain the gift of prophecy. A mantra rang through her mind over and over—*Not her Jake.*

Pirate Jake was a hundred times scarier than his mortal incarnation.

"You having trouble with this, kid?" Jake stepped right up to her and bent his head, speaking at a for-your-ears-only pitch.

"Yeah, kinda." She struggled to gather her scattered wits. To that end, she opened and closed her hands, flexing her fingers. Repetitive motion soothed her frayed nerves. She had no idea what to say to him and she was terrified. No matter what she said, it was bound to be the wrong thing. Her anger and sense of betrayal were tantamount to blasphemy. What right did she, a mere mortal, have to harbor wrath toward the king of the gods?

And what was right didn't change how she felt at all. A tremor passed through Victoria. She strove to hide it and loathed the admission. Already, she'd lost her status as Freya's priestess and possession of *Vanadium*—two of the three things that made her special. When her parents and so many of her pack mates had died, she'd believed then that she'd lost everything. Now, she realized how much more she had to lose.

"You'll have an opportunity to speak your piece but now ain't the time." He pinned her with that single, fierce eye.

She gulped and changed her mind, now convinced. *Hell yeah—her Jake.* Marshalling her composure, Victoria lifted her chin and looked him straight in the eye. "Are you firing me or am I your Valkyrie?"

"You tell me, Victoria. Are you still my Valkyrie?" The One-eyed God smiled.

"I'm your Valkyrie," Victoria declared in a voice both

strong and daring. The declaration empowered her—fear fell away. This experience also fit with *her* Jake. Maybe the human aspect of Odin wasn't so disparate from his greater entirety as one might assume. She addressed her next words to her sister soldiers, Ráðgríðr in particular. "I arrived at this battlefield first. It is my right to choose from the slain. *I* determine who goes to Valhalla."

She all but thumped her chest—*my choice. Miiine.*

Not one of the six other women spoke, but they averted their gazes and yielded in posture. As a wolf, Victoria picked up on the signs of submission. Triumph rushed through her, and it was all she could do to contain her celebration. An Alpha's instinct called for her to tilt her face toward heaven and howl in victory.

"Ráðgríðr, return to Valhalla. I want a word with you in private." Jake stepped into the moment, taking command of it and them.

"Ooohhh, someone's in trouble!" Logan heckled from the front row. His mockery earned him a one-eyed glare from Jake.

Shocked gazes riveted on the male werewolf but then turned toward Jake. The lot of them stared as though expecting an eruption and smiting. Ráðgríðr looked damn near fit to be tied. Victoria pressed her lips together to stop from smiling. Jake's sense of humor could handle Logan's worst. Still, she worried, but it was yet another thing beyond her control. She relaxed further, savoring Ráðgríðr's takedown. In her book, it was long past due.

"All Father, if I may. We were acting on Freya's orders," Ráðgríðr protested. The woman strove to sound respectful but she was clearly in a quandary.

"Ráðgríðr..." Jake cocked his head.

The High Valkyrie faltered. "Yes, Your Highness?"

"Why're you still here?"

"I'm going now." Bowing and scraping, Ráðgríðr took her leave.

Jake plowed toward the five remaining Valkyries, scattering them before him. "The rest of you, stop gawking and round up those souls. Sawyer—" He turned toward his son.

"Yeah, Dad?" Sawyer stood with Cali. Not supporting her but hovering nearby like a broody hen. Victoria refused to look at him. She averted her gaze in time to catch Logan's double take.

"Dad?" Logan mouthed while conducting an invisible orchestra with his hands.

"Why are you standing here?" Jake demanded of Sawyer. "Get Cali to the damn hospital before she passes out."

Sawyer scowled. "We'd already be gone, but she refuses to leave."

"I'm not some sissy that's gonna pass out. I'm not leaving DNR behind." Kinkaid adopted a stubborn stance. The chip on her shoulder was a dare—*Go ahead! Mess with me.* Yet, from her pallor and the tremor in her hand, she'd reached her upper limits.

Victoria knew the feeling. She also was well past her second wind.

The Hunter King stopped in front of Cali and laid his hand on her shoulder. "Kinkaid, I'll see to it that Dewey gets taken care of. Will you trust me with that?"

"Yes, sir."

The hunters exchanged a few more blurred words that were barely discernable thanks to the roaring in Victoria's head. The tide rushed in again, and the world swayed. She might have gone over like a felled tree except for Logan's hand on her elbow. She breathed deep and rested her forehead against Logan's side. He had on clean clothes—a floral fresh scent of laundry detergent overlay his earthy male aroma. His voice was a reassuring murmur in her ear as his hands stroked her hair.

Time blurred. The next time she came around, Jake was standing before her and Logan. Sawyer and Cali were nowhere in sight, having presumably left for the hospital. The male werewolf and the king of gods faced off, appraising each other like little boys on a playground. Only, Logan—dumbass—was bound and determined to get his ass handed to him.

"Logan," Victoria spoke his name in warning and tugged on his elbow.

"So, you're Odin, huh?" Logan asked. "I thought you'd be more like that *Dos Equis* guy..."

"I don't think of you at all."

"Zing. Nice one, gramps."

"Thanks, pup."

Hildr approached Jake. The redhead said, "Sir, we have the souls of the slain assembled."

Jake's heavy gaze settled on Victoria. "Are you up for this?"

"I'm ready." Victoria summoned her strength; she pushed away and set herself apart from Logan. She had half a mind to question why and how the civilian authorities hadn't arrived on the scene yet, but the matter seemed trivial compared to other concerns. It struck her as best to simply assume the sheriff and his people would arrive when Odin allowed it...and not a moment sooner.

With an effort, she focused her vision to peek beyond the veil into the Shadowlands. It took more out of her than expected, and a part of her was left wondering if her eyes had gone full-wolf. The posse of Valkyries ringed the four souls in question: DNR and the three members of *Den Valgte*, including Magdalena. It surprised Victoria that the witch's soul had been caught but she supposed death rendered them all equal in the end.

Except Odin's handmaidens *were* different. Specialized reapers. As a Valkyrie, Victoria had already died and passed the trial of being judged and chosen. In turn, she arbitrated over the worth of warriors felled in combat who hoped to enter Valhalla. Valor and skill in the martial arts were prized attributes but other traits mattered more—intelligence, cunning, and loyalty.

Verging on collapse, Victoria surveyed the four souls once, lingering on each in turn. Magdalena bristled with defiance, whereas her two male companions were more bewildered than bold. And DNR—the poor guy—was shaking in his boots. The whole time she looked, she was aware of the burden of Jake's gaze on her. Yet another test. The others watched too, but they hardly mattered. Only *his* esteem held any weight.

"Him." Victoria aimed her finger at DNR, and dismissed the others with a sweep of her arm. "They are unworthy."

Rota, who'd been silent to that point, burst out. "The woman fought well. She has skill—"

"Odin, I beseech you. Hear my pleas," Magdalena cried out, addressing Jake. "We have only sought to serve you!"

"This is my decision." Victoria dropped her statement as a ton of bricks. She glared at Rota, at all of them, daring any of her sister Valkyries to criticize or challenge her decision.

No one spoke.

Victoria swiveled to Magdalena, and bared her teeth is a feral smile. "You can rot in the Underworld for however many days we have left."

The witch shrieked as Victoria turned away, but she was

past caring. She staggered the short distance to Logan and collapsed against him. Her options were him or face plant in the dirt. He leaned over her, huffing hot, citrusy-sweet breath across her face.

"Y'know, I like you like this—all sweet and subdued..." Logan snickered. "And handsy."

"Logan?" She fought a yawn and lost. It spread her jaws so wide they ached.

"Yeah, Vic?"

"Shove it." She tried to do so but failed to stifle a second yawn. This one engulfed her. Logan's laughter echoed all around her, warm and nutty like fresh-baked brownies. She achieved weightlessness...floating. Everything was far, far away; sleep comforting.

Jake's voice impinged on the sound of silence. "You'll see her home safe?"

"Yeah," Logan said.

Then, nothing until she stirred again in the car. Victoria lifted her head, found herself buckled into the passenger seat of Logan's SUV. Music played on the radio while the night rolled along. She had no idea how much time had passed.

Logan glanced over at her. "So that was Odin, huh?"

"Yeah." She croaked thanks to dryness in her throat. "That was Odin."

The car stopped and he turned off the engine. For a second, she stared at him in blank confusion until he prodded her shoulder. "We're home. Can you walk or do you want me to carry you?"

Her face heated. "I can walk."

They climbed out of the SUV and navigated the path to the front door in silence. Victoria's sense of surrealism lingered. Everything that had happened that evening from the fight to the revelation about Sawyer had a nightmarish quality. She had a gaping hole in her heart and her soul where Freya and *Vanadium* belonged. In the course of one evening, two of the things that defined who and what she was had been stripped away.

She spoke without meaning to. "I don't know who I am anymore."

Logan glanced over at her. He frowned but then smiled. "C'mon. It was a rough evening but you're still the same short pushy blonde know-it-all you've always been."

"Shut up." She threw a clumsy punch at his side, and he made no move to dodge. Logan pivoted; a playful turn, acting like he wanted to spar. Victoria didn't have the heart. Instead, she continued onward.

"What's wrong, Vic. Why won't you talk to me?"

Logan's gaze had weight, and pressed upon her back as she trudged up the front walk toward the porch. She had no answers for him even though he deserved better. She ached from head to toe, proof she'd strained her reserves to the max. Her exhaustion was so great her natural healing had hit its limits. She needed water, something to eat, and then to sleep for about twelve hours. And a shower. She craved a hot shower more than anything.

Dear, loyal Sylvie waited in the open entrance. The older woman wore a housecoat. Deep worry lines marred the Skald's kindly face but she was there, waiting for Victoria, as always. The eye at the center of the storm. The heart of the pack.

The two women walked straight into a hug, holding one another tight. "Oh, Victory. The ruckus you created tonight —we felt it over the pack bond. I thought you were lost."

"I was." *Lost.* Maybe she still was. Victoria pulled back enough to gaze into her friend's face. "Where are the others?"

"Asleep. Should I wake them up?"

She placed her hands on Sylvie's shoulders and squeezed. "No, let them sleep."

"You both come on into the kitchen and I'll make you something to eat." Sylvie included Logan in the invitation. "Then you can get some sleep. Don't worry, I'll take care of the others."

"I don't know what I'd do without you." Verging on tears, Victoria threw her arms around Sylvie again. More than anything, Victoria longed to tell her friend everything that had happened that day. Normally, she would've. This time, she couldn't. Knowledge of Sawyer's crime was a burden she had to bear alone, as Alpha, and for the good of her pack.

The older woman returned her hug, but her face was pinched with worry when they separated. "You'd do just fine. Except, I suspect, you'd eat nothing but junk food. Now, to the kitchen with you."

"I'm starving." On cue, Victoria's stomach rumbled.

"I'm not surprised." Chucking, Sylvie herded Victoria onward, leaving Logan to bring up the rear.

It was so good to be home.

CHAPTER TWENTY-ONE

In the hallway outside of Michael's bedroom, Jake kept his vigil. He sat atop a solid oaken chair, balanced on its rear legs, the back propped against the wall. He cradled a double-barreled rifle with a black walnut stock in his arms. The hunter dozed fitfully, waking often to check on his youngest son.

The first ring of his mobile phone startled Jake wide awake. He pried the device from his pocket and glanced at the screen—Sawyer. Immediate irritation coalesced in Jake's gut. He checked the time—ten minutes to one in the a.m. Blast, it would figure that Sawyer couldn't call him at a civil hour. Jake attributed his grumpiness to a lack of sleep. He hadn't gotten more than an uninterrupted hour in the last forty-eight. Weariness had worn down his nerves to a nub.

He answered the phone. "Yeah?"

"Dad, we've got a problem—"

"Just one?" Jake asked in a tone edged with sarcasm. Grimacing, he tilted his chair onto all four legs and rose to

318

his feet. He shifted his rifle's carry strap to his shoulder, freeing his hands, and moved a yard down the hallway to muffle the sound of the conversation so they didn't disturb Michael or the twins who were also asleep in their beds.

"Okay, more than one."

"I'm listening."

Sawyer offered no immediate reply. From his breathing and the heavy cadence of his steps, he was pacing or maybe hiking. With conscious effort, Jake put a lid on his own frayed temperament. If he didn't watch his tongue, he'd snap out another curt demand which would inevitably make matters worse. His son handled like an unbroken horse. Once Sawyer got riled, he stopped thinking and started reacting. The boy had a hot temper and poor judgement—a lethal combination that had resulted in tragic consequences in the not-so-distant past.

"DNR's dead but I guess you know that."

"Yeah, I experienced his death. I'm sorry. He was a good kid." Sorrow weighed on Jake's shoulders. The young man had been too damn green to be in the field. Sierra Pines should've been a cushy assignment that kept him safe. Trouble was, safe didn't seem to be a real thing anymore. Jake took comfort in the knowledge that Victoria had chosen DNR's soul to live in on Valhalla.

Perhaps misinterpreting Jake's silence, Sawyer spoke in a guilt-laden voice. "I'm sorry, Dad. I should've protected him better."

"It's not your fault, Son. Just tell me what happened. Who started it?" Jake returned his attention to the conversation. He'd already witnessed fragments of the fight through the eyes of ravens but interpretation mattered as much as context. He wanted to hear Sawyer's version of the confrontation and the beginning was as good a point as any other.

"They did."

"Did they?" Jake harbored skepticism. Sawyer's itchy trigger finger inspired doubts. Though, ultimately, it made no difference who had fired the first shot. Sawyer was his son so Jake would back him.

Family first. Always.

"Yeah, they started it." Sawyer answered without hesitation. "Does it matter?"

"No." Jake perceived no other choice than to take his son at his word. "First shot's been fired. First blood spilled. Besides that, given who these people are—what they've done to those wolves, Victoria and her people wouldn't accept reconciliation."

"Did you see it all? Do you know who they are? Why they came after us?" Sawyer asked, terse but also—accusatory? His tone set Jake's teeth on edge.

"I saw enough—" Jake stroked his thick eyebrow, flattening the bristle. He opened his mouth to make an angry reply, cut it short, and exhaled hard to vent steam. Instead, he posed a question in a distinctly stilted tenor. "What the hell are you implying, Son?"

"Nothing. It's just... I can't—" Sawyer cut himself off. His silence conveyed the same impression of repression and restraint. Internal pressure built, testing the integrity of his son's control.

Explosive tension brooded between Jake and Sawyer. One misspoken word—one spark—would set them both off. It left him wondering how the hell they'd jumped down this rabbit hole. It was a damn shame when a man communicated better with his archenemy than his own son. Just the day before, father and son had been on the exact same page when

Sawyer had agreed to represent the hunters at the damn werewolf shindig. What had changed?

"You can't what? Just speak your mind. Stop with all the damn pussyfooting."

"The woman we spoke to said they called themselves *Den Valgte*," Sawyer said in a scathing tone. "She claimed that they serve you. That they're your 'chosen people.'"

Jake turned toward Michael's bedroom, watching to make sure nothing disturbed the child's rest. He dropped his volume but spoke with force. "Sawyer, do you still have a hunter's mark on your arm?"

"Yeah."

From the jump in Sawyer's voice, the disruption in pitch, Jake envisioned his son grabbing for the tattoo on his bicep —a frantic glance to verify it was still there. And he wasn't above gloating over the brief terror his son endured—it served his brat right for even doubting.

"My chosen people are the ones who bear that mark."

"Okay, fair enough. I had that coming. These guys insisted they were your followers."

Jake deliberated before replying. He'd had this conversation before with his sons, most recently with his oldest boy, Daniel, when he'd turned fifteen. His oldest son had possessed an intuitive understanding of how passion intertwined with knowledge; true power comprised much more than the possession of the most weapons or the best-trained warriors. In many ways, Daniel's inherent objectivity had been his greatest weakness. It cut him off from the song of the hunt.

Sawyer had the opposite problem.

"They were my followers, Son."

"Bullshit." Sawyer growled, sounding remarkably like the wolves he now kept company with. A smile tugged at Jake's lips. He supposed he should've expected the adaptation. He considered it apropos. Every god eventually found the creatures that best imbued their fundamental traits—their spirit animal. A deity might have more than one but the first was always the most vital. Odin's were the raven, the wolf, and the bear. However, clever and curious ravens had been his first—still the dearest to his heart.

"Sawyer, calm down." He infused command in his voice and naturally his rebellious son sputtered. Jake glanced over his shoulder toward Michael's bedroom; a self-reminder to keep his voice down.

He imagined Sarah's laughter—warm and bright—so vividly that her alluring scent filled his nostrils. His wife whispered in the back of his mind, *"Be patient with him, my love. He questions authority... much as his father did before he became Authority."*

"I am calm." Sawyer's feet stomped on wood—stairs? "But this is pure bullshit. They invaded our territory—killed on our lands."

Our territory—the language of a wolf.

"Long have warring tribes come into conflict. Kingdoms fight; I often have followers on both sides. It is a matter of history and the nature of men to war with one another. This cannot come as a surprise to you, Son."

"Your greater form was there, Dad."

"I'm cut off from my greater form, Sawyer. However, my division doesn't rob either of my selves of agency. You know that."

"It looked like you and talked like you so excuse me for calling bullshit. That's just a load of crap. It was *you*."

"So it was." Immense impatience hollowed his voice. In the distance, thunder rumbled, and Jake counted the many, myriad reasons he had to remain patient. "Did you imagine my aspects would be substantially different?"

Sawyer took his own sweet time to answer and when it came, he gave up the admission with grudging resentment. "Yeah, I guess I did."

His anger eased. Sawyer's frustration stemmed from honest misunderstanding. "God or man, I'm me. As I move away from humanity, I become more of what I am. Do you understand?"

"No."

Jake exhaled and his patience thinned. "I am the storm. I am the hunt. I am the searcher, the wanderer, the poet, the scholar, the knowledge seeker, the hanged man—I am all and none of these things. When men worship me, their quest brings them closer to true understanding. There are times when I test men —to determine their worth or to further their journey—"

"You're saying this was a test?"

"I'm not saying anything at all."

When Sawyer snarled, Jake smiled.

"I get it. You're saying you don't take sides in mortal affairs. But that's a lie. You're here. I'm here. We're fighting against this undead army—trying to save the world. Dad, I hate to break it to you but that's choosing a side."

"Your mother handed me a prophecy, Son. A smart man heeds his wife."

A fat spider scurried along the wall, moving toward Michael's bedroom. Jake smashed his fist down on top of the arachnid, leaving a reddish brown smear on the plaster. He wiped his hand on his jeans.

"Prophecy again," Sawyer said in a tone thick with disgust. "You're said that before but you won't even tell us what it's supposed to be."

His son's distaste reflected rather precisely how Jake had come to regard such matters—being kept in the dark and foresight. The All Father counted his relentless pursuit of premonition amongst his greatest blunders. Odin possessed one eye and the third sight. Yet, having a single eye made it difficult to perceive—his depth perception was shot. In the past, he'd compensated, relying on Frigg or Loki for advice and perspective. However, his wife was beyond his reach and Loki—not to be trusted. For now, Jake kept his own counsel, relied on his own judgement, and wondered how many mistakes he made along the way.

Jake tried to put himself into Sawyer's shoes—born human, his mother and oldest brother recently dead, and a crap relationship with his father. Sawyer had a hot head and poor impulse control, but he was also a man who preferred logic to intuition. He acquired knowledge as facts and formulas, and perceived reality as a thing rooted in logic. Math and matter, not magic and mysticism. He lacked the capacity to accept truth based on faith.

Father and son would never see eye to eye unless Jake loosened his grip and parted company with some of his secrets. So he sighed and plunged.

"Decades ago, your mother foresaw a possible resolution to Ragnarök that would allow me to save some of the Nine Worlds, and—most importantly—the tree."

Sawyer's poignant silence befitted the weighty mood. "Some. Not all?"

"People are going to die—men, elves, dwarves, and even giants. This is a numbers game. Some surviving is better than none."

On stealthy feet, Jake eased along the hallway until he reached Michael's room. He pushed the door open just enough to allow in more light. His son slept safe in his bed—

Rascal sprawled full across the foot of the bed. No sign of danger—not even a spider. He pulled the door closed, leaving only a crack. He once again retreated toward the kitchen.

"And that happens by you being mortal and taking a side?"

"It's even more trivial than that. Your mother insists that salvation turns on one insignificant mortal life." He tasted irony as he spoke.

"One—who?"

"Ain't that the million-dollar question?" His sweet, maddening wife had refused to tell him, citing need-to-know. In other words, she expected him to mess it up if he possessed too much information. He chaffed at the prohibition, but honored her wisdom.

"You think it's Victoria."

Sawyer's shrewd intuition impressed Jake but he kept his approval concealed. "Victoria is significant. Our destinies are irrevocably intertwined unless I can find some way to cheat fate."

"What the hell is that supposed to mean?" Sawyer sounded scared to death. Rightly so.

Jake hesitated, and debated, but he chose silence. His son wasn't ready. Sawyer had a fiery trial of his own to endure. If and when he survived... Maybe then.

"Fine, don't answer. I'm used to that. You still haven't answered my question." Sawyer's voice hinted at an immense ocean of frustration being kept behind an unstable dam.

Jake snorted. "I've done my best considering that you never actually asked."

"What—" The phone caught the scrape of Sawyer's nails on his scalp. "Oh."

"Oh," Jake mocked, disingenuous and Loki-like. And damn, it felt good.

"Okay, *Den Valgte* isn't your chosen. Who the hell were those guys then?"

Jake released a thin sigh. If Sawyer had shown half as much interest in his heritage as he had in math and physics, a history lesson wouldn't be necessary. "*Berserkir* were solitary warriors who wore the skin of a bear they'd slain. They weren't allowed to use traps or poison, or have assistance. They wore the bear skin into battle—"

Sawyer grunted. "Oh—yeah, I recall the stories about berserkers. They were bad asses. Right?"

The modern capacity for reducing everything significant to the trivial just chaffed Jake's shorts but it simply wasn't worth the argument. "Right. The *úlfheðnar* were the same except they wore wolf hides and fought in packs."

"What happened to them?"

He'd been getting to that if the boy could just wait... "Both orders served me centuries ago but over time, their behavior grew increasingly bloodthirsty and lawless. They slaughtered innocents—raping and pillaging—entire villages..."

"Mom made you get rid of 'em, huh?"

A wide, involuntary grin flashed over Jake's face which, thankfully, his son couldn't see. As JD would've said—*Oh burn.* With self-deprecating irony, he savored the humor. He said in all seriousness, "Both orders were banned and hunted to extinction."

"You're sure they were destroyed?"

"I'm positive. No matter what *Den Valgte* may claim, they are not descended from the original orders."

"Dad, these guys had scary-powerful magic. The bear-chick was damn near impossible to kill. If the knowledge wasn't passed down from their ancestors, then someone must've taught them. Who?"

"That's a good question." And one for which he had no

ready answer. It would've been easy to cast the blame onto Loki. Far too easy. Even though it was a convenient *cliché* —just blame Loki for everything. Jake guarded against the lazy habit. A great many other factions existed in the world. To forget was sheer stupidity.

"I know I'm missing something," Sawyer said, grim with determination. "You know something but aren't telling me."

Jake answered with a smile his son couldn't see.

Sawyer huffed. "What happened after I left to take Cali to the hospital?"

"The High Valkyrie, Ráðgríðr, lied about Freya having terminated Victoria's status as a Valkyrie..." Jake went on to provide an abbreviated account of what had transpired. For once, Sawyer listened without interruption. Once he finished, silence hung on for a time.

Eventually, Sawyer ventured a question. "What would you have done if Victoria had chosen Magdalena to enter Valhalla?"

"Magdalena would've been granted entry to Valhalla."

"What? No!" Sawyer sputtered.

"Victoria is a Valkyrie. It is her duty to decide who is worthy. Of those chosen, half go the Fólkvangr and the rest join the Einherjar."

"I don't get it."

"What don't you get?" Jake bit off his words; great was his impatience with his recalcitrant son. He confessed to wondering whether Sawyer tested him on purpose. And he already had his answer—Yes, of course.

Sawyer said, "The Einherjar are your army, those who will follow you in the End Days. Those deemed worthy to sacrifice their immortal souls in the fight to save the Nine Worlds. Mother told us the majority of warriors who seek Valhalla are denied. A select few are allowed entry to the halls of the other gods, but the vast majority enter Hel's domain where they'll dwell for eternity with their ancestors. Despite having been twisted by modern religions, her realm is not a place of eternal damnation. Though, the souls of those who are wicked are made to suffer."

"That's correct." Maybe his son had been playing attention after all.

"So why would you want someone like Magdalena or your followers with you?"

"Sawyer, you're missing the point."

"Am I?"

"You are."

"Explain it to me then."

"What happened in Broken Bend wasn't about *Den Valgte* at all."

"Who was it about then?"

"Victoria. It was all about Victoria."

Sawyer fell silent as though thunderstruck but eventually said, "You're not going to explain that at all."

"No." Jake shook his head.

His son grumbled. "There's too much that doesn't jibe, Dad. On the one hand, you're not taking sides in mortal affairs, but on the other you are. You've got a prophecy that may allow you to save the Nine Worlds, but you're still preparing for Ragnarök. And what about Daniel?"

"What about Daniel?" Jake winced at the sound of his son's name. Daniel's death remained an unhealed wound; every mention ripped off the scab. Not enough time had passed for him to have gained any sort of perspective.

"When Baldur was murdered, you lost his soul to Helheim—" Baldur was the brother Sawyer had never met— and never would.

"That was centuries ago."

"I'm just using him to make a point. Jasper, the boy I shot...".". Sawyer's tone turned harsh with condemnation. "He's there too—enduring endless torment because he died a coward's death."

"The boy was fleeing in terror when you shot him in the back, Sawyer. If he'd rushed toward you, I could've intervened and claimed him. He died as a coward, so his soul rightfully belongs to Hel. In the underworld, She is the supreme. "

"So that's what I don't understand." Sharp, rapid clicking came from Sawyer's end of the conversation—a pen perhaps? Had he been taking notes while they talked?

Jake's irritation receded as soon as he confirmed his son's barrage of questions had direction and purpose. To facilitate learning, he would willingly endure the interrogation. "Sawyer, what is it you don't understand?"

"Daniel was murdered too. Victoria told me—his back was turned to his attacker when he died. Why were you able to save Daniel, but not Baldur or Jasper?"

"I didn't save Daniel's soul, Son. Loki stole him."

"So you're saying..." Uncertainty defined Sawyer's tone.

"Loki is capable of stealing just about anything—thoughts, memories, hearts, and souls. He's not limited to physical objects." To his own ears, Jake's chuckle turned over like a strained transmission. The Trickster was another sensitive topic—difficult to discuss with any impartiality.

"How does he get away with it if Hel is all-powerful within her domain? I mean—I know they're related..."

"Good question. You just hit the nail square on the head. Loki is Hel's father. He gets away with shenanigans she wouldn't tolerate from anyone else."

"Okay, huh."

Jake imagined the gears turning in Sawyer's head,

producing an audible clatter. He decided it was past time to change the subject from existential matters to the pragmatic. "Can I still count on you to represent me at the gathering of the packs, Sawyer?"

"Yes, of course. I was just wondering whether this thing with *Den Valgte* will complicate things for us at the werewolf moot," Sawyer said, determined to dredge up the worst possible scenario. "Especially if Victoria decides we're somehow complicit. Whatever you're not telling me—I can tell when that woman is pissed off."

"Victoria's angry." Jake offered ready agreement. Sawyer hadn't caught on to the depth or source of the she-wolf's grievance yet, but he had to suspect. Jake supposed he was a massive asshole for not warning his son, but damn it—the boy needed to grow up. Victoria had proven herself—she had refused to murder Sawyer. She'd acquitted herself with honor.

Sawyer was his son, but Jake had named Victoria his daughter. He perceived the wisdom in stepping aside and allowing his children to sort out their differences... So long as the drama didn't end in bloodshed. Every man traveled his own path and faced his own obstacles—these were Sawyer's.

"What am I supposed to do?"

Jake dragged a hand over his face and looked askance at the ceiling. There were days when he suspected his genius son of being a damn fool. "You talk to her. And when she talks, you shut your trap and listen."

Sawyer huffed. "What happens if I screw this up?"

"You'll be fine, Son. I have faith in you." Jake snapped the phone shut. Afterward, he stared at the device and wondered if he'd made the correct decision.

Time would tell.

CHAPTER TWENTY-TWO

PHOENIX, ARIZONA

Three a.m. The devil's hour: a fitting time for Loki's return to Phoenix.

A burnt umber veil cloaked the gibbous moon. As a concession to the darkness, he drifted as an owl over the Phoenix suburb, flying so low his talons came within millimeters of brushing the terra cotta tiles of the Mission Revival-style homes. He found it hilarious that the King of the Aesir owned a cookie cutter house on a corner lot. Oh, the irony. The most singular entity Loki had ever known— content to hide in an unremarkable dwelling in an ordinary middle-class neighborhood.

But, Loki conceded, alighted upon the cinderblock wall that surrounded Jake Barrett's backyard, the swimming pool was damned nice. Perfect for children. He bet Michael loved the diving board, though the lack of a safety barrier concerned him. Hopping from the fence top, he assumed the identity of eight-year-old Benjamin on his way down. He skipped across the dark yard, deftly evading the motion-detectors that controlled the floodlights.

Nearing the darkened window of Michael's bedroom, the Trickster stooped like a bandit so his head remained hidden from sight. No sound came from within the room but he sensed *three* entities just inside—two living and one... not.

The *dís*.

Jake was there too, but farther away, more difficult to perceive. His magical wards protected him against scrying and second sight, but he was still mortal with all the vulgar trappings his condition entailed. The slow rate of his heartbeat and his deep, shallow respiration suggested the Hunter King was sound asleep.

Just as well. It made Loki's task easier. Of course, he could have explained his scheme to Jake. The hunter might even have agreed, but it struck the Trickster as unlikely. No, far easier to act and apologize later than to ask and get shot down.

In the plaster beside the window pane, Loki located a crack too thin to accommodate even a tape worm. Getting into inaccessible places, especially where he wasn't welcome, had always been one of talents. He changed his shape again, creating a living creature unknown to modern science, one long and thin enough to fit through the fissure. He sieved his essence into the child's room.

Loki became Benjamin again but with the eyes of a cat. Michael slept in his bed; his massive mutt stretched out across the foot. Determined not to disturb the pair before he was ready, the Trickster hunkered beside a battered oak trunk that served as a toy box. Through the cracked door, a narrow beam of light penetrated the darkness. However, the brightness caused every other part of the bedroom to seem shadier in comparison.

A spider fell on Loki's arm—eight writhing legs tickling his bare skin. Irritated, he brushed it off and tilted his head to survey the room. The walls and ceiling were alive—not his imagination. A living carpet of spiders covered every square inch of plaster. Scuttling legs. Clicking mandibles. Disgusting even by his humble standards.

Loki's manifestation sent the swarm scurrying for cover. Spiders rained from the ceiling. Some supported themselves on thin silken threads. Others just fell, dropping onto the bed and the floor. Those on the walls rushed toward the baseboard in a wave, layers of arachnids traveling atop each other, growing ever thicker as their numbers converged. Their mass was a foot high when it reached the bottom of the bed. Within seconds, the entire group had withdrawn.

Easing away from the trunk, Loki cast a furtive glance through the cracked door. His vantage allowed him to peer into the hallway where Jake slept upright in a chair, his chin resting upon his chest, arms crossed, cradling a rifle.

To the Trickster's critical appraisal, the boy's guardian appeared exhausted. Hardly surprising, considering Loki had deprived Jake of sleep the night before. Then, he'd derived amusement from inflicting misery on his old nemesis. Now, he regretted his pettiness and he wouldn't indulge it again. The thing that served as his vestigial conscience twinged but his real compunction sprang from practicality. Michael needed a vigilant guardian.

On a child's stealthy feet, Loki crept toward the bed. His approach confused the dog who lifted his head and snarled. Loki stopped in his tracks. His brow pinched in thought. Damn it, what was the blasted beast's name? Muttley? Or was it Spot?

"Rascal? What's wrong boy?" Michael's young voice was

sleepy. Beneath the covers, he stirred and reached, seeking the dog in the darkness.

Shit. Loki tensed. He'd wanted to rouse the child gently. If the pair made much more noise, Jake would awaken and charge in looking for blood. Per recent experience, the hunter woke up as grumpy as a hellhound with mange. The Trickster still suffered from the injuries he'd sustained earlier that day at the playground. He was weak. He might not survive another attack; he didn't want to find out.

This avatar—his last. If he sacrificed himself for a mortal child, he lost his foothold on Midgard but also the part of himself that kept him sane. Eternal, maddening suffering awaited him once he reunited with his greater form.

And he fumed over having lost complete control over the situation. He never worked like this—on the fly and without a detailed plan. Oh, he could scam anyone out of anything; it was his gift. But more than anything else, he regarded himself as a master of the long con; his most ingenious schemes required centuries of meticulous planning and implementation.

Loki pitched his call to a whisper, "Michael, it's me—Ben."

"Ben?" Michael twisted on the bed, turning toward the sound of Loki's voice. The boy sounded unafraid but unfortunately, the damn dog kept growling.

"Yeah, it's me. Shh, keep your voice down." Loki climbed onto the edge of the bed, extending his arm toward Rascal. He wove a hasty charm, casting friendship into the dog's mind.

Rascal whined in welcome and shoved his muzzle into Loki's open hand. The dog's great tongue bathed his fingers, leaving them slurpy with saliva. *Yuck.* With a grimace, Loki shook off dog drool.

"What're you doing here? How'd you get in?" Michael asked, unfortunately loud.

"I'm magic. Remember?"

"Oh yeah."

A solid thunk and a man's deep, disturbed snort came from the hallway, signaling Jake's inelegant awakening. His boots thundered on the tile when he stood.

"Damn it. Don't tell your dad that I'm here."

Loki ducked behind the bed and crouched on all fours. By happenstance, he found himself staring into the space beneath the bed. *It* stared back with thousands of tiny, sinister eyes. They were just two monsters glaring at each other in the dark. From her demeanor, the *dís* was wary. She wouldn't reveal herself with Jake lurking nearby. Getting the undead bitch to show herself at all was going to require guile and trickery...and probably some plain old dumb luck.

"Michael? Are you all right?" Jake asked with a burr of concern.

"Yeah, I'm fine, Dad. But I think Rascal needs to go out."

"Damn dogs shouldn't be inside at night." Jake grumbled and then snapped a command to the dog. "All right, c'mon. I'll let you out."

The Rottweiler bounded from the bed.

Yes! A grin split Loki's mouth; he aborted a fist pump. He hadn't expected Michael to prove such a deft liar—there may be hope for the kid yet. Bidding his time, the Trickster stayed hidden. When Rascal left the room, the dog's nails hit the tile, crisp clicks in contrast to the man's heavier footfalls. The sound of their movement receded.

Aware he didn't have long, Loki popped up. He bounded onto the mattress and crawled to the top. His child form wasn't much bigger than Michael, so they both fit fine on the double bed.

"What's up?" Excitement elevated Michael's naturally high voice even though he tried to whisper.

"Still wanna be a super hero?" Loki reached for the magic pocket where he'd stashed his newly stolen prize. From thin air, he pulled the mystical dagger, *Vanadium*. The dagger shimmered and danced like the Aurora Borealis.

"Whoaaaa." Michael's mouth dropped open.

"Shhh." Loki hissed. He tapped the boy's hanging jaw shut and hastily hid the weapon beneath the covers. The monster under the bed must have noticed the light show but she wouldn't necessarily understand the cause. Hell, the Trickster's entire plan banked on catching her unaware.

"Uh, what're we gonna do?" Michael fidgeted.

"We're gonna slay the monster hiding under the bed..." Loki delivered the declaration loud and clear, empowering his voice with magic. Sneering. Mocking. *This* was also one of his talents—the gift of provocation.

The mattress jolted, as though punched dead center, struck from beneath. Angered, the dead thing had finally decided to make her presence known.

"I want to call my dad." Michael waved his hands in rising panic.

"No. This has to be you. Remember what I taught you. There's a place in your mind that's devoid of fear. Go there. Just like I taught you." Loki caught Michael's wrist, slapped the dagger into his hand, and pressed his fingers closed about the hilt.

Michael gasped. "What is it?"

"Her name is *Vanadium*. Keep her hidden until it's time to strike."

"No fear. No fear." Michael recited the litany, growing steadier with each repetition, as though the words were his charm. By the third time through, he was as cool as could be.

Loki shrugged—whatever worked. Magic, once found, served each individual in a different fashion.

Loki placed himself before Michael, keeping the boy against the headboard. The Trickster altered his appearance so he looked like Michael's identical twin, right down to the PJs the boy wore. Figuring he had one good shot at this, he grabbed a gob of magic and wove it into his taunt, crafting an infuriating heckle designed to provoke.

"Inga, you coward," Loki sang out, using Michael's lilting voice. "You've sunk low—hiding beneath children's beds. Show yourself."

The bed rattled; the beast rumbled. As though caught in the grip of a terrible earthquake, the wooden posts lifted and dropped to the floor. Loki shifted his balance, riding out the tremor but he was aware of Michael's distress. The boy clung to the headboard. Pronounced cracks accompanied the splitting of boards.

Cold sweat broke out across Loki's body. Twisting his head, he scanned all sides of the bed, watching for any sign of the *dís*. The bitch could come at him from any angle—he had to be ready.

From the back of the house, Jake shouted and the dog barked furiously.

Shit. Shit. Shit. Time's up. On the verge of panic, Loki summoned reckless energy, tapping dangerous sorcery. "Do you hear—Odin's coming. Your unwiped ass is fucked."

The heaving bed smashed to the ground. The footboard shattered and collapsed into pieces, leaving it at a dangerous slope.

Loki leaned back, making sure Michael remained behind him. Barring his teeth, he threw down a gauntlet. "Inga, your ilk was birthed from my puke!"

"Loki!" A raspy female voice snarled his name—rising

with recognition and rage. *Dísir* despised him. Maybe it was the card he should've played first.

Time to deliver the *coup de grâce*. "That's right—*Loki*. You imbecilic canker-blossom. It's past time you acknowledged me as the true master of your destiny."

Dead silence—except for the pounding of Jake's boots coming on fast.

Two arachnid legs hooked the edge of the mattress. They were covered in thick, bristling brown hairs. The top of a huge square head appeared—four black eyes, round and shiny, all in a row—over a bottlebrush mustache that concealed her fangs.

"Ben..." Michael's voice shook.

"I see it." He spread his arms behind him, framing the boy, and shifted Michael to the side. Always behind him. He rotated and braced, preparing for an onslaught.

The spider's head rose higher and higher... revealing the thick thorax that sported six more hirsute limbs. Her legs were several times longer than her body, spanning the entire breath of the room from one side to the other. Her bloated abdomen dragged behind her, scraping the ground. She wasn't the svelte spring spider Loki remembered.

"Damn, Inga, you've gotten fat."

The *dís* hissed. Her black eyes glittered. Bright venom dripped from her fangs and all eight limbs shifted continuously.

Loki sucked a sharp breath. Okay, yeah, he was scared of her—scary spider bitch—way worse than Jake. Time dilated —Loki fretted. Dreaded. Had Michael lost his grip on *Vanadium*? If he had—they were both so very screwed.

"I've got it," the boy said, leaving Loki wondering if he'd spoken aloud. "No fear."

"Try not to stab me!" Loki shouted.

The spider sprang at him, running on her six hind legs—the front pair positioned to attack. Barbed mandibles—blood red chitin tipped in ebony points.

He braced and held his ground until she was right on top of him. At the last possible second, he shifted shapes to a giant scorpion and reared to meet her. His claws caught her front legs and their second set of limbs met and locked. He halted her advance but their combined force rocked the already precarious mattress.

Miscalculation: proportions to positions. One of his scorpion legs collided with Michael, knocking the boy aside. The child shouted and tumbled off the bed. Loki winced inwardly—oops. But he didn't dwell; couldn't afford to.

The *dis* had preponderance on him, enough to crush him. She pressed, shoving him. He slid, scrambled, dug in with his clawed walking legs but he only succeeded in ripping deep gouges in the mattress. He slowed her but she continued to overwhelm him, forcing him over backward. Seeking an opportunity, he lifted his tail but couldn't achieve sufficient traction. Accurate striking required his upper body to be positioned low, tail high—the opposite of his current stance.

"Michael!" Jake appeared in the entry, brandishing the molten blade of his dagger. It emanated a wave of heat—burning cinders and thick smoke that clogged the air.

"Dad!" Michael called outside of Loki's view.

Brief relief brushed Loki because he hadn't hurt the kid. It didn't last long. The entwined scorpion and spider blocked the Hunter King's path to his son. Not where Loki wanted to be, but he couldn't flee without releasing the *dis*. If she escaped, they'd never get another shot at her.

The spider's mandibles flexed, straining for him. Doom loomed in his vision. Within her mouth, poison sacks bulged with venom; droplets shimmering on the tips of wicked fangs. Those curved tusks, tipped in death, menaced him. He snapped his own jaws together, a reminder. Bite—get bit.

Weapon positioned, a reaper at his task, Jake descended on the entwined arachnids. His blade descended and struck the spider's second and third walking legs where they joined her thorax. The blow severed the limbs but also took off one of the scorpion's clawed feet.

She screeched and tipped, her balance upset.

Fearsome pain stabbed through Loki's leg. He roared and channeled his rage into an attack. His tail shot up and then struck—the stinger embedded in the back of the spider's head and delivered paralytic poison. Not as deadly as hers but it should slow her.

The second the scorpion's stinger pierced her flesh, the spider discharged a deadly spray from her fangs into his face. It hit Loki square in the eyes. Burning. Blinding. Impossible agony. He howled and thrashed.

The tangled arachnids toppled and rolled. Inga struggled to escape but Loki hung on with every ounce of petty, vindictive determination in his soul. *Taking. The. Bitch. With. Him.* Last thing he ever did.

A crunch and a splat.

Agony consumed Loki. Pain became his only sensory perception for perpetuity. Unending and infinite. He hung on a thread of lucidity but had no idea how long his rational mind could endure beneath the weight of the torment. Awful certainty overwhelmed him. The spider had killed him, destroying his avatar.

Damn it. Damn it all to hell and back. He was screwed. For centuries, he'd hidden his mind in that incarnation. His *last* life and final foothold in the mortal world. The one thing that had kept him sane all this time. Its destruction was Game Over. His cognizance had returned to his greater form, which was imprisoned in the underworld—sentenced to endure the eternal torture of having a sleeping dragon's venom drip onto his face, corroding flesh and bone. Oh irony, from spider to serpent...

From far, far away, Loki heard Jake saying, "Now, come over here..."

"Is he going to be okay?" Michael asked, his voice full of childish anxiety.

"Yeah, he'll be fine. It takes more than that to kill a cockroach."

"But he's a scorpion."

"Same basic principle. Now, son, hold the dagger like this..."

"Like this?" Michael asked.

"Yes, over its heart. You want to cut—" A roar like a wave blurred their voices out.

Loki faded into blackness.

CHAPTER TWENTY-THREE

PHOENIX, ARIZONA

Loki woke up on his back, still a scorpion with his five remaining legs twitching above him, and was surprised he woke up at all. One of his front claws and two walking legs were among the missing limbs. He groaned but a clatter emerged from his rigid mandibles. His entire body throbbed, pulsating anguish.

Without premeditation, Loki rolled over into the shape of Benjamin. Altering his form required an actual, concentrated effort; a difficulty he was unaccustomed to. He, who changed shape as naturally as he breathed, struggled through the process of shrinking from a scorpion to a boy. He lacked the guile for artistry so he settled for baggy sweats as gray as he was glum.

Afterward, he rested on his side, panting, and tried to focus his vision. No matter how hard he tried, he couldn't see. He grabbed for his face—scared beyond reason it was gone. He touched something soft and gauzy. Tore at it, ripping away bandages, and exposed his raw and swollen eye sockets.

Blinding sunshine hit what remained of his damaged eyes. Nausea slammed him. He convulsed and puked up his guts. Whimpering, he used his arms to shield his face and curled into a fetal position. Abject misery. He'd lived but the way he felt—maybe he'd be better off dead.

He hurt. He hadn't hurt so bad since the time he and Thor had gotten into a drinking match to settle such a weighty matter as who among them was the better bard. Loki had woken up a month later, suffering from the worst hangover of his entire existence, in the form of a nanny goat. He'd crawled back to Asgard with his tail tucked between his legs. The Trickster never again challenged the god of thunder to a poetry slam.

"What a cry baby." Jake's mocking voice came from close. Curtain rings scraped on the rod; the drapes shut, plunging the room into blessed darkness. He stomped closer—each reverberation of his boots on the carpeting struck like thunder in Loki's throbbing skull.

"Can you walk quieter? *Asshole.* I'm suffering here." Loki clutched his head between both hands, hoping pressure would stop his brains from leaking through his ears. And what was that crunching sound—was the bastard stomping on packing bubbles just to torment him?

"The floor is covered in shit," Jake said gruffly. "Not many place I can put my feet without stepping on something."

"Oh." Loki wheezed because snot clogged his nose and throat. Wetness on his cheeks. He still had tear ducts... or they'd healed enough that he could cry. And damn it, *they* itched. "Is Michael okay?"

"Yeah, he's asleep in my room. The twins are taking turns watching him."

"What about the *dís*?" Loki rubbed his face against the back of his arm, applying pressure since digging in with his nails wasn't an option.

"Dead. Michael cut out her heart with *Vanadium*. The curse is ended." Jake's voice came from directly over Loki, indicating he'd come nearer without making any additional noise.

"Good." Satisfaction infused his voice. He didn't bother hiding it. He stopped scratching for a second but the stinging persisted—thousands of fire ants marched across his eyeballs. Moaning, he scrubbed his face again.

"Stop that. You're not supposed to scratch."

"I can't help myself. *It itches*." Loki whined, ending on a high note. He looked up and squinted, attempting to see but all he could make out was an indistinct form looming over him.

"Damn, I'd forgotten what a wimp you are when you get hurt. Can you see?" Jake sank to his knees beside Loki. Far from being reassuring, his rival's proximity was a great, looming threat.

"Barely. Bitch got me right in the face."

"I flushed your eyes with water. No idea if it helped."

"Gee, thanks," Loki said, mixed bitterness and sarcasm. "Guess you couldn't be bothered to heal me, huh? Figures..." A painful lesson. It served him right for trying to do the right thing by the child. No good deed...

"I'm unable to use healing magic. It's one of my mortal limitations." Jake's huge hand pressed against the back of Loki's skull and the other against his forehead. The man may only be human, but his mortal vessel possessed the strength necessary to crush a child's skull. Or maybe he'd drive his thumbs through the Trickster's damaged eyeballs, thus ending him.

Loki's danger sense went off like a five-alarm claxon. He jerked and twisted, a weak attempt to escape. "Don't touch me—"

"Quiet down. If I intended to kill you, you'd be dead already. Believe me, I considered it. That stunt you pulled was reckless. You put Michael in danger." Jake released Loki's head and reached for something. In all likelihood, a weapon.

"He was already in danger. I saved him."

"The only reason I haven't killed you."

Sure enough, Loki glimpsed a flash—light glancing off metal. Jake still intended to kill him. This had all been a setup, part of a sadistic game. The Trickster swallowed around a hard lump in his throat. Real fear formed in his gut. Not the distress the *dís* had caused, but true terror because he knew the old man's capacity for cruelty better than any other creature in the universe.

"Liar," Loki hissed, barring his teeth. He briefly considered changing shapes but then dismissed it. He lacked the strength necessary to put up a fight even if he managed to shift, and besides, being a boy might be the best protective camouflage he could have at the moment. Most people shied instinctively from the thought of harming a child. Maybe even Jake.

"Are you talking to me or yourself?" Jake's tone was quick and light.

"Does it matter?" Loki sensed tension building—something scary and momentous. He didn't want to be lying here like a sacrificial lamb when violence manifested. With an effort, he marshaled his strength and scooted away. He traveled less than a foot before he hit the wall.

"No, it doesn't," Jake said gravely. "Calm down. If I meant to hurt you, I'd already have done so."

"Yeah, so you say. Or maybe you wanted me awake before

you started." Exhaustion yoked him to a great burden. He began a hard scramble for enough energy to shift again. He could manage, but it wouldn't be fast enough to evade whatever harm Jake intended to do him.

Unable to see; nowhere to flee. Loki chose the only route open to him and wailed at the top of his eight-year-old's lungs. He sobbed, turning on the waterworks, and kicked his short legs in a full-fledged tantrum. "Puh-lease don't hurt me! I don't wanna die! I'm too young to die!"

"Sonofabitch. Knock it off. Do you really think I'd torture you with my boys just down the hall?" Jake dropped his huge hand over Loki's mouth, silencing him. The hunter's tone conveyed more threat than an armed nuke. "If you wake up Michael with this shit, I will kill you."

Loki flipped the switch and shut it down. He scowled. He couldn't speak over his gag so he projected his voice. "Good point. Sorry."

Jake lifted his hand a couple inches but paused, testing Loki's word. The hunter rumbled his frustration. "Why the hell are you everything and anything—but a man—when we speak?"

"What can I say—I was the female vocalist for Berlin." He grinned.

Jake's silence spoke for itself. The joke missed its mark—probably flew right on over the rainbow. Loki couldn't see his former friend's scowl, but he was confident it was there, covering the old man's confusion. Though, really, it was inexplicable. Inexcusable. Jake Barrett must've been...

"Cripes, how old were you in the 70s?" His face skewed while he juggled the numbers.

"None of your damn business." When Jake shifted, the floor boards creaked beneath him. His movements indicated the hunter was working with his hands.

Loki's sharp ears picked up the slick sound of a knife cutting through a firm substance. He sniffed, tasting the air, and detected the delicious aroma of something tart and sweet. It set his mouth to watering.

"What're you doing?"

"Repeating the mistakes of my past."

The Trickster hissed. The unexpected blow to his pride was far worse than the sting of his injured eyes. Unfair! And uncalled for! He, **Loki,** was not a mistake to be regretted. He bit his tongue to stay silent but anger fueled his tongue.

"How can you deny me so easily? We were brothers—does that mean nothing to you?" Loki demanded with a violent gesture.

Jake grunted. "Of course it means something to me. You're getting riled up over nothing. I wasn't talking about you."

"What then?"

"Me. I seem to be set on this doomed course. Put out your hand."

"Why?" Spots of suspicion multiplied before his blind eyes like a pox.

"Just do it."

"I must be out of my mind." Muttering, Loki stuck out his arm even though doing so was insane. The spider's venom must've eroded part of his brain. There was no other logical explanation.

"Then you're not alone." Jake took hold of Loki's wrist, turned his hand over, and placed something on his palm.

"What's this?" He closed his fingers and identified... Fruit. More specifically, a piece of fruit—probably a juicy apple from the texture. Loki's brow knit. Okay, well then. Jake Barrett was trying to hand feed him sliced fruit. Oh yeah, he'd hit crazy town for sure.

"Iðunn's apple."

"What? No way!" Loki sniffed it, mistrust diamond-bright and hard in his heart. The aroma remained fresh and inviting. He didn't detect so much as a hint of poison. Still, it was impossible. It had to be a trick. "The tree hasn't produced even a flower more than two hundred years..."

"I know that."

"That would make this one of the last apples left in existence." Loki waved the suspicious prize in the air. "I can't believe you'd waste it on me."

"I can't either," Jake grumbled. "Will you knock that off and just eat it? This isn't a smart time to be screwing around. You're hurt worse than you think. Loki, I can see through you."

Loki shivered. His mind went straight to the hell that awaited him on the other side. Without hesitation, he shoved the slice into his mouth—

"Damn it. Chew!" Jake snapped.

Too late. Loki swallowed it whole. The second it had touched his lips, he'd experienced that special spark of magic. Tingling on his tongue that spread through his entire being. His eyes stopped burning quite so awfully. He squinted in an attempt to focus and detected marginal improvement.

"It helped."

"Of course it helped."

"I want more." He flexed his fingers—gimme paw.

"You're supposed to chew it. The apple's full benefit isn't realized otherwise."

"Geez, stop lecturing already. I'll chew next time." Loki struggled to sit upright. He put his back to the wall and shoved, shoulders hunched. His sight had improved marginally thanks to the regenerative properties of the apple but he wanted—*needed*—the rest of it.

"Here." Jake tossed another slice at him. It hit Loki's cheek and bounced off but he caught it against his chest. He shoved it into his mouth and—with an effort—chewed three times. The apple's flesh was firm; the juices succulent. He gulped and said, "Just give it to me already."

"No. I know how you eat."

"I—geez. Cut me a break already. You haven't spent quality time with me in centuries." Loki noted a distinct improvement in his sight already. Not quite 20/20 but soon...

"Some things don't change." Jake pared another slice with his knife and cast it toward Loki with a flick of the blade. Half the golden apple remained.

This time Loki caught it out of midair. In the same smooth motion, he popped it into his mouth. He sank his teeth into the fruit so the golden skin faced outward and flashed Jake a shiny smile. "See, chewing..."

"Yeah, I see." Jake sounded unconvinced.

Loki masticated with his mouth open so each bite was visible. Unfortunately, Jake appeared unperturbed by the gross out. But then, Loki supposed that raising sons could do that to a man. Swallowing, he asked, "You gonna tell me where you got it?"

"No." Jake paused and then countered. "You wanna tell me why you didn't come to me for help tonight? My son's life was at stake. I'd already agreed to work with you if you had a viable plan but you excluded me... I'm thinking on purpose."

"I was working on the fly—making things up as I went along. I didn't have a plan." Loki scowled because, damn it, Jake sorta had a point. And the Trickster lacked a neat answer. Honestly—and he used that phrase with only the utmost irony—including Jake hadn't even occurred to him.

"Your con is falling apart," Jake said in a tone rife with cynicism. "This whole ploy for us to work together was a ruse right from the start. I can't believe you ever intended to cooperate with me if you couldn't even overcome your hatred to accept my help."

The Trickster's shoulders jerked. He sat straighter. "You still think I'm running a scam? I almost died!"

"I think you worked hard and took the risk necessary to put me in your debt. When the time comes you'll call in the marker." Jake tossed the remaining half apple overhanded like a baseball.

Loki's hand shot up. He snatched it out of the air but he was too pissed to take a bite. The injustice of the other man's summary riled him to real anger. His first truly unselfish act in a century reduced to just another manipulative scheme. "It figured you'd twist it like that—"

"Remember who I am, Loki. I've known you too long to be fooled." Jake eyed him with unadulterated cynicism. "Let's not play pointless games. You protected my son; I owe you. I'll do whatever I have to to make you whole."

"Whole! I can't be made whole." Loki scoffed. "You wrongly imprisoned three of my children!"

Jake's hard gaze never wavered. "You sired monsters fated to destroy the world."

"No!" Loki's free fist struck his thigh. *"You made them what they are."*

"I saw what they'd become. I tried to protect the nine worlds by banishing them."

"Always with the excuses—"

"Explanations."

"Excuses! You've got one for everything. How about this? Nari and Vali were *ten* when Thor murdered them. That's four years older than Michael. You were too much of a coward to even do your own dirty work. How do you live with yourself?" Real tears streamed down Loki's cheeks but he was too far gone to care. Thor had transformed one of Loki's twin sons into a wolf who'd in turn murdered his brother. The Thunderer had gutted both children and used their intestines to bind Loki's greater form.

"That's on me. The time is coming when I'll pay for what I've done but you're not without blame." Jake's face set into a stony mask from flinty eyes to gravelly voice. No doubt, his heart was an iron ingot in his cavernous chest. "There's blood on your hands, Loki. Baldur—"

"Not my fault! I warned you! I warned Frigg! 'Don't fuck with Fate,' I said. Did you listen? No one ever listens!" He howled with frustration. His imperfect vision fogged with reddish haze.

"You could've tried harder." All the sudden, Jake sounded immensely and thoroughly exhausted. He created a dismissive gesture with his hand. "This is all pointless. We're going in circles, arguing about things done centuries ago. Our legacy is nothing but betrayal and bitterness..."

"Let's talk about what's been done lately then..." The last couple minutes had served to convince Loki that Jake was right about one thing: he should regard the aid he'd rendered Michael as a marker to be played at some future date and time.

"I could just call us even," Jake said, severe in tone. "I haven't forgotten—you engineered Daniel's death."

Loki forgot his clever retort and fell silent. Against his will, he replayed the whole sordid affair that had resulted in the murder of Daniel Barrett. An unfamiliar sense of shame flooded him. He didn't want to own it. A conscience was a disgrace for a giant to possess. His differences had always set him apart from his own people—the primary reason he'd sought a home among the Aesir; called one his blood brother over his own kin.

The silence endured, demanding fulfillment.

"You got Daniel's soul back in the end." Loki turned his child-sized face toward the apple and took a huge bite. He was beyond caring what anyone thought of him, especially Jake.

Did he care? Nope, not caring.

"Did you plan that too?" Jake's face brightened with sudden enlightenment—brown eyes gleaming with murderous intent. His hands flexed.

Aware he'd miscalculated, Loki shifted and squirmed beneath the old man's regard but it was too late. Time for a major diversion. "I saved Michael. That should count for something."

"It does." Jake leaned back, colliding with the wall behind him.

Curt but encouraging. Loki diverted his gaze, making a casual sweep of the child's trashed bedroom. The spider's mangled and dismembered body rested atop the shattered remnant of the bed. Everywhere he looked—dried ichor and destroyed furniture. "Damn, the kid's gonna need a whole new decor."

Jake grinned. "He's already said he wants to redo it in Spiderman."

"Cool." Loki tried to smirk, but was sure it bore closer resemblance to a Charlie Brown smile. Apprehension ate at him, couldn't be helped. If he failed to forge an alliance with Jake against the Norns, then they were both guaranteed to lose. Hell, the whole damn world—all nine of 'em—would burn.

"This can't work if we don't change," Jake said heavily.

Those words, coming from *Him*, shocked Loki. In the old

age, the time of mist and myth, Odin had been versatile and dynamic, but those days were long since gone. The One-eyed God had grown stagnant and apathetic centuries ago. BUT, as the Trickster had observed before, the mortal incarnation of his old friend was different.

Loki forced out the impossible confession. Truth-telling ran counter to the fundamental nature of his soul. "What I did to Daniel made me sick. I saw what I'd become through the eyes of others..." He shrugged. "I gave his soul back. I could've destroyed him. Bringing him back was the best I could manage."

"We fought tooth and nail to win back my son's soul."

"Yeah. If I'd made it too easy, you'd've assumed it was a trap."

Scowling, Jake scoured his face as though searching for a clue. "Thousands of mortals are dying at the hands of your undead army and I'm supposed to believe you feel bad about my son dying?"

"Those mortals are dying to *become* my army. I don't have a choice—"

"Sure you do. Order the Necromancer to stop."

"I can't."

"You won't."

"*I can't!*" Loki swung closed fists, bashing the wall. The impact created concentric circles on the plaster.

"You're as trapped in this as I am, ain't'cha?" Jake gave him an odd look—part soothsayer, part sage. But the truly objectionable thing was the pity that shone in the old man's eyes.

"Yes." He had more than his fair share of pent-up anger and frustration. So much of his rage was directed at Jake, but even more for the Sisters Wyrd, the witches who'd cursed them to ruin. "I'm trapped at the bottom of a pit. All my efforts to get out dig me in even deeper. There has to be some way out..."

He huffed and stared at the ground, determined to sublimate his emotions and restore his facade before he said another honest word. One of the spider's fat severed legs lay too close to his foot for comfort. The thick hairs were almost touching the sole of his shoe. Face contorted, Loki extended his leg and pushed it away.

"'This is a waste of time." Jake declared in cold dismissal. "We can't change—too old, too set in our ways. Change is hard. It'd require effort. Sacrifice—"

"You're calling *me* incapable of change? You want to talk sacrifice—do you have any idea what it cost me to steal that dagger from Freya?" Infuriated, he hurled the uneaten half of the apple at Jake. Thanks to his faulty vision, it smacked the wall beside the older man's head. Reckless words followed. "CENTURIES of plotting, manipulating, and scheming— wasted! All on the remote possibility that *you* could pull your head out of your narrow-minded ass long enough to even consider working with me. But no, that was too much to ask—"

A vicious smile of satisfaction split Jake's mouth. It set off alarms in Loki's mind. He choked off the tirade, but too late. All that talking of waste and being too old to change— calculated shots aimed right at the Trickster's soft spots, by a man who knew him too well. Fool that he was, Loki had fallen for it. Thanks to his unwise outburst, he'd given away far more than he'd ever intended.

"Ah, there you are," Jake drawled. "There's my brother. That's the first honest thing you've said since we began this dialogue."

"I hate you." Dejection enshrouded Loki. It'd all been a waste. He'd gambled and lost. Continuing the conversation was pointless. Jake believed he had an alternative agenda. The harder he pressed, the less likely he'd be believed.

"I'm well aware of that." Jake picked up the remainder of the apple, and offered it to Loki. "You may as well finish it. It'll go to waste otherwise."

The basic logic held. Loki's vision wasn't one hundred percent, and he was through with pointless, unselfish sacrifices. Martyrdom was for losers. The Trickster snatched the battered fruit from his rival and took a huge bite so juices ran down his cheeks and chin. He talked with his mouth full. "Why do you have it anyway?"

"None of your business."

"Course not." Loki rolled his now-perfect eyes and considered the core. He'd eaten down to the stem and the seeds. Polishing it off was well within his ability—he could pretty much eat anything, but he didn't need it... Tossing it constituted an even bigger waste, so he stashed it into one of the dozens of bolt holes he kept secreted about his person. The apple vanished from his hand but it remained accessible should he find a use for it.

Experimentally, he boosted his legs beneath him and sat on his calves, testing his balance and strength. The apple's magic continued to revitalize him—and would for some time to come. Soon, he'd be back to full strength, maybe better than before. At the moment, all he wanted was to retreat and recover. Hole up somewhere safe while he calculated his losses and formulated a new plan.

When Jake's hand dropped onto his shoulder, Loki almost fell over. The hunter said, "I've got to get this mess cleaned up. We'll talk more later, all right?"

"Uh—yeah," Loki mumbled, opting for ambiguity over obvious stupidity. He'd be a monkey's uncle if his eyeballs didn't cross. He hated asking, but curiosity got the better of him. "About what?"

"About how we're gonna make this alliance work." Jake used the wall as a prop and pushed to his feet. He settled his hands on his hips, surveying the remains of the spider as though trying to decide what to do with it.

"I swear, I can hear your knees popping, old man." Loki adopted a deliberately cagey tone to cover the surge of excitement that swept through him. He popped upright, rocking on his heels with boyish restlessness. Though, confusion muddled his mind. He had no idea if he'd heard right or if he was delusional. Maybe Jake was just screwing with him again... Or maybe he really had changed his mind.

"Yeah, maybe so." Jake chuckled. "You make sure Ben drops by and visits Michael later. The boy was worried sick. He's certain being bit by that spider is going to turn you into a supervillain."

"Yeah, I'll do that. Me—a supervillain. Can you imagine?" Loki grinned as his imagination opened to all the wonderful potential. Michael wanted to be a superhero...and every caped crusader needed an arch-nemesis. The games...the adventures...

He liked it. He liked it a lot.

His eight-year-old mind whirling, Loki headed toward the nearest window, intending to change shapes and vamoose. He had things to do. Big plans. A wide new world of potential to explore... But Jake's voice stopped him in his tracks.

"Are you gonna ask for *Vanadium* back?"

Loki spun, arms out, to face his old friend. He smirked. "Nah, you keep it. If I want it, I'll steal it."

Jake only grinned. "You'll try."

CHAPTER TWENTY-FOUR

PHOENIX, ARIZONA

Smoke-filled skies made for a stunning morning, marking the start of what promised to be a beautiful June weekend. The sun was a glossy pearl against a smeared canvas of orange and red. It hung over the suburban park, a painful reminder to those gathered of what they'd lost... and what they might yet lose.

A full crew of hunters stood arrayed in a semi-circle facing inward. Tough men and woman, all on edge—every last one had been with him in Tucson or known the soldiers who had fallen. The palpable strain showed on their faces— from the dark circles beneath their eyes to their haggard features. They carried tools and steel tubing, armed to the teeth with the weapons of creation. What wasn't in hand could be found in one of the half-dozen Humvees parked curbside, or was a short drive to the nearest hardware store.

"All right. That's it. Those are your assignments. Any questions?" Jake stood with his hands on his hips, stance at ease. He wore his typical uniform—t-shirt and Levis, and short work boots. As a concession to what promised to be a long day spent in harsh sunlight, he wore sunglasses and a cowboy hat, the brim tilted to shield his forehead.

"Oh, oh, oh! I do!" At the front, a scruffy twig of a man thrust his arm in the air. He didn't just wave it—he danced so his entire body bounced. He wore his trademark bandana— big, bright, and yellow—over his head, secured by a knot at the back.

Jake tilted his head back, gaze cast heavenward. Yeah, it figured. "What is it, Toucan?"

Toucan employed his best Gomer Pyle impression. "So what you're saying, sir, is this here assignment is a typical case of—*You Broke It. We fix It?*"

A stir passed through the gathered hunters—twitching lips, shifting feet. His people had too much discipline to bust straight into laughter. Jake quashed his own smile and glanced right, passing the baton to Skinner.

"What the fuck is that filth coming out of your sewer, Toucan? Do you think you're funny?" Skinner bellowed, employing his drill sergeant voice.

"Sir, no, sir!" Toucan snapped to attention. So did the rest of the soldiers.

"Extra PT for everyone! Now get your lazy asses to work! Let's get this mother-fucking rocket torn down!"

"Sir, yes, sir!" They saluted and scattered.

"Wow, that was awesome!" Michael piped up. The boy raced with his arms spread to facilitate imaginary flight. He ran circles around Jake and Skinner, chanting over and over again, *"Mother-fucking rocket!"*

The two men traded a long, shocked glance. The color drained from Skinner's face—sweat beaded on his bald scalp. It required a heroic effort on Jake's not to bust his gut laughing.

"You'd better have a word with him," Jake adopted a careful tone. "If Lucy hears him talking like that..."

"Never mind Lucy. Winnie will have my balls." Skinner leaned over and settled a huge hand on Michael's shoulder, guiding the boy's flight path toward the playground. "Son, let's talk..."

A wide grin split Jake's face. He strolled toward where a pile of equipment, tools, and supplies sat on the landscaping gravel. The collection included two new commercial playground structures and a swing set. While he watched, a squabble broke out over how to make and measure level ground.

The twins and Hal's boy, Andre, were part of a crew engaged in the energetic demolition of the ruined play structure. Unfortunately, the ruined rocket ship would have to be torn down—the cone had been damaged beyond repair. A typical case of the old making way for the new, and an inescapable aspect of the cycle. The playground would be better for it when they were through.

Considering his people were more experienced at blowing things up than construction, they were looking at least a full week's work. Jake picked up a post digger, intending to pitch in and do his fair share.

"Excuse me," said a man's cultured voice. It came from behind Jake.

Jake turned.

A clean-cut man stood too close for comfort. The fellow was handsome but in a discount-outlet fashion. Good haircut, but he wore a cheat suit of inferior materials complete with leather patches on the elbows. Fake diamond cufflinks glittered on his wrists, but his shoes were the dead giveaway—brown loafers made of Naugahyde. His most distinctive feature was a scar on his cheek. The guy had the look of a white collar professional but the air of an opportunistic predator such as a weasel. If he'd worn a logo, it would've spelled—PAPERPUSHER.

Jake figured him for a government employee who held some mid-level position that allowed him to exert an undo amount of hardship on the citizens he was supposed to serve. The guy had a clipboard, for fuck's sake.

In his experience, most bureaucrats fronted well but caved like the Cowardly Lion at the first sign of trouble. So he mustered his fiercest glare and barked, "What?'

The other man didn't even flinch. With an officious air, he pressed. "Does your work crew have a permit for this construction?"

"Who the hell is asking?"

The guy reached into the pocket of his suit coat, and Jake reached for the tattoo dagger on his forearm. But he faltered when the man drew a laminated badge and flashed it. "Nathan O'Neil. I'm an inspector with the Phoenix City Building Department."

This had to be a fucking joke. Jake scanned the area and spotted a beat up Honda parked alongside the curb, wedged in between two of the Humvees. The two-door was the exact shade of lime-green Jake would've expected a bureaucrat to choose, and duct tape kept the front bumper from falling off.

Jake blustered. "All right. So what do you want?"

"Well, from your reaction, I'm guessing you haven't filled out an RZP-12." Nathan issued a nerdy chuckle as though he'd cracked a fine, funny joke.

"What the hell is an RZP-12?" Jake's temples throbbed with the onset of a mega-headache. Oh, how he despised paperwork.

"A Residential Zoning Permit. It's the first form you must fill out in order to request permission to fill out the next form. These things do have a progression that must be followed, you do understand. There are fees and inspections... More forms. Council meetings... The whole process only takes an average of nine months on average. Seven if we fast-track it."

"Yeah, we'll see about that." He got his phone out again.

"Who ya gonna call?"

"The governor." If that didn't work, he'd go higher.

"Right to the top. That's like cutting straight to the triple-dog-dare." A wolf-like smile split Nathan's mouth—an unmistakable, and probably deliberate, tell.

"Loki." Jake flipped the phone shut.

"Gotcha." The Trickster winked.

Jake tried hard not to laugh. He fought it. And he failed.

Jake and Loki laughed and laughed. Their ruckus even drew curious looks from his men, but he was beyond caring. The years fell away and it was just like old times except it wasn't. An ominous pallor hung over their comradery which was soon to pass, doomed before it even began.

"I fooled you," Loki wheezed, hands pressed to his sides. "Didn't I?"

"Yeah, you got me." He didn't mind making the concession. Loki had won fair and square. Jake waved his hand in the vague direction of the lime-green Honda. "It was that damn car."

"Sweet, ain't it? I swiped it from the City Building Department lot."

"The clipboard was a nice touch. You've never been accused of poorly-executed pranking."

"Actually..." Loki trailed off, staring at the sky, and frowned. "Never mind."

A shout caught their attention. In unison, both men turned. They wound up shoulder to shoulder. Jake didn't sense so much as a whisper of magic to suggest Loki was employing illusions, which meant it was really him. The Trickster must be feeling his oats to take such a risk, especially after the injury he'd sustained the day before.

Michael had reported a visit from Ben AKA Scorpio, a Supervillain. Jake, however, hadn't laid eyes on the God of Lies since last they parted. They both, he suspected, needed time to recover. Change didn't come easily to old dogs or old gods.

On the playground, an argument broke out between members of the ground leveling crew. The dispute appeared to be over the placement of construction flag markers. Jake stirred but Skinner charged in to settle the matter, shouting a flurry of decidedly PG-rated insults.

"They don't have a clue what they're doing," Loki declared.

"Not a one."

"Is *Den Valgte* yours?"

That came out of nowhere. Jake slanted a sideways glance at the other man. He'd expected angry accusations and distraught declarations. Loki loved nothing more than to ham it up when the opportunity for melodrama presented. The Trickster's stake in their ongoing negotiation had to be the balancing factor. Of course, there were other issues.

"No," Jake drawled. "Yours?"

"Nope."

Jake deliberated. "Course, one of us could be lying."

"Not like that could ever happen." Chuckling, Loki shook his head.

"If it's not you and it's not me that means there's another player."

"Isn't there always?"

"Yeah..." He rolled out the wry acknowledgement. As sure

as the sun set in the west, there were always foes, some old, some new. Jake scuffed his boot against the gravel. Hell, he'd be a liar if he pretended he didn't enjoy the intrigue. Forever got boring fast without challenges and mystery.

"I'll figure out who they are. I'm already on it."

"Heh." Jake pinned Loki with a long, hard look. If they were discussing their differences again, he had an important issue to address. "What you did to Victoria was harsh."

"That was all Freya." The God of Lies drew back, pantomiming a *Who me?* reaction; authentic right down to the injured glimmer in his eyes. But the corners of his mouth pinched and he looked damn miserable for a supposed heartless asshole who didn't give a damn.

Jake shook his head. "Lookin' green there, Loki. What's wrong—your conscience finally catchin' up with you?"

The Trickster's broad shoulders rose on a deep breath. "I make the choices I have to and I live with the consequences. I don't need your consolation."

"I wasn't offering it."

Loki continued as though he hadn't heard. "However you look at it, Victoria is better off. She got a hurt but she'll recover," Loki muttered in what sounded remarkably like at attempt at self-persuasion. "Freya is a faithless whore. She would've dragged Victoria down with her."

Jake decided to try a bit of flattery to loosen the Trickster's lips. "A brilliant stroke—that. With one blow, you drove a wedge. You separated Victoria from Freya and also from me."

"Not quite the wedgie you're making it out to be." Loki's cynical tone indicated he hadn't bought into the praise. "Victoria remained loyal to you."

"I find it more interesting that you've finally given up the pretense of having no concern for Victoria." The last time her name had come up, Loki had affected indifference beyond the most-passing interest.

"We're running short on time. Subterfuge is a costly liability."

"That it is. That it is..." Jake rubbed his hands together, cracking his knuckles. "I bet my son would agree with you on that."

"Sawyer will be better off too—in the long run."

Jake tensed. "That wasn't your decision to make."

"Maybe not, but it's what you wanted."

"Who're you to say what I want?"

"Oh, give it a rest already. You put Sawyer close to Victoria because you wanted the truth to come out. If you'd meant to keep the secret, he'd be thousands of miles from here at MIT."

Jake didn't disagree, but he wouldn't admit it aloud and certainly not to Loki. But if forced, he would've owned to overwhelming relief. At least the secret was out. Sawyer didn't know yet that Victoria knew... Ah, hell, wasn't life complicated enough without *this* in his home camp? Once Sawyer wised up, at least he could get on with the business of finding some way to make things right by the Storm Pack. Or learn how to live with what he'd done. Either way was better than wallowing as he'd been doing; eaten alive by his own guilt and self-recrimination. So yeah, Jake believed it was better this way. The disposition of his son's soul was as important as any worldly concern.

The sun was rising fast; temperatures soon would soar. He fished work gloves out of his back pocket and smacked them against his thigh to shake out the crinkles. When he looked back, he discovered the Trickster's appearance had altered, but in subtle ways. Loki was taller and more muscular—about a hundred times more dangerous than that persnickety building inspector. No more weasel.

Now, he was a wolf. Undoubtedly, an Alpha.

Loki shrugged off the jacket of his suit and made it vanish into thin air. He unfastened the buttons on the sleeve and rolled one up.

"What're you doing?" Jake demanded.

"Differences aside? I thought I'd pitch in. I helped ruin this playground."

"*You* want to help."

"Yeah, I actually have some experience building stuff. Is that a problem?"

"Nah. Differences aside." Jake stomped off toward the work site but then hesitated mid-step. "Am I supposed to introduce you as Nathan?"

Loki's consideration only endured seconds. "No, Arik will do."

"Hell, you're in an honest mood today, aint'cha?"

"Lies... Repeat that and I'll deny it."

EPILOGUE

SIERRA **P**INES, **C**ALIFORNIA, ON THE WESTERN SHORE OF ***Echo Lake***

The confines of the claustrophobic closet were dim thanks to the single dying incandescent bulb. With a final stroke of the hammer, Victoria drove the nail to its desired depth and made a mental note to change it to an LED later. And maybe do some spring cleaning, too.

She spread her arms to shove aside a couple dozen or so broomsticks, leaving only a witch's crooked staff leaning against the wall beneath the nail. She gripped the rawhide cord of the wolf's cross she'd taken off Magdalena and tested the knot. Then she hung the silver amulet from the flathead nail. It dangled—brushing against the staff.

The tip of her tongue protruded between her lips as Victoria shifted the staff a couple inches aside so the two things no longer touched. There—that'd have to do.

"Hey, we're gonna be late!" Logan said in the entry to the closet. "Sylvie and Morena are already in the car."

"I'm coming." She turned toward him. "Errand boy, eh?

How'd you lose out to Morena? Or are you the pack Omega now?"

"Hardy-har-har. Very funny. I lost cause I'm still on Sylvie's shit list for trashing the kitchen." Logan stared past her into the corner. His brow knit. "Why do you have your witch trophy collection in the broom closet?"

"Oh, I dunno. It seemed appropriate?" She shoved a wisp of blonde bangs out of her eyes and pushed him out of her path so she could exit. "Why does your family own two dozen brooms? Did you father have some strange witch fetish I'm not aware of?"

His amber eyes glowed. "As a matter of fact, yeah. Plus, dad was a werewolf. Every full moon, he used to wolf out and go broom chasing..."

Victoria missed a step. She stopped and lifted her head to stare at him—inhaled. And damn it—she couldn't scent a lie on him. In fact, his basal odor didn't alter at all. Her face twisted into a frown; mixed confusion and denial. He couldn't possibly be serious... Could he?

Logan slammed the door to the broom closet shut and sprinted for the front door. "Shotgun!"

Oohh, damn it! She shot after him but yet again, her pregnant body refused to comply with the speed she expected. In her mind—a Greyhound. Reality—a Basset Hound. "Doesn't count! You can't call shotgun from inside the house!"

"Can so!" Logan waited for her at the front door, holding it open. She got past him and didn't wait while he locked up so she actually beat him to the SUV where Sylvie and Morena waited with the engine idling.

"I win." Victoria clamored into the front passenger seat beside Sylvie.

"Hey, no fair." Logan cocked his head. "I called it."

"I'm pregnant."

"What's that got to do with anything?" Despite his good-natured complaints, he got into the back with Morena.

"Everything. And if you haven't figured that out yet. Well, you need a lot more help than I can give ya." The teenager razed him from the backseat.

"Both of you—behave!" Sylvie's stern swept all three of them.

"Yes, ma'am." A mumbled chorus came from the backseat and then they were off.

Smiling, Victoria ducked her head.

ON THE DOWNSIDE, the obstetrician's office was a lot busier than it'd been on Victoria's last visit. A dozen people, including a few pregnant couples, crowded the lobby. Her own pack took up an entire corner, wedged into the adjacent chairs along the far end. Sylvie and Morena sat with her but Logan refused to be still. Instead, he paced the length of the room and back again, doing a damn good job of making the other patients nervous. He emanated an intangible air of menace.

On the upswing, Laverne, the receptionist, restrained herself from presenting Victoria with a whole new set of forms. The brunette regarded Logan with a fusion of lust and lewd speculation, but otherwise showed them to an examination room without comment.

Their numbers proved too much for the small area, but at least the wait was short. A couple minutes later, the door swung open to reveal Emanuel Luce. The young man hesitated, regarding them with wide eyes. His general nervousness over being confronted with four werewolves altered his scent to more pungent and acidic.

Victoria spoke up to offer reassurance. "Manny, this is my family. Morena and Sylvie..." She indicated each in turn, and the women offered their greetings. "Oh, and you know Logan..."

"Hey." Logan saluted with two paired fingers.

"You're here for your ultrasound today?" Manny addressed her but he only had eyes for Logan. Victoria found it amusing how Laverne and Manny had the same basic reaction to the male werewolf, but from the former it was unpleasant while the later somehow rendered it charming.

"That's right." She gestured for him to come closer. "It's okay. We don't bite."

"Speak for yourself," Logan quipped before Morena's finger collided with his side—pokey-pokey.

Manny remained in the entrance a moment longer, looking like he was debating whether to stay or run. Gradually, his tension eased and he approached, though he left the door to the overcrowded room open behind him. Victoria didn't mind. She actually preferred to have the fresh air and the escape route.

Victoria got positioned on the exam table, lying on her back, and Sylvie stood close enough beside her to hold her hand. While Manny prepared the ultrasound machine, Morena appraised the young man and then smirked.

"Hey, Logan?" The teenager affected a loud voice. "I heard a good one—how many druids does it take to screw in a lightbulb?"

"Dunno, how many?" Logan asked in scripted reply.

"You told them I'm a druid?" Manny looked askance at Victoria.

She spread her hands. "I had to tell them something."

The nurse cut off Morena's answer. "Druids don't screw in lightbulbs, they screw in stone circles." While Morena and Logan snickered, Manny returned fire— "What happened when the blind werewolf chewed a bone for an hour?"

"Oh, I know this one!" Morena waved her arm.

"Enough, look what you started," Sylvie scolded the girl.

"When he got up he only had three legs!" Logan spoke over all of them.

Without warning, Emanuel squirted ice cold lubricant onto Victoria's stomach. She startled and considered protesting but the nurse already had the ultrasound scanner positioned against her stomach. The black and white monitor blurred; the distinctive pulsating blip appeared that was the baby's heartbeat.

"This is so exciting!" Sylvie grasped Victoria's hand between her own, squeezing too hard but it was okay. The older woman's wide smile and the tears in her eyes more than made up for the minor discomfort.

"It is—" Victoria grinned, overcome even though it wasn't her first ultrasound. Nothing quite matched the wonder of the first time, but those that followed came damn close. She had tried to quantify her emotions, to put them into words, and failed.

Hush descended. Awe crystalized within the pack aura which resonated with singular unity. Over the last day or so, ever since she and Logan had reached an accord, the group's internal structure was slowly but surely altering to make room for him. Where she'd feared he'd undermine her, instead his strength reinforced her own.

Joy filled her heart, and she was so thankful to have all of them with her. She wished Sophia and the pups could've attended but concessions had to be made. Explaining four gray wolves would've been impossible, and besides, the lupines wouldn't have understood anyway. And no matter how hard she fought against it, sorrow tainted her happiness because two members of her pack who should've been present were absent.

Manny manipulated the ultrasound and obtained a better image—the fetus was visible in profile and appeared to be resting on her back. Tiny arms and tiny legs. And that racing heart beat which precisely mirrored the rate of Victoria's own pulse.

"That's it? That blob?" Logan skewed his head in an incredulous survey of the monitor.

"Oohh, look! She has her hand on her forehead." Morena squealed and bounced, unable to contain her excitement. The girl vibrated so hard she looked ready to fly apart.

"Have you already been told the gender?" Manny asked.

"Yes. I know she's a girl." Victoria quelled the impulse to cover her stomach with protective hands. Her daughter. This was her future—

"How big is it in real life?" Logan asked.

Morena jabbed him. "Her."

"Right now the fetus is about fourteen inches and weighs less than two pounds." Manny asked Victoria, "Would you like me to burn this footage to a DVD you can take home?"

"Yes, please." She mustered a watery smile.

Tears blurred her vision, but her mind was locked on the future which was far bigger and scarier than the prospect of being a mother. In less than a week, dozens of strange werewolves from other packs would descend on her territory. She not only had to convince the other Alphas of her worth, her right to address them as an equal, but she had to get them to *listen*. How was she supposed to persuade others to agree to an alliance with Jake Barrett when she was no longer certain in her own heart that aligning with the hunters was in her people's best interests?

"Victory, what's wrong? Why are you crying?" Sylvie asked softly.

Victoria bit her lower lip, choking back the damning words. She longed to explain—to tell her family what Sawyer had done. How he and his father had deceived her. But that path was fraught with nothing but misery. The truth would tear them apart from within. Morena had loved Jasper, and the teenager was rash and foolish. Logan was already spoiling for an excuse to take on the hunter. And Jake Barrett remained—a scary powerful man not to be crossed.

So Victoria shook her head while tears trickled down her cheeks. While Sylvie held her hand, Morena and Manny looked on in confusion. And Logan—

Those bright amber eyes narrowed, focused with deadly intensity. He pushed through the others and bent, resting his hand on the exam table. His breath stirred her hair; shivers ran down her spine. His ferociousness delighted her she-wolf.

Logan whispered in her ear. "Who do I have to kill?"

The End.

AFTERWORD

I hope you enjoyed Gallows God. To learn more about other
Loki's Wolves books visit my website.

Reviews are always appreciated!

ABOUT THE AUTHOR

Melissa Snark is a fantasy and romance author. She lives in Anacortes, Washington with her husband, three children and a glaring of cats.

Join Melissa Snark's newsletter to be notified of new releases.

For more information...
www.melissasnark.com